Praise for Samantha M. Bailey

Hello, Juliet

"Who do you trust and where do you go when you can't outrun your past? *Hello, Juliet* by Samantha M. Bailey is a wickedly unputdownable thriller teeming with secrets, suspense, and sly revelations. Bailey keeps the tension high and the pages turning in this searing exploration of the darker side of fame. Not to be missed!"

—Heather Gudenkauf, *New York Times* bestselling author of *The Overnight Guest* and *Everyone Is Watching*

"Samantha M. Bailey once again crafts a deliciously suspenseful tale, giving us a peek behind the curtains of a hit television show and the ramifications success has on its cast. In *Hello, Juliet*, Bailey perfectly captures the hunger for fame and the desperate measures some will take to achieve it, while also delivering a story filled with twists and surprises. A top-notch, single-sitting read."

—Kimberly Belle, internationally bestselling author of *The Paris Widow*

"Samantha M. Bailey has done it again! With exquisitely thorny characters and an evocative setting, *Hello, Juliet* pulled me in from page one and didn't let go. Bailey's fourth effort showcases her talent for executing breathtaking twists and turns. The cherry on top is an ending I never saw coming."

—Stephanie Wrobel, *USA Today* bestselling author of *The Hitchcock Hotel*

T0300690

"Samantha M. Bailey's latest thriller, *Hello, Juliet*, will actually have you saying 'OMG!' and for all the right reasons. Former actress Ivy Westcott is thrust back into the celebrity limelight for a reunion show, only to realize even darker troubles await her, which leaves her gutted and feeling more lost and alone than ever before. Bailey weaves the intrigue and allure of Hollywood, a protagonist you want to dig into, potential enemies at every corner, and a storyline that grips you from page one. With snippets of social media and a dual timeline, all the ingredients come together, making *Hello, Juliet* a riveting read and chef's kiss."

—Yasmin Angoe, Anthony-nominated and bestselling author of *Her Name Is Knight* and *Not What She Seems*

"A devilishly entertaining murder mystery set in the cutthroat world of episodic TV, *Hello, Juliet* ensnared me from the very first page. Come to gape at the diabolical antics of Hollywood stars and star-makers, stay to be gobsmacked by the stunning twists and turns. Five enthusiastic stars for this fascinating peek behind the curtain told by a master storyteller."

—Susan Walter, bestselling author of *Good as Dead*

"If you're looking for something juicy, scandalous, and truly unique and exciting, then *Hello, Juliet* should be at the top of your list. Clever, addictive, and a joy to read as we've come to expect from Bailey."

—Seraphina Nova Glass, Edgar Award–nominated author of *On a Quiet Street*

A Friend in the Dark

"Suspenseful, twisty, and addictive. *A Friend in the Dark* is smartly written and deliciously chilling. I couldn't put it down. This is Bailey at her best! I paused an episode of *Below Deck: Down Under* to finish this book. That's how invested I was."

—Jeneva Rose, *New York Times* bestselling author of
The Perfect Marriage

"Wow! Chilling, riveting . . . and page-turningly edgy. The oh-so-talented Samantha M. Bailey has created a twisted (and steamy!) world of power, passion, and vulnerability. This seductive thriller with its deep understanding of psychological trauma and the heavy secrets of the past is brave, original, and haunting. Fans of Gillian Flynn and Lisa Unger will cheer this must-read author."

—Hank Phillippi Ryan, *USA Today* bestselling author of
The House Guest

"Samantha M. Bailey never disappoints! *A Friend in the Dark* is one of the most intriguing and surprising books I've read in a while. You think you know where it's headed . . . but you don't. This thriller shocked me to the very end."

—Samantha Downing, internationally bestselling author of
My Lovely Wife

"With *A Friend in the Dark*, Samantha M. Bailey has crafted what's destined to be one of the most binge-worthy, buzzed about thrillers of the year. Wholly propulsive with twist after mind-blowing twist, richly layered characters, and an intricate plot, Bailey is at the top of her game and delivers not only a spine-tingling thriller but also a potent examination of the complexity of female desire and the terrifying, dark side of online relationships. *A Friend in the Dark* will have you glued from its first page to its explosive conclusion. An absolute masterpiece from the master of suspense!"

—May Cobb, award-winning author of *A Likeable Woman* and *The Hunting Wives*

"A tautly written story of twists, deception, and long-simmering desire, *A Friend in the Dark* is a thriller that consumed me from start to end. Samantha M. Bailey is a master of surprise endings and complex antagonists, and each chapter of this story flew by. Do not miss this one!"

—Elle Marr, Amazon Charts bestselling author of *The Family Bones*

"A sexy treat of a thriller loaded with twists and hairpin turns! Fans of Colleen Hoover should love *A Friend in the Dark*. It will keep you guessing and up way too late."

—Daniel Kalla, bestselling author of *Fit to Die*

"When you sit down with a Samantha M. Bailey novel, you expect to be nailed to your seat for the duration. *A Friend in the Dark* does that and so much more: this electrifying, layered, and psychologically acute thriller examines female desire, marriage, and motherhood while sweeping you off on a twisty ride all the way to its visceral, explosive finale. Bailey expertly crafts dark history and human foibles into an addictive narrative cocktail. Welcome to your next book hangover."

—Damyanti Biswas, bestselling author of the Blue Mumbai series

"*A Friend in the Dark*, by Samantha M. Bailey, is a knockout punch of a thriller. This wild ride starts with a marriage in freefall, then twists through a series of escalating and creepy turns before careening to a stunning conclusion. I read this one in a day and so will you."
—Darby Kane, internationally bestselling author of *Pretty Little Wife* and *The Engagement Party*

"Several lives burdened with tangled histories of desire, fear, cruelty, revenge, and murder are on a collision course until they intersect brilliantly in Samantha M. Bailey's *A Friend in the Dark*. Eden Miller finds herself suddenly without her husband, at war with her daughter, at a crossroads she never anticipated when, vulnerable and eager for attention, a long-ago flame reenters her life, igniting a forgotten passion. This is a sexy, dark, and twisty tale from a master of the genre. Highly recommended!"
—Jon Lindstrom, author of *Hollywood Hustle*, and four-time Emmy-nominated actor and award-winning filmmaker

"Clever, sexy, and compulsively readable, *A Friend in the Dark* is a pulse-pounding thriller with one jaw-dropping twist after another. Samantha M. Bailey has created a compelling cast of characters, a dark and layered mystery, and an insightful look at marriage, motherhood, and female identity."
—Robyn Harding, bestselling author of *The Drowning Woman*

"Savage secrets and desires collide in Samantha M. Bailey's *A Friend in the Dark*. Bailey is a master of misdirection, spinning twists and building tension until there's nothing to do but race to the knockout finish. *A Friend in the Dark* is a fierce, gutsy thriller, and Bailey is unstoppable."
—Tessa Wegert, author of *The Kind to Kill*

"Samantha M. Bailey's *A Friend in the Dark* simmers with palpable desire and twists that'll have readers gasping. Just when you think you know the direction of her story, you get knocked sideways with twist after jaw-dropping twist. This is a must-read for any thriller lover!"

—Heather Levy, Anthony-nominated author of *Walking Through Needles*

"Sexy, fast-paced, and deliciously twisty, *A Friend in the Dark* is Samantha M. Bailey at her suspenseful best. An unpredictable thrill ride that packs an emotional wallop, readers will be hard pressed to stop turning pages until they reach the spine-tingling conclusion. A compelling, addictive must-read."

—Laurie Elizabeth Flynn, bestselling author of *The Girls Are All So Nice Here*

"This sexy, heart-pounding thriller is everything a reader craves. Brilliant plotting and misdirection and mind games will have you flipping pages at warp speed. With twists and turns galore throughout, this is a one-sit read that will leave you shocked. A compelling look at fantasy versus reality, *A Friend in the Dark* is sure to stand out as a fan favorite of 2024."

—Jaime Lynn Hendricks, bestselling author of *I Didn't Do It*

Watch Out for Her

"Yet again, one of our most beloved thriller writers brings us a story with the heart of a family drama and the pulse of an edge-of-your-seat spine-chiller. Filled with foreboding from the very first page, this one will keep you up all night—and have you checking the locks!"

—Marissa Stapley, *New York Times* bestselling author of Reese's Book Club Pick *Lucky*

"Shows that Bailey is no one-book-wonder. It's as tightly plotted and skillfully written as her first, with a great backstory to carry it off . . . Bailey builds the suspense here with excellent pacing and clues that drop at exactly the right time. This is a great book to take on that summer holiday or the cottage weekend when all you have to do is chill, eat, and read."

—*The Globe and Mail*

"Bailey is a strong writer who keeps the reader turning pages . . . A cautionary tale about the fine line between diligence and obsession and the dangers of doing the wrong things for what we believe are the right reasons."

—*Toronto Star*

"A cleverly written, twisty, and brilliantly creepy thriller. With compelling characters intertwined with obsession, lies, simmering menace, and secrets at its heart, this is a page-turner which drew me in and kept me hooked. A real must-read!"

—Karen Hamilton, internationally bestselling author of *The Perfect Girlfriend*

"A tense and claustrophobic thriller in which Bailey makes you question whether the heart of a family is a place of safety or danger. Paranoia, obsession, and secrets ensure a twisty read."

—Gilly Macmillan, *New York Times* bestselling author of *What She Knew*

"Creepy, surprising, and relentlessly tense, *Watch Out for Her* is so much more than a thriller; it's an unflinching exploration of the roles we allow women to fill. With dark secrets and cliffhangers galore, this thrill ride will keep you up long past your bedtime. I couldn't put it down."

—Andrea Bartz, *New York Times* bestselling author of Reese's Book Club Pick *We Were Never Here*

"A hair-raising, suspenseful page-turner [that] will have one watching their back wherever they go, but what really gets to the novel's heart is the unexpected and chilling ending . . . The narrative is so well written and joined together it flows effortlessly."

—*The New York Journal of Books*

"Samantha M. Bailey's latest thriller is as propulsive as her sizzling debut. Two troubled women enter into a complex relationship that could shatter not only their lives but the lives of everyone they touch. A page-turner in the most literal sense of the word, I could not put this book down until the final shocking twist."

—Robyn Harding, bestselling author of *The Perfect Family*

"An irresistible story about what happens when we take our obsessions too far. Propulsive, electrifying, and sinister, I could not tear myself away from the narrators, two women each hiding dark secrets from their families. Bailey's assured prose delivers as enthralling a tale as her stellar debut."

—Stephanie Wrobel, bestselling author of *This Might Hurt* and *Darling Rose Gold*

"Addictive and relentlessly twisty . . . Nobody else writes a propulsive, family-centered mystery quite like this: Bailey is queen of the domestic thriller for a reason. *Watch Out for Her* masterfully deals with the shifting power of obsession, and the secrets we keep from our loved ones . . . and ourselves."

—Laurie Elizabeth Flynn, bestselling author of
The Girls Are All So Nice Here

"A compulsive and chilling exploration of trust, obsession, and voyeurism, Samantha M. Bailey knocks it out of the park with this intricately plotted domestic thriller. With dark secrets and surprising twists, this one's sure to be a new favorite!"

—Christina McDonald, *USA Today* bestselling author of
Do No Harm

"Wow! Relentlessly tense and incredibly twisty—*Watch Out for Her* proves the amazing Samantha M. Bailey is the queen of family suspense. With authentic emotion and complex and heartbreaking relationships, Bailey shows her brilliance in revealing the destructive power of love and the intensity of the need to belong. I flew through the cinematic pages, riveted and completely immersed in this propulsive and original thriller. Everyone will be talking about this—do not miss it!"

—Hank Phillippi Ryan, *USA Today* bestselling author of
Her Perfect Life

"An addictive read from start to finish, Samantha M. Bailey's talent and skill are on full display in this well-crafted domestic thriller. *Watch Out for Her* will have you second-guessing everyone you meet and rooting for characters you don't trust—and there is nothing more fun than that. Absolutely riveting."

—Jennifer Hillier, bestselling author of *Little Secrets* and
the award-winning *Jar of Hearts*

"This insanely addictive, utterly propulsive, and unbelievably tense thriller will consume you. With intoxicating, scalpel-sharp prose and gasp-worthy twists, Bailey has crafted a fresh and deeply unsettling take on obsession and voyeurism. Reading *Watch Out for Her* is like pulling a pin from a hand grenade and waiting for it to detonate. This is destined to become the most talked about, explosive thriller of the year."

—May Cobb, author of *The Hunting Wives*

"A deep dive into a world of secrets, where no one is who you think they are, and everyone has something to hide. Bailey's deft hand at ratcheting tension makes this an exquisite read. It will suck you in and you'll love every moment of it!"

—Amina Akhtar, author of *Kismet*

Woman on the Edge

"A debut that's tough to resist."

—*Toronto Star*

"A remarkable thriller."

—*Morning Live*

"One woman's struggles with motherhood and another's desperate desire to be a mother collide in this explosive debut. *Woman on the Edge* is a white-knuckle read that welcomes a bright new talent to the world of psychological suspense."

—Mary Kubica, *New York Times* bestselling author of *The Good Girl*

"This is the page-turner you've been looking for! Bailey's writing is gripping and emotionally resonant at once, and her debut novel, perfect for fans of Lisa Jewell and Kimberley Belle, will keep you on the edge of your seat until the final sentence."
—Marissa Stapley, *New York Times* bestselling author of Reese's Book Club Pick *Lucky*

"A fast-paced, twisty roller-coaster ride in which a desperate widow, a guilt-ridden new mother, and the secrets of the past collide—with a baby's life hanging in the balance . . . I couldn't race to the end quickly enough! An exciting, binge-worthy debut."
—Kristin Harmel, bestselling author of *The Winemaker's Wife* and *The Room on Rue Amélie*

"Begins with a bang and takes the reader on a tense, emotional journey of love, betrayal, and loss and straight into the heart of a mother willing to do anything to protect her child. Infused with riveting, hold-your-breath suspense, this masterful debut needs to be your next binge read. A knockout page-turner."
—Heather Gudenkauf, *New York Times* bestselling author of *The Weight of Silence* and *Before She Was Found*

"Exhilarating and evocative . . . *Woman on the Edge* had me gripped. This book effortlessly ticks all the boxes: wonderful world-building, realistic characters, and a gripping plot that made me keep flipping the pages. It's about obsession and madness, motherhood and trauma. This is a debut you'll want to slip straight to the top of your to-read pile!"
—Christina McDonald, *USA Today* bestselling author of *The Night Olivia Fell*

"With the narrative acceleration of a runaway train, *Woman on the Edge* kept me at the edge of my seat for its entire zigzagging ride; I had to remind myself to breathe. Bailey's confident prose and dark satire enrich the ingenious plot, and her authentic characters—whether damaged, yearning, or downright diabolical—make this compulsory reading for fans of suspense. An exceptional debut!"

—Sonja Yoerg, *Washington Post* bestselling author of *True Places*

HELLO,
JULIET

OTHER TITLES BY SAMANTHA M. BAILEY

HELLO, JULIET

SAMANTHA M. BAILEY

THOMAS & MERCER

Published by Thomas & Mercer, Seattle

www.apub.com

Amazon, the Amazon logo, and Thomas & Mercer are trademarks of Amazon.com, Inc., or its affiliates.

EU product safety contact:
Amazon Media EU S. à r.l.
38, avenue John F. Kennedy, L-1855 Luxembourg
amazonpublishing-gpsr@amazon.com

ISBN-13: 9781662513565 (paperback)
ISBN-13: 9781662513572 (digital)

Cover design by Mumtaz Mustafa
Cover image: © Buena Vista Images, © George Doyle / Getty

Printed in the United States of America

For Miko and Nicole,
the most brilliant, beautiful stars, who've lit up my life
since the nineties.
I wouldn't be me without both of you.

There is only one thing in the world worse than
being talked about, and
that is not being talked about.
—Oscar Wilde, *The Picture of Dorian Gray*

CHAPTER ONE

Now
January 17, 2024

"You don't know the danger you're walking into."

My head snaps up. I lock eyes with the Uber driver, who grins wolfishly at me in his rearview mirror when he stops outside Sunrise Studios. He's just reciting the tagline from *Hello, Juliet,* the teen drama I starred in almost a decade ago, but he's not wrong. I wouldn't have come back here today if I had any choice.

"You're Poison Ivy, right?" he says, like I'm in on the joke of the viral hashtag that's defined me for nearly a third of my life.

"Right," I breezily answer with a smile so he won't post on his social media about what a bitch I am.

"I saw the docuseries about you."

You and the rest of the world, I think but don't say out loud, because what's the point? This man isn't engaging me in conversation to be friendly. He wants something from me. Everyone does.

No one warned me that on Sunday night, a Tattle TV docuseries salaciously entitled *Rock Bottom: Celebs Who Never Bounced Back* was going to drop on a major streaming network. No one contacted me to verify the accuracy of episode three—forty-five agonizing minutes of interviews about my resounding public crash from grace with tabloid reporters, gossip bloggers, professors of pop culture, and even the teenage boy who does the stocking at the market where I've worked as a cashier for the last three years.

I'm not blameless, but apparently, I'm the only one the fans, the media, and surely my costars and Mack Foster—the creator of *Hello, Juliet*—blame for the tragic end of one of the most explosively popular shows ever to air on television.

Nina Johnson—the so-called *docuseries* filmmaker, who once interviewed me so deferentially that she practically bowed at my feet—doesn't know me. This Uber driver doesn't know me. And the thousands of Instagram and TikTok users reviving the #PoisonIvy trend with a clip of me drowning in my own blood in a claw-foot tub—taken from a five-year-old slasher film—definitely don't know me.

I chose to be an actress because I wanted to be extraordinary. If I'd known that landing the lead role of Juliet Jones would turn me into a meme, I'd have run away as fast as I could.

Politely thanking the driver, not making eye contact, I exit the car and watch him disappear down The Lane, which is what my former castmates and I used to call the narrow stretch of road off Higuera Street.

The morning sun beams down on the empty parking lot and loading bay to the right of the studio's front entrance. But no light filters through the towering California sycamores that hover over the dull gray one-story building where *Hello, Juliet* was shot. The soundstage looks exactly the same as it did all those years ago when I walked off the set one evening, not realizing then I'd never return.

In a thin jean jacket, I shiver in the January chill, cold dread already spreading through my weary body. Miraculously, I slept hard last night, but I still feel unrested and uneasy.

My phone beeps. For a second, when I take it out of my bag, hope flutters in my chest that it might be Lauren, texting me before a shoot the way she used to. Then I'm angry at myself for allowing that sliver of excitement. Lauren wouldn't text me; she hates me. And I should hate her for betraying me, but a tiny part of my heart still belongs to the only best friend I've ever had.

But of course, it's my mother who's texted me. She's the sole person from my life back then who's still with me now.

Mom: Break a leg.

Ivy: Knowing Mack, I might.

Mom: Cute. You've got this. Text me right after the shoot. Or before. Whenever you need me. Oh, I'm doing this . . .

There's a photo attached. I open it, and tears spring to my eyes when I see my mom in a chair under a sign that reads DR. SARITA NELSON, ORTHOPEDIC SPECIALIST.

Ivy: What???

Mom: Surprise! If you're brave enough to shoot this reunion special, I can have a consultation.

Ivy: This makes me so happy, Mom.

Mom: You okay without me?

My breath catches. My mother was as much a part of *Hello, Juliet* as me. The cast and crew loved the treats she'd bake for them and how she remembered the little details about their lives: their birthdays and kids' names. My costars would come to our house for a hug, a home-cooked meal, a sense of security none of them had with their own families.

Ivy: I'm okay.

Mom: Love you.

Ivy: Love you more.

Mom: Impossible.

The familiar affectionate exchange comforts me. And my mom's surprise makes walking into this building easier. No matter that I'm thirty-two; my mother is my safe place. I need her to be healthy. She refused to see a doctor for her debilitating back pain for years, preferring to treat herself with homeopathic remedies and ice packs. Even when we had the money for proper health insurance, she was too afraid surgery might go wrong and leave me an orphan.

But she can no longer ignore the osteoarthritis and possible spinal stenosis I'm convinced she has, thanks to Dr. Google. Her legs often go numb, and she's starting to limp. The money that Mack offered for a top-secret reunion of the *Hello, Juliet* cast is the only reason I agreed to show up at Sunrise Studios this morning. Twenty thousand dollars was Venmoed to me five minutes after I inked my name on the contract and NDA. I'll receive another $100,000 once filming is complete. If Mack sells it to a streaming network, I get another $100,000 plus 8 percent of the profit share. With that, my mother can quit her cleaning job, and I can get her the best medical care possible.

There's a part of me that's envisioned a reunion like *Friends*—the laughter, tears, joy, forgiveness. The public adoration and redemption. But *Hello, Juliet* wasn't a comedy. It was a dark teenage drama. And it bled into our real lives.

The fans ate up the palpable tension and sinister secrets between high school students Juliet, Skylar, Hudson, and Logan, never knowing who was truly a hero and who a villain. Behind the scenes, just like my character, Juliet, I never knew which of my castmates I could fully trust.

And that self-doubt I've worked hard to vanquish over the last decade rushes back as I scan my outfit—loose-fitting black dress pants I found in a thrift shop and a fitted white T-shirt that's already dampening under my arms from nervous sweat. I'm sure Mack's hair and makeup team will spackle foundation over my freckles and he'll have me change into clothes he finds more suitable. I'll let him control how I appear on camera, but I won't let him control me. Not again. I might need the money, but I certainly don't need his approval anymore.

"They can't hurt you," I whisper as I step to the side of the building, where a black gate blocks the pathway to the performers' entrance.

There aren't any security guards to protect me anymore. No one who's anyone in Hollywood shoots here. After *Hello, Juliet* ended, the soundstage became an urban legend. Sunrise Studios was rumored to be cursed. I don't believe in rumors, having been the target of so many half-truths and blatant lies, but cursed it is.

I open the email my mom forwarded to me from Ellyn Lou Mara, Mack's PA, for the security code for the gate. My mother still fields all my requests, but this is the only one I've gotten in five years, except for an offer to appear on a D-list-celebrity naked survival show. I'm not that desperate. Yet.

Dropping my phone into my bag, I reach for the keypad on the gate, punch in the code, and feel my heart in my throat when the wrought iron creaks open. It closes behind me, and as I walk down the pathway, I try not to remember the late nights when Jesse would press me up against the brick wall next to the heavy steel door, kissing me hard in between takes, before we raced back inside to the set so Mack didn't catch us together. The morning that Caleb and I got locked out during a power outage and sat on the ground playing Twenty Questions until someone finally let us in. And all the times that Lauren and I left the set together to have dinner and late-night marathon gossip sessions.

It was never fame that I sought. I yearned for validation and acceptance and to prove to my mom and myself that I was good enough, talented enough for her to have sacrificed her whole life to help me fulfill my dream. That dream turned into a nightmare, and my best friends became my worst enemies.

Blowing out a breath, I punch in the same code to open the steel door. My nerves get the best of me when I hear that familiar scrape of metal against concrete. A screech almost of pain. I don't want to be a victim nor cause any more damage. I hurt my costars to survive, but none of us really survived intact.

It's pitch dark inside the corridor that leads to four dressing rooms. Lauren and I had ours next to each other, and Caleb's and Jesse's were across the corridor. I can't see a thing, and I'm instantly disoriented.

My call time is at 10:00 a.m. It's only 9:30, so perhaps Jesse and Lauren will swan in right on time. I hope so. I want a bit of space to myself before I come face to face with the past. For a moment, I long to be that naive, hopeful twenty-two-year-old again, her whole life in front of her, as she's led to her first real dressing room with her name inside a gold star attached to the door.

I use my phone to find the light in the corridor. Flipping the switch, I can now see the entire long, narrow hallway I walked down every day. Leaning on the wall to get my bearings, I'm struck by how much I've changed but how this place hasn't changed at all.

It's eerily silent except for the tap of my boots as they echo off the floor. There's not a single sound to indicate that anyone else is here yet. I didn't even see the crew vans in the parking lot. Where's the lighting and camera team? Where is Mack? He might already be on the soundstage waiting, though I expected him to be in his office at the very end of this corridor, marking up a script, maybe manipulating another young girl into becoming the star he wants her to be, at any cost. Or maybe he wants to unsettle me so he can capture me agitated on camera. It would be just like Mack to change everyone's call time except mine at the last minute without informing me, to start me off at a disadvantage.

All the dressing room doors are closed. Despite my desire not to care, my heart twinges when I see LAUREN MALLOY in black block letters inside a gold star on her door. Before I met Lauren, I never would have believed that I could get so close to someone so fast. That anyone would want to be that close to me. And I never anticipated her disappearing from my life just as quickly.

The star with JESSE RAFFERTY in the center causes a stabbing pain in my chest. He's the only man I've ever loved and lost to another woman. Of course, there's no star for Caleb Hill. No trail of sand sprinkled along the corridor. Caleb would usually surf before his call time and come straight to set in his wet suit and grab a quick shower before heading to hair and makeup. He can't be here today.

I press my ear to Lauren's door. I don't hear her humming to herself like she used to or Jesse strumming his guitar. I don't hear anything at all. The silence is disconcerting.

I want to be inside my room and not alone in this creepy hallway. I move to my door and turn the knob to total blackness.

"Damn it, where is that light?" I feel along the wall, expecting to hit a switch, but there's only a rough, flat surface under my fingers.

The door swings shut behind me with a bang. I jump. I forgot that I need to prop it open with a doorstop. With the thin strip of light from the corridor leaking into the room, my eyes adjust to the darkness. I see that the setup in here is almost the same as it was back then. The same small two-seater couch is to the left of the door, and the vanity table is still against the wall across from the closet. But so much is different too. The pile of novels that I replenished often to read between takes no longer rests on the floor next to the couch, and it smells musty instead of pepperminty without the essential oil diffuser from my mom that I used to keep on the table.

I'm so focused on reaching the vanity that I don't see the metal chair lying on its side in front of me. I almost trip over it, my heart skipping a beat as I steady myself.

"Bruised and bloodied on camera would be fabulous," I say sarcastically to no one.

Righting the chair, I pull it over to the vanity and flick the switch on the side of the mirror. The bulbs running along the top bathe the room in a warm glow. It's too bad that the flattering light does nothing to erase the dark circles grooved under my eyes.

I put my bag and phone on the chair and lean close to the mirror. When I shake out my hair with my fingers, I'm dismayed that I've only made it frizzier. And the magenta lip gloss that suited me in the back seat of the Uber bleeds at the corners of my mouth. I'm a mess.

I find a tissue in my bag, and as I'm wiping off the gloss, I hear a creak behind me. I yelp, then laugh at myself. I'm twitchy already, and there's a whole stressful day ahead of me.

In the mirror, I see the closet door, which must have been ajar when I walked in, slowly closing. There's something hanging on the front of it.

I turn around.

Not *something*. *Someone*.

My mouth drops open, but only a terrified squeak comes out. I gape at the woman whose body is suspended from a scarf attached to the silver hook.

Her neck is bent, head lolling at a sickening angle, a sheet of hair obscuring her face. But when I see a familiar pair of red Converse dangling above the floor, I let out a cry.

Bolting over to the closet, I bang into the metal chair. My bag topples, and my phone lands with a loud crack on the cheap hardwood.

"Lo," I whisper, the nickname I haven't said out loud for years automatically falling from my lips.

I grab her wrist to feel for a pulse. Horror burns a path up my throat and panic slices into me when nothing jumps against my fingers. Her skin is cold.

Lauren is dead.

ACTORS ACCESS

BREAKDOWN EXPRESS

February 14, 2014

Ivy Westcott

Résumé

Represented by	
Elizabeth Hardwick Management (CA)	
Television	
Little Marvels series	Regular
Jamming with Jimmy	Supporting
Pretty Dolls	Supporting
Life Skills	Supporting
Commercials	
List upon request	
Training	
Luke Lawson School of Acting	
Dance Central Academy	
Raise Your Voice Training Center	
Physical Characteristics	
Height: 5'2"	
Weight: 115 pounds	
Hair color: Red	
Hair length: Long	
Eyes: Green	

ROLECALL

EXCLUSIVE ONLINE ACCESS
TO BREAKING CASTING NEWS

February 16, 2014

Auditions kick off next week for the final supporting role in hitmaker Mack Foster's newest project, *Hello, Juliet*. This gritty but glossy drama centers on a group of beautiful teenage do-gooders at Sunset Shores, a wealthy Santa Monica high school, and the clever, edgy newest arrival who uncovers the dark secrets lurking beneath their flawless exterior.

Attached to the project already are Broadway star and popular teen TV heartthrob Jesse Rafferty, whose lead role in the musically based soapy drama *Concert Hall* earned him an Emmy nomination, and fan favorite Caleb Hill—best known for his critically acclaimed role in *The End Zone*—who's back on the scene after completing a degree in kinesiology at UCLA. Word on the street is that It Girl Lauren Malloy, who most recently appeared in Foster's last smash, *Malibu Mansion*, is a shoo-in for the coveted lead role of Juliet Jones. The role of Juliet's frenemy, Skylar Rawlins, is still up for grabs.

CHAPTER TWO

Ivy was suffocating. Not just because the black leather jacket her mother had found for her secondhand at Savers was too hot and tight but also because her fear was strangling her. What if the cMail—a message via the exclusive Actors Access system—inviting Ivy to audition today for Skylar Rawlins had been sent by mistake? Surrounded by cool, composed blondes, she was the only sweaty redhead in the windowless waiting room. Ivy didn't look like a girl whose orbit everyone wanted to be in. She'd have to prove to Mack Foster that she could act like her.

But when her gaze landed on Lauren Malloy, who was sitting closest to the audition-room door, Ivy felt even more self-conscious. Effortlessly ethereal in low-rise tight jeans, a black T-shirt so cropped that her diamond navel ring visibly sparkled, and white-blonde hair gleaming, Lauren commanded attention without saying a word.

Lauren probably wasn't here for the supporting female role—she was pretty much guaranteed to play the lead, Juliet Jones, at least according to RoleCall, the most reputable site for casting news. But just being in the same room with Mack Foster's darling made the pressure of this moment so intense that Ivy's left leg started vibrating. The metal chair she was sitting on banged against the linoleum floor.

Her mother leaned over from the chair next to hers and put a gentle hand on her knee. "You've got this." She said it so quietly into Ivy's ear that it was more the closeness, her soothing scent of lavender from the soap she made herself than the words that calmed Ivy.

Only forty, with thick, wavy caramel-colored hair, her mother looked like Ivy's older, more striking friend. She instinctually knew how to move her lithe body, unlike Ivy, whose arms and legs didn't feel attached to her.

If not for her mother, Ivy would have given up on her dream of being a successful actress a long time ago. Her mom's unwavering belief in her and all the hours she worked cleaning to afford Ivy's classes, headshots, and demo reels had led to this moment. If Ivy booked this career-transforming job, their lives would finally be easier. If she failed, what then? She'd been striving toward the goal of becoming a full-time actress for ten years. How much longer could she and her mom persist before giving up?

Ivy sighed too loudly. From across the room Lauren caught her eye. Ivy felt her face redden, but then Lauren smiled. And when the beautiful, famous actress—whom Ivy had only ever seen before on the cover of magazines—got up and sat down right beside her, Ivy gasped out a squawk of shock. Mortified, she stared at the floor. But then Lauren spoke.

"Ivy Westcott, right?"

Speechless, Ivy lifted her head but could only nod, unable to hide her astonishment that Lauren Malloy actually knew her name.

"Yeah, I loved you in *Little Marvels*. Hazel was my favorite character."

Ivy blinked. Was this really happening?

Little Marvels was the only show she'd ever starred in. For four seasons, from the ages of eight to twelve, she had been Hazel Brooks, child scientist. That was the happiest she'd ever been. She loved that it made the worry line between her mother's eyebrows disappear. And even though the kids at school never seemed to want Ivy around, she had friends on the cast and fans who wanted to be just like her. Under those lights on set, Ivy felt special. She'd been seeking that kind of joy ever since.

Ivy's mom reached out her hand. "Nice to meet you, Lauren. I'm Elizabeth Hardwick. Ivy's manager."

Lauren glanced at Elizabeth, then at Ivy. "You look alike."

Ivy was startled. Few people told her she looked like her mother. From the one photo she had of her father, who had died in a car accident before she was born, Ivy knew where her red hair and freckles came from.

Uncomfortable that she seemed to be the only girl here with representation, never mind a family member, Ivy quietly said, "She's also my mom," then veered the conversation back to Lauren. "I'm surprised you have to audition, since you've already starred in one of Mack Foster's shows."

Lauren grinned like Ivy's words mattered to her. "I'm just here for a meeting with Mack."

"Did you already book Juliet Jones?" Ivy blurted, then immediately realized her mistake. If it wasn't officially announced in the trades, Lauren obviously couldn't tell some actress she'd never met before that she'd landed the role. How stupid could Ivy be?

But Lauren laughed, so prettily that Ivy laughed back. Hers was more of a rough bark, and she made a mental note to soften it. Lauren was the epitome of everything Ivy hoped to be. Merely speaking to her was momentous, as though through osmosis, Ivy might become as confident and sparkly. She needed to savor this conversation, replay it with her mom later tonight to glean any kernels of advice or insight.

Reaching over, Lauren tugged one of Ivy's curls, giggling when it bounced right back up. "Your hair is gorgeous."

"Thank you," she said automatically, smiling instead of cringing like she usually did when someone commented on her hair.

Even though it was her fiery-red curls that had gotten her discovered, Ivy actually hated that it was the only quality about her that anyone ever noticed. She was only seven when a woman in a pink pantsuit had approached her and Elizabeth at a toy store in a mall. Her mother couldn't afford to buy the expensive Barbie Dreamhouse that Ivy wanted more than anything, so they'd gone to play with the one on display.

"Those ringlets! Are they natural?" the woman exclaimed as Ivy was lost in the world of make-believe. She didn't even glance up. It was only when they'd arrived home at the converted storage unit they lived in below an Italian restaurant in Watts that her mother told her the woman was a casting director for Barbie.

A few weeks later, Ivy shot her first commercial. The lines came easily for her, and she got her very own Dreamhouse to keep. She was so excited when, for the first time, Elizabeth invited the girls in her class to come over and play. But their parents wouldn't let them, because they didn't think Ivy's neighborhood was safe. Ivy knew it wasn't only where she lived but how. Her mom cleaned some of her classmates' houses in Beverly Hills, where open enrollment meant that Ivy could attend the prestigious school with the kids her mom thought would make good friends. But she'd never belong with the girls whose lunch boxes cost more than her family's weekly food budget.

Even after Ivy had landed the role of Hazel in *Little Marvels* and Elizabeth could finally afford to buy her the trendy clothes the other girls wore, they still didn't want to spend time with her. So, Ivy pretended she really was the child prodigy whose science experiments could save the world from destruction. That was what she loved about acting most. Being someone other than herself.

But here with Lauren in real life, Ivy couldn't yet pretend to be Skylar Rawlins. And she couldn't discern if Lauren was putting on an act with her. It was so hard to tell in this town. She racked her brain for something to say that wouldn't sound lame.

"I like your shoes," Ivy said, pointing to Lauren's red Converse.

"Thanks! I wear them all the time. It sounds so flaky, but I think red is a lucky color." Then she leaned closer. "Like your hair."

Right then, the door at the end of the room opened. A smiling Black woman wearing jeans and a white button-down and holding a clipboard called Ivy's name.

"Break a leg," Lauren told her.

Elizabeth dipped her chin once, their secret sign that Ivy had this. That she could do anything she wanted as long as she tried her best. But Ivy couldn't help feeling anxious. She'd read that Lauren had been accepted to Princeton but deferred. Ivy hadn't even applied for college. Her grades were probably good enough for a scholarship, but it would have deterred her from her only goal: proving that she could make it in Hollywood.

She dug her nails into her palms and strode toward the room, standing as tall as she could, which was difficult at only five foot two. And when the woman closed the door behind her and joined the two people sitting at the long table, the ones who would decide her fate, Ivy hid that her knees buckled slightly by jutting her hip, hoping it seemed confidently coy like Skylar Rawlins and not gawky like Ivy Westcott.

The woman who'd called her name told Ivy to stand on the mark in front of the camera set up on a tripod.

"I'm Clarice Hunting, the casting director." She pointed to another Black woman at the far end, also in jeans and a white shirt, who couldn't have been more than a few years older than Ivy. "This is Vanessa Leese, the assistant director." Then she gestured to the only man, whose shaved head—and the stormy expression on his tanned face—immediately intimidated her. "And this is Mack Foster: creator, executive producer, director, showrunner."

She'd never seen Mack in person, only in magazines and on screen, walking the red carpet at events and parties. She knew he was forty-three and had a wife and twins, but he kept most of his personal life private. He had a reputation for being an exacting but loyal director who took care of his cast. But he wasn't even looking at her; his attention was on her headshot and résumé.

"Nice to meet you," Ivy said in a voice that didn't belong to her. It was husky, gravelly, a little mischievous.

After what felt like minutes, Mack finally lifted his head. "You haven't had a starring role since *Little Marvels*?"

Ivy cleared her throat. "Not yet." She let out a little laugh, hoping Mack would laugh too. He didn't, so to cover the tension, Ivy kept talking. "I was recently in *Life Skills*, that show about the guidance counselor with eight teenagers of her own?"

Squinting, Mack leaned forward, his gray T-shirt straining across his barrel chest. "Never heard of it. Role?"

"Um, I was a friend of one of her kids."

"Guest star?"

Ivy pulled at one of her curls. "Background."

Mack leveled a withering look at Clarice and turned back to Ivy. "You're twenty-two?" He said it like it was a flaw.

"Yes."

"You look a lot younger."

"I've always been small," she said, then wanted to slap her hand over her mouth.

His eyes rolled. "You're different, that's for sure."

Had Mack approved the list of actresses Clarice invited to try out? It felt like he didn't even know why Ivy was there. Maybe, as she'd worried in the waiting room, Clarice had sent the cMail to the wrong person.

Whether it was a mistake or not, she couldn't blow this chance. Every time Ivy showed up to an audition, she tried to believe that this would be her moment. Yet each time, she was told that her look wasn't exactly what they were going for; that they were aiming in a different direction, which basically meant that Ivy wasn't pretty enough or talented enough to deserve a coveted spot among the Hollywood elite. Never before, though, had she auditioned in front of one of the most successful men in Hollywood.

"I'll read the part of Juliet Jones. Whenever you're ready, Ms. Westcott," Mack said tightly.

Ivy breathed in and out through her nose, imagining for a moment that she was by the ocean, her calm place, where gazing at the endless expanse of water made her feel that her possibilities were boundless too. Ivy straightened her shoulders and grinned, zipping herself into the skin of self-assured Skylar Rawlins, who was meeting a nervous, guarded Juliet Jones for the first time.

She looked into the red light of the camera. "Welcome to Sunset Shores, Juliet. I'll be your new best friend here. Moral support, study buddy, shopping partner. Whatever you need." Her newfound rasp cracked, and heat flushed through her.

Mack narrowed his eyes but read the next line. "Oh, I didn't realize my student liaison was an actual student. You even have your own office?"

Ivy flicked her hair off her shoulder, channeling the blondes on the other side of the door. "Well, I share it with Hudson, the student body president, who's also my boyfriend." She smiled, then quickly skimmed her eyes over Mack's outfit so it wouldn't be clear whether Skylar was judging Juliet or simply taking her in. Whether she was friend or enemy. "I'm a much better person to show you around than the teachers, trust me. I have a knack for repairing broken things." Ivy laughed lightly. "Just kidding. But you'll be happy you're paired up with me."

Mack held up a hand. "Do you know how many actresses want this role?"

Ivy felt her chest burn as she nodded.

Mack appraised her for so long that she was sure he could smell the nervous desperation seeping from her pores. Ivy didn't know whether to look back at him, look at the floor, or run out of the room and never look back.

Clarice said, "We'll be in touch."

And Ivy was dismissed. She did what she was supposed to and thanked everyone for their time.

Before she'd even fully closed the door behind her, she heard Mack say, as though she were invisible, "Seriously, Clarice?"

"I liked her look. She's relatable. A diamond in the rough."

Mack scoffed. "That was definitely rough."

Quietly, Ivy shut the door, holding back her tears. She'd completely messed up her biggest shot but didn't understand exactly how.

Slumping, she crossed to where her mom and Lauren were chatting like they were at a hair salon and not the most important audition of Ivy's life. Ivy knew she wasn't being fair thinking that, but she was hurt. She wanted her mother to gather her in her arms and heal the crack that Mack's harshness had opened. She'd been to a lot of brutal auditions, but that was by far the worst. She didn't even make it through the whole scene before he'd had enough of her. She'd never experienced that kind of humiliation before.

But as Ivy stepped closer to them, Lauren stood and grabbed her arm. "So? How did it go?" There was no underlying motive in the question that Ivy could detect, just genuine interest.

Ivy only shrugged, because she didn't want to fall apart here.

Clarice called Lauren's name, and Ivy whispered hoarsely, "Break a leg," like Lauren had, hoping it was the right thing to say for a meeting.

She followed her mother to the elevator, and they were silent until they exited the imposing black glass building. Once they reached the sidewalk, Ivy burst into tears.

"Honey, what happened?" Her mother wrapped her in a hug, rubbing gentle circles on her back.

"He hated me." She didn't want to feel sorry for herself, but she knew her mother must be disappointed in her.

Besides being a background player on *Life Skills*, Ivy's most recent job had been as a murder victim in *Homicide in the Hills*, a cop drama no one watched. The only part of her that made the final cut in the scene was her left hand, before the body bag was zipped up. She tried so hard and gave every role all she had, but for some reason, her career had stalled once she hit puberty. No longer an adorable and precocious little girl, as a woman, Ivy didn't seem to stand out.

This audition was supposed to be the big break celebrities talked about in interviews, that one unforgettable moment when their lives changed forever. Ivy just ruined her shot, and their lives would be exactly the same when they woke up tomorrow.

It wasn't a bad life. But it wasn't how they'd planned for it to be. Ivy knew her mother wanted to take care of her forever, but she was an adult now and had so little life experience to show for it. But she let her mother hold her until she was all cried out.

"Let's go home. I'm sure it wasn't as bad as you think it was." Elizabeth quickly wiped away the tears under Ivy's eyes.

Ivy was despondent as they started walking toward Wilshire Boulevard.

"Wait up!"

She turned, startled to see Lauren running toward them, her keys clanging musically in her hand, her blonde hair shimmering in the sun.

"Can I take you both to lunch? My car's just in the lot." Lauren pointed to the parking area at the back of the sleek building Ivy never wanted to see again.

In the sunlight, Ivy noticed above Lauren's eyebrow a small scar that she'd never seen on her in photos or on TV. It made Lauren real as opposed to a celebrity. Still, bombing the audition felt even more significant now, because Ivy was in the company of someone she'd never match up to.

"That's lovely of you, Lauren. Thank you," Elizabeth said, since Ivy was dumbstruck.

They climbed into Lauren's shiny white Jeep, Ivy taking the back and giving her mother the front.

"Are you always this nice?" Ivy spouted, then bit the inside of her lip. She didn't spend a lot of time with girls her age. And she didn't understand why Lauren wanted to spend time with her when she probably had a contact list full of famous friends to have lunch with.

"I like to think I'm always this nice." Lauren laughed and turned around in her seat. "Very few people in Hollywood are genuine. And you seem genuine." Facing the front again, she pulled out onto Wilshire, immediately getting stuck in traffic behind a long line of cars. "I was thinking about lunch at Ivy at the Shore. Kismet, right? They do great crab cakes, if you like seafood."

Ivy caught her mother's eye in the side mirror. The dichotomy between their lives was glaring. Was it possible that Lauren didn't realize that Ivy's leather jacket, jeans, and T-shirt were all secondhand and the only seafood she ever ate was from Señor Fish?

But Ivy said, "Sure, that sounds great," as brightly as she could, looking back at the glass building. A figure loomed by a window in Mack's office on the tenth floor. She shivered. His mere presence was overpowering.

When Lauren made a left on La Cienega, her phone rang.

"My agent," she said. "I have to take this. Sorry."

Then Elizabeth's phone rang. Ivy didn't know which conversation to listen to, or neither. Lauren made the choice for her by putting her phone on speaker.

"Hi, Rayna! Just on my way to lunch. What's up?"

"You got a chemistry read for *Hello, Juliet*. With Jesse Rafferty."

"What do you mean a chemistry read? I mean, I know, but I thought—"

Ivy saw Lauren's brows knit in the mirror while at the same time her mother was saying, "Mm-hmm," into her phone. A mix of worries over Lauren's reaction to her news and whatever was being said to her mother made Ivy squirm in the back.

"Yes," Rayna said on speaker. "The chemistry read will clinch the role. It's between you and another actress. I wasn't expecting that, either, but it is what it is."

Ivy's stomach flipped. Could it be? But how was that possible when she'd tanked the audition?

"Okay, thanks. Please email me the info." Lauren ended the call.

So did her mother, who then turned around in her seat, her face glowing with excitement. "Oh my God," she mouthed. And out loud she said calmly, "You got a callback, Ives. For Juliet Jones."

Ivy's jaw dropped. "But I auditioned for Skylar."

Her mom grinned. "Apparently Mack saw something in you. The woman on the phone said something about a diamond in the rough."

Up front Lauren was silent for a moment before swinging her head to the back. "Congrats! That's so cool we're up for the same role."

Ivy wasn't sure if she should apologize to this lovely person taking them out to lunch—a person who'd clearly thought Juliet Jones was hers. This was almost too much to take in. How often did those seemingly impossible wishes come true? A chemistry read was only the first step, but it was the furthest Ivy had ever gotten before. She should be screaming with joy. But she couldn't stop hearing a little voice in her head whisper, *Be careful what you wish for.*

CHAPTER THREE

Now

"No!" I scream at Lauren's lifeless body, hanging from the hook on the closet door.

I drop my hand from her cold, smooth wrist and fall to my knees in front of her. I'm shaking so hard that my teeth chatter, and a sob tears from my throat. "I should have gotten here sooner. I'm sorry. I'm so sorry."

We were supposed to forgive each other. Now it's too late to repair the most important friendship I've ever had. I've lost Lauren forever. How can that be?

"Why would you do this to yourself, Lo? Please come back," I uselessly plead, as though the power of my voice can revive her.

But nothing will bring her back to me.

My heart hammers in my chest, because I don't know what to do first. I want to untie the scarf she's knotted around her neck, hold her in my arms, and not let her go. But I also don't want to be by myself in here with her. And yet I can't go out into the corridor and leave her all alone. Turning to the door, I yell, "Help! Please, God, someone come!"

I hold my breath for a second to listen for anyone who might be in the hall. I don't hear anything at all from outside this room, but everything is soundproofed on the stage. No one would know we're even here at all unless they're in another dressing room or an office.

Time has no meaning, so I'm not sure how long I've been in here, but surely Mack and the crew should have arrived by now. Jesse too. As tears pour down my face, I get off my knees and stumble over to my phone, which is face down on the floor. I pick it up. The screen is spidered with thin cracks. It's how my heart feels as I punch in the digits with a trembling finger and press the phone to my ear. A wail erupts from my mouth as I look at Lauren, *my* Lauren, her long blonde hair styled in waves, dark-wash jeans fitted to her long, lean legs, and those lucky red shoes that she always wore for every big moment in her life.

"Nine one one, what's your emergency?"

I'm crying too hard to speak.

"Hello? Do you need police, ambulance, or fire?"

I exhale a long, stuttered breath to stop crying long enough to explain what's happened. "There's a deceased woman"—my voice cracks—"in a dressing room at Sunrise Studios. She's hung herself. Please come. I don't know what to do."

"Okay, ma'am. Emergency units are being dispatched and will be there momentarily. How do you know the victim is deceased? Have you tried CPR?"

"I don't know CPR. I felt for a pulse, and there's nothing. She's not breathing. Please just get here as fast as possible." My explanation is garbled as I raggedly relay what I can.

"Take a breath, okay, ma'am? Help is on its way. What's your name, please?"

"Ivy," I whisper.

"Can you repeat that?"

"Ivy. My name is Ivy."

"Great, Ivy. I'm going to ask you to leave the dressing room and wait outside. Can you do that?"

I nod stupidly, like she can see me, then add, "Yes."

"Thank you. And do you know the name of the victim?"

I hang up. I don't want to give Lauren's name, in case any paparazzi have police scanners. I can't bear for either of us to be headline news before I have even begun to understand what's going on.

How can I walk away and leave Lauren like this? I did that once before, and it's left a gaping hole in my life. I can't bring her back to me, but I can get her down so she has a bit of dignity when the police find her.

I shut the closet door, horrified when Lauren's body sways with the impact, then drag the metal chair over so I can stand on it. Bracing myself, I tenderly move her sheet of blonde hair away from her face. "Oh my God!" I cry, aghast at the pinprick-like red dots splotching her cheeks and her tongue protruding from her mouth.

Retching, I focus on how to undo the blue scarf that she looped so many times around the silver hook on the door and so tightly around her neck that it cuts into her delicate skin, where angry purple bruises bloom.

Lauren clearly planned to take her own life and made sure it would work. But the Lauren I knew loved life so much. What changed since the last time I saw her, in 2014? An unbearable heaviness settles in my chest as I try to jam my finger between the thin fabric and her neck, but I only succeed in breaking a fingernail. "Goddamn it, Lo. How did things get so bad? All you had to do was call me. I would have helped you."

I pull my hand from the scarf, and with another deep sob, I hold her face in my hands, tilting it so I can see her famously turquoise eyes that are open but glazed over and bloodshot. The tiny scar above her right eyebrow—from a gash when her mother's hand slipped while tweezing Lauren's eyebrows when she was only six—is more pronounced in death than in life.

I long for her to tell me she's just acting, proving once again how much more talented she is than me. I'm dizzy as the past and present swirl in a kaleidoscope of sorrowful nostalgia. All the anger seems so pointless now that I've lost her for good.

It occurs to me that Lauren might have written a note. If she hung herself in my old dressing room, maybe she left some last words for me that will help make any sense of this.

I scan the dressing room for her bag, a piece of paper, or an envelope. There's nothing here for me, and there's nothing I can do for her. Slowly, I step down from the chair, look at Lauren one last time, and leave, closing my dressing room door so no one but the emergency unit will know that Lauren is dead inside.

If anyone else shows up and walks in the building, I don't want them to experience the trauma I have. I can't process the finality of it, the horror, and numbly I text my mom to come to the studio as soon as she can. I don't want to be without her. That's all I tell her, because I can't bring myself to message her the news that she'll never speak to Lauren, whom she loved like a second daughter, ever again.

Just the thought of that conversation makes me want to collapse. I can't be here anymore. But sprinting down the empty corridor, I can't stop the memories from flooding in. They crash into me, one recollection after another—Jesse, Caleb, Lauren, and I playing hacky sack in between takes; Lauren laughing so hard that she fell into the wall, bruising her thigh right before a bikini scene; Jesse sliding his hand down the back of my jeans as we walked to our separate dressing rooms after a long night shoot.

I reach for the handle on the steel door leading to the outside, the same one I used only a short time ago. It's locked. Panicked, I realize I probably need the security code to exit. Again, it hits me that I'm the only one here who knows that Lauren is dead. After tapping in the code that I've memorized, I grab a rock from outside and prop open the door for the emergency crew. Then I spin around and walk in the other direction, toward the soundstage.

As much as I want to leave the building, I don't want even Mack to stumble on Lauren's body. No one should see that. I have to warn anyone who might be inside.

Samantha M. Bailey

I press the red button, the gears grinding loudly as the doors open to the soundstage, which is as dark as the dressing room corridor was when I arrived. The door clicks shut behind me. Apprehension crawls up my spine, and I turn on my phone flashlight. There's not a soul around.

No crew adjusting any lights or craft services setting up a table for breakfast. This might be a very bare-bones production, but Mack should be here, at least. A tidal wave of mixed emotions slams into me, and I regret walking onto the soundstage where Mack's brutal criticisms reduced me to a withering wallflower, making me redo lines again and again until he was satisfied. But no, he was never satisfied with me.

Confused and frightened, I should go, but like back then, I can't seem to do what's best for me and walk away. Instead, I move faster across the floor, shining my light in every corner in case Mack's lurking in the background somewhere, like he used to be, watching my every move, making me so nervous that I could barely perform.

"Hello?" I call out, trying to detect any noise. All I hear is the frantic beating of my heart. "Is anyone here?" I try again.

Keeping the flashlight trained on the floor in front of me, I expect to walk through the reconstructed set of Juliet's bedroom, with its walls full of indie-band posters; a plain wood dresser with small bowls of sea glass on top; and a twin bed, covered in a black-and-white checked duvet. And a full-length mirror with a Polaroid taped to the glass—Skylar and Juliet at a picnic on the beach, much like the picnic Lauren, Jesse, Caleb, and I had after our very first day of shooting. It was also the first and last time I felt completely safe with my castmates.

But there's no bedroom, and no window for Juliet to look out from, directly into Hudson's bedroom across the shared walkway between their town houses. The windows through which they'd hold up lined pieces of paper scrawled with secret notes to each other so Skylar would never discover her best friend and boyfriend were talking late at night.

And where Skylar's bedroom used to be—with the queen-size bed topped with fluffy pink pillows, the walls covered in photos of Skylar and Hudson in various embraces from freshman to junior years, and which held Skylar's numerous framed academic awards—there's only an empty space on the concrete floor.

What's also missing is Logan and Skylar's living room with the snow-white mohair couch and the crystal chandelier shaped like a spiderweb suspended from the ceiling. The room where Hudson crushed Juliet's heart, like Jesse did to me in real life.

There is absolutely nothing and no one here. What kind of reunion is this?

Inhaling the familiar combination of sawdust, paint fumes, and the rubbery smell of the green screens makes me lightheaded. I suddenly feel like I'm going to pass out. Afraid I'll smash my head on the concrete, I sink to the floor, put my head between my knees, and close my eyes. I'll sit here for a minute, just until I get my bearings.

I hear the grate of the massive elephant door, which isolates the stage from the outside world so no sound can carry through. It could be the EMTs, so I stay where I am, too dizzy to lift my head yet. But only one set of footsteps taps across the concrete. I open my eyes, hoping to hell they don't belong to Mack. In front of me is a pair of black combat boots.

Slowly, I move my gaze up black jeans and a black T-shirt to the face that once made my heart quicken every time I saw it. Eventually, it shattered me, even though I was the one who made him disappear.

Jesse.

TWITTER

February 23, 2014

Trending topics

#TeamBlonde
#TeamRedhead
#LaurenForJuliet
#IvyForJuliet
#HelloJuliet
#WhoIsIvyWestcott
#LaurenMalloyOrNoJuliet

@tvfanatic3215
Who the fuck is Ivy Westcott? Lauren Malloy IS Juliet Jones!

💬 1.2k   ↻ 25k   ♡ 75k

Replies

@ivegotthis: Ivy Westcott probably screwed Mack Foster.

@notonmywatch: Apparently she's only 5'2, so she only reaches his waist. LOL.

@bodypositivegrl

Love seeing a curvy redhead get the chance at a starring role. Go @ivywestcott! #TeamIvy

💬 5   🔁 7k   ♡ 10k

@effthisshit

Who'd you rather?

93%	Lauren Malloy
2%	Ivy Westcott
5%	Anyone but Ivy Westcott

CHAPTER FOUR

"Hello? Juliet?"

Ivy, sitting on her bed and scrolling through tweet after cruel tweet, looked up at Lauren, who laughed.

"I've been trying to get your attention for a full minute. How about these for the callback?" She pulled a lace shirt and a pair of jeans out of Ivy's closet and held them up for her.

Ivy appreciated the help with her outfit, but she couldn't laugh about Lauren's reference to the show they both had a chemistry read for today. Lauren had finished hers two hours ago; Ivy's was in ninety minutes.

"Sorry I'm so distracted." Ivy sighed and put down her phone. "I've never trended on Twitter before. People hate me for even being considered for Juliet. And I hate being in competition with you for it."

These thoughts had been running through Ivy's worried mind since she opened social media a few hours ago and saw there was an actual poll pitting her and Lauren against each other—a poll that Ivy was losing by a wide margin.

The noon sun streaming in through Ivy's little square of window made Lauren's eyes look even bluer than usual. It was almost painful how beautiful she was. And it was definitely painful to be in this terrible situation. Ivy was finally being given the chance at the role of a lifetime, yet she had to compete for it against the first real friend she'd ever had.

Lauren tossed the dusty-pink lace top and light-wash jeans on the edge of the twin bed. "You're right. It's not funny that we both want to be Juliet. But there are only so many twentysomething actresses who can play a sixteen-year-old and only so many roles. Eventually, we're all in competition for something," Lauren said gently. "And if I read every hateful thing people say about me, I wouldn't be able to function. It's why I like coming here, being with you and Liz. It's real life."

Ivy snorted. She was pretty sure that Lauren had never set foot in a ground-floor apartment, let alone one with bars on the windows, before Elizabeth had invited her over for dinner a week earlier. At first Ivy was appalled that Lauren would see how they lived. It was a step up from their last place, but it was nowhere near what she envisioned Lauren's to look like.

Yet Lauren seemed entranced by the warmth and simplicity of their one-bedroom home, admiring their colorful wall art, most of which Ivy and Elizabeth had plucked from the "Free" bins at garage sales. And when Lauren saw the basil growing on the windowsill in the kitchen, she and Elizabeth had a fifteen-minute discussion about herbs and spices. Ivy didn't think anyone but her mom could be as obsessed with gardening, but Lauren was genuinely passionate about it.

After Lauren had gotten home from the dinner, she and Ivy talked on the phone for two hours. In her bed, with only the sliver of moonlight through her window illuminating the small space, Ivy giggled softly so she wouldn't wake her mom, who slept on the pullout couch in the living room. The whispered confidences soon deepened into nightly phone calls and a soul connection that Ivy had never experienced before.

What if she booked Juliet Jones and lost Lauren? What if she didn't book Juliet and lost her biggest chance to get the recognition she yearned for and the financial stability she and Elizabeth desperately needed?

"I'm scared, Lo." Ivy rubbed her temples, where a stress headache had been pounding all day.

Lauren pushed aside the clothes and sat on the bed. Then she grimaced and pulled a paperback out from under the sheets. "You have more books than anyone I've ever met."

Ivy smiled. "They've kind of been my only friends since my mom taught me to read, when I was four. We went to the library almost every day when I was little, because it was free entertainment."

"I was shooting commercials when I was four. No time for entertainment at all." Lauren put her hand on Ivy's arm. "You're the first person I've been able to get close to in this industry. The first woman anyway. Like you, I don't trust easily. I've been burned too many times."

A few nights ago, on a late-night phone call, Lauren had confided to Ivy that she hadn't seen or spoken to her parents since they cowrote a tell-all about her a year earlier. The book was an act of retaliation. Fame was a family business, and Lauren was her parents' best shot at the big time. She was on a path to stardom after playing Kimberly Kitt in the last season of *Malibu Mansion*. But when the show ended, she told her parents that she wanted to accept Princeton's offer and take a break from acting. They responded by trying to sell her out. Lauren spent so much time and money suing them for defamation that she never went to Princeton. She lost the case.

In turn, Ivy confessed that she was afraid her mother's sacrifices would never be worth it, that she'd never make it as an actress. It was cathartic to share her worries with someone who wasn't responsible for her well-being. Ivy could talk to Lauren about the things she held back from her mother because she didn't want Elizabeth to worry about her.

Ivy pulled her knees to her chest. "Can I ask you something?"

Until recently, having a friend over, hanging out in her bedroom, was something she could only imagine. Even though Lauren seemed open with her, Ivy was still afraid to ask intrusive questions that could make Lauren retreat.

But Lauren nodded. "Anything."

"Do you want to act? I mean, if your parents aren't involved anymore, why are you still doing it?"

Lauren bit her lip, then smiled slyly. "Probably out of spite. And honestly, I don't actually want to go to college either. Plus, I need to make a living somehow, so it might as well be with the one thing I seem to be really good at."

On the surface, Lauren appeared to have it all together. Knowing that she struggled with self-doubt, too, gave Ivy the confidence to press her further. "What do you want?"

For a moment, Lauren's eyes dimmed, then she blinked, and her sparkle was back. "I want something of my own. It's not that I don't love acting, because I do. But I belong to the fans, the directors, the media. I want something that belongs only to me."

Ivy understood. This new friendship with Lauren was her own, and it was special to her. She hoped Lauren felt the same. And Elizabeth seemed to understand, too, because she gave Ivy her space today, when usually it would be her helping Ivy relax before an audition.

"Enough talking, because you need to get ready." Lauren got off the bed. "Want me to curl your hair?"

Ivy grinned. "Yes, please."

Making herself right at home, Lauren went to the bathroom and came back with the curling iron, then plugged it into the wall next to Ivy's full-length mirror. "Sit," she instructed.

Ivy plonked down on the scratched hardwood floor.

Once the iron heated up, Lauren wrapped a section of Ivy's hair around it, locking eyes with her in the mirror. "You need to believe in your self-worth, Ives. Just be yourself today."

"Awkward and uncomfortable?"

Lauren snorted, the sound filling Ivy with joy, as did the nickname only her mother had ever used. "Well, yes, because that's exactly who Juliet Jones is," Lauren said. She opened the jaws of the wand, releasing a perfect glossy curl. "Seriously, though, if you want my unsolicited advice, use your face more than your words to express how Juliet's wrestling with her feelings for Hudson and friendship with Skylar. Emote with your eyes." She shrugged. "That's what I did for my scene with him, at least."

Ivy nodded. "You've known Jesse a long time. You already have a rapport."

"Since we were eighteen. And you'll get to know him too. Jesse's a great guy, and you two actually have a lot in common."

Ivy raised her eyebrows. "How so?"

Lauren smiled. "Like you, Jesse's a bit hard to read. Keeps his cards close to his chest. And he lost his dad, too, though his passed away recently."

A twinge pinged Ivy's heart. "That's so sad. And not really the same as me, since my dad died before I was born."

"Yeah, but a loss is a loss," Lauren said gently. "Jesse's dad was on dialysis, and Jesse donated a kidney to him. He died three weeks later."

"Oh God." Ivy pressed a hand to her chest. "That's awful. I don't think I'd be able to survive if anything happened to my mom."

"Your mom is the best," Lauren said wistfully, glancing at the phone on Ivy's bed, which was dinging just about every second with Twitter notifications. "And as your manager, she can comb through your social media so you don't have to see the stupid polls and comments. Just turn off the notifications."

Ivy was about to agree when she heard the door buzzer. A moment later, Elizabeth came to her room. She beamed when she saw Ivy. "Oh, honey. Your hair looks amazing. And there's a car for you outside."

Ivy wrinkled her forehead. "A car?"

Lauren unplugged the curling iron. "There's no way you're taking the bus to the studio after my hard work here."

Tears sprang to Ivy's eyes. She couldn't believe how generous Lauren was. "Lo, thank you."

Lauren bent down and hugged Ivy. "No, Ives. Thank you and Liz for coming into my life. Roles come and go. But real friends stay. No matter what, I'm not going anywhere." She pulled away and winked. "You'll kill it today."

———

When the driver stopped outside a nondescript gray building with no signage, Ivy texted Lauren.

Ives: I don't know how to thank you for the car. I'm much calmer than I would have been taking the bus.

Lo: It was nothing. Break a leg!!!

Ivy smiled and turned off her phone. As she stepped across the uneven sidewalk to a huge steel door, she was surprised at how run down this area was, how dark the studio looked under the California sycamores that loomed over the building, entirely shielding it from the sun.

Pausing to run her hand through her bouncy curls, Ivy said another silent thank-you to Lauren. Ivy might know the words, but without her friend, she wouldn't have looked the part of a vulnerable sixteen-year-old trying so hard to protect herself from getting hurt.

She pressed the buzzer. The door slid open to a room full of equipment—dollies, cameras, wires, lighting. Sunrise Studios was completely different from any other soundstage she'd been on. *Little Marvels* was filmed in one of the big studios on Washington Boulevard, and she'd always been accompanied by her mother. This time she was all alone. The independence was both scary and exhilarating.

There was another small buzzer next to the elephant doors. Ivy pressed it and waited. Finally, after an interminable amount of time, they began to slide open. Mack stood there, tapping his steel-toed boot.

"You're late," he barked.

Ivy was early but didn't feel like she should argue. She wasn't going to apologize either, though. Just because she wanted this job, it didn't mean he could treat her like shit. But then, as they walked through the soundstage, his tall frame dwarfing hers, Ivy swallowed her irritation.

"Wow," she said, taking in the partially constructed world of *Hello, Juliet*.

Dividers blocked sets that were clearly in progress. Mack led her to the farthest set, which was finished. It was a tiny bedroom—where a twin bed, draped with a black-and-white checked duvet, was pushed up against a wall covered in indie-band posters. A small dresser with little white bowls of sea glass stood directly across from the bed. And pretty string lights were tacked up everywhere. A simple room, but Ivy could feel the soft side of Juliet's hard-edged personality.

The room looked like so many of the bedrooms Ivy had slept in throughout her teenage years—those cramped spaces her mother had allowed her to decorate any way she liked. And it suddenly hit her how desperately she wanted to be a part of this world.

Ivy's stomach dropped to her feet when she saw Jesse Rafferty— his light-brown hair falling over his deep-set gray eyes—sitting in the pine chair next to a wood desk, under a window with, fittingly, a Juliet balcony. He lifted a tanned, sinewy forearm and waved. She wasn't supposed to be starstruck, especially since she needed to create chemistry, not infatuation, with Jesse, but his presence was surreal.

"Great. Let's start," Mack said, his voice booming. "Ivy, stand to the left of the window. Jesse, to the right. I want you to imagine you're speaking to each other through your bedroom windows late at night."

Taking a step forward, Ivy stumbled over a small dip in the wooden floor separating the set from the rest of the soundstage. She righted herself before she could fall, but she couldn't believe her clumsiness. She was so embarrassed.

Jesse moved like he was going to get up to help her, and something clicked inside her. She remembered what Lauren had said about using her facial expressions. Ivy made her voice confident but flicked her eyes downward to show the insecurity Juliet wanted to hide. "I don't need your help. I'm fine."

There was a beat of silence, in which Ivy was horrified that she'd made a major misstep. But then Jesse winked at her. Mack didn't react at all, only handed them each a few pieces of lined paper and a Sharpie and flipped on the camera.

After placing the paper and Sharpie on the desk, Ivy folded her hands under her chin, as though gazing out her bedroom window, contemplating her first day at Sunset Shores.

"Action," Mack called.

```
INT. JULIET'S BEDROOM—NIGHT
(HUDSON looks out his bedroom window and waves
    at JULIET. She rears back, surprised that
    HUDSON also lives on Pico Boulevard and
    not in a Beverly Crest mansion like SKYLAR
    and LOGAN.)
HUDSON. (Scrawling on a piece of paper and
    holding it up.) Hello, Juliet.
(JULIET bites her lip to stop a wide smile.
    They met briefly outside her locker earlier
    that day, when he introduced himself as
    the student body president, and she felt
    an immediate spark. But she's been told
    that he belongs to SKYLAR. She grabs the
    paper and Sharpie.)
JULIET. (Scrawling her own message.) Hey.
HUDSON. (Writing back.) Meet me outside?
JULIET. (Plays with her fingers, debating.
    Writes another message and holds it up to
    the window.) Why?
```

"Cut!" Mack practically yelled. "I don't buy it. Do it again without blinking like you have sand in your eyes, Ivy. And I don't know why the fuck you're screwing up your face like you're sucking a lemon. Stop it."

Ivy froze. She'd followed Lauren's advice. Wasn't this what she was meant to do? "Sorry."

"Don't apologize. Do it better." He waved the sides—the excerpt of the script. "Who is Juliet Jones?"

Ivy blinked back tears, scared to make any move with her eyes at all. But the answer to his question was easy. *She* was Juliet. She'd lived this life. Ivy said, "Juliet's been ostracized and misunderstood her whole life because she's poor in a world of wealth and privilege. She's desperate to fit in at Sunset Shores but wary of trusting her new friends. She's shy but wants her voice to be heard. She wants to mean something to people."

Mack watched her with an intensity that was unsettling. Ivy was used to being scrutinized by casting agents and producers, but this was different. It felt possessive. She'd never heard anything predatory about him, but would anyone really talk about it?

Jesse coughed, shifting from foot to foot, obviously uncomfortable with the tension. Ivy thought of her mother on her hands and knees, using a toothbrush to clean the grout of marble floors. And she blocked out Mack's crossed arms, his biceps bulging in a black T-shirt to try to intimidate her.

She focused on Jesse and redid the scene from the beginning as herself, thinking of everyone who'd said no to her, every group that hadn't invited her to join them, and every time she'd been scared to ask if she could.

"Cut!" Mack said loudly.

Exhausted, Ivy longed to sink onto the twin bed. Glancing at Mack, though, she saw that he looked as unimpressed as he had during her first audition. She had nothing left to give.

But when Jesse grinned at her, a zap of excitement woke her right up. "Great to meet you, Ivy."

High from the connection between them, so disconcerted with Mack watching them, Ivy blurted out what Lauren had told her. "I'm sorry about your father's passing."

The grin on Jesse's face fell so fast that Ivy knew she'd overstepped.

"Ivy, maybe wait more than three seconds before intruding in Jesse's personal life." Mack glared at her.

Chastised, Ivy could only nod, struggling not to cry or say anything else.

Jesse stepped over the cables and gave her a sympathetic smile. "Can I walk you out?"

"Sure. Thanks," she said weakly, hoping Mack would give her some kind of encouragement or at the very least cut her off right now so she could let go of any hope.

But he only cocked his chin at her. "Thanks for coming in."

Humiliated, she didn't really want to be alone with Jesse. She wanted to go straight home, curl up on the couch with the springs poking through the fabric, and share a bowl of popcorn with her mother. She winced when she thought of having to tell her mom that she messed up. There was no way that Mack would offer Ivy any role ever again. He seemed to despise her.

She followed Jesse off the soundstage to the dressing rooms, where he stopped, so she did, too, dropping her bag on the floor.

Mack came into the corridor and walked straight down the hall like they weren't even there. She wanted to ask Jesse if he was always like that, or if it was only Ivy who annoyed him. But she couldn't, of course. Jesse and Mack obviously had a history from their easy rapport together.

Once Mack was no longer in sight, Jesse smiled at her. "Don't take Mack too seriously. He's hardest on the actors he sees potential in. You did good."

"Really?" Ivy didn't want to sound unprofessional or inexperienced, but something about Jesse put her at ease, despite the belly flutters he gave her.

"Really. I think we'd make a great team." He blushed. "Thanks for what you said about my dad. Not a lot of people do, because it makes them uncomfortable. I appreciate it."

Ivy smiled, relaxing with this larger-than-life figure. As with Lauren, she was recognizing that Jesse was a real person with his own struggles.

After a genial wave, Jesse walked away. Ivy opened the exit door and stepped outside. As it began to close, she realized that she'd left her bag on the floor in the hall. Grabbing the edge of the door before it slammed shut, Ivy went back in. Jesse was already gone. But she heard his smooth voice from a room down the corridor.

"But I thought Lauren was Juliet."

Ivy stopped dead, not sure if she should stay and listen or leave right now before she heard something she didn't want to. Curiosity won out, and she strained to hear more.

"That's our new Juliet," Mack's gravelly voice responded.

Before she could process that shocking information, Jesse spoke again.

"Why?" he asked.

Ivy sagged. He'd told her that she'd done great. Had it been a perfunctory compliment he gave every actor he did a read with? Sometimes she hated this town.

"Don't ask why. Just keep an eye on her."

"Me?" Jesse's tone rose in pitch.

"Yes, you. Help a man out, okay?"

"I still don't get it, but whatever you need."

"I need her. Because that girl's either going to be my greatest triumph or my biggest mistake."

CHAPTER FIVE

Now

Tearstained and grief-stricken on the floor of the soundstage isn't how I want to see Jesse again. I don't want to see him at all.

He drops to a crouch beside me, and scent memory hits me so powerfully that I try not to breathe in his familiar, crisp clean-soap and fresh-laundry smell. When we met for the first time right here, I thought he was a god. Now I know he's just a man, flawed and maybe dangerous. Jesse is a convicted felon.

"Ivy, are you okay?" he asks in that deep, resonant voice that transfixes fans and, for a time, transfixed me as well.

And damn it, hearing that voice again now soothes me when it shouldn't. Not after everything that he's done to me. Did he do something to cause Lauren so much pain that she took her own life to escape it?

Perhaps Jesse takes my silence as evidence of a mental breakdown, because he says softly, "Hang on. I'm going to get some light in here."

I hear a switch, and the lights on the pipe grid running along the whole length of the ceiling beam down, making the soundstage feel like a cave. Jesse returns to my side. I lift my head, and we stare at each other for a beat.

This close up, I see what time, trauma, and three years in prison have done to him. His stubbled cheeks are gaunter than they used to be, and there's a dimness in his expression. But his shaggy light-brown hair still falls over his gray eyes, which immediately fill with concern over my obviously distraught state.

"Um, can you stand? I mean, do you want some help getting up?"

"I'm fine." I'm not, but I don't need his help. Balancing with a palm on the cold floor, I slowly rise, and he does, too, until my face is level with his chest.

The corner of his mouth twitches, as though he wants to make a quip about how small I am, like he used to tease me when we were together. But the twitch quickly vanishes as his gaze roams around the room. "Why is it so empty here? I figured they'd reconstruct the sets. One, at least."

"Did you go to your dressing room yet?" My throat is raw, and my upper body shakes in the chill of the vacant soundstage.

"No. I'm late, so I came straight here. Why?"

We're in the space between before and after I ruin his life. For the second time. I don't want to hurt anyone this deeply, even though Jesse destroyed so many lives with a reprehensible, senseless crime.

So, I'm gentle when I say, "Jesse, something bad has happened."

"Okay," he says slowly. "What is it?"

Taking a deep breath, my stomach twisting, I destroy him. "It's Lauren. I'm so sorry. She's . . ." This is brutal. I open my mouth again, and the words come out. "She's dead."

He blinks. "What?"

"She . . ." My tongue feels thick. "She hung herself. I called 911. They told me to leave the building. I'll explain outside. I don't think we should be here."

But Jesse only crosses his arms over his chest. "What the hell are you talking about? Tell me right now what game you're playing."

I bristle, but now's not the time to rehash old grievances. All I can do is tell him what happened. "I got here for my call time, and no one else was around. I went to my dressing room and found Lauren."

He bolts toward the steel door leading to the dressing rooms, jams his finger on the red button, then squeezes through the small opening before it finishes sliding apart. I hesitate. Do I follow him or leave the building, like the 911 dispatcher instructed me to? My feet make up my mind for me, and I trail behind him into the corridor.

The heavy door closes, and I watch Jesse turn the knob on my dressing room. "Wait. Just a second. Please." My heavy breathing echoes off the white walls.

He turns around, jaw tight and his hands balled into fists. "What the actual hell, Ivy. I don't know what you want from me."

Then he whips around, opens the door, and vanishes inside. The door slams shut with a loud crack.

I press myself against the wall, closing my eyes as though it will ease his devastation to come. Three seconds later, there's a horrific howl.

The last thing I want is to go inside that room again, but Jesse's suffering is agonizing. There's a fine line between self-preservation and compassion. He broke my heart, but I can't ignore the sound of him shattering inside that room. I move away from the wall, open the door, and prop it open with the orange rubber stop for the EMTs.

Seeing Lauren hanging by the hook is worse the second time because I don't have shock to numb me. I let out a sob, then cover my mouth with my hand before it becomes a wail. I'm not sure I even have the right to feel as broken as I do. "I'm so sorry, Jesse."

I am sorry. For his anguish, and for the secrets I've kept from him.

"No. She wouldn't do this," he whispers gruffly, his voice cracking as he looks from his wife to me. It hurts to see the love crumpling into torment on his face, love that I'd always wanted him to feel for me.

Over the months and then years since I last saw Jesse, though I tried to put my hope into a little mental lockbox, I still waited for him. I'd picture the knock on my door, his name flashing across my phone screen, or even a message he'd slide into my DMs. But he and Lauren cut me off like I never mattered to them. They never really wanted me. All they wanted was each other.

"Why, Lo?" He takes two steps forward, reaches a hand toward Lauren, then stops himself.

As he lowers his hand, his gold wedding band catches the lights from the vanity. His knuckles are scraped with cuts, dots of fresh blood seeping out.

He moves away from Lauren, toward the small sofa. "I just saw her a few days ago. She was fine. Happy."

He still has his back to me, so I can't read his expression, but his words trigger confusion. Didn't they live together? Was he on location filming? Was she?

Once he sits down and faces me, I see the tears streaking down his face, soaking into his black T-shirt. He holds my gaze. His voice turns cold. "Why is Lauren even in your dressing room? What did you say to her, Ivy? What did you do?"

"Me?" I bite back. "I haven't spoken to Lauren in close to *ten years*. Maybe I should be asking you the same question."

He slumps against the couch. "I'd never hurt her," he says. "She's . . . she was my best friend."

When Jesse was convicted, Lauren stood by him instead of being on my side. She and I should have been taking care of each other. Every audition I've failed since *Hello, Juliet* was canceled, every tabloid story that places the demise of the show and cast squarely on my shoulders, and every time I've stayed up all night, worry gnawing at my stomach because my mother is in pain and I'm not financially able to help her— I've thought about *them*. Anger is easier to handle than despair.

While I became poison, they remained the power couple. Jesse has written and directed three critically acclaimed independent films, and Lauren's starred in them all. I guess she found the thing of her own she always wanted: making a life with Jesse. He's the embodiment of the redemption arc, and Lauren was never subjected to the vicious attacks like I was. Of course, she wasn't filmed flying into a frenzied rage. There seems to be no redemption for me for that single mistake. Not with the fans, not with Lauren. Never with her now.

"She was once my best friend too," I say shakily as a harrowing thought occurs to me. What if Lauren hung herself in my dressing room so I would find her, as a punishment, a message that this is my fault?

He lifts his head. "Ives," he whispers with what sounds like deep regret.

The nickname that only my castmates and my mother use stirs such agony inside me that I don't hear the slapping sound from the hall until the thwack thwack is right outside the door.

"Ivy! Where are you?"

My body sags in relief. "We're here, Mom! But wait!" I race to the doorway to block it. I need to warn her about what she's seconds from seeing.

But she doesn't wait, and because she's four inches taller than me, I can't prevent her from looking over my shoulder. She makes a choking sound. "Oh my God." Then she leans away from me, inspecting me from head to toe. "Are you hurt? What the hell is going on? Is that—"

"It's Lauren. I . . . She hung herself, Mom. When I got here, the whole place was empty, and I found her in here. Like that." I bury my face in my mother's soft white sweater, her fingers gently stroking my hair. "I called 911. They're coming."

I don't often see my mom lose her composure, so when her shoulders shake beneath my cheek, I hesitate to look at her. Her distress will make this final. My mother can't bring Lauren back to me.

"Why? Why would she do this to herself?" She wraps her arm around me and emits a breathy gasp of surprise. "Jesse, is that you?"

I lift my head, shocked as Jesse crosses the room in a single stride and collapses into my mother. She gathers him to her, and he leans in, like a little boy in need of comfort. And that's exactly what my mom offered—to him, to the entire cast. When Jesse lost me, he lost her too. A needle of jealousy spears me, because I want her to choose me over him. But my mother, who was neglected as a girl and discarded like trash for choosing to have me at eighteen, would never abandon the people she loves no matter what they've done.

"It's going to be okay." She pats his back. "We were a family once. And family sticks together." A cry breaks free from her mouth. "I think we should get her down."

"I tried, but the knot's too tight," I tell her.

She releases both me and Jesse and rummages in her bag, then pulls out the small white first aid kit she takes with her everywhere. She clicks it open and removes the little scissors. "This is all I have."

She climbs on the metal chair and runs a finger over Lauren's hair and face. "She's so beautiful. Even now." A horrendous choke heaves out of her. "Hold her legs, Ivy, while I cut through the material. I don't want her to fall."

I wrap my arms around Lauren's legs, and her body sways sickeningly against me as my mom snips at the blue scarf tautly pulled between the silver hook and Lauren's neck.

Suddenly there's shouting and stomping from the hallway.

"In here!" I cry as two paramedics, a police officer, and a woman in a navy pantsuit storm into the dressing room.

Jesse backs as far away from Lauren as he can. I feel her body drop, and I catch her and fall to the floor with her in my arms. I want to close her bloodshot eyes for her, take away the tiny red dots mottling her creamy skin, and unsee the look of terror frozen forever on her face. Did she regret what she'd done the moment it was too late?

The woman in the pantsuit flashes a gold badge. "I'm Detective Katie Tanaka with the LAPD homicide division. Everyone, place your hands where I can see them."

Jesse, still backed into the far corner next to the vanity table, looks like he wants the ground to swallow him whole. He immediately raises his palms out in the air. My mom does the same, dropping the nail scissors. They clatter to the floor.

Cradling Lauren, I follow suit, the weight of her body keeping me on the floor. I don't want to let her go yet.

The detective scans the room. "Anyone at risk of physical injury inside or outside this room, to the best of your knowledge?"

We all shake our heads, and Tanaka whips a small spiral notebook out of her pants pocket, then speaks into the radio on her shoulder. "ME/C needed at Sunrise Studios." She reels off the address, then points to the two paramedics. "Please carefully remove the ligature around the victim's neck while preserving as much evidence as possible."

They walk over, and with gloved hands, the male holds Lauren's wrists while the female paramedic takes her by the ankles. Lauren's lucky red Converse are the last thing I see as they move her out of the room and into the corridor. I'm relieved I don't have to watch Lauren zipped into a body bag. I couldn't bear that being my last view of her. But I'll never touch her again, and I wish I could have held on for a bit longer.

I remain on the floor, because I don't know what I'm supposed to do. The lights flick on, and the room floods with a stark coldness. I hear the female paramedic say from the corridor, "No vital signs. Indications of preliminary rigor mortis. Terminating resuscitation."

Of course I knew that there was no chance for Lauren to have survived, but the official statement makes my chest cave in. That hole that's been there since Lauren vanished from my life will forever gape open. I weep into my hands. My mother cries loudly too. Jesse is silent, though when I look up, his face is blanched.

The detective is soft spoken when she says, "Identify yourselves and how you know the victim, please."

I wipe my eyes. "I found her and placed the call to 911. I'm Ivy Westcott. Lauren Malloy was my friend and costar on *Hello, Juliet*."

I wait for Tanaka to react to both my name and that of the show, but she doesn't even raise an eyebrow, simply jots the information down in her notebook and turns to my mother.

"Elizabeth Hardwick. I'm Ivy's mother and her manager. Lauren and I were close when the girls were on the show together."

Tanaka looks at Jesse. "Jesse Rafferty. Lauren was also my friend and costar."

Now Tanaka's eyes narrow for a second. She likely knows Jesse's criminal record. And I wonder why Jesse didn't call Lauren his wife.

"Is there anyone else in the building besides you all and the victim?" Tanaka asks, watching us carefully.

"I don't think so. We were supposed to be meeting with Mack Foster for a secret taping. A ten-year reunion episode. But he's not here, and neither is any crew." I turn to my mom. "Unless you saw someone?"

"No. Not a single person other than us." Her voice warbles.

"Did any of you touch anything?" The detective directs the question to Jesse. "Other than the victim."

Jesse nods. "The entrance to the soundstage, the lights in there, and Ivy's dressing room." He says it so meekly that I can barely hear him.

"I touched Lauren too," my mom says with a hitch. "I wanted to get her down. I don't know what I've touched in the corridor and in this room. I'm not thinking clearly."

Tanaka nods and looks at me.

"The same. I tried to undo the scarf around her neck." I close my eyes for a moment, wishing the director would call "Cut" and this gruesome scene would end.

"May I hold my daughter, please?" my mother asks.

The detective shakes her head, her auburn ponytail swinging and tiny diamond studs in her ears catching the light. For a moment, I'm envious that she gets to investigate death, not be a part of it. "Not just yet. I'm going to ask you all to wait outside while we maintain the scene for the medical examiner and field investigation unit." She cocks her head at the male officer standing off to the side. "Sergeant Reyes will escort you out of the building. Has anyone spoken to Mack Foster today?"

My mother and I say no. I glimpse at Jesse, now stone-faced. Out of the three of us, Jesse might be the only person who keeps in touch with Mack, but his lips are pressed tightly together. He's holding himself as stiff as a board.

I look at my mom. "Maybe we should call Mack? Tell him what's happened."

"Please don't inform anyone of anything at the moment," Detective Tanaka instructs, then says to Sergeant Reyes, "Please take Mr. Rafferty to your car. Put the ladies in mine." Then she faces us again. "Have any of you opened that closet door?" She points to where the shreds of the blue scarf dangle from the silver hook.

"I did. Actually, it was open when I got here, and I closed it so I could try to get Lauren down," I say nervously, feeling like everything I've done today is wrong.

"And have you seen a note?" the detective asks us. "Her bag and phone?"

"All I saw was Lauren," I tell her.

My mom and Jesse echo my response. His is cautious, wooden.

"We'll take you to the station to ask some questions, rather than here. The second this hits the scanners, the hungry piranhas will show up to feed."

My God, the paparazzi and social media will tear us—well, probably just me—apart the moment the news of Lauren's death breaks. Instantly I'm ashamed. All that matters is finding out why Lauren took her own life, here in my old dressing room, at the soundstage that was our second home. The thoughts buzz around my head so loudly that I almost miss the detective's next question.

"Do any of you know Ms. Malloy's emergency contact or next of kin?"

Jesse's eyes meet mine, then he says, "She's estranged from her family. I'm her emergency contact."

I wince without meaning to. I shouldn't be surprised; she's his wife after all. But the cleft between them and me is glaring. They chose each other and left me out in the cold.

I'm sad, too, that Lauren will never have the chance to repair the broken relationship with her parents. Was she happy with Jesse as her only family? It looked that way from afar. But all I really know about Lauren's real life in the last nine-plus years is from what I've read online.

There were the usual rumors of arguments and breakups between her and Jesse, but I know better than anyone how the media manipulates innocuous photos for clickbait. And most of the shots of the two of them were with wide smiles on red carpets, out at fancy restaurants, and on exotic beaches, clasping hands on the sand. I hope there was truth in their smiles and that they genuinely loved and cared for each other.

I hope, too, that Jesse's not the reason I've lost Lauren forever. He was quick to accuse me of foul play. Perhaps it's a tactic to protect himself.

Sergeant Reyes says, "Follow me, please," and ushers me, my mom, and Jesse into the hall.

I lower my head so I won't see Lauren, lifeless on a stretcher, eyes devoid of the sparkle that first drew me to her. Later I wondered if it was guile. I'll never know if our bond was a lie, all for ratings and to catapult her already-skyrocketing career.

When we get outside through the door to the performers' entrance, I gulp in the fresh air. Reyes leads us through the back lot and over to the parking area closest to the street. There aren't any crew vans here, either, but there is an ambulance, two fire trucks, two police cars, and an unmarked black sedan. I try not to watch as Jesse's led to the police car, from which another male in uniform emerges and presses on Jesse's head, like he's a criminal, to get him into the back seat.

Jesse turns and catches my eye through the back window. I think I see him mouth, "I'm sorry." My pulse quickens, because I'm not sure which wrong he's apologizing for.

My mother takes my hand, like she used to when I was a little girl, and we follow the sergeant to the sedan.

"I'll open the windows, and you can wait here for Detective Tanaka to take you to the station. It's safer than being exposed to the street."

"Thank you," I say as he opens the back door and, without touching our heads, gestures for me and my mom to sit in the back.

He walks to the car with Jesse in it, and once he's inside and has shut the driver's side door, I throw myself into my mother's arms and cry until I have no more tears left. She cries with me, and I feel her wince against me with every breath.

I lift my head. "Did you even get to see the doctor today?"

"No, but I'm fine. Don't worry about me." She rubs her forehead. "Mack's not here. Lauren committed suicide. It's wrong. It's all wrong, and I should have come with you to the set."

Shifting so she doesn't need to wrench her back, I take off my jean jacket, fold it into a makeshift pillow, and put my head in her lap. "I needed to go alone. But I wish I'd never said yes to the reunion at all."

"Some reunion." My mom wipes the tears, streaking her mascara under her eyes.

As I reach up and clean the stains away, I hear tires on gravel. I move from my mother's lap and look out the window to see a white van pull through the open gate into the parking lot, CORONER stamped in blue letters on the back. I shudder when a man hops out and unravels yellow crime scene tape around the perimeter of the studio, from the front doors all the way around, through the pathway. Two more police cars show up, and another male and female officer duck under the yellow tape and enter the building.

I need to stop crying and start acting. This is all so fucked up. My mom and I are in the back of a detective's car. Lauren is dead. Mack didn't bother coming to the reunion he planned. There was no crew. No sets. I have that horrid sinking feeling I used to get on set, when it felt like I was the outsider looking in. And often I'd end up in the press soon after—a leaked photo or some tabloid gossip that made me look stupid, out of control, unworthy of being in the company of such talent.

But when Tanaka finally exits the soundstage and strides toward the sedan, her austere, commanding presence comforts me. The police will get to the bottom of this. Then my mom and I can go back to Santa

Cruz and I'll figure out the rest of my life. There will be no more money coming in from the reunion. If I could undo what's happened today, I would, but it's closed the door to the comeback I've left open as a secret possibility in my heart for far too long.

The detective drives through the open gates, turning onto The Lane, the crime scene tape flapping in the wind. I will never go back to Sunrise Studios. And I'll never see Lauren again. Tanaka navigates to the end of the road, and the anvil of grief on my chest gets heavier as we pass the redbrick wall between the decaying buildings where Lauren and I would sometimes eat lunch and talk about things we both swore we'd never tell anyone else. I kept her secrets. I'm not sure if she kept mine.

Beside me, my mother flexes her feet. She's been doing it more over the last year or so to shake out the tingling and numbness in her legs.

"Can you feel your feet?" I ask her quietly.

"Yes," she snaps, then puts her hand on my cheek. "Sorry. I moved too quickly back there, but I'll be fine."

I lean my cheek into her hand. When we get on the 10 headed toward Santa Monica, Tanaka's radio crackles to life. "Not a 10-56. It's a 187," the disembodied voice says.

Tanaka catches my eye in the rearview. "Copy."

A cold tremor spreads through me, and I shudder against my mother's palm. I've been an extra on enough cop shows to know exactly what *187* means.

It's the police code for homicide.

FAME FRENZY

March 2, 2014

In a shocking upset, Lauren Malloy has been cast in the supporting role of Skylar Rawlins in Mack Foster's *Hello, Juliet*. The coveted lead of Juliet Jones has been snagged by the relatively unknown twenty-two-year-old Ivy Westcott, a mostly bit player except for a single starring role on *Little Marvels*, a show about child geniuses, when she was twelve. Fans are furious. They're threatening to boycott the upcoming teen drama unless Foster gives Malloy the headlining role that they've all been waiting for since her sensational performance as Kimberly Kitt in *Malibu Mansion's* final season. Filming begins this week. We've reached out to Foster's, Malloy's, and Westcott's reps, but they have yet to respond to the uproar.

CHAPTER SIX

Under the hot lights on the set of Skylar's bedroom, Ivy's skin prickled. All she had to do was take the tank top Lauren was holding out for her. Instead, she fumbled, and the shirt fell onto the floor.

"Cut!" Mack boomed, then tore off his headset and handed it to Vanessa, the AD. Vanessa had what must have been her fourth cup of coffee in front of her at the monitor, and she looked as frustrated as Ivy felt.

Elizabeth had visited the set earlier in the day but left because she thought she might be distracting Ivy. Ivy wanted her mom to come back to reassure her that twenty takes was normal. That there was a learning curve, and Ivy was doing the best she could. Without her mom, she felt like a failure.

At the table read and rehearsal the day before, Ivy had a handle on the blocking, the lines, and the best way to convey her guilt-ridden envy over Skylar's relationship with Hudson. But she had also been haunted by the fans, how they'd promised to boycott the show because she'd been cast as Juliet.

She was already finding it hard to focus on this first day of shooting. Once she'd gotten in costume—tight black jeans, which dug into her waist, and a black crop top—she had become self-conscious. Then, no matter which way she sat on Skylar's queen-size bed, Mack asked her to move. The angles weren't translating well on camera, which Ivy understood meant that her body didn't look good.

"Fuck it," said Mack. "This isn't working. We'll have to reshoot tomorrow." He turned to Vanessa. "Text Caleb that he can stay in Malibu as long as he wants. We've lost the light for the Beverly Crest scene." Then he glared at Ivy. "Stop touching your hair. You curl it in your fingers every three seconds, and it's annoying."

Her face burning, Ivy dropped her hand from her hair. She was holding everyone up. Jesse had been singing and playing guitar in his dressing room for hours, waiting for Ivy and Lauren to finish their scene so he and Lauren could film theirs, which would also be on the soundstage. Later that day, Ivy and Caleb were supposed to shoot on location at the six-thousand-square-foot midcentury home in Beverly Crest that served as the front facade of Skylar and Logan's mansion.

In that scene, Juliet would exit Skylar's house just as Logan pulled up in his red Porsche, and he'd offer her a ride home. When he dropped her off, he'd discover that Juliet and Hudson lived right across the walkway from each other. He'd keep that information to himself for now, in case he needed it as leverage against the sister he secretly despised and her boyfriend, whom he didn't trust.

But now they'd have to reschedule the shoot.

"Go home, girls. And Ivy, you'd better be prepared tomorrow. We've lost valuable time and money," Mack barked, then stormed off the set.

Lauren gave her a sympathetic smile, but Ivy couldn't make eye contact. She was mortified. Leaving the set, she went to the bathroom off another corridor down the hall from her dressing room and splashed her mottled face with cold water. Kai, the makeup artist, had worked hard to even out Ivy's skin and cover her freckles. Now they stood out like splotches of humiliation.

The bathroom door opened.

"Hey," Lauren said softly. She jangled her keys like she had the first day they'd met, at the audition. "Want to go for a drive?"

"Where?" Ivy asked, really wanting to go home and curl up in her mother's arms. But she also didn't want to tell her mom how horribly she'd messed up. Elizabeth wouldn't make her feel bad about it; she'd probably blame Mack. Elizabeth had already complained to him about his curt tone and harsh critiques of Ivy. It had only made things worse. Ivy just wanted her mom to be proud of her. She wanted to be proud of herself.

"The beach?" Lauren suggested.

That made her smile. She and Lauren might have only known each other for less than a month, but Lauren seemed to understand what Ivy needed right now more than Ivy did herself.

Lauren was quiet on the fifteen-minute ride, and so was Ivy, ruminating over every mistake she'd made today. When Lauren spoke, Ivy jumped a little because she was immersed in her thoughts.

"I'm sorry," Lauren said, pulling into a parking garage across from the Santa Monica Pier.

Ivy couldn't imagine what Lauren was apologizing for. Ivy was the one who'd ruined the whole day. "For what?"

"Giving you bad advice last night." Lauren gestured to Ivy's hair.

"You were only trying to help. It's not your fault I went overboard with it."

The night before, they'd had a video call to run lines again. Lauren thought it might be good for Juliet to have a signature gesture, something she did when she was nervous, like twirling her hair or jostling her knee up and down.

"Still, I'm sorry. You only made a couple of small mistakes, and Mack went hard at you. It wasn't fair."

"Thanks," Ivy mumbled, not wanting to talk about the scene anymore.

Lauren pulled a red baseball cap and huge sunglasses from the console, popping them both on herself. Ivy burst out laughing at how ridiculous Lauren looked. It felt good to release her pent-up stress.

"Laugh now, my friend, but you should cover up too. Your hair is so easy to spot. Twitter polls and gossip bloggers are only the beginning." She took a blue ball cap out and handed it to Ivy. "You're not just Ivy anymore. You're Ivy Westcott."

A thrill and a shiver coursed through her at the same time. She wasn't sure if being Ivy Westcott was a good or bad thing right now.

Lauren grabbed a blanket from her trunk, and as they strolled toward the beach and down to the shore, Ivy watched the parents chasing after their kids and the die-hard sunbathers braving the seventy-degree weather in tiny string bikinis. At 5:00 p.m., no surfers rode the choppy waves, but there were some young people in their twenties hanging around at the edge of the water. Was anyone watching her? That was what she'd always dreamed of. Being noticed. Now Ivy wasn't certain she could handle it.

They found a secluded spot near the cliff at the far end of the beach, where Lauren spread out the blanket. The wind rocked the water, and the palm trees rustled. But their serenity was short-lived.

Ivy yelped when a hand landed on her shoulder. She turned. It was Jesse, with Caleb beside him. They were both in T-shirts and jeans, carrying blankets and coolers.

Ivy was torn about their arrival. Had they heard about how Mack had berated her on set? Were they here out of pity? She felt embarrassed. And she still wasn't sure what kind of help Mack had requested of Jesse when she'd overheard them talking on the day of their chemistry read.

"Hey, Ives." Caleb grinned, adopting the nickname that, up to this point, only Elizabeth and now Lauren ever used.

"Hey." She smiled at him.

They'd only met yesterday at the rehearsal for their scene, but she'd immediately liked him. Affable and easygoing, he didn't make her nervous like Jesse did. She also wasn't attracted to Caleb the way she was to Jesse. Every time Jesse was in her physical space, she was flustered.

Caleb dropped the cooler and spread out his blanket next to her. Jesse did the same with his on Lauren's side.

Lauren stretched out her long legs, leaning back in the sand, tilting her face toward the setting sun. "Nice you guys had a day off," she teased.

Ivy stiffened. Lauren must have noticed, because she mouthed a quick "Sorry" at her.

"We lost the light," Jesse and Caleb said in unison and laughed.

Ivy wasn't sure what was funny, but she chuckled nonetheless.

"It's a running joke with Mack," Jesse said to Ivy, clearly sensing her confusion, his gray eyes searing into hers. Jesse was intense, so Ivy couldn't tell if he gave everyone his full attention or if it was different for her.

Caleb nodded. "He's constantly worried about the light. He loves shooting in the magic hour, so we're always scrambling to get to set and film."

"Have you all worked with Mack before?" Ivy asked lightly, but the all-too-familiar pinch of being the most inexperienced on the show stung. How was she going to catch up? Mack probably regretted hiring her at all.

"Caleb did a few guest spots on *Malibu Mansion*, and I had a recurring role for a few episodes," Jesse said. "But I've known Mack since my early teens. He was the showrunner on my first series, but I had to drop out because my dad got sick." He pushed his hair out of his eyes. "Anyway, we'll shoot tomorrow. It's fine."

They knew how poorly Ivy had performed today. She could see it in their forced joviality. And they also must have seen her face fall, because Caleb shifted closer. "Hey, it's fine," he said. "We've all had off days. That's why we're here. We need to get to know each other if we want this show to work. We're a team."

Caleb had struck on exactly what Ivy was terrified of. As the lead, she was driving the show. It was too much responsibility. She didn't want to be the star; rather, she yearned for acceptance in their group.

Jesse opened the cooler. "I've got soda, still water, and sparkling." He winked at Ivy. "I was a singing waiter in New York while on Broadway to make ends meet."

"Still water, please," she replied, trying to maintain eye contact, even though he unsettled her. She'd had crushes on a few of the guys in her acting classes and some stolen kisses with other background players and guest actors on the few jobs she'd booked. But never before had an electric charge shot through her veins just from looking at a man. There was no way Jesse felt the same, though, so she'd better get over it.

She listened as the three of them chatted about Caleb's upcoming surfing competition that weekend and Jesse's songs that he wrote in his off time. Lauren described the marigolds she was planting around her front walk, while the guys' eyes glazed over. But Ivy hung on their every word. Each of them had other passions, and fuller lives compared to hers. She'd been homeschooled since *Little Marvels* ended, awaiting her next big break. She'd never done anything beyond school but act.

Caleb gave Ivy a sidelong glance. "I think we should play an icebreaker game."

"Like Truth or Dare?" Lauren asked.

Jesse groaned. "What are we, fifteen?"

"Our characters are. Or close to," Ivy retorted, surprising herself. But she wanted in on that easy banter the other three shared, even if she had to fake it until it was more natural for her.

"First, snacks." Lauren took bags of chips, a vegetable-and-fruit plate, a box of crackers, and sliced cheese out of the coolers and laid them in front of her. "This is never ending. How long were you planning on staying here?"

"However long it takes for us all to be comfortable," Jesse said, then took out a blue-and-white Tupperware container with "cupcakes" written across masking tape on the lid. Ivy recognized the tight, neat lettering.

She pointed at it, with a questioning look.

Jesse grinned. "Caleb and I went to your place first to see if you might be there. Your mom told us you were at the beach and gave us cupcakes."

Ivy had to laugh. "Only my mom has cupcakes at the ready and marks it on the container in case you forget what's in there."

"She's very cool," Caleb said.

"Much cooler than me. I'm a bit shy," Ivy admitted. "I'm sorry."

"Don't be sorry. I'm pretty introverted myself until I really get to know someone." Jesse smiled at her. "Why don't you tell us something about you that you wish people knew?"

It was a good question. Ivy pulled her knees to her chest, looked out at the ocean, and said hesitantly, "I wish people knew how scared I am to fail."

Sharing that with the three companions on her greatest journey in life was both relieving and terrifying. Now she felt even more vulnerable. But she was never going to be Juliet Jones or a true part of this cast unless she opened herself up.

"We all are, Ives," Caleb told her. "Impostor syndrome is the downside to putting yourself out there. But without risk, there's no reward, right?"

Ivy took his words to heart. As the sun set, Jesse got his guitar from his truck, and they stayed on the beach, singing and laughing until the stars twinkled in the black sky above the Pacific and they were the only ones left on the beach.

And for the first time in her life, Ivy had a glimpse of what it felt like to belong. She never wanted it to end.

CHAPTER SEVEN

Now

Lauren was murdered?

My gasp must have been louder than I realized, because Tanaka glances sharply at me in the rearview mirror, and my mother jerks back, dropping her hand from my cheek. I subtly shake my head at her. I certainly can't explain that the 187 code I just heard through Tanaka's radio might mean that Lauren didn't take her own life. The information could have been about another case entirely, but my gut tells me it's not.

This ride in the back of the detective's car is suddenly more ominous than it was a moment ago. Am I a witness or a suspect? And who would ever want to kill Lauren?

Tanaka pulls into a lot full of police cars, adjacent to a nondescript brown building, and I recall the last time I was questioned by the police in a death, just about ten years ago. This station looks similar to the Hollywood Division I was escorted to then, but though I was a legal adult, my mother had been allowed to stay with me. I'd been at the scene of a crime, but I was never considered the culprit. This time, once Tanaka has ushered us inside, our shoes sliding over the brown-and-beige tiles, she points to a small wooden bench.

"Mrs. Hardwick, please sit here, and someone will be with you shortly."

"It's *Ms*. Ivy's father passed away. And she has his last name," my mother tells the detective as she gingerly lowers herself onto the bench.

"My apologies."

My mother offers a sad smile. She looks older than she did last night when we passed each other in the lovely kitchen at the Airbnb. I was on my way to the shower, and my mom was making tea. We exchanged a silent look of hope. We were grateful to be staying in such a nice place for free, courtesy of Greer, our mutual boss in Santa Cruz. And the reunion was finally a chance for me to free myself of Poison Ivy, put the past to rest, and truly start over. That little moment feels so clear and in direct contrast to the fear and confusion we're experiencing now.

I squeeze my mom's hand before following Tanaka down a too-bright corridor to a small interview room. She gestures for me to go in first. I do, and my stomach curdles further. There's a long, light wood table, bare except for a box of tissues, and three black plastic chairs: one is at the head of the table, closest to the wall; another is in the middle; and the last, at the far end near the door. Under a white stucco ceiling, LED lights beam down on me, draining any energy I have left.

The room is otherwise empty, except for the camera I can't see but know is there. I expected the reunion to be the last time I ever appear on film. I expected to do it with Lauren.

I keep my tears at bay, because I don't know what's going on here. Tanaka smiles, one bottom tooth slightly twisted, which endears her to me, despite my wariness. I've always been drawn to those unique qualities that other people might perceive as flaws. It makes me less self-conscious about my own.

"Can I get you a coffee? Some water? You've had a terrible shock," she offers, gesturing for me to take the seat at the end of the table closest to the back wall.

"No, thank you." I sit down, not sure if I should put my bag on my lap, the floor, or on the table. I choose my lap.

Tanaka sits down, moves her chair closer to me, and pulls out a black recorder from her pocket. I notice a small coffee stain on the corner of her white blouse and a tiny hole next to her left eyebrow, where a piercing must have been. She's human, doing her job. Hers is to save lives. Mine was to play make-believe. But I have nothing to hide. I don't need to pretend I'm anything but broken.

But when Tanaka's deep-brown eyes soften, as though in sympathy, the back of my neck tingles, the tiny hairs poking at me. I've become a fairly good judge of character. Understanding the depths of the human psyche is vital to embodying all different types of people. And I've been burned enough to become skilled at deciphering whether kindness is genuine or calculated. Tanaka is being too nice.

I lean back slightly.

She pretends not to notice. "Is it okay if I record our conversation?"

"Do I need a lawyer?"

Tanaka blinks. "Do you think you need a lawyer?"

"I don't know. I want to be protected." And it seems that Tanaka isn't the one who's going to do that for me.

"I just have a few questions, Ms. Westcott. But if you'd like to call an attorney, please do."

I don't know any attorneys and can't afford one anyway. I'd have to get a public defender. I'm a member of SAG-AFTRA, but since I don't make enough money to qualify for health insurance, I doubt I can get legal representation, if they even offer that in a case like this. I don't have anyone but my mother handling my failed career.

"You can record this," I tell her, because I don't feel I have a choice.

She presses the button. "This is Detective III Katie Tanaka, LAPD Pacific Division. Please state your name and address for the record."

"Ivy Westcott. One one seven three four Sandy Way, Watsonville, California."

"Do you permanently reside in Watsonville?"

"Yes."

She peers closely at me. "When did you arrive in Los Angeles?"

I hold her gaze so she won't think I'm nervous, but my body betrays me, my knee bobbing up and down. "Last night."

"And where are you staying while you're here?"

"Greer, the owner of the town house I live in on La Selva Beach, gave me and my mother a place to stay in Culver City for a couple of nights." I don't know how much or how little detail to give, what exactly Tanaka is looking for. But my curt answers clearly aren't conveying the magnitude of my despair and sorrow, because Tanaka silently stares at me, betraying no emotion.

"I'm a wreck, Detective Tanaka, and not myself right now." All I can picture is Lauren's neck compressed in the blue scarf and those red Converse dangling above the floor.

The detective reaches into the jacket of her pantsuit and pulls out a phone. She checks it, looks at me, and slides it back inside her jacket. Suddenly she stands. "Excuse me for a few minutes."

She walks out, closing the door behind her. I'm frightened. I look down at the scratched, stained table and wonder how many criminals have sat here too. Hours seem to pass, though I can't be sure, because there's no clock in here. I'm afraid to reach into my bag and even check my phone, certain every move I make could be misconstrued. So many times I've been accused of acts I never committed, my words twisted and expressions bent to suit whatever story the press wanted to tell.

The last time I saw Lauren, I was trying to make her understand what Jesse had done, how wrong it was. She'd stood there stone-faced, refusing to listen, making my screaming accusations seem unhinged. On camera, it looked like I was attacking her.

I shiver and put on my jean jacket. The room is even colder with the door closed, and I fight to stay awake, but my eyes droop with stress, fear, and utter confusion. I jerk when the door opens.

Tanaka's face looks harder than it did before. In one hand, she holds a tablet, and in her other, a manila file folder. She sits down again, places the tablet on the table, and pulls out a paper from the folder. Then she turns the paper over and pushes it toward me. "Lauren was strangled."

I already knew, but I lurch back anyway. "Please don't make me look at that," I beg. "I can't see her like that again."

"I understand. But if you want to help find out who did this to her, I need you to look. Can you do it for her?"

Do it for her. By the end of the show, I'm not sure what we were doing for each other as much as *to* each other. We'd become Juliet and Skylar, constantly locked in battle over a man.

Bracing myself, I move my eyes to the blown-up color photo. I think I'm going to throw up. I swallow again and again, until Tanaka drags the wastepaper basket over to me. Someone killed Lauren. If I'd shown up on set before her, would I be dead too? It's that realization that halts my nausea. I look at the photo.

The second I see Lauren's skin, stippled with red dots, and a thick band of purple bruises—whether from fingers pressing into her or that blue scarf yanked around her throat—my hand circles my own throat, imagining the violence and terror Lauren must have experienced.

There are also long, thin vertical scratches running above the thick line branded around her neck. I point to them. "Did I . . ." I exhale a shuddery breath. "Did I scratch her when I tried to undo the scarf?"

"We only have preliminary findings at the moment. An autopsy will tell us more about what Lauren suffered. But those seem to be defense wounds."

I look at Tanaka. "She fought for her life."

"Hard."

A sob fragmented by my struggle to catch my breath gets stuck in my throat. I cough to clear it. "She didn't want to die." I think about the scrapes I saw on Jesse's hands. I don't know what prison might have done to him, and I'm aware how passionately he reacts when he's backed into a corner and can't emotionally shut down. But his anguish seeing her hanging from the hook in my dressing room was real. I also know how deeply Jesse loves. I just wasn't worth fighting for. And yet could he have done this to Lauren in a moment of extreme duress?

"Someone tried to stage the scene to look like a suicide. Poorly and quickly. Lauren's bag and phone are missing." There's an expectant look on Tanaka's face, like she's waiting for me to solve this crime for her.

When I don't say anything, she continues, "Can you walk me through your day, from the time you arrived at the building to when you discovered Lauren?"

"An Uber dropped me off right out front at around nine thirty a.m. As instructed by Ellyn Lou Mara, Mack's assistant, I went through the gate to the side door, where we always went to access the dressing rooms. I was given a security code, so I punched that in and went inside the building." I wish I could undo what happened next.

"Earlier you mentioned that you were there for a reunion of some kind?"

"Yes. Mack Foster planned a secret reunion shoot with me, Jesse, and Lauren. It's been almost ten years since the show ended. I imagine that if the reunion had sold to a network, it would have aired at the ten-year mark. My mother, who's my manager, received an email from Ms. Mara that she forwarded to me."

Tanaka tilts her body closer. "Can you send me that email, please?"

With her eyes boring into me, I take my phone out of my bag and open my email. She reels off an address, and I send her all the messages from Ellyn Lou, including ones for my rider and call time. I watch as she reads them, then taps something out on her own phone.

She lifts her head. "Were the yellow tulips and bottled water you requested on your rider in your dressing room when you arrived?"

"I don't know." I sniffle. "After I saw Lauren hanging from the hook on the closet, I didn't care about anything else."

The detective's eyes drop to her screen again. While she's doing that, just in case, I switch off the location on my phone. I feel scrutinized enough as it is. I don't need to add *hunted* to the mix.

Tanaka slides her phone back into her jacket. "Do you know if Lauren and Jesse received the same email from Ms. Mara?"

I shake my head. "I don't know anything about Lauren and Jesse. Today was the first time I'd seen them in close to a decade."

Tanaka steeples her fingers under her chin. "How would you characterize your relationship with Jesse and Lauren before the show was canceled?"

I don't know how to answer that, because I still don't know what was real and what wasn't. The detective is clearly fishing for something. I don't want to give her anything she can ultimately use in a news conference as bait to feed the hungry press out for my blood.

"Don't believe what you read online and in the tabloids. That's all I can say. It was a long time ago. I moved on and only came back to shoot the reunion for closure and income."

"Your mother fields all your requests and offers?"

I don't have any, but I answer, "Yes."

"And did you sign a contract?"

"Yes, and an NDA. Mack didn't want word of the reunion to leak in case it all went awry, I assume." I huff out a sad laugh. "Which it did."

"Were you surprised to suddenly be offered an appearance on a reunion special after all these years?" Tanaka asks, observing me carefully, like she's waiting for me to crack.

Did Tanaka watch the Tattle TV docuseries? "Not after a celebrity exposé, in which the third episode was all about me, dropped on Sunday night and streamed at number one all over the world." I bite my lip. "I almost expected it."

She nods grimly. "How soon after that exposé did Ellyn Lou Mara contact you?"

"Tuesday morning."

"Today is Wednesday. That's a quick setup for a reunion special," she says, as though I planned it myself. The detective drums her fingers on the table. "You haven't had an easy time of it in the press. Do you think you've been portrayed unfairly?"

I don't know if she's referring to then or now. If she's seen every vicious word written about me. I can't tell if she's younger or older than me. Her skin is smooth and unlined, but even detectives probably get Botox in LA.

Instinctually, I cross my arms over my chest, but I drop them quickly. I don't want to look defensive, even though I am. "Not to sound conspiratorial, but I think I was sabotaged from the minute Mack chose me over Lauren."

In response, I get a thin-eyebrow raise. "Interesting choice of words. So you and Lauren were in competition. And you both had a relationship with Jesse Rafferty?"

White noise fills my head. A warning, a coping mechanism— whatever it is—stops me from answering. Instead, I glance around the interrogation room, because that's exactly what this is.

Tanaka clicks her tongue and redirects, asking me to describe the scene when I found Lauren hanging from the hook on the closet door. Taking a deep breath, I start talking. By the time I end with my mom using tiny nail scissors to slice through the material wrapped like a noose around Lauren's neck, I'm bawling.

The detective pushes the box of tissues toward me.

"I'm sorry." I take a tissue and blow my nose, but I can't get hold of myself. "It was so awful."

"I understand how difficult this is," Tanaka acknowledges. "I don't want to keep you here any longer than I need to. Just a few more questions, okay? When you arrived on set, you were alone?"

I crumple the tissue in my hand. "Correct. I thought it was odd that there were no crew vans parked in the lot, that I could see, and everything was dark. But it was a closed set, so maybe I shouldn't have assumed there'd be any crew."

"How long after you found Lauren in your former dressing room did Jesse Rafferty arrive?"

"I'm not sure. It felt like seconds between when I first saw Lauren and called 911. The dispatcher told me to leave the studio and wait outside. I was doing that when I ran into Jesse."

"Ran into him?" She squints.

"I was on the soundstage . . ." I hesitate, because the dispatcher told me to leave the building and I didn't. "I went to the soundstage to warn anyone who might be there because I didn't want them to be traumatized finding Lauren like I was. I turned on my phone flashlight to look around, expecting to see some of the old sets reconstructed, like they do on other reunion shows and reboots, but the whole stage was empty."

"I see. And your mother was also there. How does she factor into this?"

"I panicked after calling 911, so I texted my mom to come to the studio. She was at a doctor's appointment but left and rushed over. She got there only minutes before you arrived."

Tanaka leans ever nearer to me. I can smell her flowery shampoo. "The entrance you used is access controlled. Each person allowed in is given a separate PIN. So, the only people who ostensibly could have gotten inside are the ones Ellyn Lou Mara gave the code to. But the system only logs the day the PIN was used, not how many times. So Jesse could have come in and out without detection after he first arrived. So could you." Then all false camaraderie vanishes. "That email address for Ellyn Lou Mara doesn't exist."

I wrinkle my forehead. "I don't understand what you mean."

She smiles, but it's chilly, sending terror straight into my bones. My leg vibrates again, knocking against the metal chair. She zeroes in on it. I press on my thigh to stop it from moving.

"Ms. Mara's entire email account has been deleted. I sent a message for her to call me and received a bounce back that the account is no longer valid."

I don't know why that would be, but it's clear Tanaka thinks I do. "Well, why don't you ask Mack about it? It was his reunion. His show."

She nods curtly. "We have yet to locate him to ask."

The walls in the room feel closer than they did a moment ago. Mack's assistant sets up a reunion where Lauren is murdered, then her entire email account disappears, and so does Mack? My blood goes cold.

Tanaka and I stare at each other for a beat, then there's a knock on the door. It opens without her saying a word.

A man with bushy salt-and-pepper hair and wearing an expensively tailored charcoal suit steps into the room. "Sorry to interrupt. I'm Wyatt Gibson, Ms. Westcott's attorney. I'd like to sit in on the interview, if I may."

I slump in relief, but I'm also very confused—that is, until I see my mother behind the attorney I definitely don't have.

"It's fine, honey. I'll explain later. I'll wait for you right outside the door until you're done here."

The attorney smiles at my mother. "I don't think we'll be long, Liz."

Liz? This man I've never seen or heard of before touches my mother's shoulder before closing the door and approaching the table.

He picks up the chair closest to the door and places it between me and Tanaka, so she has no choice but to move farther away from me. I can see my reflection in the high gloss of his patent leather shoes. We can't afford him. But I don't care, because I need him. I'm clearly a suspect.

"Where were we?" He notices the photo of Lauren and flicks a disapproving glance at the detective. "Why is this necessary?"

"It's necessary, Mr. Gibson, because your client was first on the scene of a murder victim who was once her colleague and a close friend until they stopped speaking. The victim was found in your client's dressing room."

"Which I've explained," I say.

Mr. Gibson shakes his head sharply at me. I shut up.

"I'm certain my client is traumatized from finding Lauren Malloy's body hanging from a hook on a closet door, when she was supposed to be on set for a job she was contracted to do. A job for which she was already Venmoed twenty thousand dollars upon signing. Have you questioned Mack Foster? Jesse Rafferty, who was also on the scene?"

"Mr. Rafferty is being questioned by Sergeant Reyes. Mr. Foster's wife will contact us when she is in communication with him." Tanaka picks up the tablet next to the manila file. "May I see your Venmo account, Ms. Westcott?"

"Why?" Mr. Gibson asks.

"To verify the payment Ms. Westcott received."

Mr. Gibson looks at me, and I nod.

She hands me the tablet, and I open my account for her.

"You received and accepted a payment from MF Productions just yesterday."

"My manager did, and it goes into my account," I say.

The detective scrolls and taps for so long that I'm jumping out of my skin. Mr. Gibson nudges me with his thigh. I stop fidgeting.

The detective gives a tight smile. "The payment was sent from Ellyn Lou Mara's email on behalf of Mack Foster. That email account, as we know, is gone, and Ellyn Lou Mara doesn't seem to exist at all. After going through your Venmo account and payments, I can't seem to find the corresponding account for MF Productions." She tilts her head. "That company and all their information appears to have been deleted, as well."

"What are you asking, Detective?" my new attorney says curtly.

"I'm just stating the facts. We've discovered that Sunrise Studios was rented for a music video shoot by MF Productions. That's not Mack Foster's company, or at least not according to Rachel Foster or preliminary searches. It seems to be a fake." Eyes gleaming at me, she says, "We believe that someone set up this reunion to murder Lauren Malloy."

I reel at the tacit accusation. "I certainly didn't. I barely have the money to pay my bills, much less hand out thousands of dollars for a fake shoot. And Jesse would know far more than me about booking the studio for a video, with all his experience in the music industry."

Tanaka nods. "Noted. But didn't you or your manager think it was odd that Mack's production company changed names and that he used Venmo instead of direct deposit or a check, as is the standard method for payment?"

I won't answer, but the truth is that I needed the money so much I didn't think about it. Maybe my mother did, but I'm sure she noticed the relief on my face when she told me how much Mack was offering and disregarded any suspicions for my sake.

"Both Ms. Westcott's manager and Ms. Westcott signed an NDA. Clearly Mack wanted this to be as confidential as possible."

"So confidential that he used an assistant, when he hasn't had one or even worked in years?" The detective licks her lips, as though she's eager to see my reaction.

I'm stunned. While I knew that Mack hasn't created a hit show since ours, I didn't realize he'd stopped working altogether.

"What does any of this have to do with my client? She's clearly been set up, lured to Sunrise Studios so she would find Lauren Malloy's body, implicating her in a crime she didn't commit." He points to the photo of Lauren's mutilated neck. "It's impossible for my client to have strangled the victim. Ms. Westcott is only five foot two. Ms. Malloy was . . ." He looks at me.

"Five ten," I say, hope rising, because he's right.

Tanaka shrugs. "There was a metal chair right there that Ms. Westcott could have stood on. She could have done it if Ms. Malloy bent over or crouched, perhaps to hug or touch Ms. Westcott."

I didn't kill Lauren, and I'll do anything to prove it. This morning I hoped to find vindication and change the public's perception of me. If I'm officially named a suspect, I'm not sure I'll survive the fallout.

Mr. Gibson slides a card from his wallet and hands it to Detective Tanaka. "We're done here. Until you track down Mack Foster and get answers from Lauren's husband, we have nothing else to offer." He pushes his chair back.

My head is spinning. The attorney pats my shoulder, my cue to get up. I do, and on wobbly legs, I follow Mr. Gibson to the door.

"Just one more thing, Ms. Westcott."

Withering, I turn around.

"Lauren Malloy filed for divorce from Jesse Rafferty yesterday."

I can't conceal my shock.

The detective captures it. "Someone's got a reason to want Lauren Malloy dead. If you didn't kill her, you might very well be a target."

THE CUTTING ROOM

D.O.A: Dull on Arrival

Is *Hello, Juliet* Star Ivy Westcott a Slow Burn or a Deadweight?

Rick Newman

March 24, 2014

Like anyone who loves a juicy teen drama, I was chomping at the bit to get a sneak peek at the CB's most anticipated new show, premiering this fall. With a coveted straight-to-series 13-episode order, the slick Santa Monica–based soapy suspense is poised to be Mack Foster's biggest hit yet. So no one was more surprised and disappointed than me after watching the press screening of the first episode (they were supposed to release two to media, but there were filming delays). To say I was underwhelmed is an understatement. Don't get me wrong. Caleb Hill as Logan Rawlins and Jesse Rafferty as Hudson Hayes light up the screen, and even I swooned every time they appeared in front of me. Handsome, talented, and commanding, these boys know how to capture attention and keep it there. Lauren Malloy, who possesses that elusive It Factor and who many believe should have played the lead, Juliet Jones, instead is cast in the supporting role of Skylar Rawlins. And like every character Malloy has ever played, she steals the spotlight, making you forget there's anyone else in the scene.

But there is someone else in the scene: Ivy Westcott, who swooped in and nabbed the role of a lifetime. With her mane of red curls and adorable freckles, the curvy Westcott defies typecasting. But she stumbles in Malloy's shadow, shrinking so much that she almost seems like a background player, which is what she mostly was before ending up at Sunset Shores. The fast-paced, tightly written, fiery script burns out in Westcott's dull presence. But anything can change under Mack Foster's direction. Rumor has it that the more-experienced Rafferty, Malloy, and Hill are propping Westcott up as best they can. Hopefully, Juliet Jones will wake up and set us all ablaze.

CHAPTER EIGHT

Then
March 25, 2014

A heavy hopelessness settled in Ivy's chest. The weight of it wouldn't budge. She had barely slept last night, and she yawned loudly.

"Wow. The acoustics in here are intense." Lauren giggled from the stall next to hers in the grimy bathroom at the Santa Monica Pier. Mack had gotten permission to close the pier for two hours for a private promotional shoot. Today was the cast's first official photo call for *Hello, Juliet.*

"Sorry," Ivy said, stifling another yawn. "I was up too early."

Until dawn, Ivy had obsessed over the malicious review on *The Cutting Room.* The clever, biting television trade website used to be one of Ivy's favorites. Now that she was the subject of one of its hit pieces, she realized how damaging schadenfreude could be to the person whose performance was being slammed.

She mashed her lips together so not a trace of yesterday's makeup would get on the snow-white bandage dress she had to change into for the shoot. Mack would kill her if she got even a faint stain on the HERVÉ LÉGER that Stella, head of wardrobe for the show, had borrowed from a contact who owned a boutique on Rodeo Drive.

"You okay?" Lauren asked gently.

"Yup," Ivy answered, once the dress was over her head. "Just making sure I can fit in this thing." She wasn't okay, but how could she talk about it with the person she was unfavorably compared to?

The worst part was that Rick Newman was right.

"It's one review, Ives. One opinion from some guy who makes a living being a dick. It's not fair for him to pit us against each other when we're a team."

Her mom had comforted her, too, when she'd found Ivy sobbing into her pillow the night before.

"I just got off the phone with Mack," she'd said, sitting down by Ivy and stroking her cheek. "I made sure he went to bat for you with the CB. He gave you the role because you're different. And sometimes *different* takes a while for people to get used to. You're memorable and unique. Embrace it, instead of fighting against it. Trying to be someone else will only backfire."

Ivy had to take heed of her mom. So, with those words in mind, she walked out of the stall to the row of sinks outside the bathroom. Lauren was already there. Ivy made a valiant effort to admire but not envy how Lauren's black dress hugged her every curve, making her look even more statuesque, while Ivy, despite the four-inch heels that Mack had insisted she wear, barely came up to Lauren's shoulder. She focused on Rick Newman describing her as adorable and curvy instead of boring and basically invisible.

Lauren beamed. "You're beautiful, Ives. The white is so you."

"Thank you." The compliment erased Ivy's self-pity. In the mirror, she saw that the white dress did make her pale face glow. "You look amazing too."

"Not too tall?" Lauren glanced at them both side by side in the mirror.

Ivy laughed. "Is there such a thing?"

The sparkle in Lauren's eyes dimmed. "It's not as wonderful as you might think to tower over everyone," she said, then cleared her throat.

"I can't imagine you any other way," Ivy told her friend, who hid her insecurities so much better than Ivy did. And she felt special, because Lauren shared them with her. "Turn around, and I'll zip you up, then you can do me."

Ivy pulled up Lauren's zipper, lightly squeezed her arm, then spun around. Lauren's soft, cool fingers drew up her zipper, then stopped. Lauren tugged and grunted.

"Um, it only goes up a little more than halfway, and I don't want to pull too hard and break it."

Ivy reached her arm around her shoulder to feel where the zipper wouldn't go up any farther. "Is it stuck?"

"I don't think so. It doesn't matter, though. Your hair will be down, and they're only going to shoot the front of us."

"No, it has to zip up. It did just yesterday when we tried the dresses on." Panic constricted her throat. The dress did feel a lot tighter than the morning before, when they'd done a quick rehearsal with Stella at the boutique. It had zipped up, no problem.

Lauren patted her back. "Don't worry. I'm sure Kai or Renata has a safety pin, or they can quickly stitch the back up."

"They do makeup and hair, not alterations." Ivy faced Lauren. "How bad is it? The truth."

Lauren bit her lip. "It's . . . not perfect, but there's magic in Photoshop. Seriously, no one's going to notice." She touched one of Ivy's curls. "Your hair already looks gorgeous, and your makeup will be stunning. It's fine. But we're going to piss off Mack if we don't shoot before we lose the light." She smirked.

They exited the bathroom and walked down the empty boardwalk, the ocean sparkling under the orange glow of the sun. Ivy took off her heels so they wouldn't get stuck in the slats, and they quickly walked past the closed shops that sold T-shirts and beach gear, until they reached the end of the pier. Red umbrellas and black bounce boards to reflect the light were already set up around Jesse and Caleb.

"Ladies! Makeup now, please. We're going to lose the light. Come on!" Mack strode over, with Stella right behind him.

Lauren nudged Ivy in the waist. Ivy wished she could laugh, now that she was in on the running joke about Mack's obsession with the light. But she couldn't. She was terrified he'd find out about her dress snafu.

She and Lauren headed toward the makeup tent, where Kai spread tinted moisturizer over Ivy's cheeks and nose. "Please stop scrunching your face."

She relaxed her muscles, but even with the cool breeze coming off the Pacific below them, Ivy's skin felt hot. "I need help with my dress," she whispered.

Kai dotted a sponge under her eyes. "What kind of help?"

"I can't zip it up. Do you have a safety pin or anything?"

Kai put down the sponge on the tiny folding table and stood behind Ivy, peeking down the back of her robe. "Shit. A safety pin isn't going to work. What did you eat for breakfast?" She laughed. Then she stopped. "Hey, hey. You'll ruin your makeup." Gently, Kai flicked the tears gathering at the corners of Ivy's eyes. "I'll get Stella. Hang tight."

Kai walked away, leaving Ivy to watch Renata curl Lauren's thick blonde hair into beachy waves.

Staring straight ahead, Lauren said, "Can they fix it?"

"I don't know." Ivy was close to bursting into tears.

Lauren flashed Ivy a sympathetic smile in the small mirror in front of her.

Stella marched over, her long braids swinging behind her. "Stand up and let me see."

Ivy did, and Stella made a frustrated sound in the back of her throat. "Suck everything in."

Ivy tried, but the dress was so tight it was impossible.

"Damn it." Stella walked in front of Ivy. "The dress is the wrong size." She pulled out her phone. "I'm going to call the shop and see if they can bring the eight you tried on yesterday that actually fit. This one is a six."

"There's no time. Do you know how much I've spent on this already? We'll edit it later. Just get in the shot, Ivy. Jesus." Mack stomped off.

Ivy hadn't realized he'd overheard everything. Her insides quaked. Mack was scary when he was angry, and he was definitely angry with her, even though this time it wasn't her fault.

"What a fuckup," Stella said, ending her call. "Someone called in a dress size change this morning, and now the eight's not available. There's nothing we can do." She pointed to Renata. "Hair for Ivy. Quickly, please."

Renata yanked sections of Ivy's hair from the root, apologizing over and over while she curled them into ringlets. At least her hair looked full and glossy when she threw off her robe and sped to the end of the pier, where the photographer was snapping shots of Lauren, Jesse, and Caleb. They looked perfect together, all shiny and glamorous.

One of these things is not like the others, Ivy said in her mind. But when she joined her cast, she felt fingers splay across her upper back. Both Jesse and Caleb were trying to cover the back of her dress.

Ivy turned around and mouthed, "Thank you," and the photographer shouted, "Facing front, Ivy!"

As the sun dipped low—turning the sky cotton candy pink—and the temperature dropped, Ivy started enjoying herself. The photographer shot her with the whole cast, then only Lauren and quite a few shots just of Ivy. In the excitement, she forgot about the dress and the scathing review. Ivy proved her worth today by being herself; she was proud of her resilience and how far she'd come.

Once the shoot was done, the photographer packed up and left. Jesse and Caleb helped Renata and Kai carry their equipment down the pier while Lauren and Ivy huddled together against the railing, warming each other from the chill. Mack came over with a canvas bag, pulled out two red-bound scripts, and gave one each to Ivy and Lauren.

"Rehearsal tomorrow. Nine a.m. sharp. We'll shoot at one."

Before Ivy could assess Mack's mood with her, he surprised her by reaching into the canvas bag again and handing them two navy hoodies.

Ivy unfolded hers. On the front, in white block letters, it said, **HELLO, JULIET.** On the back was **STARRING IVY WESTCOTT.** Touched by the sweet gesture, she put hers on immediately. Mack smiled at her. Ivy was so shocked that she didn't realize until later it must have been more of a sneer, conveying dominance rather than reward and affection.

That night, she sat on an overstuffed cashmere couch surrounded by plants in Lauren's gorgeous four-bedroom Beverly Hills oasis—the first time Lauren had invited her over—as they both opened their new scenes. It was cozy sitting in comfortable silence, neither pretending they wanted to do anything else but prepare for the following day's shoot.

With a flutter of excitement, Ivy opened the binding to her first scene. Mack didn't reveal anything about the episodes until they were ready to start rehearsing.

INT. JULIET'S BEDROOM—NIGHT
(JULIET is getting ready for bed. She gets
    a Snapchat notification. It's from HUDSON.
    JULIET's nervous to open it because she
    has no clue what he wants from her. He
    doesn't pay any special attention to her
    at school. It's only late at night when
    they're both alone in their bedrooms that
    he shows any interest in her. But she
    can't resist reading the message.)
HUDSON. (Message.) Outside?
(JULIET doesn't respond. Turning away from
    her window, she debates whether to meet
    HUDSON on the walkway. She decides to do
    it, if only to confront him about their
    secret blossoming attraction. She fears
    he's playing her for reasons she can't

understand. And she's scared to hurt
SKYLAR, her new best friend.)
EXT. WALKWAY—NIGHT
(JULIET gets to the walkway, where HUDSON
is waiting for her. (Car engine guns in
background.) They both turn to the road,
where a red Porsche peels away. HUDSON's
face fills with fear.)
HUDSON. I think that was Logan.
JULIET. So what? We weren't doing anything
wrong.
(HUDSON just shakes his head and takes off for
his house. JULIET stays on the walkway,
bewildered and hurt.)

Poor Juliet, Ivy thought, flipping to her next scene. Lauren was
equally engrossed in her own pages beside her.

INT. JULIET'S BEDROOM—NIGHT
(It's Saturday evening. JULIET gets a text.)
SKYLAR. (Message.) I have a massive headache.
So sorry to bail on our sleepover, but I
won't be any fun.
JULIET. (Typing back.) No worries. Another
time! Feel better!
(Not even a minute later, JULIET gets another
text. It's from an unknown number. She opens
it. Her face falls. She's devastated.)
JULIET. (Reads anonymous message) Hudson
belongs to Skylar.
(JULIET sees a photo attached. It's of SKYLAR
and HUDSON making out on SKYLAR's white
mohair couch.)

"Savage!" Lauren said, looking up from her script. "Who do you think sent Juliet the text?"

"So brutal," Ivy agreed. And she laughed. "We'll find out when Mack wants us to."

Then her phone rang.

"Hi," she said to her mom. "I'll be home in a couple of hours. Lauren and I are reading our scripts for tomorrow."

"Sweetie, did the dress tear when you took it off?" Elizabeth asked in a worried tone.

"No." Ivy's knee bobbed up and down. "Why?"

"I'm going to text you a photo."

An attachment came through of the white bandage dress that Ivy had never wanted to see again. There was a long, jagged rip down one side. She sucked in a breath. "I swear that wasn't there when I took it off and gave it back to Stella on the pier."

"I believe you. But I just talked to Mack. He said"—her mother sighed—"he wants you to lose a little weight before the upfronts in May. Or he'll make you pay for the dress."

Make her pay for the dress or for not being exactly who he wanted her to be?

Ivy glanced over at Lauren, who was pretending to be reading more of her script and not listening to the call. She ended the conversation with her mother.

"Everything okay?" Lauren asked.

Ivy was about to tell her how upset she was, when an odd expression crossed Lauren's face. It was only for a split second, but Ivy could have sworn that her best friend looked . . . satisfied.

A sick feeling churned in her stomach. Surely Ivy had imagined it. But someone *had* phoned in the size change and torn the dress. Was it Mack, to force her into losing weight?

Or—like in the anonymous text that Juliet had received—did someone else want Ivy to suffer?

CHAPTER NINE

Now

Mr. Gibson steers me out of the interrogation room, and Tanaka's warning rings like a distress signal through my mind: *I might be a target.* My hand flies to my throat. Does someone want me dead because of what I did so many years ago? Because of me, lives were ruined.

When she sees me, my mom instantly rises from the bench she's waiting on, her movements slow. Today has taken a physical toll on her.

The attorney puts a finger to his lips and guides us toward the front doors. When we exit the building, it's already late afternoon. The sun is behind the clouds, and it's cold. But that's not what makes me freeze. On the sidewalk and across the street—anywhere that can be considered public property—photographers and reporters teem with their cameras, waiting to capture my exit.

"Going out the back way isn't any better. My car's parked at the strip mall across the street. Stay with me. Head down. Don't say a word," says Gibson. He strides ahead, looking behind him every few seconds to make sure my mom and I are still there, his red-and-white-striped silk tie tossed over his shoulder.

Holding hands through the throng, my mom and I stick as close to Gibson as possible. I try to ignore the screaming, but it's so loud, and the reporters don't care that I'm scared. They shove microphones in my face while boom operators circle me.

"Poison Ivy! Did you murder Lauren Malloy?"

"Are you still in love with Jesse Rafferty?"

"What did it feel like to find your nemesis dead on the old set for *Hello, Juliet?*"

I lose my mother in the crowd, and I'm more worried about her getting injured or trampled than myself. Jostling forward, I feel someone bang into me. I'm pulled backward by my hair, a yank that makes tears spring to my eyes. Instantly, I cry out and cover my face with my hands, frightened that acid, blood, or feces could get thrown at me. That someone could pull out a gun and shoot me right here.

Mr. Gibson must have heard my shriek of fear, because I feel him drape his suit jacket over my head. I hear a muffled, "I'll get you across the street. Hold tight to my arm."

I remove my hands from my face and grab his arm, unable to see anything but the ground in front of me. Fingers circle my wrist, and I instantly recognize my mother's skin, scarred from years of scrubbing with bleach through thin latex gloves. I hear the pain in her huffing as she drags me for what seems like miles. Until finally, I'm pushed somewhere, a door slams shut, and an engine turns over. It's not until we've driven away that the jacket is taken off my head.

My mother holds my face in her hands. "You're white as a sheet. Wyatt, do you have any water up there?"

He rummages in the glove compartment and tosses a bottle into the back. "It's probably warm."

"Doesn't matter." My mom opens the bottle, pours some into her hand, and gently wipes it on my face. "Are you okay?"

I nod, afraid to speak because if I open my mouth, I'll howl. I'm in danger and can't help myself. I'm hit with a wave of grief-laden terror so immense that I lean against my mother. The force of it is too great to carry by myself.

She wraps an arm around my shoulder, pulls me closer, and kisses me on the top of my head. "It's going to be all right. I promise. We'll find our way forward, honey. We always do."

We don't, though. I've been in limbo for practically ten years, with one foot in the past. I'm stuck in a dead-end job bagging groceries while also managing an Airbnb just to afford to live in a somewhat decent home, and I'm being accused of murder. But I'll let my mother believe she can fix this for me, because her face is so pale and she's clenching her jaw every time she moves her legs. She needs my success more than I do.

"There's no way you two can go back to Santa Cruz tonight or to wherever you're currently staying in LA. We have to get you somewhere secluded. Do you need anything for the night?" Gibson says, his voice strained as he maneuvers onto Culver Boulevard through the photographers chasing after his car.

None of these people care about our safety, or even their own, as long as they get the shot that will make them the most money. I keep my eyes on the back of the attorney's head, which swerves left and right at the camera flashes through the windows.

"We don't have toothbrushes or anything to sleep in. My car is at our Airbnb here in Culver City," I tell him.

"Okay. Let me think of a motel in Santa Monica. Away from Beverly Hills and West Hollywood is probably the safest," Mr. Gibson says. "Once you're in a room, I'll grab you some stuff. Your car will have to sit where it is for a bit." He makes a sudden right turn, tires screeching, and my mom and I are thrown against the door. "Sorry. Hopefully, if I can lose the paparazzi behind us, I'll be able to get you into a spot no one would look to find you."

Now that we're getting farther from the police station and the storm of thoughts thrashing around my mind calms slightly, I realize I still don't know who this attorney is. "How do you two know each other, Mr. Gibson?"

He smiles at me in the rearview mirror. "*Wyatt*, please. No need for formalities. Your mom cleaned for me a long time ago and saved my ass when she found an important document that I'd mistakenly thrown away. I told Liz I owed her one. I'm happy to do this pro bono."

My mom reaches over the front seat and touches his shoulder. "Thank you, Wyatt, but you don't owe me anything. We'll reimburse you once we find our footing again. This is just a blip."

My mother never ceases to amaze me. Her unwavering confidence in me and herself and her determination to support us no matter the physical and emotional cost are her greatest strengths. I'm not sure what mine are. Tears spill down my cheeks for what feels like the hundredth time today.

I laugh sadly. "Mack always hated that I couldn't cry on command. If only he could see me now."

"We do need to see him. Where the hell is he?"

"Good question. The detective told me that his assistant, Ellyn Lou Mara, doesn't even exist. Neither does the production company that paid me." I explain about the bounced email and fake Venmo account.

My mom's mouth drops open. "None of this makes any sense, Ivy. You didn't kill Lauren, so who did?"

I nod. "Mack was an asshole and treated me like his marionette, but a murderer? Why would he ever want to kill Lauren? She was his favorite. His true star." I imagine his large hands wrapped around Lauren's neck. "I won't go down for this, Mom. And I won't let Lauren's death go unpunished."

She tilts her head, her silky hair falling over her shoulders. When I was little, I thought one day my hair would become smooth like hers. Instead, it only got curlier and frizzier. "It's not your responsibility to get justice for Lauren, honey. All we need to do is make sure we listen to Wyatt and let the police do their jobs. There's no evidence against you."

I grunt. "It certainly felt like there was in that room with Tanaka."

And something in me snaps. I'm being driven to an unknown location, unable even to get myself a change of clothes. I have no control over my life. From the paparazzi who chase me; the filmmaker, Nina Johnson, who created an exposé to capitalize on my suffering;

the influencers who post vile videos for clout—someone always profits off my pain. Now I'm being framed in the murder of my once closest friend. Someone set up that reunion to hurt us both.

Was I supposed to be the one hanging from that hook? Did the murderer mistake Lauren for me? It was so dark in that room. Maybe I *was* the target. What devastates me the most is the possibility that Jesse murdered her . . . or meant for it to be me. His hands were all cut up, and I have no clue when he actually arrived on set. Then there's another detail to consider: Lauren filed for divorce yesterday.

Lauren needs me. I can't undo all my past mistakes, but I can get justice for my friend and protect myself like I never have.

I won't voice my thoughts now. I don't know this man, Wyatt, taking care of us. My mother might trust him, but I don't. I've learned the hard way that everyone, regardless of how kind and giving they might seem, is looking out for themselves.

With that in mind, I'm less frightened and more determined when Wyatt pulls into the gloomy parking lot of a seedy, run-down pink building streaked with dirt. It reminds me of my last horror-movie role. If this place—the SEAVIEW MOTEL, it says on a gaudy pink neon sign—has a claw-foot tub, I'll lose it more than I have already.

I scan the lot from left to right—only a few empty cars are parked. Craning my neck, I check the road as the vehicles pass by to make sure no one has followed us. I think we're safe. I unbuckle my seat belt.

"It's not the Chateau Marmont, but you should be okay here for the night, at least," Wyatt tells us, his headlights illuminating a small rodent or large bug scurrying across the parking lot.

My mom unbuckles her seat belt and leans over to open her door. "Thanks, Wyatt," she says weakly.

Wyatt opens his door. "Stay here. Lie low. I'm going to check you in under my name."

He walks off to the main doors, and once he's inside, I ask, "When did you work for Wyatt?"

"Right before you landed *Juliet*. You don't remember I told you about the fancy office building in Beverly Hills with the spa on the main level? Sometimes I took their free shampoo samples." She lets out a little laugh. "I thought life was so hard then. If I could only make your wishes come true, we'd have everything we needed."

"You always gave me everything I needed, Mom. Maybe I should have been content with less."

Wyatt is back quickly, with a pink plastic key chain dangling from his hand. "Let's go inside."

I peel myself away from my mother. Exhausted, I trudge over the slippery cobblestones, glancing in every corner for paparazzi or, worse, a murderer. It's too poorly lit to really see if anyone is watching us as we make our way up a steep, rickety flight of stairs to the second floor.

There's a terrace with umbrellas and seating to the right. To the left are three rooms with large windows that face the parking lot and street. As terrifying as it is to feel like I'm being watched, it's also the rush of adrenaline I need to uncover the truth. Not just behind Lauren's death but also behind every moment on the show. Someone wanted to get rid of me from day one.

Wyatt unlocks the door to the room at the far end, next to the terrace, and we enter quickly. He closes the door behind us, then immediately shutters the white blinds over the window.

"Lock the dead bolt and put the chain over the door. Don't use social media or tell anyone where you are. Try not to look at the news, because you both know better than anyone how skewed it is. If I find out anything, I'll contact you immediately." He looks at me. "I think it's best if you aren't in communication with Jesse or any crew from the show, should anyone reach out. Even Mack. If he gets in touch, call me immediately."

My mom and I nod. My throat is raw, my body aches, and being sequestered in this room makes me feel like ants are crawling all over my skin, but I have no intention of following all his orders. I'll do whatever it takes to gain control over my own narrative.

"I'll be back as soon as I can with some stuff for tonight." Wyatt opens the door, looks over to the terrace, down to the parking lot, and then toward the rooms next to us. "I think the coast is clear. Stay safe."

After he's gone, I lock and bolt the door and slide the desk chair under the knob. I'm used to people lurking in bushes to photograph me, but this time my life—and my mom's—could really be at stake.

She's pacing back and forth across the terra-cotta tiles, favoring her left leg. I want her to get into bed, but I know better than to suggest it.

Suddenly, she stops. "Ivy? I'm scared."

The vulnerability in my mom's voice distresses me. She's not young anymore, and she needs me. I cross the room and take her into my arms. It's unnatural at first, and she doesn't seem to know where to fit herself against me. But then she relaxes and lets me hold her.

"This too shall pass. That's what you've always told me, right?" I say into her ear.

She emits a sad chuckle. "That's what your dad used to say to me when I got pregnant with you and my latest and last foster family kicked me out." Her body shakes. "I'm sorry."

"For what?"

"For ever encouraging you to live in the public eye. I'm your mother. I should have said no. I should have protected you so much better than I did."

Her tears dampen the collar of my jean jacket. I pull away so she can see my face. "You did your best, Mom."

Exhaling heavily, she lifts her head and points to the floor. "Is that blood?"

I peer down at the long brownish-red stain between the tiles. In this run-down motel, it could be anything. "Who knows? But you're not cleaning it." I take her hand. "Come on, let's get in bed."

The role reversal is odd but comforting for me. I need an action plan. After tucking my mom under the covers, I grab my phone from my bag. There's no way I want to search social media for my name and any hashtags. But there must be something I can research to give me a bit of knowledge and power.

I slide in next to my mom and prop my pillow against the wood headboard. "If Detective Tanaka is right and Ellyn Lou doesn't exist, who would create a fake reunion. And why?"

My mom follows my lead, sitting up too. "And where the hell is Mack?"

I nod. "All we know is that someone wanted us all together in the same place. Someone besides Lauren got there before I did. It could have been Jesse. He could have left and come back. Tanaka said the number of times the PINs are used isn't recorded." I remember what the detective also told me. "And Lauren filed for divorce *yesterday*."

My mom widens her dark-brown eyes, shot through with thin red lines. "She did? God. What a mess."

"But why now? Right after the docuseries, we get an email about a secret reunion. Then Lauren files for divorce? There's got to be a connection."

I don't want to, but I download the Tattle TV app on my phone. Right at the top is the exposé, still streaming at number one. The graphic is an eye-popping hot-pink square with twelve close-ups of "rock-bottom" celebrities on a four-by-three grid. I'm on the top far left, with my old headshot from when I auditioned for *Hello, Juliet*. I look so young and hopeful.

There's no time to go down the nostalgia rabbit hole. I click on episode three, titled "The Meteoric Rise and Staggering Fall of Ivy Westcott."

My mom sighs and watches over my shoulder as Nina Johnson, hiding behind the camera, asks questions to each person she interviews, starting with Vanessa, the AD on *Hello, Juliet*.

"Did I think Ivy was talented enough to lead the show?" Vanessa bites her lip. "No. And I hate saying that, because Ivy worked so hard. And she was kind to everyone. But she was always like a deer in the headlights and never seemed to accept that she *was* the lead. I'm not sure she actually wanted that. She shrunk in Lauren's presence, and her infatuation with Jesse overshadowed her work. Then when Jesse and Lauren were together, Ivy lost it."

Stiffening, I keep watching, even though I'm hurt. Vanessa never once said any of this to me. Maybe if she'd helped me instead of following Mack's orders and being silent when he berated me, I might have found my way on set. I was young and scared, and I needed a mentor I could trust. But Mack held all the power on that show; he wouldn't have listened to her even if she'd tried.

I look at my mom, whose hand has been stroking my arm as I watch. "Maybe we should reach out to Vanessa? I don't even know if she's still in the industry," I say. "Stella, Kai, and Renata, too, are all interviewed. They probably know more than they're saying on camera."

My mom raises her palms midair. "Maybe. None of them were there today. They might know nothing at all."

"True, but it's worth a shot." I fast-forward through the frames to the end to make sure I didn't miss anything the first time I watched the episode on Sunday night. "Neither Jesse, Lauren, nor Mack did an interview. They gave me that grace, at least."

My mom pulls me into her. "You have so many talents, Ives. I hate seeing you broken like you were when we moved to Santa Cruz. I was so frightened."

"I'm fragile, maybe. But I'm not broken, Mom. I'm going to figure this out."

There's a knock at the door. It's only been about twenty minutes since Wyatt left, but maybe there's a store close by and he did a speed shop. I get out of the bed and look through the peephole. I jump back.

"What is it?" my mom asks in a reedy voice, like she can't take much more.

I turn to her. "Jesse found us."

SCOOPS AND SCANDALS

Upfronts, New York City

May 14, 2014

Nina Johnson. I'm Nina Johnson with *Scoops and Scandals*, your only show for all the entertainment news and celebrity gossip. It's the last day of upfronts, and I'm here at the Javits Center with the gorgeous cast of *Hello, Juliet*, the most buzzed-about show premiering this autumn on the CB network. It's a pleasure to meet all of you! Mack, you're known in the industry as the hitmaker. What's your secret?

Mack Foster. I can't take the credit, Nina. It's all in the casting.

Nina Johnson. And what a cast you have. Of course we all know Lauren Malloy, Jesse Rafferty, and Caleb Hill, but we have a new face gracing our screens come September. How does it feel to be the newest It Girl in Hollywood, Ivy?

Ivy Westcott. I'm thrilled that Mack gave me the chance to be part of such a talented cast on an incredible show. It's been an amazing experience so far.

Nina Johnson. And you look amazing! Let's get a before and after shot of you up on the screen. Wow, from soft to svelte! How did you lose the weight so quickly?

Ivy Westcott. I consulted with a nutritionist, and Caleb has been working out with me.

Nina Johnson. Is there perhaps romance in the air between you two?

Mack Foster. You and the viewers will find out this fall, Thursdays at nine p.m.!

CHAPTER TEN

Then
May 14, 2014

Ivy stepped out of the limo, her only goal not to trip in her three-inch heels. Her black off-the-shoulder dress was molded to her body, and she shuffled rather than glided across the uneven sidewalk toward Requiem, the restaurant where the CB network was hosting an after-party for the upfronts.

"Ivy, I love your hair!"

"Your freckles are so cute!"

"Hello, Juliet! I love you!"

"Well, you certainly have admirers." Lauren, in an ice-blue halter dress with flowing pleats, laughed beside her.

But Ivy was overwhelmed, grateful that Lauren was with her. After her brief suspicion that her costar might have purposely changed her dress size and torn the expensive HERVÉ LÉGER, Ivy had felt awful for even thinking it. She'd confused Juliet and Skylar's on-page drama with her real life. Lauren had immediately realized that Ivy was upset and invited her to sleep over. They didn't discuss the dress or the scene they were shooting the following day. They had a spa night. Ivy even showed Lauren how to make a face mask, like Elizabeth had taught her, from extracts of the lavender and sage that grew in Lauren's garden.

Now, Ivy stuck close to her as they made their way through the crush of fans and paparazzi standing behind the two barricades set up on both sides of the entrance to the restaurant. There were so many camera flashes, so many people screaming for her attention that they were all a blur. Since she'd landed at LaGuardia on the red-eye, Ivy had been rushing from interview to interview, presentation to party, no time to enjoy or even understand that her life had changed in an instant. She was famous and hadn't even done anything yet.

After their stage presentation that morning at the Javits Center, the official trailer for the premiere episode of *Hello, Juliet* dropped on YouTube, racking up over a million views by early afternoon. Even Mack was surprised by the sudden attention on Ivy. So was the network. They told Mack to announce that *Hello, Juliet* was landing in the most desired—and lucrative—9:00 p.m. time slot on Thursday nights. This was the best result any of them could have hoped for from the upfronts.

But for Ivy, the pressure of living up to the hype of her newfound stardom terrified her. What if she was never good enough? What if she couldn't possibly measure up to the rest of the cast?

And as Ivy got closer to the restaurant entrance, something wet landed on her cheek.

"Holy shit, Ives. Someone just spit on you." Lauren grabbed Ivy's shoulder.

Ivy froze, then felt an arm around her waist, pushing her forward. She knew it was Jesse, because she smelled soap and fresh laundry detergent. Caleb was in front of her and took her hand. She let them guide her into the lobby of the restaurant, where a bouncer closed the door.

In shock, Ivy leaned against the host desk.

"You okay?" Jesse asked, taking a tissue from his pocket to wipe the spit from Ivy's cheek. "You're shaking."

She wasn't okay; she was humiliated. "Why would someone do that to me?"

"People are going to both love and hate you, no matter what you do, simply because you're a celebrity. And there's nothing you can do about it but try to separate the fame from the work." Jesse laid his hand on the small of her back.

His wise words and warm touch shot sparks into her skin. Ivy didn't know how to read his attentiveness. Jesse was always keeping an eye on her, as she knew Mack had instructed, but it often seemed more affectionate than compliant. And with his fingers all over her, she could barely focus on anything but whether he possibly felt the same electricity she did. Ivy wasn't even sure if he was single. Though the cast spent most of their time together, there was so much she didn't know about them. She could be pining for someone unattainable, just like Juliet was for Hudson.

As she tried to deal with the frightening attack outside and Jesse's heady proximity in the restaurant lobby, Lauren rushed in with Mack. She grabbed a champagne flute from a server passing with a tray and handed it to Ivy. "Here. I'm so sorry! The security guard jumped the barricade to try to catch who did it, but there are too many people."

Ivy took the cold flute.

"I can go out there and find out who did it." Caleb started walking toward the door.

Ivy pulled him back. Caleb was all brawn and no bite. "Thank you, but no."

"You have to get used to that, Ivy. Shake it off. There are a lot of important executives and advertisers here." Mack cocked his square chin at the room, packed with beautiful people dressed to impress. He, too, was transformed from his usual tight T-shirt and jeans into a well-cut black suit that made his tall, fit stature even more imposing. "I need you to be on." His hand rested on her shoulder. It didn't feel comforting but authoritarian.

"Mack, she was just assaulted. Give her a minute?" Jesse said.

A look passed between him and Jesse that Ivy couldn't decipher. She didn't want to cause any tension. "I'm fine."

"Good. Have a drink and mingle." Mack gestured at the flute in Ivy's hand.

Even though she was twenty-two, Ivy had never tried alcohol, because it scared her. Her mom had been a foster child from the age of three after her heroin-addicted parents lost custody of her, and Ivy's father had been killed in a head-on collision with an intoxicated driver. But tonight, she needed something to take the edge off. Lifting the cold flute to her mouth, she took a tentative sip, the bubbles tickling her nose. Within seconds, a calm warmth spread across her chest. She had one more sip and put the glass on the host desk.

Ivy grinned at Mack, who gave her an approving nod. It made her stomach flutter, and she wanted more of it. She wanted to make him proud. Prouder than she felt when she looked around the dimly lit restaurant, where art deco lamps hung from the vaulted ceiling, shining a spotlight on the power brokers milling about the main seating area and lounge. The floor-to-ceiling windows were covered with blackout curtains so people outside couldn't see in. But what caught Ivy's eye was the giant poster board promoting *Hello, Juliet* tacked up to the brick wall, next to all the other posters of the CB shows dominating the ratings. It was the shot from the pier, Ivy front and center in that damn white dress.

Ivy's pulse palpitated at the bloodred tagline in a bold font underneath her image on the poster: SHE DOESN'T KNOW THE DANGER SHE'S WALKING INTO.

Mack waved at someone, his face lighting up. Curious who could make Mack Foster look so happy, Ivy turned away from the poster and watched him walk across the restaurant and hug a slim brunette in a classic black sheath.

"Who's that?" she asked Lauren.

"His wife, Rachel. She's really nice. Come on, I'll introduce you."

"Selfie for my mom first?" Elizabeth was relaxing at the Carlyle, where the CB network had booked a block of suites for the cast on the top floor.

No one else had brought their manager or any representative along to New York, but there wasn't a question whether Elizabeth would be joining Ivy. Without her mom's unwavering support and endless sacrifices, this wouldn't be happening. Her mom was probably lounging in her queen bed next to Ivy's, eating room service and watching a movie. Imagining it filled Ivy with glee.

Lauren took the shot, and Ivy texted the photo to her mom. Sliding her phone back into her black beaded clutch, Ivy snatched up her half-full glass of champagne and, following Lauren and the guys through the crowd, wove her way toward Mack and his wife.

"Is this the famous Ivy?" Rachel, only a few inches taller than her, held out her hand. "Rachel Foster, better half of this guy." She laid her head on Mack's shoulder.

Ivy put her flute down on the table behind her and shook Rachel's hand, momentarily distracted by the stunning sapphire ring on her wedding finger. "So nice to meet you."

"Your hair is extraordinary." Rachel extended her fingers toward Ivy, then laughed and dropped her arm. "Sorry. I'm used to running my fingers through my kids' hair."

Ivy laughed too. "Thank you. How old are your kids?"

Rachel nudged Mack with her elbow. "Nice to know their father talks about them. They're both eleven. Twins. A boy and a girl."

Ivy had known that Mack had a family, but he was all about work on set. In his office at the studio—where Ivy had been summoned a few times with her mom, who always defended her when Mack crossed the line from constructive to cruel criticism—there were no pictures of Rachel and his kids. She wondered what he was like as a father, if he pushed his children the way he pushed Ivy. Around him, she questioned herself all the time. But the way Rachel gazed at him in adoration made her wonder if perhaps she was being unfair.

Hollywood could eat her alive and spit her out if she didn't toughen up. It was possible that Mack was teaching her how to handle criticism by being the first to attack.

"How's everything going for you, Ivy? This experience must all be a lot for you."

Ivy was unsure how truthful to be, and in the moment she hesitated to answer, Rachel leaned in and whispered, "Don't let Mack give you too much shit."

Ivy didn't know how to react, because it would surely get back to Mack. She just smiled, but inside, her chest loosened. Rachel clearly knew firsthand it must be a rough go for Ivy and was on her side. It alleviated some of her worry, knowing that she wasn't Mack's only target.

"I should head back to the hotel. The twins are probably jumping up and down on the beds and tormenting their sitter." Rachel grinned. Then she kissed Mack on the cheek and said her goodbyes, and he walked her to the entrance.

A server approached Ivy with a silver tray of chicken skewers. She took a plate and a skewer to be polite, but she wasn't hungry. She took her champagne from the table, had one last sip, and looked for where Lauren, Jesse, and Caleb had gone.

Suddenly, her left hand spasmed. The plate smashed to the ground. Mortified, she bent to pick up the pieces of shattered ceramic, and her head began to spin. Desperate to act like everything was fine, she blinked again and again to get her bearings, but that only made the dizziness worse. All Ivy could do was stay on all fours on the restaurant floor, hoping no one would notice her until she felt able to stand.

"Ives? What happened?" Jesse crouched beside her.

Caleb was on her other side. Moving a jagged white shard away from her hand, he said, "Careful. You'll cut yourself."

"I . . . I don't know what happened. One minute I was fine, then the next I thought I was going to pass out."

Jesse put a hand to her forehead. "You're all clammy. Drink a bit too much?"

Ivy shook her head but immediately stilled, because everyone's legs—all she could see from this angle—were playing Tilt-A-Whirl. "I only had a few sips. But it was the first time I've had any alcohol, so this probably wasn't the time to try it."

"Did you eat today?" Caleb asked gently.

"I wasn't really hungry. There was just so much going on."

"I think you're losing weight too fast. You have to eat." Caleb was firmer now.

"I do eat. I'm not trying to lose any more weight, and I'm healthy. That's not what this is. I feel really weird." Her heart was beating too quickly, and the fear that everyone, especially Mack, was watching her made it worse. "Is everyone looking at me?"

"No," Caleb assured her. "They're too busy schmoozing. We need to get you outside."

"If we both take her, that'll call attention. Find Lo and tell her that Ivy's not feeling great and I'm getting her fresh air. Distract Mack so he doesn't notice that Ivy's gone."

"Got it. Text me with updates." Caleb kissed Ivy's cheek, then left her alone with Jesse.

It was like she had no control of herself, which was exactly why she never drank. But surely a few sips couldn't cause this extreme a reaction unless she was allergic to alcohol. Whatever the reason, she couldn't ruin this party for Mack or herself. She couldn't believe this was happening tonight of all nights.

"Okay, I'm going to lift you slowly from under your arms. Then lean into me like we're talking so it doesn't look like you're wasted. Can you do that?" Jesse asked, but his voice sounded faraway.

"I think so." Ivy wasn't sure, though, because once Jesse held her, her body flopped in his arms. What the hell was wrong with her?

But she managed to get on her feet with Jesse's arm tight around her waist. He held up a finger to someone behind her and basically carried her in one arm, so she looked like she was walking close to him. He took Ivy to a back entrance, kicked open the door, and brought her into an alley, where he sat her down on a little curb. The cool air and quiet helped clear the fog a bit.

Jesse sat beside her and stretched his long legs out, then brushed her matted hair away from her face. "Panic attack, maybe?"

"I've never had one before, but it's possible. It's been an overwhelming day."

His eyes ran the length of her body. "You've lost a lot of weight."

Ivy bristled. "Not you too. I'm taking care of my body better."

He nodded. "Just making sure. It's harder for actresses than actors, and I know that Lauren's struggled with body image."

"It's not that." Ivy was embarrassed, talking with Jesse about her body and the scene she'd caused inside the restaurant. "Did anyone see us?"

Jesse shook his head. "I don't think so."

"I think I can go back in now. Maybe I just needed a little breather."

"You sure? I'm pretty wrecked. It's been a long day. We could go back to the hotel so you can get a good night's sleep."

He smiled at her, and Ivy had vertigo for a different reason. What should she do? Return to the hot, stuffy room and mingle for another hour or be alone with Jesse for a while longer? But would Mack be furious if they left the network party early?

"I'll text Mack that you're not feeling well and I took you back to the hotel." He got his phone from his pocket.

Ivy held his wrist. "No, don't. He already gets upset with me. This will make it worse."

"I think he's tough on you because he sees a unique opportunity to . . ." He rubbed the back of his neck. "I don't know how to word it."

"Create something from nothing?"

Jesse laughed. "Not nothing. But in a way, yes. You're like his ball of clay." Then he scraped a hand through his hair. "This is all coming out wrong. Let's just go?"

Ivy looked around her. "I left my bag inside."

He gave her the beaded clutch. "I picked it up from the floor."

He called a car, then took her hand and laced his fingers with hers. Her heart pounded from his tender care as he led her through the shadowy alley past the exits of other restaurants, both of them ducking their heads until the car arrived.

Ivy barely registered the ride back to the hotel, because Jesse was so close to her and they were alone for the first time. She wanted him to touch her, but he kept a respectable space, sneaking glances at her every few seconds. Should she touch him?

Ivy debated for so long that the driver had pulled up to the back entrance of the Carlyle and let them out before she could make up her mind. In the elevator to the top floor, Jesse stood a foot away from her, his hands in his pockets.

"My mom's asleep in my room," Ivy whispered hoarsely, her pulse jackhammering at the base of her throat.

"I'll get you inside without waking her up," he said.

That wasn't what Ivy meant. She wanted to go to Jesse's room. She wasn't drunk or even dizzy anymore. She had no clue what had happened to her at the restaurant, but she felt fine now. Better than fine. She was wide awake and clearheaded.

They got off the elevator, and Ivy quickly scanned for anyone lurking. Rachel must have been at the hotel already; Mack could have come back early, his kids might have snuck out to use the vending machine, or any paparazzi or fans who discovered where the *Hello, Juliet* stars were sleeping might pop out. Luckily, the hallway was empty.

They tiptoed toward their rooms, which were right next to each other. Jesse stopped at her door. "Do you have your key card?" he asked.

Instead of taking it out of her clutch, Ivy turned to face him, looking at his full lips. She put her hand on his chest.

Jesse stepped back, so Ivy's hand dangled in midair. "I think we should both get some sleep." He looked pained.

Ivy's cheeks burned with humiliation. She dropped her hand and ducked her head, draping her hair around her face. She wanted to disappear into the crimson carpet.

Jesse sighed. "Ives, look at me. It's not you."

She snorted.

"I mean it. I've liked you from the moment we met, but this isn't the time or place for us to be together. It wouldn't be right after what happened at the restaurant. I'm not that guy."

The ache in her chest eased slightly. Finally, she lifted her head. "But I told you that I'm fine."

"I know, but it was scary to watch you drop to the floor like that." He cocked his head toward the other rooms. "Why don't we talk about this when we're back in LA and not in a hotel hallway?"

"Okay," Ivy said quietly, unsure whether he was being genuine or trying to let her down gently. And though she knew he was right, she was crushed.

She slid her key card into the slot, and Jesse held the door open while she went inside, where she could hear her mother's faint snores.

"You'll be all right?" he whispered.

Ivy nodded.

"See you tomorrow. Sweet dreams." And he left, closing the door with a soft click.

Without wiping off her makeup, brushing her teeth, or even taking off her dress, she slid into bed and texted Lauren.

Ives: Tonight was awful. I got dizzy at the party and don't know why. Jesse brought me back to the hotel. I basically hit on him, and he turned me down. I can't tell if he's a good guy or so not interested in me, and I messed everything up. I need you! Love you.

The message was read a few seconds later, but Lauren didn't respond. She was probably in the throes of partying and preening. Tonight was important to Lauren too. She wasn't responsible for Ivy's mistakes.

Yet Ivy tossed and turned all night, hoping for a text and replaying every disastrous moment. At 4:00 a.m. she heard a noise in the hallway.

There was still no response from Lauren, but it sounded like a door opened and closed in the direction of Jesse's room. Maybe he'd changed his mind and wanted an early breakfast with her, before the press junket and their flight home, to check on her and talk more about what had happened between them. Perhaps he was going to slide a secret note under her door, like the notes Hudson held up to Juliet from his bedroom window.

She got out of bed to peer through the peephole. Her mouth dropped open. Lauren was running down the hall toward her own room in her bare feet, holding her heels in her hand.

She was wearing Jesse's light-blue dress shirt.

CHAPTER ELEVEN

Now

I look through the motel-room peephole again. Jesse's still standing there.

"You're shaking. Are you afraid of him?" My mom gets out of the bed.

"Aren't you? He might have killed Lauren," I whisper as quietly as I can, leaning my back against the door. He knocks again, and my pulse ratchets up. "How did he even know where we are?"

"There's only one way to find out, and I'm not afraid of the guy who cried in my arms more than once. He made a terrible, terrible mistake, and he's paid for it. He lost his wife. I think we need to talk to him."

"Ex-wife," I mutter before I move the chair from under the doorknob.

I stand back to let my mom answer, and I run my hands through my tangled hair and drag a finger under each puffy eye. God, why do I even care what I look like? Lauren is dead, and I could have been the intended target. An ex-convict who also happens to be my ex-boyfriend is about to enter my motel room, where the only weapon is the seashell lamp on my bedside table.

But after my mom brings Jesse inside and relocks and bolts the door, I think of nothing but how awful he looks. His ashen face is hollowed out.

"Hey."

Even his throat sounds stripped of the resonant power he's famous for. Jesse's musical talent is even more impressive than his acting. But writing and directing are his true gifts. He had so many passions when we were together. I thought I was one of them.

I never knew how to read Jesse, because he guarded his true feelings under a good-natured smile. Without a hint of that smile, I can see how shattered he is. But is that because he killed Lauren on impulse and regrets it? There's a reason romantic partners are often the prime suspect. And it was Lauren, not Jesse, who filed to end their marriage. Maybe he didn't want anyone else to have her.

My mother doesn't seem to share my dark thoughts, because she takes Jesse's elbow and leads him to the small wood desk across the room from our bed, where I moved the chair that was under the door handle. "Sit," she says gently.

Jesse does as he's told, folding his long body into the chair while I try to slow my pounding heart. I don't want him here, and I don't want him to affect me the way he does. But as I sit on the edge of the double bed and hear the creak of the springs, a memory of the first and last times he and I were in bed together in his cabin on Castaic Lake flashes through my mind, no matter how much I try to stop it. No one could make me feel as loved and as worthless as Jesse.

"Why are you here?" I finally ask. For our entire relationship he held the power over my sensitive soul, and he crushed it in his fist. I want the upper hand for once.

He catches my gaze, staring at me so intensely that I'm the first to look away.

"I just want to talk," he says hoarsely.

My mom takes a place next to me on the bed, and her presence centers me. Jesse hurt my mother, too, and she never deserved that. She invested a lot of time and love into the cast. Now half of us are gone.

I regard Jesse coldly. "How did you know where to find us?"

A muscle in his cheek jumps. "I followed you from the police station and waited until that man left. I'm sorry. But we really need to talk. You're the only person I can talk to." He looks at my mom. "Both of you." He clears his throat. "I'd never hurt Lauren. And I never wanted to hurt you."

"Well, you did. But that was a long time ago. I haven't even thought about you in years," I lie.

My mom lays her hand on my lower back, but I don't know what her message is, whether she wants me to go easy on Jesse or she wants me to ask him something specific.

"I've thought about you—both of you," Jesse says, shifting so he can look at me and my mom at the same time. "A lot." He rubs his lips, like he used to when he measured his words before speaking.

I notice he's taken off his gold wedding band. The cuts along his knuckles are etched deeply into his skin. An image of the purple bruises and deep red lines around Lauren's neck floods my vision. Even when Jesse was arrested ten years ago, I didn't believe he was dangerous, just reactive. But uncontrollable reactions can lead to murder.

"What happened to your hands?" I ask him bluntly.

He doesn't flinch. "They're from working on my truck. I still have the red pickup."

My mother has been uncharacteristically quiet. Finally, she clasps her own hands and tucks them under her chin. "Guys, tensions are really high, and we're all a mess."

Jesse immediately focuses on her, like he used to when he came to our house. He respected my mother and loved being around her, because all she ever wanted was to take care of us. But there's another person who took care of Jesse, whom he often chose to side with over me.

"Where's Mack, Jesse?"

A peculiar look that I can't pinpoint crosses his face. "I don't know."

I'm not sure I believe him. And I lower the boom. "He could have killed Lauren, and he's framing us. Because you're also a suspect, aren't you?"

He nods slowly. "I haven't spoken to Mack in seven years. Not once since I was released from prison."

My mom and I both flinch at Jesse's casual mention of his incarceration. But when he tugs a shaky hand through his hair, I realize it wasn't nonchalant. It must be difficult for him to talk about. Now's not the time to go backward, so I don't. I wait for him to continue.

"I don't think Lauren was in contact with him anymore, but I can't be sure. What I am sure of is that I didn't kill her."

"Neither did I," I say curtly. "Why did you really come here? What do you want?"

His eyes fill with sorrow. "I want to make amends."

"It's too late for Lauren." My leg vibrates, like it does whenever my body can't contain my emotions. And the dam breaks. Tears leak out of my eyes.

And finally, Jesse, too, lets go. He hangs his head, shoulders shaking, us together in our shared love for Lauren but separate in our grief. His is about the woman he lost today. Mine is about the friend I lost a long time ago and the chance to ever be part of each other's lives again. My mom, too, weeps beside me.

But after I'm cried out, I know that our collective anguish isn't going to solve anything. I make a decision that might be completely stupid, but it's better than sitting in this motel room waiting for Tanaka to arrest me, the paparazzi to hunt me down, or someone to attack me and my mom.

"I want to find Mack or, at the least, Rachel. She might know something that she hasn't told the police to protect Mack. But maybe she'll talk to me." I wipe my eyes with my sleeve. "She was always nice to me."

My mother looks sharply at me. "I think we should stay and wait for Wyatt."

"I'll go with you," Jesse says, immediately rising from the chair.

I knew he would offer. I don't know if it's because he wants to keep an eye on me, because he wants to lead me in the wrong direction, or because he's innocent. I definitely want to keep an eye on him. I don't exactly feel safe, but I doubt he'd be stupid enough to risk going back to jail by hurting me when my mom knows exactly where I am.

My mom stands. Her feet must be numb, because she drops and almost hits the floor, but Jesse bolts over and catches her arm. "I've got you, Liz," he says in such a gentle tone that it breaks my heart, both for my mother and for me.

It's not healthy that she and I only have each other.

"Thank you." My mom lets out a little laugh. "Not as young as I used to be."

"Do you want to sit down again? It's been such a horrible day. We're all exhausted." I'm concerned but trying to play it off in front of Jesse. My mother is so proud. She barely talks to me about her struggles.

"I'm fine." She removes Jesse's hand from her arm, shakes out her feet one at a time, then points at him. "Everything you did to Ivy, and going to jail, it forever changed us. You hurt us, Jesse. I want to trust you and believe that Ivy is safe with you. I really do."

His shoulders slump. "I don't know what I can say to assure you that Ivy is safe with me. You're safe with me, Liz. But I'm not sure that any of us is safe from the person who killed Lauren," he says gruffly.

I turn to my mom. "Do you want me to wait until Wyatt comes back?"

My mom shakes her head, a few silver strands peeking through the chestnut brown. "It's already getting dark, so I think better to go now." She looks at the windows, shut tight, blinds drawn. "I'm worried about the press and fans, though."

Jesse rubs his thighs, where his jeans hang loosely. He's thinner than he used to be. "I'll watch her, Liz. I promise."

I can watch out for myself. After giving my mother a tight hug, I leave her in the motel room and follow Jesse to the parking lot. We both scan every corner for paparazzi or fans who might have sniffed out our location. Seeing no one, he asks, "Your car or mine?"

"Mine isn't here."

"Okay." He heads to the red pickup, and I follow a few steps behind him, trying to catch up with his long strides.

I hope that's not a metaphor for tonight.

The windows of his truck are all open, as he always left them. He told me he didn't worry about break-ins because everything truly irreplaceable goes with him. I climb in, noticing that same tiny guitar charm his dad got him hanging from a silver chain on the rearview mirror. Without thinking about it, I flick it like I used to. Memories of me and Jesse together, and us with Caleb and Lauren, rush into my mind. It's torturous, so I deflect to hide my agony from him. There's nothing Jesse can do to alleviate my sorrow when he's caused so much of it. "I can't believe you still have the truck."

"It's a classic. I keep it in mint condition between films." He touches the tiny red guitar, his arm brushing mine. "I try to keep everything that's important to me, but it doesn't always work out that way."

I ignore the electric zap of his skin on mine and his comment. "Congratulations on all your success."

My tone is flat, and he sighs before turning the key in the ignition. "What's written about you online, that stupid pseudo-docuseries, none of it is fair."

I tip my head back and look out the window. "No, it's not, but whoever said life is fair?"

Jesse doesn't respond, because what else can he say? He turns down the road and places his phone in a holder above the dashboard, then smiles at me. "Old car. No GPS or anything fancy. I was thinking we'd start with Mack's house. I want to take a back route to be as careful as possible."

I shrug.

"It's going to take about forty-five minutes through Wilshire. That okay? We'll avoid the 10."

It's longer than I expected to be alone with him, but I'd rather be careful too. And I know he's asking because Wilshire Boulevard is where

Mack's production offices used to be, where *Hello, Juliet* and Lauren and I began. "It's fine."

I gaze out at the lights of the surprisingly light traffic and the wintry sky that's black at only 6:00 p.m. There are no stars I can see, only the twinkling glow from the restaurants and streetlights as we pass the pier. And the mood in the car is dark too. I used to love talking to Jesse. I could be myself with him. Now there's so much unspoken between us that the silence is heavy with regret and sadness.

When he mumbles something, I'm not expecting it, and I jump, banging my head against the window I'm leaning against.

"I didn't catch what you said."

"You were always adorably clumsy."

I sigh and rub the side of my head. "You can't act like we're friends, Jesse. Or co-anything. The only reason I came with you is because I'm scared for my life and for my mom. And I came back to LA to shoot the reunion, pocket the money, and move on."

Only one of his hands is on the wheel. The other rests between us on the long seat. The vintage truck has no console to separate us.

"For what it's worth, I was happy about this reunion show. Scared, too, but I've wanted to talk to you for so long. Lauren and I wanted to see you, but we were afraid you didn't want to see us."

Us. That was always the issue. It often felt like they were on their own island, and I was treading water around them. He and Lauren were a unit no one could penetrate.

I face him because I'm tired of this nervous agitation, of constantly biting my tongue. "You never even tried reaching out. Neither did Lauren."

He looks at me. "Did you?"

"Yes," I say curtly. I don't want to talk about Lauren. I don't want to talk to him at all. But I did reach out to Lauren, once. Five years ago, I emailed her after she was nominated for an Independent Spirit Award for Jesse's first film. I hadn't watched the movie or even contemplated reaching out to him, but I read a few reviews. Lauren was luminous and raw and deserved to win, but she didn't. I thought that with both of us getting close to thirty, it was time to lay the past to rest. I was proud of her. She never emailed me back.

"She never told me you got in touch."

I raise an eyebrow. "Did she tell you everything?"

He shrugs sadly. "I really did love you. It was never an act."

"I don't want to talk about this, Jesse." I shift so I'm as close to the door and as far from him as possible. "I work in a market and book guests into an Airbnb. I'm so far out of Hollywood, or trying to be, and that whole time in my life is over. I'm not the same girl who fawned over you and was so scared of Mack that I could barely think for myself."

"I'm sorry."

It's not the first time he's apologized only to hurt me again. Stupid me, for going back to him.

That ends the conversation, and the drive stretches on in silence for the next half hour. My mom texts that Wyatt has come and gone, bringing sandwiches, some toiletries, and a change of clothes for each of us. She adds a laugh emoji with a shot of the too-big sweats and T-shirts, in pink, of course. Men. But at least we can find a moment of humor. Wyatt told my mom that he wished I hadn't left with Jesse, because it could compromise my reputation and influence Tanaka's assessment of my involvement in Lauren's murder. But what's done is done.

My mom doesn't ask how long I'll be, but I assure her I'll be back at the motel with her as soon as I can.

Jesse makes a left onto North Beverly Drive and is more cautious than he used to be when we get to the winding road and sharp turns on Coldwater Canyon. He wasn't reckless, but Jesse loved to motor up Mulholland Drive, music blasting as he rounded the dangerous bends that overlooked the dizzying basin of the San Fernando Valley. Fearless, Jesse brought out the adventurer in me. He made me feel alive. Until he killed someone. But he did his time, and perhaps I need to find some forgiveness within myself, instead of being at odds with him. I simply don't know what I'm doing either. On that, he and I understand each other.

He turns right onto Mulholland, where massive houses perch high on the cliff, untouchable except to the wealthiest and most powerful. This was never what I wanted. Having a home of our own and enough money in the bank to sleep well at night was all my mom and I strove for. For a very short time, we had that, until I realized that the price of fame would cost me my happiness and security.

Jesse pulls up to the gate guarding the enclave—a stunning all-white split-level mansion looming above a treetop canopy. Jesse used to have the code, which I imagine Mack and Rachel have changed over the years. The only time I've ever been here was at a dinner party Rachel had organized as a thank-you to the cast for bringing Mack's dreams for *Hello, Juliet* to life. After we left that night, Jesse shot down the windy road above the canyon, his hand on my leg, the wind whipping my hair into my face. I was so happy with him, despite how insecure I'd been around Mack.

Now I'm leery. Jesse could have easily lied about not staying in touch with Mack.

"Do you want to stay in the car or come up to the gate with me?"

I debate for only a second. If Mack is hiding inside and evading the police, which wouldn't be too hard, considering there are five bedrooms, a pool house, a movie theater, and an array of nooks and crannies, I don't want him to see me on camera until I'm ready to see him. I want the element of surprise. My own plot twist.

"I'll stay here."

Jesse nods and turns off the ignition. Through the open windows, I hear his sneakers strike the pavement as he walks slowly to the gate. He's hesitating, but I don't know why. I shift so I can see him better, my knee knocking into the glove compartment, which pops right open. I stifle a harsh laugh. Mack helped Jesse install a hair-trigger release because the door had kept getting stuck. I'm about to close it when I

see something purple sticking out from under loose papers, a flashlight, and a small tool kit.

After checking to make sure Jesse is focused on the intercom, I slide my hand in. And I pull out a small lavender Coach bag. Quickly, I unzip it. There's a black wallet. Opening it, I gasp, though I already knew what I'd find: Lauren's driver's license. And there's something else at the bottom of the bag. I lift it out.

It's Lauren's missing phone.

DIRT ALERT

Wasted Westcott Wrecks the Upfronts

May 19, 2014

We have all the exclusive intel on Ivy Westcott after she collapsed at the CB after-party during the May upfronts in New York City. Our reporters spotted Westcott leaving a medical office in Beverly Hills, looking worse for wear. Inside sources on the set of *Hello, Juliet* tell us that the shrunken starlet needs rehab stat. The pressure of sudden fame and an unrequited crush on costar Jesse Rafferty might be too much for an inexperienced Westcott. But Rafferty and Lauren Malloy, a.k.a. "Lesse," are lapping up the attention as they go public with their burgeoning romance. It looks like Westcott got the leading role but Malloy got the man.

CHAPTER TWELVE

Then
May 20, 2014

Curled in a ball on the small mustard-colored couch in her dressing room, Ivy flung the red binding with the new pages for today's scenes at the wall. It landed with a soft, unsatisfying flutter on the floor. Episode four was originally supposed to capture Juliet and Hudson's first stolen kiss. Hudson would climb up the trellis of Juliet's town home and through her window. But Mack had rewritten it to reflect Ivy's current turmoil. Having that truth thrown back at her on screen would be unbearable.

"Ives? You in there?" Caleb's sweet voice called from the hallway.

Ivy didn't want to get up and open the door. She didn't have the energy.

"Ivy, let me in, okay? I want to help."

Ivy sighed. "The door isn't locked."

The dressing room door creaked open, and Caleb walked in, his black wet suit unzipped to the center of his muscular chest, pink roses in his hand. He closed the door, then handed the flowers to Ivy. After picking up the bound pages from the floor, he sat down next to her, smacking the script against his knee. Poor Caleb was caught in the middle between his friends, and he only wanted everyone to get along and do their jobs.

This job was only one of Ivy's stresses. Since the news had broken over her apparently drunken fall at the after-party and the coupling of "Lesse," Ivy couldn't go anywhere without being mobbed by reporters. She was sure her eyesight was damaged from the constant flash of hundreds of cameras in her face. She couldn't even visit the dentist without it ending up in the tabloids, warped into a titillating scandal where none existed. A simple filling became medical help for a drinking problem she didn't have.

"Why would Mack do this to me?" Ivy asked, pointing to the script in Caleb's hand.

Instead of Juliet and Hudson finally giving in to their attraction, the new scene called for Hudson to choose Skylar and crush Juliet's heart.

Ivy was mortified just reading Jesse's lines and thinking about the confusion and humiliation Juliet was supposed to feel. Mack had done it on purpose, either to put Ivy in her place or to morph her into her character so it would be authentic on screen.

Juliet Jones had started out as a girl who wouldn't take shit from anyone, no matter how desperate she was to fit in. She'd become a facsimile of Ivy, though. Ivy was so eager to please that she allowed Jesse and Lauren to lie to her, said nothing when the tabloids denigrated her, and stayed on the show despite constantly feeling used and abused.

In the third episode, it was revealed that Skylar was the reason Juliet had been accepted into Sunset Shores. She'd found out about Juliet's expulsion from her former school through an acquaintance and cajoled the principal into giving Juliet a second chance, promising to look out for her. Did Lauren convince Mack to hire Ivy after they'd met in the audition room? Did she have an ulterior motive from the beginning?

Ivy's head spun. She couldn't tell fact from fiction anymore.

She stroked one of the soft pink rose petals. "I want to quit," she admitted to Caleb, who'd been quiet on the couch while she ranted in her head.

"I know," he said. "I've wanted to walk off sets and go back to Vermont more times than I can count."

Ivy was surprised. Everyone loved Caleb Hill. He was considered one of the nicest guys in Hollywood. "Really?"

He nodded. "Of course. Life on the farm, despite the ass-crack-of-dawn wake-ups and my parents' stress over money, was easier than this." He plucked one of the rose petals and tucked it behind Ivy's ear.

The gentleness of his touch made her want to cry. She was sick of crying over this show. "I'm a fucking GIF, Caleb."

Someone at the after-party had taken a shot of Ivy at her lowest, literally. A video of her on all fours on the floor at Requiem was spliced on a loop with another video of "Lesse" holding hands on their way into NOBU for a romantic dinner. The GIF made it look like Ivy was crawling toward Jesse and Lauren, begging for a scrap of their attention. Any footage of Jesse and Caleb helping Ivy at the party had been conveniently snipped.

Ivy's stress was the network's boon. Videos of her received the highest clicks online; she was the leading story on the entertainment shows. The only place she could go was the studio, where a team of security guards covered the front entrance and parking lot in case anyone found out where the cast filmed. So far, the location of Sunrise Studios was the only well-kept secret. Mack made sure of it.

He also made sure that he squeezed every drop out of Ivy's infamy, leading the CB to push the premiere ahead to mid-August. The fans were panting for the show to release; Ivy was dreading it. The sudden onslaught of meetings that had poured into her mom's inbox immediately after the upfronts presentation—from respected film producers who'd never given Ivy a callback before—were canceled. They were replaced with requests from B movie honchos seeking to leverage the hot mess Ivy was purported to be. This wasn't how she'd imagined her newfound stardom playing out.

Ivy twisted a curl, then immediately dropped her hand from her hair. She couldn't even indulge in her coping mechanism in private anymore without feeling shame. Mack had conditioned her. God, why was she doing this to herself? Was the money really worth it?

Caleb squinted at her. "You know Lesse is a PR stunt, right? They're not really together."

Ivy scoffed. "So *Lauren* said. Jesse only talks to me on set."

Caleb was the only person on the show who Ivy trusted. Lauren and Jesse had used her to become more famous, more well liked, more relevant. Why else would they let this public humiliation happen to her? It was Caleb who picked her up all the way in Watts, even though he lived in Laurel Canyon, to take her to the set. And he drove her home every day. All because Mack wouldn't pay for a car service only for her. In the safety of Caleb's 4Runner, when it was just the two of them, Ivy told him everything about that night in the hotel hallway with Jesse. She finally unloaded on her mother too.

Her mom had the same take as Caleb. Yesterday, when the photo of Ivy stumbling out of the dentist's office, still a little groggy from the laughing gas they'd given her, made the cover of every splashy gossip magazine, Elizabeth had hugged her and said, "I wish I thought of this fake-couple PR genius first." Then she smiled. "We could put out a statement that you weren't drunk, but I think it's best to let it blow over. Another scandal will explode soon, and this will be but a memory."

Another scandal hadn't come out yet, though.

Caleb leaned back against the couch and winked at her. "We could do our own PR stunt. 'Civey'? 'Calive'?" He blushed.

Ivy laughed, then felt bad when she saw Caleb's face fall. Was Caleb interested in her? If he was, she'd be far gentler with him than Jesse had been with her. He hadn't even texted after the night when he'd said they'd talk about everything when they were back in LA. He'd never asked if Ivy was okay after the media fallout. "I really liked Jesse," she said. "I stupidly thought that he liked me too. And Lauren knows how I feel about him, but she's going along with the supposed charade that they're together."

There were footsteps in the corridor. Someone slid a piece of paper under Ivy's door, and it landed by Caleb's sneaker. They looked at each other.

Ivy held up her hands. "You can read it."

Caleb bent down, retrieved the folded paper, and opened it. His awkward attempt at possibly asking Ivy out seemed to have been forgotten, because the serious look on his face morphed into a grin. "It's better if you look at it."

Ivy groaned and took it. She was still furious, but a small smile played at the corners of her lips. On the bottom of Lauren's *New York Times* crossword, already completed in pen, *I'm sorry* was written out at least twenty times in her loopy cursive. On the top, above the crossword, *Please forgive us* was written in chicken scratch.

Ivy pointed at Caleb. "Did you make them do this?"

Caleb snorted. "As if. I can't make them do anything. They're really sorry, Ivy."

"We're really sorry, Ivy!" Two voices, one deep and smooth, the other a pretty soprano, called from behind the door.

It wasn't healthy for Ivy to be this angry. She hated the off-screen drama that consumed her. This was supposed to be the happiest time of her life. "You can come in," she relented.

The door creaked open, and Lauren's and Jesse's heads popped in. "Can we talk to you?"

"This is my cue to leave. I've got to get ready for my scene with you, Ivy." Caleb got up.

"Thank you, Caleb. For the flowers. Being here for me. You're a really good friend."

Caleb gave a smile, but it was a bit sad and longing. Ivy wished she felt the magnetic pull toward him that she did with Jesse. Caleb was the safer choice; he'd never hurt her.

"Hey, man." Jesse walked into the room and clapped Caleb on the back.

"Thank you for dealing with all this shit. It's not fair for you to get caught in this stupid fake love triangle," Lauren said, entering the room too.

"You all need a hobby." Caleb walked out, closing the door behind him, leaving grains of sand on the floor.

The joviality was gone. With Jesse and Lauren standing side by side in her space, Ivy was overpowered. But she wouldn't back down. "I'm really pissed."

Lauren sat on the couch where Caleb had, crinkling the bouquet of pretty pink roses. She shifted and held them out for Ivy. But Ivy didn't take them. She didn't want anything from Lauren right now. Lauren retracted her arm and kept the bouquet in her hand, while Jesse stood, saying nothing.

"You have every right to be pissed. But we never meant for any of this to happen," Lauren said. "I tried talking to you this week, but you didn't seem to want to hear the truth. So here it is. I was only in Jesse's hotel room that night because he texted me after he got you back to your room, freaking out that he did the wrong thing."

Ivy narrowed her eyes. "Which part was wrong?"

"All of it, Ivy." Jesse finally spoke, pushing his hair back from his face. "I meant what I said. I liked you the minute I met you. But this role is really important to me. And it's really important to you and Liz. You weren't feeling good, and I didn't want to take advantage of you in any way. Or screw things up on set. I didn't want to hurt you."

"But you didn't even text me the next morning!" Ivy swerved to face Lauren. "You didn't text me back at all! And I'm sorry, but why were you wearing his shirt?"

Jesse jerked. "How did you know she was wearing my shirt?"

Ivy's face heated up. "I heard a noise and looked through the peephole. I wasn't stalking you."

Lauren cringed. "I spilled a whole bottle of water down the front of my dress. I was cold, Ives. That was it. But someone must have spotted me on my way out of his room and made an assumption"—she pointed at Ivy—"and ran with it, like you did. Even though there was no photo proof, before Jesse and I could say or do anything, we were Lesse. And with what happened to you at the after-party, that video of you on the floor, Mack wanted to deflect the attention off you onto us. We were trying to protect you, for fuck sakes."

Lauren's plausible explanation and the genuine distress on her face slightly chipped Ivy's hard shell. Still, she had feelings to express to Jesse. "You didn't even speak to me for the last week, except when you had to. Not a word of support or sympathy about that video that's all over Instagram and Vine. I'm the face of drunken desperation."

"Ivy, I was trying to protect you by not bringing you to my room that night. But I wanted to, okay?" Jesse shifted from foot to foot, a faint blush rising on his neck. "I'm not great at expressing how I feel, but there you have it. And Lauren and I didn't know what to do about the media backlash."

Did Jesse mean that he wanted to be more than costars and friends with her? "So now what?" she asked both of them.

Jesse and Lauren looked at each other. Ivy couldn't tell if it was a glance of pity or perhaps concern. Did they believe what the news was reporting about her?

"We'll 'break up' as soon as we can," Lauren said, focusing on Ivy. "We promise. But we all have a huge opportunity to make this show a hit. We have to stick together."

"Where the fuck is everyone?" Mack shouted from the corridor.

"Shit." Lauren scrambled to her feet as Jesse strode to the door and called out, "We're all here. Rehearsing." He turned and winked at Ivy.

She rolled her eyes, grabbed the script, and stood up. The roses on the couch were already wilting. Either Ivy could do the same and stay despondent, not trusting two of the people she cared about the most, or she could forgive them and move forward, see if they would be true to their word. With no time to put the flowers in water, she left them and her anger behind.

Then together, she, Lauren, and Jesse headed to makeup and hair, Ivy's whole being suddenly lighter. She could now do whatever scene Mack wanted, even if it meant reliving the pain she had experienced after the upfronts. She was an actress, not a social media star. She couldn't control what the public posted about her, but she could control how she reacted to it.

After she changed into Juliet's black cargo pants and black crop top, Ivy stepped toward the set of Skylar and Logan's living room to shoot the next scene, determined to show Mack that he couldn't break her.

They all landed on their marks. Ivy's was at the bookshelf across from the couch. She looked over to where Mack usually sat next to Vanessa. But he wasn't there.

"Mack just left. He's going to Lucy and Liam's soccer game," Vanessa said. "Quiet on set!" she called out. "And action!"

INT. SKYLAR AND LOGAN'S LIVING ROOM—DAY
(SKYLAR and LOGAN are at their front door
    getting pizza from a delivery driver.
    HUDSON and JULIET are alone.)
HUDSON. I'm sorry if I gave you the wrong
    impression, Juliet. I'm not interested in
    you that way.
JULIET. (Hides her shock and pain. Shrugs.)
    Whatever. You're not my type. I'm bored
    of you already.
HUDSON. I didn't mean to hurt you.
JULIET. I think you're a liar. Either you
    want me and you're too afraid to break
    up with Skylar for some reason. Or Skylar
    told you to flirt with me and the game is
    now over.
HUDSON. (Whispering.) It's not what you
    think. Not exactly. I—

(*HUDSON is interrupted by SKYLAR and LOGAN entering the living room. HUDSON takes the pizza from LOGAN's hands.*)

HUDSON. (*To JULIET and LOGAN.*) Sky and I will take care of the food. You guys choose the movie.

SKYLAR. Nothing scary.

(*HUDSON and SKYLAR go to the kitchen. JULIET is reeling from HUDSON's cruel dismissal of her and her suspicions about HUDSON and SKYLAR's motives. She sits on the couch. LOGAN sits beside her.*)

LOGAN. (*Sotto voce.*) What's going on? You okay?

(*JULIET shakes her head. If she speaks, she'll cry.*)

LOGAN. He's not worth it, Jules.

(*JULIET blinks. She's taken aback by the overly familiar nickname and LOGAN's perceptiveness.*)

JULIET. (*Whispering.*) You saw us that night on the walkway, didn't you?

LOGAN. Look, you don't want to get on the wrong side of my sister. Trust me. Hudson will never leave her. She knows too much about him. (*Brushes a tear from JULIET's cheek.*) I'm just watching out for you.

(*JULIET stiffens under LOGAN's possessive touch.*)

"Cut! Excellent, all of you." Vanessa took off her headset and rubbed her eyes. "That's a wrap for today." She shut down the monitor and walked off the set.

"I'm wrecked. Going home. Want a lift, Ives?" Caleb asked.

"I'll take her," Jesse said, walking onto the set.

Ivy jumped, because she didn't even know he was still there.

Caleb grinned. "All's well that ends well? You guys good?"

Ivy nodded. "We're good."

"'Kay, see you. Just be careful not to get caught together."

Caleb left through the door to the front entrance, not even bothering to take off his makeup and change back into his street clothes. He walked out in Logan's jeans and white T-shirt.

"Meet you in the lot in ten minutes?" Ivy asked Jesse.

"I have a better idea. Come here."

Ivy did, and when she fell into his arms, she let herself fall for him. He gathered her hair in his hand and kissed her hard. He tasted exactly like she'd imagined—sweet and a little spicy. She slid her hand up the back of his neck and pulled him closer, and her other hand skated up his T-shirt and over his muscled stomach. She heard breathing.

It wasn't Jesse's.

She leaped back and pressed her finger to her lips. Something on the soundstage skittered across the floor. But no one stepped out from the shadows.

"Let's go," Jesse mouthed, and they went through the doors to the corridor, where he stayed while Ivy went to grab her bag. She opened her dressing room door.

Pink petals were scattered everywhere, ripped from the roses, the stems snapped in half.

CHAPTER THIRTEEN

Now

Lauren's missing phone is cold in my hand. I press the button to power it on, but the screen instantly lights up and shows her background, which undoes me. It's a photo of her in jeans and a white tank top, grinning next to a wild spray of hot-pink bougainvillea. I don't have time to give in to my grief. Jesse is still speaking into the intercom, but he could come back to the truck at any second.

Jolts of fear replace my sadness. If Jesse has Lauren's bag and phone hidden in his glove compartment, the only logical conclusion I can come up with is that he was at Sunrise Studios with her before I arrived. He could have killed her and taken her things. But why would he keep the phone on, possibly triggering a signal that the police could locate?

I don't want him to know I've found the phone, so I shove the lavender bag back into the glove compartment, push the door closed, and slide the phone deep into the pocket of my dress pants, hoping that he won't notice it's gone until I'm back at the motel with my mom. Then I'll give the phone to Detective Tanaka. I'm out of my depth here.

Jesse heads back to the truck, shaking his head, and climbs into the driver's side. "Mack and Rachel moved a few years ago. The current owner doesn't know where they live now, not that he would tell me if he did. He's lucky that the paparazzi and fans never knew that Mack ever lived here. He was so good at keeping secrets when he wanted to."

I widen my eyes without meaning to.

Jesse cocks his head. "I mean like where Sunrise Studios was."

"Yeah," I say, my voice too high pitched. I grip my thighs so my legs won't shake. He can't know how scared I am of him. Lauren's phone burns a hole in my pocket. What if he sees it? Or opens the glove compartment to get something and the bag isn't in the same hiding place?

He squints at me, illuminated by the yellow motion-activated light over the security gate. "Everything okay?" He laughs sadly. "I mean, nothing is okay, but did something happen? You look shaken."

"I'm so tired, Jesse." Which is the truth. "I think I need to stop for tonight."

He nods. "I'll take you back to the motel."

I wish he didn't know where we're staying. And I don't know if I should go straight to Tanaka with Lauren's phone. Then I have an idea. "Actually, can you take me to get my car? I left it at my Airbnb."

He gives me a sidelong glance. I can't tell if he's suspicious of my motives. The only way to play this off is by being as calm as possible. I picture the ocean to get my bearings, but of course it doesn't work. I might be sitting next to Lauren's killer.

"Sure. Of course." He carefully drives down Mulholland and suddenly lets out a chuckle when we pass Coldwater Canyon Park.

"What?" I ask, trying to be as normal as possible. On the inside, I'm spiraling. Jesse is strong and smart. If he's trying to frame me for Lauren's murder, I have to watch every single thing I say or do. He could be recording me, for all I know.

"Remember when we snuck into the playground after Mack and Rachel's dinner party?"

Of course I do. Not only because we made out like teenagers in the gazebo, the thrill of getting caught only heightening the intense emotions he stirred inside me. But also because even then I was wary of his motives with me, yet I ignored my gut because I wanted him so much.

It occurs to me that Jesse might know exactly where Mack is, that somehow they're working together to bring me down. Jesse went to jail because of me. Mack lost his show and the reputation he'd built for decades as a respected, powerful hitmaker. His downfall wasn't as widely publicized as mine; nevertheless, he's since disappeared from the television industry. Jesse could still be as close to Mack as he ever was.

"Yes, I remember that night," I say hoarsely.

"I wish we could go back to the very beginning, when we first met, and do it all differently."

This feels like an opening to ask about things I've always worried about. But how can I trust anything he'll tell me? I do it anyway, because we have at least twenty more minutes together in this truck, and talking is the only thing keeping me from outright accusing him of murder, which doesn't feel safe or smart. And a tiny part of me hopes that maybe Jesse has Lauren's bag and phone because the search team found it at the studio and gave it to him, because he's her next of kin. But I don't really believe that.

"Did you start a relationship with me because Mack told you to?" I ask.

His hands tighten on the wheel. Then he glances at me. "No. I loved you from the moment we met."

I cry silently inside. People we deeply cared for are dead. I'm afraid of the only man I've ever loved. My acting career is truly over. My mother is in pain. It's all too much.

Maybe it's too much for Jesse, too, because he wipes his eyes while focusing on the road in front of us. We say nothing else for the rest of the ride, because we can't change the past. We're each on our own for the future. Whatever happened between Jesse and Lauren, and Jesse and me, is over. My only goals need to be protecting myself and my mom and finding justice for my friend. No matter what Lauren might have done to me, she deserves that.

Thankfully, there are no photographers or gawkers lurking around the white guesthouse where my mom and I stayed only one night before all hell broke loose.

Jesse stops at the curb, and I hear him swallow hard. "For what it's worth, I hope one day I can explain everything to you."

I bristle, because all that tells me is that he has something to hide. Nodding, I exit the truck, and I don't look back when I get into my car. The glow of his headlights only moves once I've turned the key in the ignition.

I'm not going back to the motel.

Instead, I let Jesse get far enough ahead, following him all the way north along La Cienega, then right onto Sunset, and left onto Laurel Canyon. I think Jesse knows where Mack is, and if that's where he's going, I'll follow him straight to the man who ruined my life. I'm not stupid enough to confront Mack by myself. But if I can lead Tanaka to Mack, and the truth about what happened to Lauren, I have to try. I don't want to call the detective or Wyatt, because I'm afraid Mack will be tipped off somehow and he'll run before he can be caught.

I'd rather risk my safety than let these two men destroy my well-being for a moment longer.

I keep a few cars in between Jesse and me and tie up my hair when we're stopped for a moment so he hopefully won't recognize me. I know he's checking his rearview mirror for paparazzi, but I don't think he'll be looking for me.

Usually, Laurel Canyon at night is a beautiful drive. Through the smog and light pollution, LA twinkles with hope and promise. But I focus directly on the road ahead of me as Jesse merges onto the 101 South, then turns onto the 134 East. Traffic is heavy, and I'm glad his red truck is easy to spot. He makes a sudden exit onto Vineland Avenue. No other cars do, and I have to go the same way or give up the chase.

Slowing, I keep as far back from the truck as I can, sweating now, even though the air is chilly through my open window. Jesse stays on Vineland, then turns. I can't make out the name of the street in the dark. His taillights disappear. Hoping this street is short enough that I can catch up, I count to thirty. Then I also make the turn. His truck is about fifty feet away, lights off, stopped at the curb.

I immediately brake and switch off my headlights. At first, I'm not sure if he's still inside the truck. Then he emerges, shuts the car door, and heads down a cobblestone path. I park right where I am and wait.

From here, I can see that the house is a modest terra-cotta bungalow. Mack could be inside. I stay in the car, suddenly frightened I might see him. Maybe I'm not as brave as I want to be. It's time to let Tanaka handle this. I reverse, catching the street name this time—Ridgewood Avenue. At least I have information that the police can possibly use. I'm about to head back to the motel when Jesse exits the bungalow, alone. And he gets back into his truck, thankfully driving forward instead of backtracking, so he won't spot me.

It's then that I see something flapping in the wind on the front of the bungalow. It's yellow like the crime scene tape surrounding Sunrise Studios after I found Lauren's body. If this is Mack's place, I don't think he'd be allowed to stay at a crime scene. I wonder if this is Jesse and Lauren's house.

I park a bit closer, then unbuckle my seat belt and open my door quietly. Ducking down so neighbors won't notice that I'm skulking down their street, I walk quickly to the bungalow and up the cobblestone path to the front door, where the yellow tape dangles from the wood on my left, like someone ripped it from the other side. Maybe it was Mack, Jesse, or even the police. I don't know. But from the purple irises and white daisies lining the pathway to the hot-pink bougainvillea hanging artfully over the front porch—the same flowers in the background on her phone—I know instantly this is where Lauren lived.

Through a small opening in the white curtains covering the front window, I peer in. There are plants everywhere. Lauren once told me that she was passionate about plants because they were something she could take care of that would never hurt her.

I shouldn't try to get inside, but I have to. There might be security cameras and an alarm, but I'll explain to Tanaka, and Wyatt, why I'm here if I get caught. I have Lauren's phone as evidence. Though they might believe that I've had it all along. Unless I can find some kind of proof that exonerates me and points to Lauren's real killer.

Heart jammed in my throat, I scan the front porch for a hidden spare key. I might be searching too quickly, because I'm scared to be here, and I don't find anything. I look at the type of lock on the door. It's a standard keyhole entry. Rummaging in my purse, I find an errant bobby pin, then laugh at myself as I attempt to pick the lock. Then I swallow the laugh, because I'm getting my fingerprints all over everything and I'm a suspect. What the hell am I doing?

I start sliding the bobby pin out of the lock, giving up for the night, but I inadvertently turn the knob as I pull it out. The door is unlocked. I check behind me for anyone watching. The coast is clear. I enter Lauren's home, closing the door behind me.

No alarm blares, announcing an intruder, but that doesn't mean there aren't cameras recording my every move. I'm already committed, so I step forward into the main living area.

Bright, airy, and spacious, it's neatly organized. If the police did search, they were respectful of Lauren's home. And as I saw through the front window, there are plants hanging from the ceiling, resting on shelves, and sitting in colorful pots on the polished hardwood.

I need to keep moving, so I walk down a wide hallway with the same glossy flooring and to a bedroom with an elegant black wrought iron bed under a window overlooking the vibrant garden in the backyard. There's another window to the left of the bed, through which the moon shines, casting shadows on the white tiles. Plants hang from this ceiling, too, their healthy leaves lush and green. Will Jesse care for these plants that meant so much to Lauren?

Being in their home feels like an intrusion into a world that I have no part of. I don't even know what I'm hoping to accomplish. Find the password to Lauren's phone? That seems impossible. Evidence that

Jesse murdered her? Or that he and Mack planned it together to frame me? Maybe they hired someone to kill me and the hit man strangled the wrong woman. Perhaps I'll find something that the police missed in their search. I knew Lauren better than they ever could, no matter how many years have passed since we last saw each other. We shared *Hello, Juliet*—and Jesse.

"Jesus. Now I'm writing a script to a really bad movie," I say out loud.

I text my mom, not telling her where I am, just to check in and let her know that finding Mack was a bust. I explain that Jesse took me to pick up my car and I'll be back at the motel soon. She texts back that she's holding steady. But I want to get back to her.

I turn on a Tiffany lamp on the small table next to Lauren's bed, where there's a paperback with a bookmark. A book she will never finish reading. And I'm struck by the black-and-white photos on the bedroom wall, set in tasteful white frames—Lauren on red carpets, at parties and galas; pictures, of course, of her and Jesse, making funny faces or simply enjoying each other's company on beaches and at restaurants. Their happiness is obvious.

I turn to the other side of the room, where there's a simple white dresser, above which is a color photograph. I walk forward. And I have to hold my stomach, because a terrible pain rips into me. The picture is of me and Lauren, taken at the only birthday party I've ever had, in the only home I could ever truly call my own, when my mom and I lived in Culver City.

Lauren and I are cheek to cheek in the kitchen, and my mom is in the background putting away the remainder of the cake she'd baked for me. I'm wearing the silver link chain necklace, the nicest gift I've ever been given, that Lauren presented to me in the iconic robin's-egg blue Tiffany box. It was my twenty-third birthday. And I later threw the necklace in her face.

Any residual anger simmering beneath my grief drains away. I use the hem of my white T-shirt to wipe my eyes. "I wish I'd known you still cared about me," I say to the young, extinct version of us.

I head back to the living room and gaze at the white couch and armchair, the white built-in shelves, and the rows and rows of books, games, and puzzles that must be Lauren's. She loved all kinds of games, especially competitive ones, because she knew she'd always win. She had a gift for word games, like the unfinished crossword I now see behind me on the glass coffee table, filled out in pen, as always. Where is all Jesse's stuff, like his guitars, his Independent Spirit Awards, posters of his films?

Then something scratches at my brain. I grab that pen, looking for paper I can write on. I don't feel right using Lauren's last crossword.

"Fuck. Why don't you have paper anywhere, Lo?" I say, scouring the spotless room for an errant receipt or envelope. I don't want to lose my train of thought.

Giving up, I flip over the crossword, and at the top of the newspaper, I write out letters, rearranging them in different ways, crossing ones out as I go. Finally, the answer is in front of me.

I think I know who Ellyn Lou Mara really is.

Then I hear something. At first, I'm not sure what it could be. I still and listen carefully. A creeping sensation crawls up the back of my neck. It's footsteps.

Someone is in the house with me.

TWITTER

June 19, 2014

@lessestansonly

Lesse spotted at the Chateau Marmont, snuggled up in a corner! Ivy Westcott has given up and is now getting her hooks into Caleb Hill!

💬 2k   🔁 10k   ♡ 83k

Replies

@laurenjesse4evs: Photo evidence? I won't believe it until I see it. Hudson & Skylar BETTER be together on Hello, Juliet. This isn't a Brenda/Kelly sich.

@ilovelesse: Who the eff are Brenda & Kelly? Don't care. Lesse is SO HOT! Perfect couple. Ivy & Caleb? Ew. Caleb is fiiine. Ivy is . . . just there. Lol.

@lesselust: Ivy's cute. Maybe a five or six? But Lauren? A ten. I hope she & Jesse get married! Can you imagine their beautiful babies?

CHAPTER FOURTEEN

Then
June 20, 2014

"Liz, we're leaving!" Caleb called out from the front door of Ivy's apartment before Ivy could tell her mom herself.

Since Ivy had found the snapped stems of the pink roses scattered all over her dressing room, she and Jesse snuck around on set as discreetly as they could. Caleb covered for them—like tonight, when instead of Jesse, he was the one driving her to Mack's for a dinner party. And Caleb was already at Ivy's house anyway. In fact, he'd been there almost every night that week.

Ivy was torn about that. On the one hand, Caleb's protection comforted her. But though he hadn't made any outright overtures toward her or directly expressed his feelings, Ivy knew he cared about her as more than a friend. He gazed longingly at her when he thought she wasn't looking and accepted Elizabeth's offer of a home-cooked meal whenever he could, lingering until late into the night.

"His family is all the way in Vermont. I think he needs a mom," Elizabeth had told her when Caleb had left a few nights ago after hugging Elizabeth tightly.

"Maybe you need a son," Ivy joked, then realized she'd hit a nerve as a wistful look crossed her mom's face.

Ivy had assumed her mom didn't want more kids, but she shouldn't have. Having Caleb in their lives expanded their family of two. But she wasn't sure it was best for Caleb. It seemed as though he wanted to be around Ivy as much as possible, yet as little as possible around the whole cast. He'd been half an hour late to their shoot the day before—a tense scene in which Logan hid on the walkway, recording Juliet and Hudson's first secret kiss in her bedroom, after Hudson had begged her for another chance. Logan then used the footage to convince Juliet to fake a relationship with him to throw Skylar off track.

The steamy kiss Juliet and Logan shared in front of Hudson and Skylar, coupled with the rampant rumors of an off-screen liaison between Ivy and Caleb, might give him false hope. Ivy never wanted to hurt Caleb, and she wasn't sure whether to openly talk about the boundaries of their relationship with him. Unlike Juliet, who was frightened of Logan's creepy attention, Ivy wanted Caleb in her life, but only as a friend.

She stopped stressing about it, because Elizabeth walked slowly toward them at the front door, smoothing her mussed hair.

"You okay, Mom?" Ivy asked, taking in the fogginess in her mother's eyes.

Elizabeth laughed. "You mean because of how schlubby I look compared to the two of you? Yes, I'm fine. I lay down for a power nap, and the next thing I knew, an hour went by."

Ivy didn't believe her. The money coming in from each episode she filmed of the show was finally paying her mother a small salary, so she'd been able to stop cleaning, but years of manual labor had done damage. Ivy worried that it could be permanent.

"Stop examining me, Ives, and let me look at how gorgeous you two are." Her mom adjusted one of the straps of Ivy's mint green maxi dress—which she'd bought with Lauren the other day at a gorgeous boutique in Beverly Hills—then smoothed her hand over the front of Caleb's black dress shirt.

Ivy caught a whiff of what she hoped was cologne. But Caleb had been at her place since 2:00 p.m. and hadn't smelled sharp and tangy when he'd shown up. Ivy and Elizabeth didn't have any alcohol in the apartment, so that meant Caleb had brought his own, drinking it in secret. She wasn't going to ask him about it. Not now, at least. She trusted that he wouldn't put her life in danger by driving over the limit.

They left the apartment, and when Caleb held the lobby door open for her, the heat smacked Ivy in the face.

"God, it's sweltering."

"It'll be nice and cool in Mack's mansion." He laughed. "Did you ever imagine going to a famous producer's house for dinner?"

"I imagined it. I didn't think it would really happen."

"Yeah," Caleb said flatly.

Ivy couldn't read his mood. One minute, he was his usual affable self, then the next he seemed sad. She didn't want to push him to talk when tonight was so important. Being invited to Mack's mansion was momentous. Ivy wanted to believe that it meant he accepted her, that she belonged in Mack's closely guarded world. So she silently followed Caleb to his black 4Runner, in which his boards and other surfing gear took up the whole trunk.

Ivy slid into the passenger seat, and she was shutting the door when Caleb said, "Liz is right. You look beautiful. The dress matches your eyes."

Ivy felt herself flush, both because of the compliment and because she wasn't sure how to respond. She simply smiled and lightened the suddenly tense atmosphere by pointing out all the places she and her mom used to pick up secondhand clothes and furniture as Caleb drove through Watts.

By the time he pulled onto Vista Bay Drive, an impressive tree-lined street with one property after another hidden behind large security gates and tall foliage, they were chatting and laughing like the good friends they were. Mack's house was at the very end, so high up on the hill that Ivy could see a slanted white roof with skylights, peeking out from the top of a thick cluster of sycamore trees.

"Holy shit," she said, after Caleb had given their names into the intercom and the gates had yawned open, allowing them access to the large circular driveway.

Caleb stopped the car, and when Ivy slid out onto the creamy stones, her mouth fell open. The house was unlike any other she'd ever seen up close. Angular and elegant, the mansion had four different levels, and there were at least ten windows per floor that Ivy could see. Was each a separate room?

Caleb pointed across the road to the other side. "Fitting."

Ivy followed his finger to where the Hollywood sign loomed like a beacon.

Exhaling, she whispered to Caleb, "It's amazing."

They passed Jesse's red truck, with the windows open, and before they could even walk up to the wide white front door, Rachel Foster stepped out. In jeans and a plain black T-shirt, with a grin on her youthful face, Rachel was a natural beauty. Ivy wondered how much younger she was to Mack's forty-three years.

"Welcome! Did you find the place okay?" Rachel asked, beckoning them inside.

Rachel's friendliness dispelled the last bit of awkwardness between Caleb and Ivy and lowered Ivy's shoulders from where they almost touched her ears. And once they had walked through the resplendent front hall, Rachel leading them toward the living room, Ivy was soothed by the sleek white-and-blue design with a coastal vibe.

The ceilings were so high that Ivy felt tinier than usual, but the modern chandeliers and lamps emitted a warm glow that lit up the gray-and-white marble floors. Papers, books, and magazines were tossed on pine coffee tables, and taupe throw blankets lay scrunched up on the two low-slung baby blue couches. A family lived here.

Mack had a whole separate life away from *Hello, Juliet*. It softened Ivy's defensiveness toward him.

"What can I get you to drink? Mack's getting dressed, and Jesse's out back with the kids, playing basketball. After swimming with them all afternoon." Rachel laughed. "I should pay him as my babysitter, he's here so much."

Jesse had never told Ivy that he was hanging out with the twins today. That irked her. They certainly couldn't reveal their secret relationship to anyone but Caleb and Lauren, and they only snuck around the studio when they were sure that Mack and the crew weren't looking. Illicit, heady touches—his hand sliding down the back of her jeans; her fingers grazing his arm; and stolen kisses inside her dressing room. They didn't label what they were; Ivy didn't own Jesse. Still, she expected a simple text from him to let her know what his plans were before the dinner. He knew how important this night was for her, how much she wanted to impress Mack.

Ivy realized that Rachel was staring at her. She hadn't answered her question about drinks.

"I'd love a club soda, if you have it. If not, water is great," Ivy said.

Rachel laughed. "You're very easy." She turned to Caleb. "And for you?"

"A beer, please. Thanks." Caleb sat on the couch, flinging his arm over the back of it. He seemed much more relaxed than earlier. Ivy would follow his lead.

She sat next to Caleb, and while Rachel went to get the drinks, Mack came down the spiral staircase, his steps hard. Always a formidable presence, in his own home Mack took up even more space. But instead of his usual T-shirt and jeans, he wore a burgundy-and-cream pin-striped button-down and black dress pants that gave him an air of elegance instead of gruffness.

Ivy stood, but Mack waved his hand.

"Sit! Get comfortable," he said good-naturedly, looking around the large room. "Lauren's not here yet?"

Caleb shook his head. "No, but Jesse's still with your kids outside, I think."

Mack grinned. "Lucy and Liam adore him. They call him Uncle Jesse, which, of course, any TV producer would find amusing."

Ivy laughed a bit too loudly, not used to this friendly Mack.

Rachel came back in with the drinks and handed them to Ivy and Caleb. "Ah, you chose the shirt I suggested?" She winked. "Sometimes my husband listens to me."

Something buzzed loudly, and Mack pulled his phone out of his pocket, then slid his finger across the screen. "Lauren's at the gate."

"I'll drag the twins in for a shower and get Jesse." Rachel walked back toward the kitchen.

Once Lauren was inside, Jesse came in, sweaty, with his dress shirt sleeves rolled up, his pants wrinkled.

Ivy's chest ached with longing. To distract herself from how much she wanted to touch him, she said, "The windows on your truck are open."

He grinned. "I know. I always leave them open. Everything irreplaceable goes where I go."

Caleb cocked his head. "You're not worried someone will steal the truck and your guitar?"

"My dad once told me that if someone really wants to take something I have, they probably need it more than I do." Jesse cleared his throat. "I'd hate to lose my truck, but that stuck with me."

An odd expression crossed Caleb's face, but Lauren came in and Rachel steered everyone to the dining room before Ivy could assess what it meant.

"Take a seat, guys." Rachel pointed to the long teak table, where there were only five chairs.

"You're not joining us?" Lauren asked, ethereal in a white strapless dress that came to just above her knee.

Rachel shook her head. "I'll be upstairs with the twins. Our staff will serve you dinner. I nudged Mack into having this celebration, but this is for all of you. To thank you for your hard work, dedication, and for bringing Mack's vision to life." She swiped a light-pink polished nail under her eyes. "Sorry. I'm emotional because Mack came up with this concept when the twins were born. A story of people who seem good on the surface but battle demons underneath. And the audience never knows who to trust and who to root for."

It felt like Rachel was looking right at her. But then she swept her eyes so swiftly around the room, Ivy convinced herself she must have been imagining it. Then Rachel was gone, and it was only the cast and Mack.

He stood and got the bottle of Dom Pérignon from the silver bucket. "To *Hello, Juliet*!" Then he popped the cork, the sound ricocheting off the walls.

After pouring each of them a glass, from which Ivy pretended to take a sip—she wasn't going to make the same mistake twice—a team of servers dressed in black laid out course after delicious course. Ivy couldn't help but notice how many times Caleb drained his glass and refilled it.

She poked Jesse, who was seated next to her, in the thigh. He took her hand under the table, rubbing his thumb across her palm. She was trying to privately tell him to keep an eye on Caleb, but his touch shot fire through her.

"Maybe slow down on the alcohol, Ivy? Your face is all red," Mack said.

Ivy tugged her hand away from Jesse's. With Mack's attention on her, she watched Caleb get the second champagne bottle that the servers had set out. He lifted it, a dark look crossing his face upon finding it empty. This time, Ivy knew he was frustrated.

She pushed her chair back, ignoring Mack's inaccurate comment. "You know what? I am a little warm. LA summers, right?" She caught Caleb's eye. "Can you come outside with me for a minute to get some fresh air?"

The hope that filled his blue eyes crushed her. But more importantly, she needed to get him out of this room. He was a bomb waiting to detonate. She could see it in the stiffness of his gestures, the tightness in his jaw. Caleb was seconds from exploding.

They left everyone behind and went through the kitchen to where a door led to the most stunning backyard. The turquoise water shimmered under pink lights surrounding the entire perimeter of the pool. And there was a cedar pool house that appeared larger than Ivy's entire apartment. Nearby, two light-gray couches and two armchairs were clustered around a firepit. Just beyond was the basketball court where Jesse must have played earlier with Liam and Lucy, who Ivy had yet to meet.

"Oh my God," she exclaimed. "This is unreal."

Caleb scoffed. "Money and power. Gets you whatever you want."

Ivy sighed. "Can we sit for a sec?"

Unsteady on his feet, Caleb flopped onto one of the couches and patted the area next to him. Ivy sat, but a few inches away from him.

"What's going on?" she asked.

He turned to her, his blond hair sweaty. "You don't see it, do you?"

Her pulse sped up. "See what?"

Laughter from the living room carried out to the backyard.

Caleb shook his head. "I'm fine, Ives. Worry more about yourself and less about me." He scrubbed his hands over his face, no longer looking at her. "Go back inside. I'll stay out here for a bit to sober up."

Uneasy, Ivy stood, wanting to touch Caleb, let him know she was there for him, but he was staring at the ground. She went back through the kitchen, where she could hear low whispering from the other room. Plastering on a smile so Mack wouldn't know how worried she was about Caleb, Ivy stepped into the dining room. No one was at the table anymore. She glanced over at the living room, where Mack, Lauren, and Jesse were huddled in a corner, next to the shelf of Mack's Emmy and Golden Globe Awards.

She got closer to them. Everyone's heads snapped up and swiveled in her direction. There was a beat of awkward silence, when no one said a word. Then Lauren smiled at her.

"Hey, everything okay?" Lauren's voice was higher pitched than usual.

Ivy had the disturbing sensation that they'd been talking about her. But she couldn't ask, so when they all, including Caleb, gathered in the living room for dessert, she pretended that Caleb wasn't trashed, that Jesse didn't spend more time with Mack and his family than he did with her, and that she was privy to the behind-the-scenes machinations of her own show.

At midnight, Mack ushered them to the front door. Rachel never came back downstairs. After Lauren and Caleb got into her Jeep— Caleb would get his car when he was sober enough to drive—Jesse offered to take Ivy home. She hoped that meant he'd come inside. Her mom would probably be asleep. She could sneak him into her bedroom, like Juliet did with Hudson. If Mack could use Ivy's life for the plot of the show, Ivy could take ideas from the plot. It gave her a sense of power, and Mack would never find out.

As she followed Jesse down the front steps, she felt a hand on her back. She turned.

Mack waited to speak until Jesse was at his truck. Then he said in a low but urgent tone, "Be careful."

Ivy had no idea which of the cast members she needed to be careful of.

CHAPTER FIFTEEN

Now

I hear breathing behind me in Lauren's living room. I slam the crossword down on the coffee table, then whip around, clenching the pen tightly in my fist, because it's my only weapon against whoever's in the house with me.

"I knew you'd follow me," Jesse says, hands on his hips, shaking his head at me.

I drop the pen onto the floor, but my heart is still racing. I stand, and with only the couch between us, I glare at him. "You think this is funny?"

"Of course not, Ivy. But you're the one who broke in."

"The door was open," I retort.

"I left it open on purpose. We need to have an honest conversation." He moves around the couch, closer to me.

I panic and bolt to the front door, which I yank open before racing into the street. It's quiet. The lampposts burn brightly, but the neighborhood is devoid of people.

I take off, my stupid heeled boots digging into my ankles, slapping the pavement as I run toward my car. I can hear him following me, our heavy breaths the only sound in the night other than the crickets chirping.

"Stop!" Jesse whisper yells. "I'm not going to hurt you!"

I don't stop, but I slow down, a stitch under my ribs and nowhere to hide. "I'll bet Caleb believed that too."

"Fuck you, Ivy. You ruined my life."

He knows.

I halt and slowly turn around. Jesse's bent over, panting, his hands on his knees. "I'm begging you to come with me back inside Lauren's house before we end up on TMZ."

He's right. It might seem serene out here, but anyone could be watching from their windows—recording us on a phone, live streaming our fight on social media. It's safer to go with him. And I've got the element of surprise. Lauren's phone is in my pocket, and I think I've solved at least one mystery. The name of the person who planned the reunion is on her coffee table.

"I need to tell my mom where I am first." I take my phone out of my bag.

Ivy: I'm at Lauren's house with Jesse. I'll explain later. Just want you to know where I am.

Mom: Are you safe?

Am I? I don't know, but I don't want my mother to worry.

Ivy: Yes.

Mom: Love you.

Ivy: Love you more.

Mom: Impossible.

"Let's go," I tell Jesse.

As we trek back, what Jesse had said, which I repeated to my mom, hits me. *Lauren's house.*

After we go inside and he closes the door, I say, "You don't live here, do you?"

"No. I still have the apartment I did ten years ago." He moves in front of me, arms crossed. "I never lied to you, Ivy. Lauren and I were only ever friends."

I take a step back. "Why marry her then?"

He doesn't answer. It's infuriating, yet there's something else we need to get out into the open. Something that I did to him.

"I never lied to you either." But Jesse might have gotten away with murder had I not anonymously phoned in the tip that nailed him to the wall. "How long have you known it was me who turned you in?"

"Since I was arrested."

All these years I believed it was a secret and only I carried anger—toward Jesse for how much he hurt me. He must have been so angry with me too. "Why did you run that night?"

"I was so scared, Ivy. And I'm scared now. I know you think I killed Lauren. But I didn't. There's someone out there who murdered my best friend." His face twists. "I don't want to lose you too."

"You lost me a long time ago." I pull the phone out of my dress pants. "Why the fuck were Lauren's bag and phone in your glove compartment?"

His face pales. He reaches for the phone, but I curl my fingers around it.

"I did not put anything of Lauren's in my glove compartment." A muscle twitches in his jaw. "If I actually took her bag and phone, do you think I would be stupid enough to hide it where anyone could find it?"

I shrug. "That's perhaps a perfect defense."

He glowers at me.

"Nothing else to say?" I ask, seething.

"What's the point, Ivy? You never listen." He sighs a grunt of frustration. "There wasn't some grand conspiracy against you then. And I'm not part of some plot now. It was never about you at all."

That takes the wind out of me. Because there's truth in his harsh statement. It did feel like the firestorm of media gossip, roller coaster of fan opinion, and the dynamics between Jesse, Lauren, and me revolved around me. Maybe I am self-centered. I'm also furious.

"Are you saying that someone else placed the phone in your truck? To frame you? Or so I'd find it and they could frame me?"

Now he looks at the floor. "Maybe. I always keep my truck windows open. You know that."

I huff a laugh. "I know nothing about you."

Sighing, he walks away from me and over to the coffee table, where he points at Lauren's crossword. "You decided to do a puzzle while hanging out here, looking for evidence against me?" he says incredulously.

I have no idea what happened between him and Lauren during their marriage, why she filed for divorce, or why they got married in the first place if they were only friends, as he's insisted. But my gut, which has admittedly been wrong before, tells me that he's not going to hurt me. Right now, at least. And I need someone to help me figure out who killed Lauren, if he is innocent. My mom can't handle much more. I want to take her home.

"I was doing an anagram. I know who set up the reunion."

He narrows his eyes. "Who?"

I pick up the crossword from the table and show him the two columns of jumbled letters I scrawled down on the paper to arrange into the words I was trying to put together. "Look at the letters in the name *Ellyn Lou Mara*. Then look at the last column."

Jesse leans over the paper, looking from left to right. His head jerks back.

"Yes. *Ellyn Lou Mara* is an anagram for *Lauren Malloy*."

Jesse doesn't say or do anything, but then his shoulders shake. I think he's crying, until a silent laugh becomes a rolling belly bray that makes me laugh, too, even though the situation isn't funny at all.

"Only Lauren," he says, when he finally stops and wipes his eyes.

"Only Lauren," I agree.

"How did you even think of an anagram?" he asks with a trace of awe.

I wave my hand across all the board games on the shelving unit. "She loved all kinds of games." My heart pinches. "And she knew me well enough to know that the only way I'd see the two of you again was if I could redeem myself on camera." I lower my voice. "And if there was money involved."

Jesse's face turns serious. He rubs his chest. "Lauren thought about you every day. I know she did, because she looked at your photo on her bedroom wall all the time. When we saw that exposé, she was devastated for you. She wanted to reach out, and I guess setting up a whole fake reunion was the only way to get all three of us in the same room together."

I want to believe him. "Then tell me what you're hiding. Why did Lauren want a divorce?"

"I can't," he whispers. "You need to hear it from Mack."

Throwing my hands in the air, I shout, "Goddamn it, Jesse! Why are you still protecting him? Lauren is dead! And he's disappeared, leaving you to take the fall for him."

I push past him for the front door. I don't want or need any more of his help. I'm so tired of coming second to the puppet master who controlled our lives then and still does now. A man who might have murdered the person Jesse and I both loved.

Without another word, I leave the house. As I head toward my car, parked haphazardly up the street, I don't look back to see if Jesse is behind me, or to look at Lauren's place. Her entire life there has nothing to do with me. It's only a matter of time before a shrine is erected on her doorstep. And I'm tied to a stake.

I drive on autopilot back to the motel, constantly checking for paparazzi or anyone else who could be following me. By the time I pull into the lot, where only one empty black hatchback is parked, I'm exhausted. After dragging myself up the stairs to the second floor and inserting my key into the lock, I hear a snap, like footsteps on a twig, from somewhere close to me. Instantly alert, I whirl around, staring down into the murky gloom behind the trees surrounding the picnic tables. I don't see anyone, but it doesn't mean someone's not there.

Rushing inside the room—where my mother is fast asleep with the lights on—I do the whole routine of locking and bolting the door, then jam the desk chair, which Jesse sat in only a while ago, under the knob. I make sure the blinds are tightly drawn.

There's half a BLT on a paper plate on the desk, and another wrapped sandwich on another plate—food from Wyatt. I haven't eaten a thing all day, but I'm not hungry. There's a gnawing ache in my stomach, and my eyes are gritty from tears and fatigue. Depleted, I change into the pink tracksuit and climb into bed next to my mom as quietly as I can, wishing for sleep to take me away from reality.

I'm jolted awake by a loud banging. At first, I don't know why I'm lying next to my mother in a bed covered in a scratchy flowered duvet. The banging starts again. Someone's at the door.

"Ms. Westcott? Ms. Hardwick? It's Detective Tanaka."

Now I'm fully aware of my surroundings and circumstances and gently shake my mom's shoulder. She startles, rubbing sleep from her eyes, clenching her jaw when she turns on her side to face me.

"It's Tanaka," I whisper. "She's outside our door."

"I hope it's for a good reason," my mother whispers back, immediately getting out of bed.

I do, too, though I don't think there's any good news that precipitates a detective bashing her fist on our door. Smoothing the pink tracksuit, I haul myself out of the bed. I feel awful. I need a hot shower and food. "Should I answer?"

"Yes, and I'll text Wyatt. Let's be polite but not say anything until he gets here. I still don't know what happened between you and Jesse last night."

"I have so much to tell you, but later." I open the door.

"Good morning, Ms. Westcott. May Sergeant Reyes and I come in?"

I do a quick scan of the second-floor landing, the small picnic area, and the parking lot below for anyone holding a camera. There's only one man getting into the black Mazda that was parked there last night. He doesn't give me a moment of his attention.

"Yes," I tell Detective Tanaka, and I bring them inside. I gesture to the bed and desk chair. "There aren't many places to sit."

"We can stand." Her tone is terse, and her red-rimmed eyes drill into me.

She looks as drained as I feel. Her sleek auburn hair is coming loose from her ponytail, and there's a slight odor of gasoline and brine wafting off her. I glance at her navy trousers, the same ones she wore yesterday, the bottoms of which are wrinkled and damp. Instantly, I'm on guard. Something bad has happened.

"My attorney will be here soon." I look at my mother for confirmation, and she nods.

"That's fine. But Mack Foster won't be. He's dead."

GOTCHA

24/7 Access to Celebs Behaving Badly

Redhead Ruins Everything

July 18, 2014

This drunken mess of a drama queen is doing everything she can to split up Hollywood's hottest couple. The dumpy lead of the most-talked-about show, premiering next month, was spotted climbing all over her hunky and taken male costar in his truck. Clue: Hello, Red.

Comment anonymously below with your best guess!

Guesses

Ivy Westcott. What a bitch.
Ivy Westcott. I heard that she's screwing Caleb Hill too.
Ivy Westcott. That chick needs a stylist.
Ivy Westcott. She is NOT Juliet.
Ivy Westcott. Get rid of her.

CHAPTER SIXTEEN

Then
July 19, 2014

Jesse drove up a road so steep that Ivy was worried they'd roll right back down. When he finally pulled into a gravel driveway, she leaped out before he'd even put his truck in park. After a hellish escape from LA and a few near misses with the paparazzi following them, they were finally at his cabin on Castaic Lake.

Jesse hopped out, too, and came around to hug her. "I've never been so happy to be here."

Ivy rested her head against his chest. "I don't know if I want to go back."

Jesse laughed, but Ivy wasn't kidding.

Insulated in Jesse's arms, where no one could find them at his cabin, which was hidden in a copse of trees and shrubs, Ivy could forget about the viral gossip piece. Ivy really thought no one would ever see them in Jesse's truck in the pitch-dark parking lot after a late-night shoot.

The buzz about the show was already at a fever pitch. The blind item rocketed it into the stratosphere. She was relieved, at first, hoping this would be the impetus for Lesse to end and Ivy and Jesse to go public with their relationship, like Juliet insisted Hudson do in the ninth episode, which they'd filmed that night before the parking lot rendezvous.

Skylar was suspicious of Logan and Juliet's sudden romance; Juliet just knew it. And only a day after the foursome had a double date at a bowling alley, Juliet was accused of plagiarizing an English essay. Skylar went to bat for her with the principal, but Juliet suspected that Skylar was playing games, arranging the pieces for some kind of secret revenge. Juliet gave Hudson an ultimatum: tell Skylar the truth about them, or they were done.

Ivy was sick of sneaking around too. Maybe a part of her wanted to get caught. But the *Gotcha* snippet enraged the fans so much that the CB instructed Lesse to lay it on even thicker in public, pushing Ivy to the back burner.

"It smells so good here." Ivy breathed in the potent scent of pine and cedar, her pulse slowing in the fresh air and the cool breeze off the lake.

"That's just me."

She laughed. Jesse kissed her on the top of her head and went to grab their bags and groceries from the back of the pickup. Together they brought everything up the wooden stairs to the front door of his cabin. "It's not luxurious, and I haven't been here in a bit, so it might not be too clean."

Ivy didn't know what to absorb first. The A-frame was stained mahogany, surrounded by a wraparound porch and trees with pretty purple flowers. She reached out and plucked one of the shiny black fruits.

Jesse held her wrist. "Don't eat that. Those trees are poisonous. The fruit's called *devil's cherries*."

Ivy dropped the berry. Jesse released his protective hold on her, and she wiped her hands on her jean shorts as she followed him inside the one-floor space that was his private retreat. The cabin was chilly despite the sticky heat outside, but when Jesse wrapped his arms around her, she instantly warmed.

She snuggled into him. "Thank you for bringing me here. I'm sorry I've been such a mess."

He moved his arms to her shoulders and pushed her back gently so he was facing her. "You'll hate me if I tell you that it only gets harder."

"I will, so let's stop talking."

Jesse grinned and pressed his lips against hers. She fell into him, like she always did when they were together. Deepening the kiss, she slid her tongue into Jesse's mouth. He moaned softly, tracing his finger along the back of her neck.

When it was just her and Jesse, Ivy was bold. She loved to feel his heartbeat race against her chest, and his hardness against her. He laced his fingers with hers, kissed her once more, then led her over to the floor-to-ceiling windows that took up almost the entire back wall. Ivy momentarily forgot everything else as she pressed her forehead to the glass, taking in the magnitude of the lake, shimmering under the golden sun, and the rugged Sierra Pelona Mountains, which rose in the distance. She couldn't imagine anything bad happening here. "That is the most gorgeous view I've ever seen." She pointed to the water. "That's Castaic Lake?"

"Yup." He moved her finger to the left. "And over there is a really cool lookout." He chuckled. "There's a private, secluded trail straight there from the cabin. It's not for the faint of heart, because it's completely in the woods, but I used to go off on my own to explore, scaring the shit out of my dad." His face turned serious. "Do you know you're the first person I've ever brought up here?"

Ivy's chest fluttered. "I am?"

"You are. You're the only person I've ever wanted to share this with."

"Yet you've never shown me where you live in LA," she teased.

"That's because your place is a home. Mine is just a stopping ground. Once I fix this place up, I'll live here full time. It's not that far from LA."

Ivy imagined living here with him—the fantasy both intoxicating and terrifying. She was afraid to completely open her heart to Jesse, because he was also dependent on Mack. She'd never asked Jesse what Mack had meant about keeping an eye on her when she'd overheard them on the day of the chemistry read. And she didn't know what Mack meant after the dinner party when he'd warned her to be careful.

"Does Mack know about us?" What she was really asking was whether he had tipped off *Gotcha*.

Jesse shook his head. "Not from me. But I think Rachel senses something going on."

Ivy widened her eyes. "How?"

"At our guitar lesson, she told me she felt a spark between us when we all had dinner at their house."

Ivy blinked. "Guitar lesson?"

"Nothing formal. I show her a few chords every now and then." He smiled. "She's not exactly a natural, but I like teaching people, especially music, because I don't get to do enough of it."

"That's nice of you." She meant it but also wondered what else he'd failed to mention. "What did you tell Rachel about us?"

"I neither confirmed nor denied." He moved closer to her. "Now, enough talking about everyone else. We came here to get away from that. I want to show my girlfriend around my favorite place."

My girlfriend.

The words made her giddy. They'd only been together, and in secret, since the end of May. Ivy had no idea what the future held. But right here, right now, she tucked her hand in the back of her boyfriend's jeans, quieted her worries, and followed him through the main room, furnished with brown leather couches and a thick black rug lying invitingly next to a fireplace. The area wasn't that large, but the vaulted ceiling made it seem spacious and cozy at the same time.

They took the grocery bags to the kitchen and unpacked steak, corn, fruit, bagels, cream cheese, and coffee. Jesse pulled a bottle of sparkling water from a bag and lifted it. "Yes?"

Ivy smiled. "Sure. I'm sorry if you'd rather have wine or something stronger."

"This is great." He walked to the tall cupboards—painted a soothing sage—and took out two glasses.

Ivy rested her elbows on the Formica counter. "Do you think Caleb is okay?"

Jesse poured the water and scratched his chin. "He will be. We're all dealing with the pressure of filming and the unexpected attention the best we can. I mean, we knew there'd be gossip and paparazzi, but none of us have experienced anything like this."

That made Ivy feel so much better about her own struggles with sudden fame and like less of an outsider. She had wanted to give Caleb his space after the dinner party, but she'd reach out as soon as they got back to the city. Now, though, this weekend was about her and Jesse.

As the sun set and the light in the cabin painted them with an apricot glow, he guided her to the living room. "Get comfy. Let me just get some firewood. The temperature drops even faster here than in the city once the sun is down." He nipped at her neck, then left the cabin.

Alone with her thoughts, and her veins hot with how much she wanted Jesse, Ivy wondered if she should simply wait or take off her clothes to surprise him. Trying not to dwell on how her body might look to him—this man who'd probably slept with so many lithe, beautiful actresses—Ivy pulled her black tank top over her head to reveal the red lace push-up bra, part of a matching bra-and-underwear set that Lauren had given her the day before.

It had been on a break between scenes. They'd been sitting on the low brick wall outside the studio, when Lauren slipped something wrapped in white tissue paper into Ivy's bag and told her to open it at home. The lingerie was perfect. Once again, Lauren had instinctively known what Ivy needed. As a thank-you, Ivy had a purple orchid delivered to Lauren's house. Lauren told her that it was the most special gift she'd ever received, because it was the first anyone had given her that was entirely unconnected to her appearance or acting.

Now Ivy stood, slid her jean shorts down her legs, and tossed them into a corner. Then, in the lingerie, she lay on her side on the rug. But after a few seconds, she felt ridiculous and dragged a pale-yellow cashmere throw blanket from the couch to drape on top of herself.

It felt like an hour had gone by before Jesse finally returned, a stack of logs tucked in his arms, and more in a canvas bag he carried. Sweat lined his forehead, and he was flushed.

"Did you chop all that wood yourself?"

He laughed. "I'm pretty handy with an axe, but not this time. I had to go into the shed to get it, and it was full of crap I had to take out and put back in." He sniffed himself. "I should probably shower."

"No, don't. Come here."

He dropped the wood, and Ivy threw off the blanket. Jesse sucked in a breath. "You're so beautiful. Like a Pre-Raphaelite Botticelli painting."

She snorted. "I'll bet you say that to all the girls."

He shook his head. "I only say what I mean, and I would only say that to you." He ran his fingers over her goose-bumped thigh. "You'll be a block of ice if I don't get the fire going."

It wasn't the cold but his touch that spread shivery delight over her skin. Impatiently, she waited as Jesse laid the logs and kindling and struck a match. Flames rose from the fireplace, heating the whole room. Jesse stripped off his shirt, then stoked the fire, his back muscles straining. Finally, he joined her on the rug.

Ivy let go of her inhibitions and fear. With Jesse's expert hands and mouth making her come alive in ways she'd never felt before, she brought him inside her body and as close to her heart as he could get.

———

A noise awoke Ivy from a deep slumber. She held her breath. It was footsteps on the deck outside the window.

"Jesse." She patted his chest, near where her head was. "I hear something outside."

"Mmm. Lots of noises here at night."

"No. I think it's a person."

Jesse opened his eyes, looked at her, and smiled lazily. "It's probably an animal. We get bears, coyotes, even mountain lions, but probably not up on the deck." Gently, he eased away from her and, fully naked, got out of bed. "I'll check so you can feel secure. You're so little. I wouldn't want an animal to snatch you away."

She scoffed. "I'm stronger than you think. And you can't go out there without any clothes."

"There aren't any neighbors for miles, Ives. It's fine. Can you hand me the flashlight? It's on the table next to you."

She didn't want to send him out there alone and naked, so she grabbed the flashlight, wrapped a sheet around herself, and followed him to the back deck. He turned the latch. It was unlocked.

Ivy sucked in a breath.

Jesse laughed huskily. "It's a tricky latch. It doesn't lock properly, but don't worry. Go back to bed. I can handle this." He waggled his eyebrows at her. "I'm a big boy."

Despite her worry, the sight of his hands that had driven her wild more than a few times and the sound of his rich, honeyed voice made her weak. She wanted him all over again. She did what he'd said and climbed back under the smooth sheets, listening to make sure he was okay outside.

A few minutes later, he slid into the bed. "There's absolutely nothing out there except a raccoon scrounging for scraps."

Ivy giggled. "Sorry."

Jesse kissed her on the mouth. "Sleep time, so I have enough energy to love you in the morning."

Love? Did that mean Jesse loved her? She definitely wasn't going to ask, and she couldn't say it back until she knew for sure. He fell asleep in seconds, and she lay awake, replaying his sentence and his touch in her mind.

When the morning sun shone through the windows in the cozy bedroom, Ivy wasn't sure how much she'd actually slept. But she felt invigorated and wide awake. She stretched, a bit sore from the night before with Jesse. She felt amazing. Reaching for him, she only felt the sheets. He wasn't in the bed.

She wrapped the thick capri blue duvet around her naked body and, smiling from the inside, she padded to the kitchen, her skin still carrying Jesse's scent—clean and fresh with a hint of spiciness. A half-full pot of coffee was on the counter. Maybe Jesse was outside. She was about to take her coffee to the deck and see if he was out there—together, they could watch the steam rise over the lake, then go straight back to bed—but before she could open the sliding glass door, she heard clicking sounds.

Following the noise, which sounded like tapping on typewriter keys, led her to the second bedroom. The door was closed. She hesitated. She didn't want to interrupt Jesse's flow of thought when he was writing. He'd confided in her that he'd been drafting his first screenplay on his grandfather's old black Underwood. While he loved acting and music, his secret dream, which he was scared to fail at, was to write and direct films. Ivy wondered if Mack knew.

Her need to see Jesse the morning after ruled against her sense of etiquette. Ivy opened the door a tiny crack. His hands stopped moving. He must have heard her. She stepped inside the room, but Jesse didn't turn around. Instead, he angled his body to the right and bent his head over a piece of paper on the oak desk.

Ivy wasn't sure whether to leave and let him create or kiss him on the back of the neck. As she tiptoed toward him, she tripped over the bottom of the duvet and let out an "Oof."

His head whipped up. Quickly, he slapped his hand on the paper, before spinning around in the chair. "You scared me."

She laughed. "I was trying to be stealth but almost broke my neck on the blanket."

"Give me a few minutes, and I'll join you in bed?" His voice was higher than usual, and his cheeks were pink, eyes dilated.

"Sorry. I don't want to interrupt. Just checking if you want a refill." She jutted her chin at the coffee mug resting next to the paper he still had his hand on.

"I'm good, but thanks. I'll be finished with this scene in about ten."

His speech was rapid, and from the way he kept blocking the desk with his body, it was clear that there was something on that paper he didn't want her to see. Her stomach curdled.

Ivy held his nervous gaze and walked close enough that she could see granules of what looked like raw sugar spread out on the paper under Jesse's palm.

Her voice quivering, she asked, "What is that?"

Jesse removed his hand and pushed his chair back. "It's not what you think."

"I think it's cocaine," she said in a steely tone.

"It's not cocaine."

"Is it a drug, Jesse? Are you doing drugs first thing in the morning?"

He sighed. "Listen, okay? It's Molly. That's it. I use it to open my mind a bit more." He winked. "I didn't sleep much. Last night was incredible."

"Don't deflect." She pulled the blanket more tightly around her, because she suddenly felt exposed. "How often do you do it? Snort it? Lick it? Whatever it is you were doing before I came in."

A muscle jumped in his jaw. "You can't judge what you don't know, Ivy. Just because you don't touch something that you consider wrong doesn't mean it is wrong."

Her lip curled up in disdain. "You're making no sense."

He started to get up from the chair, but Ivy shook her head.

"Fine. I'll stay here. What I mean is that you don't drink, and you've never done drugs, so you can be a bit self-righteous about it. I'm not hooked on it, and I'd never ever drive on it. It's just something that kick-starts my writing."

Ivy stepped back even farther. "Were you high last night? Is that why it took you so long to get the wood for the fire?"

He hung his head and blew out a breath. "Yes. Not because I needed it to sleep with you, but sex feels really, really good on Molly." He reached out his hand, but she reared back. "And I was nervous. You're special to me, and I didn't want to fuck up your first time."

Ivy laughed, cold and hard. "But you did, Jesse. I'll now always remember my first time being with a guy who had to be high to be with me." Her voice cracked with the tears threatening to spill. She forced them back. She didn't want him to have any access to her vulnerable emotions right now. "You know my father was killed by a driver high on cocaine and my mother had no parents because of heroin. So it's not that I'm self-righteous but that I lost half my family because of someone's reckless actions. But the worst part is that you snuck around and lied to me."

He crossed his arms. "I'm not the only one."

"Excuse me?"

"Almost everyone I know does Molly. It's not cocaine or heroin."

"So Lauren and Caleb do it too?"

"I don't think we should talk about it when you're this upset." Now he stood. "Please. Let's go for a hike, breathe in the clean air, remember why we came here."

"I came here because I love you." The words tumbled out, and she didn't want to hold them back. What was the point? He'd already broken her heart.

"And I love you. I'm in love with you." He stepped closer, pressing his palms together. "I'm begging you, okay? I only started using it when my dad got sick. I gave him my kidney, and he died anyway. The only way I could keep the cabin my grandfather built was to take the role of Hudson, when all I wanted to do was curl up in a ball and cry like a baby."

Ivy took in Jesse's pleading, his ill-timed declaration of love, and the terrible loss he'd suffered. She thought about her mother and the pain she dealt with; everything she and her mother had survived together. Jesse had no one to share the burden with. But he had snuck out to get high and slept with her on a completely different mental plane than she'd been on. That was what made her feel sick and used.

Ivy turned on her heel, wanting to stomp out of the room, but she had no fight left in her. So she simply trudged out.

161

"Where are you going?" Jesse followed her into the hall and to the kitchen, where her bag sat on the counter next to the coffee machine.

"Calling my mom to send a car for me," she answered while taking her phone out of her bag.

Jesse reached for her phone, but Ivy snatched her hand away.

"Seriously? Who are you?" she hissed.

"You can't tell Liz what you saw. You can't tell anyone." His face was ghostly.

She gawked at him. "Don't tell me what to do."

"Please," he pleaded, eyes wild. "I promise I'll never do it again."

"Never hide anything from me again? I don't believe a word you say." She picked up her bag. "You're an actor through and through."

Ivy left Jesse in the kitchen and didn't let the tears flow until she had gotten dressed and rolled her suitcase out the door.

The devil's cherries were smeared all over the deck right under Jesse's bedroom window, smashed beneath two large footprints, the dark-purple juice staining the wood with its poison.

CHAPTER SEVENTEEN

Now
January 18, 2024

How can Mack be dead?

My mother gasps, sinking to the bed, and I can only stare in shock at Tanaka.

"Presumed dead, to be more accurate. His SUV was found submerged in water at around five a.m. by a hiker. The vehicle was empty, but his phone was found inside the console. His wife confirmed it belonged to Mack." The detective pierces me with a sharp look. "Divers are doing a recovery mission."

I sag to the bed beside my mom, who touches the back of my head. I lean into her hand and ask the detective, "Did he . . . Was he . . ." I stumble over my true question. "Was it an accident?" I don't expect the tears that trickle down my cheeks. Mack made my life a living nightmare. He might have killed Lauren. But he was a husband and a father. I never even knew my father, but I feel his loss nonetheless. Rachel, Lucy, and Liam have only ever known their family whole and together. They don't deserve to suffer like this.

"We don't know much yet. We're hoping you can fill in some of the missing pieces." The detective tucks a strand of hair behind her ear and scans the room, like there might be evidence in here . . . and there is. I have Lauren's phone in the pocket of my dress pants, rolled in a ball on the floor, and the knowledge that Lauren was likely Ellyn Lou Mara. But Tanaka's penetrating stare makes me want to hold onto that information until she tells us more.

I glance back at my mom, who's checking her phone. I assume she's waiting for a text from Wyatt.

"Where were you both last night?" Tanaka asks, while Reyes keeps his coal-colored eyes trained on me.

I need to do something with my hands, because they're shaking. Both Tanaka and Reyes are assessing me like I've done something wrong, when all I did was try to get some answers and protect my mom and myself. "I want to help. I really do, but I need to hear from Mr. Gibson." I turn to my mom again, angling my head so Tanaka won't see me widen my eyes at her.

She dips her chin, our old silent exchange that means that I should go ahead and that I've got this. Tucking my hands under my legs, I tell the detective that I was with Jesse last night, and my mother says that she was in the motel room all night long.

Tanaka flips open that spiral notebook again. "Why did you go out with Jesse when you're both involved in a murder investigation?"

"We went to Mack's old house to try to find him."

Her eyebrows shoot up. "And did you? Find him?"

"No."

"Your attorney thought that was a good idea?"

I shake my head. "I left before he came here to drop off some food for us." I hesitate. How much do I tell? I don't know if Tanaka's here to arrest me. "I found out some information, though, about Lauren and Jesse."

I'm hoping Wyatt will come through that door any second now and instruct me on what to do without implicating myself. But there's no knock, call, or text from him, so I take a deep breath and tell the detective that I found Lauren's bag and phone in Jesse's glove compartment; followed him to Lauren's, where she lived alone; and solved the riddle of Ellyn Lou Mara.

Tanaka listens, face impassive, but her hand is quickly jotting down everything I say in her little notebook. My mom's been making noises of surprise after every sentence I utter.

"Let me get this straight," Tanaka says, rubbing her forehead with a finger. "You're now in possession of Lauren's phone?"

I nod, walk over to my pants on the floor, and pull out the phone.

Tanaka gets blue latex gloves from her pocket, slides them on, and takes the phone. "Did you try to gain access?"

"No. I wouldn't know her password."

The detective presses the power button. "It's dead." She hands it to Reyes, who produces a clear plastic bag, stamped with **EVIDENCE** in black letters, from the tool belt around his waist and pops in the phone. Then she directs her attention back on me. "You believe Lauren set up a fake reunion as Ellyn Lou Mara, Mack's nonexistent assistant, because it's an anagram of her name? Why would she do that?"

I try to recall Jesse's exact words last night. "Jesse told me that Lauren thought about me all the time. There's a photo of us on her bedroom wall. He thinks she set up the reunion to get the three of us in a room together." Pointing at myself, I say, "I think she wanted to tell me something about Mack. Something that Jesse is hiding."

"Any idea what she wanted to tell you?"

A sick turbulence roils my stomach. "Jesse and Lauren didn't live together. He keeps calling her his best friend instead of his wife. I don't know the exact nature of their relationship, but I do think the timing of her filing for divorce and her death are linked."

Tanaka nods crisply. "Spousal privilege, perhaps. They got married before Jesse was arrested for involuntary manslaughter."

"What does that mean?" my mom asks.

"Lauren likely knew something about Jesse that she didn't want to be forced to reveal in court. As long as they were married, she legally didn't have to."

"Have you talked to Jesse?" I ask, in pain for him. No matter how furious he makes me, how much I distrust him, Mack is the second father who Jesse has lost.

"We haven't located him yet. We do know that Jesse owns a cabin on Castaic Lake," she says grimly. "That's where Mack's car was found, below a lookout. We surmise that he either drove over the cliff intentionally or someone else made that car go over with Mack inside. The windows were smashed, but we don't know yet if that's from the impact of the drop or not."

I draw in a breath that feels like a razor blade against my throat. "Jesse once told me there's a private trail from his cabin to the lookout. Does that mean . . . Are you saying that Jesse could have killed Mack?"

Tanaka doesn't respond to my question but asks her own. "What time did you last see Jesse?"

"Around nine p.m. We parted ways at Lauren's."

Jesse's cabin is less than an hour from LA. It's possible for him to have driven there after he drove away from me.

"Do you know the address of the cabin? We haven't found a listing yet," Reyes asks, the first time he's spoken since they walked into the motel room.

I shake my head. "His grandfather built it a long time ago. It was at the top of a really steep dirt road. There aren't any other cabins close by, I don't think. It's on Upper Castaic Lake." I close my eyes to picture it. "It has a wraparound deck. Oh"—I remember the shiny black berries—"and there are devil's cherries growing all around the front of the cabin."

Reyes nods. "Okay. Thank you. That's very helpful."

My mom, who's still clutching her phone, likely waiting to hear from Wyatt, asks, "Are we in physical danger? Can we go home?"

The detective presses her lips together. "I think you should be vigilant. We'll track down the address of Jesse's cabin. And the digital forensics team will make Lauren's cell top priority. But these things take time to get right. Please remain in LA until I tell you otherwise.

I'm sure we'll have more questions for you if and when Mack Foster's body is recovered."

There's a noise from outside. A car pulling into the lot. I hope it's Wyatt. "Are you sure that Mack is dead?"

"Without a body, we can't be definitive, but we're fairly certain he couldn't have survived because of the conditions—hypothermia, the current; getting trapped in the thick weeds in that lake would kill him if drowning didn't." The detective hands my mom and me each a card. "My personal cell number is on the back. Call me anytime, day or night, if anything happens or you remember anything. No detail is insignificant."

Thanking her for what, I don't know, I watch her and Reyes leave, and then lock the door once again. When I face the room, my mom's deflated, curled up on her side of the bed. Instantly, I sit beside her and rub her back, like she's done for me countless times.

"Can I get you anything?" I ask lightly so she won't know how worried I am about her.

She shakes her head. The half-eaten sandwich Wyatt brought last night is still on the desk. The fact that my mother didn't throw it out and wipe the desk clean frightens me. Making everything look nice, no matter how filthy it might be below the surface, is what my mom does.

She reaches around and holds my hand. "I can't process any of this."

"It's hard to know how to feel right now," I say. "Mack was awful to me, but he gave me a chance when no one else would. And Jesse—" My voice cracks.

My mom faces me over her shoulder. "You deserve to be loved the way you love. You'll find it one day."

Her eyelids flutter. I don't like how weak she looks. "I think we should order some food. We haven't eaten, Mom."

Groaning softly, she sits up, propping the pillow under her hips. "I'm being a terrible mother. There are some granola bars in my purse. Please eat one. For me."

"You're an amazing mother. And you've pushed yourself too much." I look for her purse and see it on the stand under the television. I reach in and take out two granola bars, along with the little first aid kit to see if there's anything in there to ease the pain that I know my mother is in.

But seeing the white box reminds me of how she used tiny nail scissors to slice through the blue scarf that Lauren's killer had used to stage her suicide. If Mack is dead, the only other person besides me left from the show is Jesse. I'm having a hard time coming to terms with the very real possibility that he's a ruthless murderer.

"Ives, is it that hard to find a granola bar?"

I wave the bar, rip open the packaging, and take a bite. It forms a sticky lump in my mouth, and I struggle to swallow it, but I need the energy for what I'm about to do next. And to lie to my mother.

I hand her the other granola bar. "Okay if I go out and get us something more appetizing? I also need some air."

"But Jesse's out there. I don't think it's a good idea." She throws off the covers. "I'll come with you." But her voice is groggy.

"Why don't you rest? I won't be long. And I'll be very careful."

She nods, her eyes already drooping. "A nap is probably a good idea."

I hop in the shower, not bothering to wash my hair. When I emerge from the bathroom, my mom looks less pale.

"Wyatt finally texted. He was in court this morning. He's coming by this afternoon." She points to a bag under the desk. "He also got us flip-flops."

"Thank goodness to both," I say, getting mine and slipping them on. "Sure you're okay on your own for a bit?"

She grins cheekily, more like herself. "I was on my own forever until you showed up."

"And with Dad."

"And with Dad for a short time." She sets her jaw. "Stay in touch. And be safe. Please. I love you."

"I will. I promise. Love you more." I run over and kiss her on the cheek.

She holds onto me for a moment. "Impossible."

I hesitate before walking out of the room and leaving my mom alone. I've never seen her this low. Through poverty, literal back-twisting manual labor, fighting tooth and nail for me to have a career, then to save my life when it imploded, Elizabeth Hardwick has been a fierce warrior. When we go home, I'm going to find a new career that will provide for us both, out of the public eye, away from Hollywood forever. I won't let anyone tear us to shreds any longer.

We are the survivors.

FACEBOOK

Hello, Juliet Fan Forum

Public Group
150k members
About: A no-holds-barred forum to discuss all
things *Hello, Juliet*. Haters encouraged.

August 14, 2014

Top Contributor: CJ Smith
OMG, guys, did you see the video of Ivy Westcott outside NOBU
last night with the cast?

Comments

> **Lisa Sanders:** She was brutalized. It was awesome.
>
> **Jeanette Collins:** Calling her a whore is slut-shaming.
> But she kinda deserves it? Who does she think she is
> stealing Jesse from Lauren?
>
> **Tom Rigsby:** Fucking bitch.
>
> **Netta Fortin:** She looked scared. She doesn't deserve
> that.
>
> **Mandy Lincoln:** I've watched the video over and over.
> Caleb Hill shoved a photographer. Now he might be

charged with assault and Ivy gets to screw the hottest guy on the planet. Not fair.

Netta Fortin: THIS is unfair. Why so much hate for Ivy? I love her natural look. She isn't trying to be a Barbie. She's real. We need more actresses like her to represent us regular girls!

Tom Rigsby: Bitch.

CHAPTER EIGHTEEN

The air in the projection booth was hot and electric, in complete contrast to how heartsick Ivy felt inside.

Since she'd walked out of Jesse's cabin—taking a car home and not telling her mom, or anyone, the details of their breakup—she and Jesse only spoke when they needed to on set and for promotions.

Even Lauren didn't know why Ivy had ended things with the love of her life. But she did tell Ivy that Jesse was the one who insisted on putting out a public statement about Lesse's "amicable, better as friends and costars" breakup. Now Ivy was dealing with the fallout, once again, branded the whore who'd broken up the hottest couple since Brad and Jen.

Not even at last night's requisite cast dinner at NOBU, which the network had arranged to celebrate this evening's premiere of *Hello, Juliet*, did Jesse say a word to her. Granted, Ivy ignored him, too, but it was Caleb who jumped in to protect Ivy from the vitriol shrieked at her after they exited the restaurant. And Caleb who shoved the photographer who'd stuck his camera right in Ivy's face, asking her how she felt about stealing her best friend's boyfriend. All lies. Now Caleb might be charged with assault.

Ivy tugged up the waistband of her baggy jeans, wishing Stella had chosen something sexier for her. But Ivy's appeal to her small but mighty fan base was how accessible she was. She got letters and DMs praising her for her authentic appearance, unlike Lauren's unattainable beauty in her high ponytail, skintight jeans, and low-cut white tank top. The only imperfect part of Lauren was the battered red Converse on her feet.

Stop it. Stop comparing yourself. That was her mother's voice in her head. Tonight, before the car Mack had hired picked Ivy up at their new two-bedroom rented bungalow in Culver City, her mother had marched her over to the oval mirror they'd hung in the hall between their bedrooms.

"What do you see?" her mom demanded.

"Frizz. Boobs that are too big for my body."

Her mom laughed. "Most girls would kill for those natural curls and boobs. Be proud of who you are, Ives."

"How can I, Mom, when being a celebrity feels like I'm walking naked straight into traffic all the time?"

Elizabeth had spun Ivy around and cupped her face. "Ives, I think somewhere inside, you do believe in yourself, or you wouldn't put yourself in the position of being seen by the world. The fans and media—they're like vultures. They'll tear apart your flesh and gnaw on your bones if you let them. Don't let them."

"Fake it until you make it," Lauren, next to her, now whispered as they stood in the projection booth.

"I'm trying," Ivy answered. "My braids are too tight." She touched her head, where her hair was pulled back. She longed to let her curls loose.

They watched Jesse and Caleb hold court on the stage, tossing *Hello, Juliet* swag—T-shirts, sweatshirts and sweatpants, bumper stickers, and posters—to the audience. Mack wanted the cast to be as approachable as possible tonight, and more like the teenagers they played than the adults they were.

The crowd filled every seat in the movie theater. The CB network had run a massive online and grassroots ad campaign, partnering with a soda company. For every purchase, buyers had been entered in a raffle, and two hundred would win tickets to the private screening of the first episode with the cast.

Outside on the Third Street Promenade, paparazzi and the fans who hadn't been lucky enough to win a ticket to the premiere party surrounded the movie theater in droves.

Ivy was so afraid she'd be booed tonight, or worse. The behind-the-scenes drama of the show had become bigger than the show itself. It almost didn't matter what public opinion of the first episode would be after it dropped. Ivy's reputation was defined by gossip and rumor, not talent and skill.

Mack appeared at the top of the stairs in the projection booth, his gaze firmly on Ivy, unsettling her. He checked his gold Rolex. "Ready, ladies? Jesse and Caleb have gotten the crowd all hot and bothered."

Lauren laughed. Ivy tried to join in, but her laugh came out as a nervous titter. Lauren squeezed her hand. Ivy didn't know what she'd do without her best friend, who was more like the sister she'd never had. Lauren had been by her side to commiserate after months of reshoots, countless takes, degradation, and heartbreak. And she knew that Lauren felt the same.

After Lauren had called in tears that morning, because she felt responsible for the NOBU drama, Ivy showed up at her place with giant sunglasses and wigs—brunette for Lauren, blonde for Ivy. She hired a car to take them to Hollywood Boulevard, where they strolled with Starbucks cups in their hands, buying tourist trinkets. No one looked at them or chased after them for a shot. They were just two average girls hanging out. Sometimes Ivy longed for that to be her life.

But now she and Lauren had to follow Mack down the stairs of the booth, through the middle aisle of the theater.

He leaned in close, because the screaming in the theater hadn't stopped. It only got more intense as a white screen lowered over the stage and the lights dimmed in the audience so Jesse and Caleb were under a spotlight. "Stick close to me," Mack said. "We'll get you both on stage for the intro, then we'll head back to the booth."

For a moment, no one noticed them, so Jesse, in a tight white T-shirt, yelled into the microphone, "And here come the gorgeous ladies who make me and Caleb look great on screen! Ivy Westcott and Lauren Malloy!"

A roar went up in the audience, and every eye focused on Ivy, whose underarms pooled with sweat. She pressed herself as close to Mack as she could get. She didn't like feeling his body against hers, but he was built like a tank and provided a protective barrier down the aisle, where security guards were also stationed every few rows. She could smell his sweat through the black silk shirt he wore. Maybe Mack was nervous too. Ivy softened toward him, the way she did every time he acted human around her.

They all clambered up to the stage, and Mack directed the guys to stand on one side of him, with Ivy and Lauren on the other. Taking the mic from Jesse, he boomed, "Okay, everyone! It's time! Thank you so much for coming to the exclusive showing of the premiere of *Hello, Juliet*! Please take your seats. After the show, the cast will be available to sign autographs!"

The room went dark, and a security guard with a flashlight led the cast and Mack down the stage stairs, through a back room, and up to the projection booth. Mack passed a tray of champagne flutes down the row.

Ivy took one to be polite, but there was no way she was drinking tonight. Everyone else plucked a glass from the tray, and once Mack was seated at the end, closest to the door, he lifted his glass in the air.

"To all of you. I'm so proud of what we've accomplished. Here's to reaching the greatest heights!"

Everyone but Ivy took a sip, and as Mack stared at her over the rim of his glass, she wondered whether she was becoming his greatest triumph or his biggest mistake, as he'd described her to Jesse the day she booked Juliet.

The opening bars of *Hello, Juliet*—the theme song that Jesse had written and sung, accompanied by a soulful, raw melody on his acoustic guitar—reverberated off the theater walls.

> Hello, Juliet, we've been waiting for you.
> We all have sins. Few of us are true.
> Break our hearts, and we'll darken your soul.
> But together we might finally be whole.

Jesse's gravelly voice entranced the crowd, who were completely silent. To Ivy, the lyrics felt like they were written for the two of them. She missed him so much that her chest throbbed all the time, but lying and then avoiding her meant he didn't care about her enough to try to stay together.

Her attention shifted when the montage began—Ivy in a motorcycle jacket and combat boots stomping up the steps of Sunset Shores, really a high school in Laurel Canyon that they'd used for the exterior shots. The audience went wild.

This was also the cast's first time seeing the fully produced premiere. To watch herself so large on the screen, her name listed first in the opening credits, Ivy went through a gamut of conflicting emotions. Pride at what she had accomplished; reassurance that she had a steady income to support herself and her mom. But it was daunting to be so exposed, unable to control what the critics thought of her performance and what the public thought of her as a person. Ivy wasn't even quite sure who she was anymore.

Caleb leaned over and whispered, "I can hear you thinking from here."

She chuckled. They hadn't talked about his feelings for her, or their awkward interaction at Mack's dinner party. But she had texted him today to thank him for protecting her outside NOBU and asked if he'd been charged with assault. All she got back was a thumbs-up emoji.

"Caleb, about last night—"

"Nope," he interrupted. "It's what I'm here for, and luckily that photographer has a kid who wants to learn to surf, which is what I did today. It's all good." He winked. "Want me to grab you a soda? There's a whole case in here, courtesy of Sparkle Splashers."

Ivy giggled, relieved that at least she and Caleb were in a good place. "Sure."

Mack scowled at her, but Caleb got up, bringing her back a can, which she popped open and drank gratefully. The cool liquid slid down her parched throat, and Ivy leaned back in her plush velvet seat, trying to revel in the gasps and excited yells from the crowd in her first scene with Jesse. Their chemistry was electric. The magnetic pull when Juliet smirked at Hudson and he grinned back jumped off the screen. Caleb must have noticed it, too, because he said, "Hot," under his breath. Ivy didn't detect an undercurrent of resentment, so she whispered, "On screen. Off, it's as cold as ice."

He squeezed her arm as the scene on the screen below them switched to the first meeting between Juliet and Skylar in the student-liaison office at Sunset Shores. The crowd cheered even louder when Skylar appeared on screen. Ivy watched herself wilt next to the effervescence that naturally bubbled out of Lauren. Ivy had been trying too hard to match her effortless energy. She cringed inwardly, not daring to look at anyone else until the next scene with Caleb. He was the one with whom she'd felt most at ease sharing a screen.

Ivy knew the first couple of episodes weren't her best work, but she tried against all odds. By the time episodes ten, eleven, and twelve had wrapped—with Hudson and Juliet no longer speaking after she'd issued him the ultimatum about Skylar, and Logan and Juliet staging their own fake breakup—she'd found her footing and her voice.

Ivy wanted to text her mom, who was watching at home, before the episode ended and the night got too busy with the cast meet and greet and the partying that was sure to ensue. Mack wouldn't be happy if she wasn't on her game with the fans. She reached into her purse for her phone, and her hand hit the edge of something sharp. An envelope.

Curious, Ivy pulled it out. It was white and blank. A card, maybe? But who had put it in her bag, and when? There was a huge crowd of non–ticket holders who'd lined up outside before she and Lauren entered the theater. And despite the security guards ushering them inside, Ivy's hair, back, arms, and hands had been groped. She'd gotten so used to the unwanted touches that she'd just kept walking forward.

A creeping sensation, a barb of unease, pricked at her. She opened the envelope and slid out the white paper, folded three times. And she read the warning, typed in Comic Sans font.

You don't belong here. Enjoy this while it lasts. Goodbye, Juliet.

CHAPTER NINETEEN

Now

Locking the motel-room door, I hope I'm not making a mistake by leaving my mom all alone. She's obviously not feeling well. But I have the only key. I'll do what I need to as fast as I can. I check three times to make sure the door is secure and scan the entire area around the motel. It's empty. I appreciate that Tanaka isn't a detective who leaks information to the press just so she can be on camera. She's not looking for fame but justice.

I jump into my car and take a back route through the alley behind the motel until I park on the palm tree–lined Ocean Avenue. Quickly covering my head with the hood of my pink sweatshirt, I get out and duck into a little shop, grateful that it's only about sixty degrees, so my tracksuit doesn't stand out as conspicuous.

"May I help you?" a woman immediately asks, coming out from behind the counter, where a row of vibrant scarves is on display.

Thinking of Lauren and the blue scarf knotted around her neck—an image that I'll never unsee—I shake my head. "No, thank you." Before she can recognize me, I scoop up a wide-brimmed sun hat and pull an oversize pair of sunglasses off a spinning rack. Both will swallow my face and head, which is exactly what I want. The bright hoodie can't contain my famous red curls unless I cinch it around me so tightly that I won't be able to think.

Pulling out my wallet, I'm relieved to find some cash, because I don't want a paper trail. Not because of Tanaka but so this lovely shop owner won't see any identifying information about me.

I exit the store and immediately don my ridiculous disguise—something Lauren taught me to do—and take cover behind a tree.

Even though we shot on location on the beach a few times, I don't know this part of Santa Monica that well, and the unfamiliarity adds to my growing unease about being alone. I feel like there's a red bull's-eye in the center of my chest, never mind the photographers who could be anywhere. The dysfunctional family I belonged to, that someone tried to push me out of, is irretrievably broken. I have my little family of two to protect now.

What Detective Tanaka said about spousal privilege gave me an idea. There's one person who might know what kind of secret Mack would kill himself to hide or that'd make him the target of a murderer. His wife.

I download Instagram, which I deactivated a long time ago. I have no desire to be on any social media, torturing myself with how much people hate Poison Ivy. But I need it to contact Rachel, whose own account is private. Quickly, I make an Ivy Westcott fan feed, which I'll delete immediately after I get what I need. I send Rachel a DM with a photo of my face.

Hi, Rachel. I'm so very sorry for what's happening. May I stop by? I know today might not be the best time, but it's important.

It will go into her requests, maybe even her hidden messages, but hopefully she'll see it and believe it's really me. Then I check my texts. Nothing. I assume my mom fell asleep and Tanaka doesn't have any urgent updates.

I go back to my Instagram notifications. Rachel has sent me a DM in a new message thread in Vanish Mode.

Hello, Ivy. Thank you. Yes, I'd like to see you. Don't park on the street or come through the front door. There are reporters everywhere. You can take 17th Street and come through the backyard. Just DM when you're at the back door, and I'll let you in. You'll have to hop the fence. I can't come outside.

Rachel gives me the address, and before it disappears, I commit it to memory. My ability to quickly memorize is one of the only things I haven't lost.

I look every which way for anyone who's figured out who I am as I get back in my car. Satisfied no pedestrians have recognized me, I still keep my eyes trained all around me as I drive the four minutes to Seventeenth Street and park. Rachel failed to mention that I'd have to walk along the path of another house to access her yard. Running so no one catches me trespassing, I'm panting when I reach the tidy square of yard with neatly trimmed hedges that coincides with the address Rachel gave me.

I'm struck by how modest this neighborhood is, with mostly average-size bungalows. Mack and Rachel went from a mansion in the Hollywood Hills to a house that's the smallest on this street. It's clear that Mack, too, has fallen prey to the *Hello, Juliet* curse. Then I banish that thought from my mind. He could very well be dead, and no one deserves that.

Nervous at how exposed I am to Rachel's neighbors, I hesitate, then shimmy up the fence, hoping none of them think I'm breaking in and call the police. Once I hop over and reach the back door of a sand-colored house with white trim, I'm breathless and take a second to collect myself.

I can hear the whir of helicopters nearby—a reporter probably trying to get an aerial shot—and the voices screaming Rachel's name from the front of the house. My sympathy for her expands, because she isn't in Hollywood, except by marriage. She didn't choose to be in the public like I did; she was thrust there because of love. I think about her twins, Lucy and Liam, whom I never had the chance to meet.

I DM Rachel that I'm here, then text my mom the truth about where I am.

Mom: You're very kind to see Rachel. Please be careful on your way back. I'm going to take a nap now. Wyatt texted me that Jesse hasn't been found yet.

I'm afraid that Jesse will go to the motel to find me again, and I don't want my mother alone with him. I'll be in and out of Rachel's as quickly as possible.

Ivy: Any more news on Mack?

Mom: Nothing yet. Divers haven't recovered a body. They're going to dredge the lake at some point.

Ivy: Rest, Mom. I won't be too long. Don't answer the door to anyone but Wyatt and the police. Promise me.

Mom: I promise.

Hearing footsteps from inside the house, I anxiously dig my nails into my palms. I don't want to be out here much longer and become the lead story.

The door opens. I startle. It's been years since I last saw Rachel, and she's aged a lot. Her hazel eyes are swollen, and her face is puffy. Of course it is. She's just lost her husband, and in the worst way, because they haven't found his body yet. Mack might have been my Svengali, but he seemed weak in the knees for his wife.

"I'm so sorry, Rachel."

She nods. "Thank you. Come in." She closes the door behind me. "Did anyone see you?"

I shake my head. "I don't think so. I parked on Seventeenth Street."

Rachel nods. "That's where I'm parked, not that I'm going anywhere right now."

She leads me through the storage room at the back of the small house, to the living room, where all the blinds are shut tight. The whole place is dark and stifling. And quite empty. The walls are bare of any photos, and the furniture is sparse. There's only a beige couch, a silver floor lamp, and a simple pine coffee table piled with used tissues.

"Sorry for the mess. This was supposed to be temporary until Mack got back on his feet, but that's lasted seven years. We're renting the place from a friend."

I don't know what to say, because Rachel was always commanding. Now she seems drained of her soul, which is heartbreaking. "I get it. I rent, too, in exchange for taking care of the Airbnb I live in."

She smiles sadly. "It's been a hard time for all of us. Can I get you anything? Tea? Coffee?" She lets out a strange laugh. "Something stronger?"

Her energy is manic, making me prickle with apprehension. I breathe in for a count of four, hold it for a few seconds, and release it as quietly as I can. I have a lot of questions to ask, and I need to be calm and gentle when I do.

"A glass of water would be great. Thank you."

She guides me to the compact kitchen, opens the plain white fridge, and retrieves a bottle of water. After handing it to me, she steeples her fingers under her chin, which wobbles.

"Why?"

I don't want to assume what answer she's seeking, so I sip my water to give her time to elaborate.

She flops into a chair at the round white table, and I follow suit.

"Why would Mack take his own life? My life. Our kids'. I know things haven't been easy"—she waves her hand around the shabby kitchen, the paint peeling on the walls and the counters scratched and dinged—"but it would have gotten better. And none of it was his fault."

"Are they sure it was suicide?" I ask, and I immediately regret it when her eyes harden.

"Are you not?"

"I . . . I don't know." My hand automatically goes to my hair, and I tug at a curl.

"You've always had the most gorgeous hair." She laughs that odd, high-pitched sound again. "Mack used to call you Little Orphan Annie at home."

I bristle. "He didn't like me very much, did he?"

The doorbell rings and rings again. Rachel stiffens but doesn't say anything about it. Her eyes narrow. "How did you feel about him?"

"That's a complicated answer. I was grateful he gave me the role of a lifetime. But he made me feel like I'd never measure up to the image he had of Juliet." I came for answers, so I have to ask them. "I always wondered if he wished he'd given Lauren the role. Did he?"

"He did everything to make that show a success." She points at me with a trembling finger, the nail torn and sharp. "Everything for you."

Her sudden shift from collaborative to combative is distressing. I change the subject from me. "How are Lucy and Liam?"

She moves her finger from my face, and her features slacken. "Awful. I mean, they're doing great in their lives. Both twenty-one and at UCLA. But Mack was their hero. He was everyone's hero, except yours. Do you think—" She stops and abruptly stands up.

I'm not sure if I'm supposed to stand too. I regret coming here at all. I've left my mom alone in the motel room, and Rachel's demeanor spikes my already frayed nerves. Of course she's grieving a shocking loss, but she vacillates so wildly between kindness and accusation. I'm not getting any of the answers I came here for. I only have more questions: Why hasn't Mack had a show air since *Hello, Juliet* was canceled? Why did he hire me? Did he kill Lauren? Could Jesse have killed him in revenge?

"Stay here for a minute. I want to show you something."

She leaves the kitchen, and in the silence, I hear the paparazzi and fans shouting outside. My defense mechanisms relax. It's unfair that she and her kids will be a paragraph in the tabloids, forever followed because Mack's SUV went off a cliff.

Rachel returns with a cardboard box filled to the brim with papers and drops it heavily on the kitchen table. I twitch from the noise, curious what's inside.

She palms her chest. "This is the worst pain imaginable."

"I can't imagine," is the only thing I can say, because I'm not sure if she's talking about this box or losing Mack.

"All Mack ever wanted was to create a legacy for the kids. To entertain audiences but also teach them something. He was a mentor. Did you know that? He helped so many young writers and producers. Read their scripts, introduced them to the right people. He was going to help Jesse with his screenwriting, though he did just fine on his own." Her eyes soften at the mention of Jesse.

"Jesse told me—there's something that Jesse knows about Mack." I don't know if I should tell Rachel about Lauren planning the reunion or leave it to the detective.

"No kidding. The police have been here three times since Lauren died, looking for Mack. Today, though, they had a search warrant." She lets out a hoarse sob. "Do you know what it feels like to watch strangers take away your possessions?"

The question seems rhetorical, because she barrels ahead without waiting for any response from me. I don't know what to say anyway. I just want to leave.

"They took our computers, Ivy, and cleaned out his whole desk. All they left behind were his awards and this box I found hidden in the garage under yard tools—like Mack ever used those." She shoves both hands into the box and lifts out stack after stack of manila files. "Guess what's in these files?"

I shake my head, confused and more than a little frightened, because she's boring a stare of absolute hatred at me. "I . . . I don't know what's in there."

"No? How about in this?" She takes out another box, this one steel with a clasp, and pushes it toward me. "You should know what's in these, Ivy, because every single thing is about you."

REDDIT

r/ruinaceleb
RuinACeleb

2.5 Million Members
What hot tea is being spilled? Share, comment,
upload, and link to all the receipts.

New Comment: @diggingupthedirt I found a leaked police
report! OMG. What a scam. But Ivy Westcott's home address is
on it. Let's harass her. LOL.

Full Name	Ivy Westcott
Home Address	325 East 105th Street Watts, California, 90002
Classification of Crime	
Harassment	
FOR POLICE USE ONLY	
Was the individual injured? The alleged victim was unharmed.	

CHAPTER TWENTY

Then
August 28, 2014

So thankful she and her mom had moved before their address was shared all over Reddit, Ivy felt awful for the residents who lived there now. She could only imagine the people staking out the property, skulking through the yard, and peering into the windows, hoping to get footage of Ivy Westcott naked to post online. Filing a report after finding the frightening letter in her bag at the premiere party had not only been useless but also put her in more danger.

"There's no real physical threat here, ladies," the male officer had told Elizabeth and Ivy in a condescending manner.

"*Goodbye, Juliet? Enjoy this while it lasts?* What else do you need? Can't you dust it for fingerprints or something?" her mom had insisted, hands on her hips.

The officer had given her a patronizing smile. "Do you know how many celebrities have ardent fans? I suggest you get a dog."

They couldn't get a dog, because Ivy worked all the time, and though her mom did most of her management work from their living room, it hurt her to sit for more than thirty minutes at a stretch. A dog would add even more physical stress to her day.

Since that night, Ivy felt eyes on her back wherever she went. A constant dread took up space in her stomach, next to the confusion she felt over Jesse. When *Hello, Juliet* rocketed to number one in the ratings after the first episode, Jesse texted her a congratulations, as though they were friends. When the show remained at number one for three consecutive weeks, the cast had been invited to shoot a *Rolling Stone* cover, set in a boxing ring. Ivy and Lauren had worn gold lamé leotards, while the guys, of course, got away with tight shirts and board shorts. Jesse had every opportunity to talk to her alone that day, but he didn't. He made sure Lauren and Caleb were close by any time he was near Ivy.

Now, five days after the cover shoot, in her room, Ivy flipped her pillow over to get the cold side. It was the twentieth time she'd done it since she'd woken up this morning and decided not to leave her bed at all. The clock on her nightstand read 6:00 p.m., so she'd met her goal.

There was a knock on her door. She'd smelled the roast chicken—her favorite—and heard the clatter of bowls and spoons for the cake her mother was making for her twenty-third birthday, which was today.

"I'll come out soon, Mom," Ivy called, her voice raspy from not speaking to anyone the whole day.

Another knock.

"Ugh. I'll get up." Ivy peeled herself from the sheets and went to open the door. It wasn't her mother standing there.

"Hey," Jesse said, running his hand through his thick hair.

Ivy's stomach dropped. "I don't want to talk to you."

"Will you hear him out, Ives?" her mother asked, appearing behind Jesse in a gray sweatshirt dotted with pink frosting.

Enraged that her mother and Jesse were handling her behind her back, Ivy wanted to slam the door. But Jesse's sad eyes and the worry line indented between her mother's eyebrows made her mutter, "Fine."

Jesse wrung his hands, shifting from foot to foot while Elizabeth sat on Ivy's bed. Ivy stood, arms crossed, wincing when she caught a glimpse of her wrinkled pajamas and bedhead in the full-length mirror on the closet door.

"I'm so sorry, Ivy. I never want to do anything to hurt you. I love you so much that losing you hurts more than losing my father."

Her head warned her that Jesse was a writer who knew how to charm with his words. But her aching heart took precedence, and Ivy dropped her defensive stance. "Do you have a problem with drugs?"

Jesse shook his head. "No. And I won't do it again if it bothers you. I don't need it." He rubbed his chest, shooting a look at Elizabeth. "You're braver than me. You're not afraid to feel. I am."

Ivy huffed a laugh. "Do you know me at all? I'm so afraid to feel. That's why it's been so hard to play Juliet. She's too much like me."

"Can I say something?" Elizabeth said softly.

Ivy shrugged. "Sure. Since this is an ambush."

Her mom pressed her lips together, shooting Ivy an apologetic look, then addressed Jesse. "My daughter is the most important thing in my life. She is my life. It's been the two of us since I was six months pregnant. Ivy grew up with no family but me, because of drugs."

"I know," Jesse said, looking down at the floor.

"But you don't really know. You might think pot, Molly, whatever else you've been doing isn't that dangerous. It's not only how it affects your body and mind, but the people who love you. One mistake ruins lives." Elizabeth stood, grimacing when her right foot hit the floor. "Now I'll let you two talk alone."

She left the bedroom, closing the door behind her.

Ivy and Jesse looked at each other. He took a step forward, but she held up a hand. "I don't trust you, Jesse. I can't be with someone who hides things from me and runs every time there's a problem."

"I hid it because I knew it would upset you, but I wasn't trying to lie. And I was afraid to talk to you."

Ivy fingered a curl. "I'm talking about Mack too. I get that you see him as a father figure. But you follow his directions, on and off the set. I know he told you to keep an eye on me." She blew out a breath, afraid of asking the next question and finding out the truth. "Was it

Mack's idea for you to fake a romance with Lauren to show me he's in total control?"

Jesse's face contorted with what seemed to be genuine pain. "Yes, it was his idea to fake Lesse, but only for publicity. That kind of shit happens all the time. Mack doesn't know you and I were ever together."

"Promise me you're telling the truth." She wanted so desperately to believe he was. She wanted to be with him, touch him, and love him. But not if he was going to make her miserable.

He reached for her hand, and she let him take it. He held it over his racing heart. "I promise, Ives. You're more important to me than Mack and the show. I also promise never to take drugs again. I've never been in love before you. I've never let anyone close enough. This is new for me too."

"You can't keep hurting me like this," Ivy said, splaying her fingers over Jesse's chest.

"I know I won't get another chance with you. I won't do anything to screw it up again."

There were voices outside Ivy's room.

Jesse turned over her palm and laid a gentle kiss on her skin. "Get dressed, okay? There's something for you in the living room."

He walked out. Ivy's head spun. She wasn't going to simply fall back into Jesse's arms. But she would get out of her pajamas, because it sounded like there were a lot of people in her house. And once she'd changed into a white eyelet dress that dipped low enough to highlight her ample chest, then clipped her unwashed hair back on both sides so her curls flowed down her back, her suspicions were confirmed.

"Surprise!"

In the living room, Jesse, Caleb, Lauren, and Elizabeth beamed at Ivy from under a silver **HAPPY BIRTHDAY** banner tacked up to the pale-pink wall above the first flat-screen TV Ivy and her mom had owned.

Ivy blinked back tears. "Oh, fuck it." She let her feelings out because Jesse was right. She was brave. And with all their arguments, sensitivities, and insecurities, these four people were her family. She was glad Mack wasn't there, that he hopefully hadn't been invited. He probably didn't even know today was Ivy's birthday.

"Thank you so much." Ivy wiped under her eyes. "I had no idea you were doing this for me."

"It was their idea," Elizabeth said. "I'm just the chef."

"You're so much more than that, Liz," Caleb said, his shaggy hair damp, probably from surfing. "You're like our mom too."

"Then do what I say, and let's get this party started." Elizabeth grinned, leading everyone to the gleaming walnut dining table that she'd shined to a high polish.

Tapered candles in small white glass votives surrounded a stunning bouquet of coral dahlias in a crystal vase Ivy hadn't seen before.

"Because of you?" Ivy asked Lauren.

"From my garden, of course." Lauren smiled. "But that's not your gift. This is." From the black tote bag slung over her shoulder, she handed Ivy a Scattergories box.

"Seriously? You should host a game show one day. You're obsessed." Ivy laughed.

"I know, right? There's another little something for you, but after dinner." Lauren wrapped her arms around Ivy. "Love you."

"I love you too," she whispered into Lauren's soft hair.

Caleb also gave her a wrapped gift. "For you, old lady."

"Still younger than you," Ivy responded, kissing Caleb on the cheek, and added the gift to the small pile already on the buffet.

After Lauren had brought in the roast chicken and Elizabeth had carried in a salad, they all sat down at the table for dinner. Lauren, Elizabeth, and Caleb on one side; Ivy and Jesse on the other. Ivy laughed to herself, because she knew her mother had made the seating arrangements.

Light from the candles flickered over the faces of everyone Ivy loved. This right here was all she really needed in life.

"Thank you. I've never . . ." She cleared her throat. "I'm very lucky to be a part of our family."

Jesse raised his glass of sparkling water. "Ives, this is only the beginning. Happy, happy birthday!"

Everyone raised their glasses and drank to Ivy. Caleb was drinking water, which Ivy was glad to see. It didn't bother her if people drank; she wasn't that self-righteous. It wasn't even that Jesse, and maybe Lauren and Caleb, did drugs. That was their business. It was the lies and the excess that scared her. Celebrity culture could eat anyone up and spit them out, if they weren't careful.

After dinner, the guys insisted that Ivy and Elizabeth relax on the couch while they stacked the dishes, and Lauren brought out the cake. Sparklers crackled, and Ivy blew out her candles, wishing for her mother to be healthy and for Jesse to be honest and not break her heart again.

Caleb piled the presents from the buffet into his muscular arms and deposited them gently onto the coffee table. "In case there's anything fragile." He smiled shyly.

She lifted the top off his gift first. Inside the box was a black-and-pink wet suit in her size.

"You're going to teach me how to surf?" Delighted, Ivy beamed so widely that her cheeks hurt.

"Yup. The fall's the perfect time to surf in Santa Monica, so after we shoot the season finale." He pointed to another wrapped box on the table. "There's that too."

"You didn't need to get me all this!" She laughed. "But I'll take it."

Caleb's handsome face lit up when Ivy unwrapped a stunning blown glass vase in all different shades of red. It was one of the most beautiful things Ivy had ever seen, and she told him that.

"It reminded me of your hair when I saw it in a gallery."

"I love it. Thank you so much." She hugged him hard, and he held on tightly. But it was a brotherly hug. Now that her relationship with Jesse was back on track and Caleb seemed to have accepted that he and Ivy would only ever be good friends, maybe the dynamics off screen wouldn't be as contentious as they were written to be on the show. They could all move forward from here.

Lauren reached into her tote. "I didn't wrap this." And she gave Ivy a rectangular box in the iconic robin's-egg blue.

Ivy squeaked, "Tiffany? Lo . . ."

"Oh my God, just open it."

Ivy took the top off the box and gasped. Inside, nestled on a soft bed of cotton, was a stunning silver link chain. It was cool in her fingers. She put it around her neck, lifting her hair, and asked Lauren, "Will you clasp it for me?"

Lauren moved behind her, and there was a tinny click. The chain was surprisingly heavy but comforting rather than cumbersome.

"I'm sure you're used to wearing delicate necklaces, because that's how you see yourself. But that's not who you are, Ives. You're tougher than you think."

Ivy touched the chain, absorbing Lauren's words. "Thank you."

"That's beautiful, Lo. And I agree," Elizabeth said, looking at the chain. "It really suits you, Ivy."

"And my best friend, we're now linked forever," Lauren whispered in Ivy's ear. "No one can separate us. You see me the way I want to be seen. And I'll always choose you."

"Stop your lovefest so I can give Ivy my gift," Jesse said, nudging Lauren out of the way. "Unless you want to go first, Liz."

Ivy's mom shook her head. "Since Ivy was little and we didn't have a lot of extra money to spend, we've made each other gifts every year."

"This year she made me a mug at a pottery place for my tea. I'll show you guys later."

Elizabeth laughed. "Please don't. It looks like shit, but it's the thought?"

Everyone else laughed too. Jesse, though, was fidgety.

"Your gift, please." Ivy wanted to put him out of his misery, because he was clearly impatient to show her what he'd gotten her, and she was curious.

Jesse jumped up to get the last remaining box on the table, his hands shaking slightly when he handed it to her. Ivy lifted the lid, confused over the MP3 player inside.

Jesse coughed. "I, uh, well, I made you a mixtape of sorts. My own songs and some that make me think of you. I'm singing them." His cheeks flushed. "Maybe that was stupid."

Ivy was overcome by a rush of love for this thoughtful, humble man, who had hordes of women screaming for his body and his voice. Who hid his writing because he was scared to be judged. Who made mistakes that he wanted to rectify. She feared what might happen if anyone found out that the rumors about them were true, but here and now, she didn't care who was watching and leaned over to kiss him hard. "This means so much to me. I'll listen to it tonight."

The doorbell rang. Ivy stiffened. She wasn't expecting anyone else.

"Let me check the camera," her mom said, opening her phone.

They'd put in an expensive security system that had cameras on the front and back doors, and an alarm. They weren't taking any chances with their safety since Ivy had been doxed.

"It's a guy in jeans and a T-shirt. No idea who he is," Elizabeth said.

Caleb got up, but Jesse stopped him. "I'll go."

Jesse left. The room was tense.

"Anyone get you a singing telegram?" Caleb asked, obviously trying to lighten the suddenly somber mood.

No one laughed. They were all craning their necks to watch as Jesse answered the door. Ivy heard a collective exhale when the door shut and Jesse waltzed back into the room, shaking his hips and hiding something behind his back.

"Guess what I got," he sang.

"Too small for a naked telegram," Caleb quipped, making everyone relax.

"That's what she said," Lauren added.

Elizabeth groaned.

"Ta-da! It was a courier." Jesse flung his arm out, the red binding Mack always used for the scripts in his hand. "The finale!"

"No way." Lauren jumped up. "Give it to me!"

Ivy was quiet. Was it selfish of her to want her birthday to be about her and not the show? She was excited to see the season finale, but every single thing in her life was about work. Did Mack know it was her birthday and do this on purpose? No, she had to stop catastrophizing. They'd been waiting eagerly for the finale. The twelfth episode had left off with a shot of the police pulling a bag of steroid pills from Logan's locker, the mystery of whether they belonged to him—or if Hudson, Skylar, or Juliet had planted them—to be revealed later.

"Let's sit at the dining room table and prop the script up so we can all see it?" Ivy suggested.

They all gathered around the table, and Ivy blew out the candle on one of the votives to lean the script against it while Elizabeth turned on the lights. They all began reading. Ivy was the fastest, so she waited for everyone else to catch up before turning the pages.

The episode was very well written, propulsive, and gripping. Ivy expected nothing less from Mack. He wasn't the kindest director or showrunner, but he definitely knew how to create ominous tension and emotional depth that kept viewers coming back for more.

Ivy turned the last page.

INT. SKYLAR'S CONVERTIBLE—NIGHT
(A foggy night at 2:00 a.m. SKYLAR, HUDSON, and JULIET have just picked up LOGAN from the police station. SKYLAR bailed him out. LOGAN is driving, because he insists. HUDSON is next to him in the passenger seat, with JULIET and SKYLAR in the back.)
SKYLAR. You have a serious drug problem, Logan. I have to tell Mom and Dad. You

know that. If you're convicted, you'll lose your scholarship to Oregon.

LOGAN. I know things about you too, Sky. Do you really want to play this game with me? I know what you've done.

HUDSON. Shut up, Logan! Take some goddamn responsibility and stop blaming everyone else for your issues.

LOGAN. My issues? That's hilarious. I know why you stay with my sister.

JULIET. Stop! Everyone just stop! I can't stand the secrets anymore!

(Tense silence fills the car.)

LOGAN. You're right, Jules. But do you know how my sister won all those academic awards? How she's going to get into college? She hasn't studied a day in her life. She cheats. Your perfect best friend with the perfect boyfriend pays him to do all her work for her. He's got a lucrative side hustle going on.

HUDSON. You don't know anything, man. We just bailed you out. Who do you think you are, throwing accusations around?

LOGAN. Skylar is Hudson's best client and the keeper of his secrets. That's why he'll never be with you, Jules. He can't get rid of her.

SKYLAR. (Laughing.) You're such a loser, Logan. You can't even run around the block without amping yourself up. Watch yourself, big bro.

JULIET. (*Slamming her palm against the car door.*) Do I matter to any of you? Or has it been a hustle from the beginning? "Let's involve Juliet so she'll be the scapegoat when anything goes wrong." You're all so goddamn worried about what everyone else thinks of you that you're destroying me! And you don't care!

HUDSON. My feelings for you are real, Juliet.

SKYLAR. He's lying to you, Jules.

LOGAN. You're all liars! One of you planted those drugs in my locker. And one of you is going to pay for it.

(*LOGAN doesn't see the car careening toward them in the wrong lane. Only JULIET notices. Leaping toward the front seat, she grabs the wheel, the tires screeching as she frantically steers them away from the other car. The convertible flies over the embankment off the highway and flips, heading straight for a ditch.*)

Ivy got to the end of the scene before anyone else. She gasped, feeling like she'd been punched in the stomach. Lauren was wrong that no one could separate them. Mack had the power to split them apart.

Ivy turned around and looked at her castmates. "One of us is going to die."

CHAPTER
TWENTY-ONE

Now

I stare at the manila files on Rachel's kitchen table, and at the steel box. My heart skitters. "What do you mean, this is all about me?"

"Open it. All of it."

With Rachel's wild eyes trained on me, I bend my head and flip open the first manila file. There are pages and pages of clippings from tabloids. Every story ever written about me, collected in a neat stack, inches high. In the next file are what seem to be every Twitter, Instagram, Facebook, and Reddit post; every message board ever made about me; all printed out. They date back from when I was cast on *Hello, Juliet* to the day the show ended.

And yet another terrifying file is filled with Polaroids—not printed from the internet, but originals. Me opening the door to my apartment in Watts and to my house in Culver City. Me sitting in Caleb's car and Jesse's truck, including the night Jesse and I kissed in the parking lot and someone outed us to the press. The most horrifying photo of all was taken from what appears to be the deck of Jesse's cabin, right outside his bedroom window, because we're in his bed under the blue duvet.

Jesse's hidden under the blanket, so it's just the shape of him. But I'm fully visible, the duvet tucked under my bare arms.

I was right that night when I heard footsteps on the deck. Someone was watching us. Not someone. Mack.

Shocked, I look up at Rachel.

"Now the steel box."

I don't even want to touch it, but do I have a choice? My only other option is to walk right out her door. And a part of me needs to know what's in there. What other private moments in my life Mack infiltrated without my ever knowing. I pop the clasp. Inside are five thumb drives. Swallowing hard, I can only shake my head at Rachel.

"Those thumb drives? They seem to be every YouTube, Vine, TV, and radio interview with you and about you." Her tone is hateful, like I've collected all this myself. "And secretly recorded videos, like the one of you on the floor at Requiem."

I feel sick. "I don't understand why he had this . . . or why he did this."

"Neither do I." She tugs a hand through her tangled hair. The prongs holding the sapphire in the center of her wedding band catch on a few strands and pull them from her head. She doesn't seem to notice. Her attention is solely on me. "Were you sleeping with him, Ivy?"

I lurch back. "No! Never. I don't know what all of this is, but I swear that I had no interest like that in Mack. Ever." I can't even believe she'd think so.

I need to leave, but I don't know how to get up safely. I'm in danger. I can feel it. My bag is slung over the chair, and if I reach for my phone, she might stop me. I hope I'm being dramatic, but she just accused me of sleeping with her husband, who, it seems, was watching me every time I felt someone's presence where no one should have been. Capturing my most vulnerable, personal moments. And for what?

I try not to visibly shudder in front of Rachel, but I feel so violated. Yet I'm also relieved to finally know who'd leaked everything to the press, including that humiliating video of me crawling on the floor at the upfronts after-party.

I've long suspected my champagne was spiked that night. Mack was beside me from the moment I walked into Requiem to when I placed my drink on the host desk, then down on a table while I was with him and Rachel. He could have slipped me something. Again, though, what was his motive? To stoke the flames for the show by throwing me into the fire? Frighten me into quitting? And how does Mack stalking me connect with Lauren's murder and his death?

Staring at the files, Rachel says, "I've never seen Mack as obsessed with a show as he was with *Hello, Juliet*. He always worked hard, since he was a little kid. He grew up dirt poor, the oldest of six kids, and helped take care of them. He took whatever jobs he could to go to AFI and make his short films. Even now, with what little money we have left, he sends them—" Her voice catches. "Sent them money every month. And he was almost always home with us for dinner. His family was everything. Until you came along."

"I truly don't know why he did this, Rachel. I swear that there was absolutely nothing going on between us."

She lifts her eyes from the repulsive dossier that Mack collected and slaps the table. "There must have been, Ivy!" She points to the photo of me in the bedroom at Jesse's cabin. "If it wasn't to see you, why else would Mack drive up that treacherous dirt road in the middle of the night?"

She grabs my hand, her ring digging painfully into my skin. "Did he touch you in a way he shouldn't have? Please. I need to know."

Gently, I pull my hand away, and as softly as I can, I say, "No, Rachel. Mack never touched me. I never touched him. I promise you."

"The role was Lauren's. Then you swan into that audition and nab the job of a lifetime. No experience. No stage presence."

I don't have to take this. "I didn't ask to be Juliet Jones, and I did the very best I could under unbearable circumstances." I stand and grab my bag from the back of the chair, wishing I could take photos of

Mack's treasure trove to show my mom and the police. I'll call Tanaka the minute I get out of here. "I need to be with my mom. I really am sorry for your loss."

"How is your mom?"

It's an odd question, considering I don't think Rachel and my mother ever met.

"She's okay. Why?"

"It wasn't until after I saw her at the memorial that I made the connection."

I squint at Rachel. "What connection?"

"That she cleaned Mack's office building. The one on Wilshire. Only for a short time, but still, I probably should have said something to her before now. It's just been . . ."

"I'm sorry. I think you're mistaken. My mother was a cleaner, but not for Mack's offices."

"It only occurred to me when I saw her again in person. But she definitely worked there. I saw her one night when Mack forgot something at his office. I was in the area, so I went to get it for him. Your mom was in there cleaning."

I feel the blood drain from my face without understanding exactly why I'm so stunned. My mother cleaned a lot of office buildings, often at night when I was old enough to stay home alone so she could be available to take me to auditions and classes during the day.

"I—I had no idea. So, are you saying my mother knew Mack before he cast me as Juliet?"

Rachel lets out a sad laugh. "Highly unlikely. I don't think he chatted with the cleaning staff. Not to be rude."

I think we're past worrying about social etiquette at this point. I'm more concerned about why my mother never told me she cleaned Mack's offices. Unless Rachel is totally wrong. She's been wrong about a lot.

Thankfully, she seems spent from our conversation and walks me out. "Be safe," she says in a chilling tone before she closes the door behind me.

My head swimming with more questions than the answers I came here for, I throw on my huge hat and sunglasses before skulking back through Rachel's yard. Mack was obsessed with me. My mother might have cleaned his production offices on Wilshire. But the biggest question is if Mack is really dead.

I slide into my car, nervous sweat making my skin sticky, despite the chilly weather. After tossing my inane disguise on the passenger seat, I text my mom to see how she is, but she doesn't respond. I call, but that goes unanswered too. Though I leave a detailed message about going to Rachel and Mack's and everything I discovered while I was there, I don't mention that I know she worked at the Wilshire building. That's a conversation we should have face to face. If it's even true.

I call Detective Tanaka, who also doesn't answer. There's too much to explain in a message, so I ask her to phone me back. I don't know if Jesse's been found.

I have to get back to my mom, but I can't seem to even turn on my car. There's so much to process. So I sit, watching the few people on the street walking their dogs or simply enjoying the fresh air. I envy them their seemingly simple lives, though of course I'm sure they each have their own trials. But these people are unknown, able to stroll the sidewalks with their heads held high. I'm so used to keeping my eyes to the ground that I miss most of my surroundings. I chose that life the moment I auditioned for Juliet Jones and lost myself.

I've fallen so many times. But I've always gotten up. I'm Elizabeth Hardwick's daughter, after all. Maybe she never told me that she worked for Mack because she didn't want me to think I'd gotten the role for any reason other than my merit and worth. But did I? Or did Mack feel sorry for the young single mother whose daughter needed her big break? Mack never struck me as particularly charitable, but the way Rachel talked about him as a father and a husband makes me see a different side to the man who never seemed to want me around. Yet my skin crawls, thinking of the files and photos, and all the storylines he ripped from my pain. Mack hated me, but I never did anything but try to make him proud.

I don't know what it was he wanted from me. Now, I probably never will.

I call my mother again. Still no answer. She said Wyatt would be by at some point, so perhaps he's there. Perhaps she's still sleeping. I now regret telling her, especially in a voicemail, what Mack's done to me. My mother's entire adult existence has been devoted to protecting me. I don't want her to blame herself for his transgressions.

But I will blame myself if I affect her health. I'm a grown woman who didn't even hire my own lawyer. I shouldn't expect my mother to communicate with Wyatt. That's my obligation, their connection aside.

"Jesus, Ivy," I say to myself when I realize that I don't even have Wyatt's number in my contacts. I google Wyatt Gibson criminal defense attorney Los Angeles. A whole slew of links come up, but none for a criminal defense office. I hit "Images." There he is. I click the link, and it opens to a landing page for Gibson and Associates, Personal Injury Lawyers. That's strange. Swiping through the pages at the top of the website, I look to see if there's a link for criminal defense. Nothing. I quickly scan the about page, testimonials, and cases Wyatt has won, becoming more and more confused.

I look at the time on my phone. I've been in my car for almost an hour. I need to get back to the motel. I'm heading down Seventeenth when my phone rings. It's my mom. Slowing, I press the speaker.

"Mom, I don't know if you listened to my message yet. Don't. I'm on my way, and I'll tell you everything when I get there. But I did just find out that Wyatt's not a criminal defense attorney."

Silence. Then I hear a sickening wet gurgle.

"Mom? Are you okay?"

"Ivy," she croaks in a brittle rasp. "Help me."

THE CUTTING ROOM

Take Two—Westcott Awakes

Rick Newman

September 15, 2014

This cynic critic is nibbling his words. Though Ivy Westcott doesn't possess Lauren Malloy's natural talent, she's come a long way from the first two offerings of *Hello, Juliet*. In the subsequent episodes, Westcott finally displays that Mack Foster magic of transforming a dull rock into a shiny diamond. Westcott isn't flawless in her execution of Juliet's inner turmoil between her friendship with Skylar and her attraction to Hudson, plus her uncertainty about Logan's intentions. But her dialogue is crisper, and the light has come on in her green-as-envy eyes. Fans, too, are gobbling up the tension and high stakes in such massive numbers that the show has been given an early season-two renewal. The ferocious backlash against Westcott's casting has died down, but another cast member might be at risk. Word on the street is that someone is getting axed from the show. For now, I'm Team Ivy.

CHAPTER TWENTY-TWO

"Is Liz home?" Jesse asked, entering the second Ivy opened her front door.

"No. She went grocery shopping."

"Good." Jesse kicked the door shut with his foot, then gently pushed Ivy against the wall, devouring her mouth with his.

She ran her hands through his silky hair, moaning when he stopped kissing her mouth and nipped at her neck with delicate little bites. "Let's go to my room. We only have about an hour before we have to be at the Snake Pit."

Ivy had never been to the notorious bar on the Sunset Strip, where no photographers were allowed on the premises and celebrities could engage in all sorts of debauchery without getting caught. The raucous, edgy scene wasn't where she was comfortable, but tonight was special. Tonight, Ivy was finally someone other people valued. Someone who people wanted to know.

Jesse shrugged off his battered brown leather jacket, hung it on a hook, and swept up Ivy in his arms. Laughing, she threw her head back as he carried her down the hall and tossed her onto her bed.

"Early renewal, baby!" He whooped, sliding down the straps of her black tank top, taking one of her nipples in his mouth.

"Oh God. Don't stop." Jesse's mouth felt amazing. Everything he did to her gave her a natural high. And she was truly happy that Rick Newman from *The Cutting Room*, one of her harshest critics, was the first to do an about-face. The tides had turned in her favor. Though she'd never escape being compared to Lauren, Ivy didn't care anymore. She was being recognized for her worth and praised for her acting, and she had a secure job for the next season, at least.

If Mack was going to kill off a character—as was rumored in the press, even though they hadn't even shot the season finale yet—it wasn't Juliet. The fan fervor had prompted the CB network to send Elizabeth Ivy's contract for the second season the night before, with a note that she wasn't to discuss it with her fellow cast members.

But as Jesse's tongue trailed between her breasts, Ivy struggled to keep it from him. How could she be this intimate with him, expect honesty from him, but not give it in return?

She blew out a breath and asked, "Did Mack get you and Caleb a gift? He got me a black Birkin bag. I'm not sure about Lauren."

Jesse snickered. "Subtle. And I was going to ask you the same thing." He flicked his tongue over her skin, then said, "He got me a really cool flask with a compass in it and my name and the show engraved on the back. Plus a very expensive bottle of scotch. I'll show you later. I assume he got the same for Caleb."

Despite the intoxicating rush, Ivy winced. "A flask and scotch? Is that appropriate, considering Caleb's trying not to drink as much?"

Jesse sighed. "I think he's fine now, Ives. It was a rough patch. We've all had one."

Sometimes Ivy felt like she was the only one who took Caleb's issues with alcohol seriously. Yes, he was back to his happy-go-lucky self, but

Ivy didn't see the twinkle in his eyes that had been there when she first met him. But perhaps they were all more jaded now.

"I think the finale is just a cliff-hanger and we'll all be back second season. Stop talking and show me where you want me to touch you, Little Red."

Jesse's hands on her body made every worry vanish. She was so into him that she didn't even know her mom had come home.

"Ives? Where are you?" Elizabeth called out.

"Shit."

Jesse laughed. "Relax. It's not like you're a teenager sneaking your boyfriend into your room. She knows what we're doing."

"Yeah, but she doesn't need to have it thrown in her face. She's still my mom."

He kissed her, then moved from the bed to put on his clothes. "I'm meeting up with Caleb. But I'll drop you at the Snake Pit to meet Lauren."

"Oh, you're not coming in with us?" Ivy was disappointed.

"A bit of boys' time first, but we won't be long." He pulled his black T-shirt over his head and grinned. "I'm going to help your mom with the bags so she likes me more."

"I think she likes you more than me," she said as Jesse bounded out of the room.

It was true. While her mother treated Caleb like the son she never had, Elizabeth relaxed more when Jesse was around, as though she could take a step back from the responsibility of Ivy's happiness and security. Jesse played guitar for her, and they even watched classic movies together that Ivy wasn't as keen on.

Elizabeth had encouraged Jesse to visit his father's grave, where he hadn't been since his dad's funeral last January. She gave him flowers from the small garden in their backyard, and Ivy went with him, holding Jesse as he cried in her arms. They were all healing from the ups and downs of the first season and their tumultuous lives.

Ivy tugged on her jeans and tank top and clasped the silver link chain that Lauren had given her around her neck. Then she touched it like a talisman—a wish that none of them would be leaving the show.

Jesse and her mom were just coming in the door with the groceries when she reached the front hall. Her mother looked her up and down. "Aren't you guys going to the Snake Pit soon?"

Ivy smirked. "I think this is actually perfect for the Pit, but I'll shower and change super quick after I get the rest of the bags from the car."

The week before, Ivy had surprised her mom with a baby blue Mini Cooper, their first vehicle.

"I'll get the rest of the groceries." Jesse smiled. "Oh, I wanted to show you the flask." He reached into the pocket of his leather jacket. "Hmm. It must be somewhere in the truck. I'll go get it."

"It's fine. Show me later."

"What are you two on about?" her mother asked, cheeks flushed as she moved her attention from Ivy to Jesse.

"Mack's gifts for the early renewal." Jesse winked at Elizabeth, who winked back. Then he turned to Ivy and asked, "Can you be ready in thirty?"

She nodded, left Jesse and her mom, and headed for the shower. Half an hour later, dressed in a silver chain mail dress that she'd bought with Lauren on Rodeo Drive, Ivy looked at herself in her bedroom mirror.

"You did it," she said to her reflection. "All those years of wanting and hoping and waiting—your time has come. It only gets better from here."

Never again would they experience the fear of not knowing if they had enough money for food and medical care.

She walked out of her bedroom and found her mom and Jesse in the living room.

"Holy shit." Jesse's mouth fell open when he saw Ivy. Then he looked sheepishly at Elizabeth. "Sorry."

Elizabeth laughed. "You said it before I could. You look very sexy, Ives."

"Is it too much for the Snake Pit?" Ivy didn't want to be overdressed.

Jesse grinned. "Nothing's too much for the Snake Pit. You'll see."

Elizabeth walked them to the door, where Ivy kissed her goodbye, then she got her Birkin from the front hall table and climbed into Jesse's red pickup truck. She flicked the tiny red guitar charm hanging from the rearview mirror. When she shifted, her knee knocked into the glove compartment, and it popped right open.

"Is it broken?" she asked.

"Nope. Mack helped me put in a quick release."

Ivy let out a peal of laughter. "You tricked it out because you're too lazy to press hard on it?"

"Vintage car but modern times, my love. Gotta keep up." Jesse reached over, then pulled out a silver flask. "Mack must have put this in here before we added the release."

She took the flask from him and smiled, then ran her fingers over the smooth metal. "This is really nice." She didn't want it to bother her how close Mack and Jesse were, and she wanted Mack to see in her what Jesse and her mom saw. Gifts weren't as good as words of praise, but the luxurious bag in her lap was a start.

Jesse tilted his head. "What are you thinking about so deeply over there?"

"I love you."

"I love you too. Maybe let's just make an appearance tonight, then you can sleep at my place?"

"Your place?" Ivy raised her eyebrows. "Wow, that's a first."

"I only want to be with you. I don't care where we are."

"We can have a secret signal to each other when we want to leave the Snake Pit?" she suggested.

Jesse laughed. Then he crooked a finger at her and winked. "Like that?"

Ivy giggled. "No, you idiot. Not *A Night at the Roxbury*. And something other people won't notice."

He let out a belly laugh. "*A Night at the Roxbury?*" He pressed his index finger to his lips and kissed it. "That?"

"That," Ivy agreed.

They turned onto Sunset and passed the famed Chateau Marmont, the long street in front of them lit on both sides with the bright awnings of the bars and restaurants. Lined with storied landmarks like the Roxy and the Rainbow, the Sunset Strip represented a legendary Hollywood, where regular people became extraordinary, an elite circle to which Ivy now belonged.

Jesse pulled up right outside the bar, where a bouncer blocked the black door. "God, you're gorgeous," he said, leaning over to kiss her. "I want everyone to know you're mine, Ives." He took her hands. "Let's go public."

"Now?" Ivy laughed. Warmth radiated through her body. She'd waited for Jesse to take the initiative.

"Well, not right now, but tomorrow, okay? I don't care what Mack and the network want. I want you. Not for the show or anyone inside that bar, but because you make me happy."

"You make me happy too," Ivy whispered. Keeping secrets was unhealthy.

So when she spotted Lauren standing by the wall next to the bar, Ivy waved her over. Lauren leaned her elbows on the window frame, her mouth a slash of red that made her look like a stunning vixen. "You and Caleb will come in soon?" she asked Jesse.

He nodded. "Yeah. We'll find you inside."

Ivy touched Lauren's arm. "Lo, Jesse and I got our contracts for the second season. Did you?"

Lauren grinned. "Yes. Not sure about Caleb, though."

"I'll find out and text you in our group chat." Jesse ran his thumb over Ivy's lips. "I messed up your lip gloss."

"Good. Do it again," Ivy said, kissing him quickly.

"Guys, you have all night to paw each other," Lauren said, opening Ivy's door. "Come on already."

Ivy giggled, hopped out, and watched Jesse drive away. Floating, she and Lauren sauntered over to the bouncer right as a small group of photographers descended on them. Ivy didn't know where they'd suddenly come from but decided not to shy away. So when they yelled out, "Congratulations, girls, on the early renewal!" Ivy thanked them while Lauren smiled placidly.

"How does it feel to be a star, Ivy?"

Ivy grinned. "We're a family and support each other. Now Lauren and I are going to celebrate. Have a good night, guys!"

She took Lauren's hand, leading her for once, as the bouncer waved them across the threshold and let them inside the bar to safety.

Ivy gazed around the gritty, cavernous room, where shiny red leather banquettes were tucked into all four corners, and even though smoking inside was illegal, cigarette butts littered the concrete floor. Framed platinum records and band posters covered every inch of the black walls, spotlighted by the pink-and-green neon over the bar and stage.

No live band played tonight, so music pounded through the speakers, making Ivy's chest vibrate. When Lauren pointed to the bar, Ivy yelled, "Why not? But it's on me," and got them each a sweating glass of whiskey sour.

A few sips of the tangy drink and the raw beat of the bass made her feel reckless. Here she was free to do whatever she wanted. What she wanted most was to feel Jesse's hands and mouth on her. To press her body against his like the other couples on the dance floor.

Lauren, though, didn't look excited. She was staring at her phone.

"Everything okay? Hear from the guys?" Ivy asked.

"No. Keep dancing. I'll be right back. Going to pee."

Ivy wasn't sure she wanted to be without Lauren but knew she should let go of those fears. Always cushioned by other people, Ivy needed to be her own person. She smiled at Lauren and turned back to the crowd, raising her arms above her head, swiveling her hips, carefree.

The buzz started low and slow. A murmuring, and necks craned toward the bar. She saw the bartender holding something in his hand, then move toward a door behind the stage. He disappeared inside. Seconds later, people began walking in the direction of the front door, heads down as though they didn't want to be recognized. What was going on?

She texted the group chain.

Where are you all? Something weird is happening. Everyone's leaving.

No response.

She didn't know whether to stay where she was, follow the crowd out the front door, or see if Lauren was still in the bathroom. She opted to find Lauren, but every stall was empty. Then the music stopped.

She came back to the now-vacant bar and saw the black door behind the stage. On instinct, with a terrible sinking feeling in her stomach, she walked toward the door and pushed it open. Then she froze, taking in the scene playing out before her in horror.

Caleb was on his side, shaking uncontrollably on the floor in the middle of the dark room, where the black lights made the sight of him even more frighteningly macabre. The burly bartender was injecting a syringe into Caleb's right shoulder, while Lauren, on her knees beside Caleb, stroked his hair back from his face, yelling something that Ivy couldn't discern. Next to the bartender was a black box, with NALOXONE stamped into the center of a red cross.

Ivy heard something that made her look toward the exit. The door swung shut as a figure in a battered brown leather jacket slipped away into the night.

It shook Ivy out of her shock, and she rushed over to Caleb. Lauren and the bartender were by his side, both screaming, "Come on, Caleb!"

Cold sweat breaking out all over her body, Ivy dropped to her knees on the other side of Caleb, shouting, "What happened? Did Jesse go to get help? Did anyone call an ambulance?"

Lauren looked up for only a second, tears streaming down her face. The bartender injected another dose of naloxone, this time into Caleb's thigh, right through his jeans. Neither answered her.

Ivy whipped out her phone and pressed Emergency Call while Lauren moved Caleb onto his back, made a fist, and rubbed her knuckles on his chest.

"Help!" Ivy screamed at the 911 dispatcher on the line. "The Snake Pit back room! Someone's collapsed. Hurry!"

As the 911 operator assured Ivy that help was on the way, there was a gurgling from Caleb's throat, then a horrifying rattle from his chest. Lauren's rubbing became ferocious until the bartender shook his head at her. Caleb was silent. His body was still. Lauren unfurled her fist and laid her palm over his heart.

With a guttural howl, Ivy fell forward, crumpling on top of Caleb, dead beneath her.

CHAPTER
TWENTY-THREE

Now

"Mom? Mom!" I yell into the phone.

There are no other words, just the faint sound of staccato gasps, like my mom is trying to catch a breath. I slam on the gas. At a red light, I call 911. I notice that my location is enabled. What the fuck? I know I turned it off when Tanaka interrogated me at the police station. I could have swiped over it by mistake, but I don't think so. I think someone else wants to know where I am and somehow got access to my phone.

I tune out the noise in my head to focus on the dispatcher who comes on the line. "Something's wrong with my mother. Seaview Motel. Room 203. I'm going there now."

The dispatcher says something, but I hang up, because I need to call Tanaka. She's still not picking up, so I leave the same rambling message I gave to 911.

I make a left too widely, narrowly missing the car that's coming up beside me. For a moment, I wish Jesse were driving, because he'd know how to get me to my mother as quickly and safely as possible. Could he have hurt her? Unbearable guilt crushes my chest for wasting precious time sitting in my damn car instead of being with her.

Finally, when my heart is punching my throat, and with my hand on the door handle, I turn onto Main Street and see the pink building in the distance. I gun it to the parking lot, turn off my car, and am out of my seat belt in seconds.

Bolting toward the stairs, then taking them two at a time, I race to our room, my legs and chest burning. The door is open a crack. I step inside. And I scream.

My mother is on the floor, lying in a pool of blood. So much blood that when I get down on all fours next to her, my hand slips, crimson staining my skin.

"Mom!" I cry.

She doesn't move. I press two fingers to her wrist, bursting into tears when I feel a faint pulse. My phone rings from my bag. I scramble for it, seeing LAPD flash across my screen.

"Help! It's my mom. She's unconscious and bleeding on the floor of our motel room. She's got a pulse but . . . just come. Please come!" Suddenly I realize that if someone hurt her, they could be nearby. I drop my voice to a whisper. "I'm not sure if someone is in the motel room. Like in the bathroom. What do I do?"

"I know you don't want to leave her, but if you feel unsafe, go outside," Tanaka says firmly. "I'm on my way."

"I'm not leaving her," I insist.

"Okay. Do you know where the wound is?" she asks.

I scan my mom's entire body. The blood is thickest under the right arm she's lying on. "Her arm, I think. I don't know if she was attacked or fell because . . ." Because her back finally gave out, and I didn't help fast enough.

"Stay on the line with me. I'm right around the corner. Is she still bleeding?"

I scoot as close to my mom as I can get without moving her, because I don't know what kind of wound she has. If she hit her head. If she'll survive. As carefully as I can, I lie flat on my stomach to look at the area around her right arm. A choking sound of revulsion comes out of my mouth. "There's a metal nail file in her arm. She's losing a lot of blood. It won't stop. Should I remove the file? Try to tie something around it?" I will her to open her eyes. "Mommy, please. I'm here."

I feel a rush of air, and in bursts Tanaka, with an EMT crew right behind her.

"Ivy, I need you to step back. Let the paramedics look at her."

I don't want to leave my mother's side, but I nod, sitting only a few inches from the man and woman in uniform who are kneeling next to my mother. Tanaka heads to the bathroom, while the woman wraps a long band of navy nylon around my mother's arm, cinching it tightly while the man checks all her vitals.

"Deep laceration and possible severing of the radial artery." He inserts a tiny needle into my mother's uninjured arm and attaches an IV to a bag that he holds in his hand.

With my arms wrapped around my knees, I look to the ceiling. If there is a higher power, now's the time for me to believe. I can't lose my mother. "Will she be okay? Please. Just tell me she'll be okay," I beg.

Tanaka comes out of the bathroom and steps over to me, crouching down. "The room is secure." In a gentler tone, she says, "Ivy, they'll do everything they can. I want you to come outside with me, please."

I sob. "I wasn't even here. I should never have left her."

"We need to preserve all the evidence in this room. This might be a crime scene, Ivy." She offers to help me up.

I ignore her outstretched hand and stand by myself. "A crime scene? Lauren, Mack, and now my mom? What the hell is going on? Where's Jesse?"

"We'll find him. But right now, we need to get your mom to the hospital."

"Jesse lies. Over and over, he lies. Lauren only married him for spousal privilege. She died because he's been hiding a secret about Mack since Caleb died. And now my mother is bleeding out on a floor." I grind my teeth together to control the howl trying to rip free from my throat. Then I remember why I called Tanaka twice today. "I saw Rachel

Foster earlier today. I found out that Mack was stalking me. There are files and photos of me in a box at Rachel's house. Maybe that's what Lauren knew. Maybe she died because of me."

Now my mother might die too.

Tanaka speaks into the radio on her shoulder. "SID to Rachel Foster's house. Stat. And bring her in."

The paramedics put their hands under my mother. "Three, two, one," the woman says, and they lift my mother, place her on the stretcher, and carry her out the motel door into the sunshine. "Transport to UCLA Santa Monica," the woman calls out over her shoulder.

"I need to go with you." To the detective I say, "Find Jesse, please." And I follow the paramedics down the stairs to the ambulance in the parking lot.

They open the doors and place my mother inside. The man heads to the front while the woman stays in the back. "Get in," she says to me.

I scramble inside. The doors slam shut, the lights flash red, and the siren blares as the ambulance screeches away from the motel, weaving through thick traffic. I can't hold in my wail any longer. The paramedic, whose name tag I finally see reads "Radhika," glances over and says, "We'll do everything we can."

But *I* didn't. All I can think about is how scared my mom must have felt and how after she'd spent years battling chronic pain, someone tried to end her life in mere minutes.

Meanwhile, Mack is presumed dead. Jesse is missing. My mother hired Wyatt, a man I'd never heard of until yesterday, to represent me in a homicide, though he's a personal injury attorney. Where is he right now? He was supposed to stop by the motel. Was there more between them than my mother let on? Could he have hurt her?

My anxiety ratchets higher when something beeps, as the ambulance careens from lane to lane. Radhika adjusts a button on a monitor. Blood drips from under the tourniquet wrapped around my mother's arm.

"What is it?" I ask, panic coursing through every muscle in my body.

She gives me a comforting smile. "Just her blood pressure rising a bit. It's to be expected with this kind of arterial injury."

Nothing is expected. I look at my mother's matted hair, chalk-white face, and closed eyes. I notice another long red line on her collarbone. Pressing my hand to my mouth, I can't do anything but hate myself for not protecting her.

After what seems like an interminable ride, the ambulance pulls into the bay at the UCLA Santa Monica Medical Center. Radhika pulls a lever, the doors open, and the man who was driving runs out to help her lower the legs of the stretcher onto the ground.

I jump out, but they've already disappeared with my mom through the hospital doors. That could be the last time I see her. I race after them, and it's not until I'm in the packed emergency area, where every seat is filled, that I realize I didn't cover my head. Faces snap toward me, shocked. Many of my gawkers have phones in their hands. Then the murmurs start.

"Oh my God, it's Ivy Westcott."

"She's covered in blood. She probably killed someone else."

"Maybe she's filming."

"She hasn't been in anything in forever."

The whispers are vicious; the cruelty is astounding. But nothing can hurt me as much as possibly losing my mother. I ignore everyone and head straight to the desk, barely stopping to breathe before I reel off my mother's name.

"They've taken her into surgery." A woman hands me a clipboard full of paper. "You can fill out most of these forms while you're waiting, but the one on top, with her medical history, we need immediately."

I don't know where to go or what to do. I want someone here with me, but there's no one who can come right now. No one from home whom I can ask to drive all the way from Santa Cruz to sit with me while my mother might be dying. My coworkers at the market are acquaintances, and though my boss Greer and I are friendly, it's a professional relationship. I haven't let myself get close enough to anyone to rely on them.

I move down the hall, away from the crowd who seems to be reveling in my agony, nearer to the doctors in white coats and nurses in blue scrubs. Scanning the form about my mother's history, I fill out everything as quickly as I can and give it back to the woman at the desk, who tells me I can wait in the surgical unit.

I've never been in a hospital, except when I was born. The smell of sickness and sounds of sadness pervade the elevator. It's worse when I get off on the fourth floor and pass a too-brightly-lit area filled with children coloring on the floor while stricken adults are staring into space under blankets. No one seems to notice me. This is where people wait to find out if their loved ones have made it through surgery. I now better understand why my mom didn't want me to go through this.

Stepping toward the desk, I'm about to speak, when the man behind it does a double take. I brace myself for a vile comment, but instead, he whispers, "Let me find you a private space to wait for your mother."

I follow him to a small, tidy room, which he unlocks with a key card attached to the lanyard around his neck. Once we're inside, he says, "I loved you on *Hello, Juliet*. I'm supposed to pretend I don't know that you're a celebrity, but you made me feel that I could do anything without having to be like everyone else."

His kindness undoes me, and through a flood of tears, I tell him, "My mother only has basic health insurance. I don't think it will cover any of this." Money isn't what matters right now, but I'm afraid she'll refuse care, if and when she's conscious, because of the financial strain.

He nods. "We'll take care of her no matter what. It will be okay. I'll make sure you can stay in here until your mother is out of surgery, and I'll tell the doctor where to find you when it's time."

"Thank you so much." I reach out and touch his arm. I wish there were someone here to touch me.

"All the positive thoughts for your mother," he says before closing the door.

I didn't even get his name, this wonderful man who's shown me there are good people in the world who don't want to bring me down. It's so quiet in here that I can hear my heart break. Sinking into the dove-gray chair under the window, I let myself feel every emotion—the shame over my failures and the guilt that I've ruined my mother's life.

My phone rings.

"Hello?" I answer immediately, without checking the screen.

"What time did you leave Rachel Foster's?" Tanaka asks curtly.

"Around noon. Why?"

"She's not at home. I'm going to send you a video clip of the CCTV from the motel. Can you watch it now?"

"Yes. They took my mom into surgery, and I'm in a private waiting room. What am I looking for?"

"Someone went into your room at twelve thirty p.m. I want to know if you can identify them."

My hands shake when I open the link Tanaka sent. The video is dark and grainy, so I hold it as close to my face as I can. "I see someone in a dark hoodie and sweatpants. Walking through the parking lot from the street?"

"Yes, keep watching."

The person's gender and build are unclear because the clothes are oversize, and the hood of the sweatshirt is pulled tightly around their face, which they keep as low as possible. They head up the stairs to the second floor, straight to my motel-room door, and lift a hand to knock. Something catches the light on their left hand. Oh my God.

"Is that a sapphire ring on the person's wedding finger?"

"Yes. Do you recognize it?"

"It's Rachel's."

"Stay where you are. Lock the door in that room. I'm on my way to the hospital. I don't know where Rachel is, what her motivation was for going to the motel, or what happened when she went inside, but Rachel went in and came out ten minutes later."

"Enough time to stab my mom. But I was right there on Seventeenth Street. She must have been close to my car, and I didn't see her. I could have stopped her."

"This isn't your fault, Ivy."

"Isn't it?" I cry. "Why would Rachel ever want to hurt my mother? She didn't know her. Rachel told me today that she once saw my mom when she apparently cleaned Mack's office building before I got the role as Juliet, but they never saw each other again until Caleb's memorial."

"Maybe Rachel was looking for you and things got out of hand. But I think you've been blamed enough for things out of your control. We'll find Jesse and Rachel. You focus on your mom."

"My location on my phone was enabled. I didn't turn it on. Rachel could have, when I was at her house." I clutch my clammy forehead.

"Hang tight. I'll text or call you when I have any updates."

I'm so alone, with only my phone for comfort. I should be relieved that Tanaka has clearly ruled me out as a suspect, but it underscores how much danger I'm in. As a distraction from unhelpful intrusive thoughts, I busy myself with the forms, but there's so much I can't fill in. My mother's parents' names and any of their medical history, except their addictions to heroin. I know so little of my own medical history on my father's side. There are two people out there who never wanted to know me, but I'm lost and need any tether to family I can find. My mother might be furious, but perhaps she'll understand my desperation.

I google Millicent and Robert Westcott, Oregon. That's all I know about them from the one time, on a whim, I looked up my dad's obituary online. It was only a few lines about his sudden, tragic death, and not one word about my mom and me. Yet I still want to talk to my grandparents, because I don't have anyone else.

I get a hit immediately for Westcott Motors, a car dealership in Salem, and a phone number. It's just after 1:30 p.m. I have no idea if they run this dealership or how many they have. I don't know how old they are, if they're retired. My dad was only nineteen when he met my mother, so I could venture a guess that his parents might be in their seventies or older. I have to try.

My pulse jackhammering, I dial the number.

"Salem Motors, how can I help you?"

"I—" I'm so scared to do this that I can't finish my sentence.

"Yes?"

Breathing out a long stream of air, I say, "I'm looking for Millicent or Robert Westcott."

"I'll transfer you. One moment, please."

I almost hang up. I didn't expect it to be that easy. I have no clue how to start this conversation, because I've been angry at them for so long.

"Hello, Millie here."

My grandmother's voice is sweet but strong. "It's Ivy," I say in such a hushed tone that I'm not sure she can hear me.

"Who?"

"Ivy. Your granddaughter."

There's a pause so long that I think we've dropped the connection, but suddenly she yells, "Robert! Come quick! Oh my heaven. Come!" Then to me, "Ivy, don't hang up. Please don't hang up. Is this really you?"

"It's really me." I'm so stunned at how happy she sounds to hear from me that I start to cry. I realize that she's crying too.

"Honey, we are so glad you found us. Your mother must be gone."

"What? No. She's in surgery. I . . . I know that you don't want anything to do with me, but I didn't know who else to turn to. Or what to do. I don't even know who you are."

"We've waited thirty-two years for this phone call, Ivy. Wait. Robert's going to pick up the other line."

"Ivy, we're so proud of you. We've watched everything you've been in." A man laughs a deep, chesty chuckle, then sniffles. "Sorry. Millie and I are just shocked. Absolutely shocked and over the moon."

I press the phone closer to my ear. "I . . . I don't understand."

"We know, dear. There's a lot to discuss," my grandmother says. "Is your mother's condition serious?"

It's asked in such a hopeful lilt that I go silent.

"I apologize. You love her. Of course you do. But we've missed your whole life."

My mind trips over itself. This isn't at all how I anticipated the conversation to go. "But you wanted to miss it. You tried to pay my mom off to leave my dad and terminate her pregnancy after he died."

"Terminate?" my grandmother repeats in an incredulous tone. "Darling, we wanted to keep you and raise you. When Josh fell asleep at the wheel and died—"

"Fell asleep at the wheel? No, he was killed by an intoxicated driver."

There's a long pause, and all I hear is a wheezy sound. "Is that what your mother told you?" my grandfather asks sternly.

I don't like how he's speaking to me. I debate hanging up. Calling my grandparents, especially now, was a mistake. "If you wanted me so much, why haven't you ever reached out all these years?"

"We couldn't, Ivy." My grandmother exhales a rattly breath. "Your mother made it very clear that if we ever contacted you, she'd destroy us."

INSTAGRAM

@thecb

September 17, 2014

All of us at the CB network are deeply saddened by the sudden and unexpected passing of beloved *Hello, Juliet* star Caleb Hill. Only twenty-five years old, Caleb was a highly valued member of our family whose remarkable talent was matched by his loving warmth, which he bestowed on everyone with whom he worked. Revered by fans, creator Mack Foster, and Caleb's costars Ivy Westcott, Lauren Malloy, and Jesse Rafferty, he will be forever missed. A private memorial will be held in his honor. In lieu of flowers, Caleb's family has set up a donation fund for a scholarship in his name at UCLA, his alma mater. If you or anyone you know is struggling with substance abuse, please seek help. You're not alone. #RIPCalebHill #HelloJuliet #TheCB

CHAPTER
TWENTY-FOUR

Then
September 30, 2014

The crowd of mourners numbered in the thousands, many of them fans who wept behind the barrier the police had set up on the boardwalk overlooking the Santa Monica beach. A wall of brawny men separated Caleb's family and friends from the celebrity gawkers and paparazzi, who couldn't even give Caleb the private send-off he deserved. But as a former competitive surfer, Caleb should be laid to rest in his favorite place in the world. His mother had given birth to him in a tub on their Vermont farm, and in the water was where he would remain forever.

Ivy was shattered. She gazed at the waves that rolled through a light breeze from swell to shore. It was a perfect beach day. Caleb was supposed to teach her to surf here. Instead, she was saying goodbye to him.

Though the autopsy report listed his manner of death as an accidental overdose resulting from a lethal combination of MDMA and alcohol, questions lingered about how the quantity of substances in Caleb's system could have killed a man of his size. Ultimately, it was determined that a grand mal seizure stopped Caleb's big, beautiful heart. Nothing stopped the online trolls from slaughtering his character and memory.

Ivy and her mom found a place by Lauren on the sand. Caleb's mother, father, and younger sister stood directly at the shoreline, while Mack and Rachel were next to Lauren. Every few seconds, Mack wiped his face with a handkerchief as though he were sweating in the midday sun. Ivy was sure he was wiping his tears but didn't want anyone to witness his grief. Whether his tears were caused by Caleb's loss or the death of *Hello, Juliet*, Ivy didn't know. Perhaps it was both.

Hello, Juliet had been canceled ahead of its second season. The final episode to air would be the twelfth, in which police searched Logan's locker and found a baggie of steroids. They never had the chance to shoot the finale. Viewers would never know who tipped off the police, how the drugs got into Logan's locker, and who the true antagonist was on the show. Once again, the plot mirrored their real lives. But for Ivy, Jesse was the villain in her story.

She hadn't spoken to or even seen him since he'd slipped out the back door of the Snake Pit. He had vanished like smoke and hadn't bothered to pay his respects to his best friend. Jesse wasn't the man she believed him to be. He wasn't hers anymore.

All she cared about now was how she'd never laugh with Caleb again nor receive one of his trademark tight hugs and words of comfort. Never again see his wide grin. Never thank him for being her steadiest, most protective friend. And never apologize for hurting him for not loving him like he loved her.

The breeze carried the sound of the wails from the fans on the boardwalk. They mourned a character, not the loving, genuine, kind, and funny man Caleb was. His celebrity, all their celebrity, was a facade. It meant nothing to her anymore.

Ivy's hair whipped her in the face, and her mother brushed it back. She caught her mom's hand and held it against her cheek as an anchor. Lauren quietly wept beside them. All three women wore yellow dresses.

Caleb's parents had asked for everyone attending the memorial to honor him by wearing his favorite color, the hue of sunshine.

Ivy heard the faint whir of rotor blades in the distance. She couldn't see the helicopter, but she knew that three miles away, Caleb's ashes were raining down into the Pacific. There was a deep keening howl. Ivy turned, shocked to see that the gut-wrenching cry came from Mack, held up in Rachel's arms. He looked smaller and weaker than she'd ever seen him. He was just a man, not the master of their lives anymore.

Ivy squeezed her mother's arm, stepped over to Lauren, and took her hand. "Lo, let's take a walk, okay?" she said.

Ivy wasn't ready to go home. Once she left the beach, her future without Caleb, the show, and Jesse would stretch endlessly before her. For the first time in her life, there wasn't a schedule or a plan. She simply would *be*. But that young woman was an enigma she was too sad to contemplate.

In silence, they strolled together down the stretch of beach toward the pier and away from the few fans and photographers still rubbernecking above them as security blocked them from stepping down to the beach, which was closed for the next hour.

"Can we sit?" Ivy asked, nervous because, while she understood Lauren's suffering, her friend was nearly catatonic.

Lauren sat cross-legged, trailing her fingers through the sand and staring out at the ocean. Ivy joined her, saying nothing for a little while, matching Lauren's breathing. When the silence became too painful, because Ivy needed to share her grief with Lauren, she spoke.

"We'll get through this. Together, okay?"

"There is no *together* anymore. Everything's over, Ives. Caleb is dead." Tears spilled down her cheeks. "It was supposed to be our best night. The start. Not the end. None of it makes any sense."

Ivy ventured to ask the question plaguing her since she'd watched Lauren rub her fist over Caleb's chest. "You weren't giving Caleb CPR that night. What were you doing?"

"Sternum rub. For an opiate overdose," Lauren answered quietly. "I didn't know what Caleb took."

"Did he . . . I know Caleb drank a lot. But drugs often too?"

Lauren shrugged. "I don't know. Caleb was private like me. He wanted everyone to love him, like you do." She smiled sadly. "It's so easy to get caught up in the Hollywood lifestyle, want to find something to deal with the pressure."

"And you? Do you do drugs to deal with the pressure?" Ivy wanted to know if she could lose Lauren too. If she was naive to think they handled fame better than she did. They were better actors than she was; they could have hidden so much from her.

"I can see the wheels spinning up there." Lauren pointed at Ivy's head. "We didn't party together. I mean, Jesse and I did years ago, but not recently."

His name was a knife in her chest. "Do you know where Jesse is?"

Lauren looked back at the sand.

"Lo?"

"It wasn't Jesse's fault. It was Caleb's decision to take the Molly. He asked for it."

Everything around Ivy faded except Lauren's statement. Her mind scrambled to make the words coherent in a way that wouldn't implicate Jesse in Caleb's death. But there was no other way to interpret what Lauren had said.

Ivy grabbed Lauren's arm. "Did Jesse give Caleb the Molly?"

Lauren kept staring at the sand.

"Lauren," Ivy said again, in a sterner tone, "did Jesse give Caleb the Molly that night? Was that their plan? To meet in the back room first?"

No response.

Ivy shot to her feet. "You knew right away that Caleb overdosed! And you know that it was Jesse who gave him the drugs that killed him! Why are you protecting him? Caleb is dead!" she screamed so loudly that it echoed off the water.

Lauren got up too. "Shut the fuck up, Ivy," she hissed. "What the hell is wrong with you?"

"With *me*? Are you out of your fucking mind? You're defending a liar! A criminal!" She spit the words at Lauren, who goggled at her.

Lauren stepped forward, maybe to calm Ivy down. But Ivy saw red. Uncontrollable rage made her tear off the necklace Lauren had given her, breaking the clasp. She threw it at Lauren, and the chain smacked her in the face. Gaping, her friend held her hand to her cheek, where a welt had already risen.

Ivy was aghast. She hadn't meant to hurt her, but she needed to make Lauren listen to her. "You promised you'd always choose me. But you're choosing Jesse, again. And I'll never forgive you for it!" She pushed past Lauren.

All she wanted was space, but her jostle against Lauren's shoulder was too hard. Lauren fell to the sand.

There were flashes of light, one after the other. Ivy looked over at the sidewalk, where cameras were pointed straight at her. On the pier, there were other people holding up their phones.

Elizabeth came running and inserted herself between Ivy and Lauren, holding Ivy's arm tightly. Ivy finally registered that she was on the beach at Caleb's memorial, his family possibly still lingering, his ashes floating in the water.

Tears blurred her vision as her mother used one hand to guide Ivy up the steps to the pier, her other arm outstretched as though to ward off anyone who tried to come near them. Ivy glanced back to see if Lauren would follow them.

But she was already gone.

CHAPTER
TWENTY-FIVE

Now

Furious, I hang up on my grandparents. My mother was right. They hate her. And she'd do anything to protect me. She kept my grandparents away from me, because they're awful people, despite how happy they seemed to be to hear from me.

I'm famous. Maybe they know how little money I have, how desperate I've been to book a job, any job. They might be thinking of using me, my face and infamy, to drive their business. Even as a has-been, Poison Ivy would still draw a crowd, if only to watch me fall apart in real time.

I'm more upset than I was before I called. My phone rings in my hand. I almost don't want to look at who it is, because if it's my grandparents, I absolutely won't speak to them again. But I do look, because it could be the surgeon or front desk nurse. It's Tanaka.

"Did you find Rachel and Jesse?" I ask immediately after I answer.

"Not yet. But we found some other evidence that I want to discuss with you. Do you have a moment?"

"I'm still sitting in the private room." I won't tell the detective about my horrible grandparents. It's irrelevant to what's going on, and she's not my therapist, though I could definitely use one.

"We got into Lauren's phone. You were right. She was Ellyn Lou Mara. She planned the reunion. We found Google searches on Sunrise Studios, how to make a fake Venmo account, and email confirmations of payments made from her account to MF Productions so she could pay you. We matched those with her bank records."

The news isn't surprising, but I wish it weren't true. If she'd ever answered my email five years ago, if she'd just gotten in touch after the Tattle TV exposé, she might still be alive. We could have found our way back to each other. Lauren put so much effort into reuniting us, spending tens of thousands of dollars to get me back to LA.

"Do you know why she planned it?" I ask nervously. I'm desperate for resolution and retribution against Lauren's killer, but I'm scared of who it might be.

"I was hoping you might shed some light on that. We found a text from her to Jesse. I'll send it to you."

My phone dings. This is the moment of truth. Did I fall in love with a cold-blooded murderer? A man who still affects me in ways he shouldn't.

Lauren: If you don't tell Ivy the truth, I will.

I slump in the chair. "Did he respond?"

"No. Lauren filed for divorce a few hours later and set up the reunion." Tanaka pauses, and I hear voices in the background. "I need to take care of something. If Jesse or Rachel contact you, call me immediately."

We hang up. I bring my knees to my chest and rest my chin on them as I try to figure out what secret Lauren took to her grave. How it all relates to Rachel, Mack, Jesse, me, and possibly Caleb.

I think back to the times I saw Rachel: at the upfronts after-party when I was certain my drink had been drugged, and at her house for the dinner when she noticed the chemistry between me and Jesse.

Then something Rachel said to me today sets off alarm bells. I squeeze my temples to recall her exact words.

If it wasn't to see you, why else would Mack drive up that treacherous dirt road in the middle of the night?

It's plausible that she made an assumption about how steep the road to Jesse's cabin is. Maybe she's seen other photos of the cabin than the one from the deck she showed me today. That photo definitely didn't include the road. But if not, Rachel must have gone to Jesse's cabin at some point.

I open the CCTV footage from Tanaka of the Seaview Motel. Rachel in her black hoodie and black sweatpants, hiding her face. But she can't hide her feet. The sneakers she's wearing are plain and black. I zoom in. I can't tell the precise size. They could be a nine or ten, though, maybe even larger. Maybe as large as the footprints I saw that night at the cabin, marked into the devil's cherries staining the deck.

Did Rachel think I was in bed with Mack, and she'd come to confront us? And then snapped the photo as evidence. But if that's the case, did she take those other photos of me too? Was Rachel, not Mack, the one stalking me?

But why show me the evidence of her husband's supposed obsession with me? Perhaps to throw me off track . . . I'm missing something. And I can't think in this tiny space. I need fresh air.

I leave the private room and head to the nurse's desk. "Excuse me?" I ask as calmly as I can. My heart's beating out of my chest. I'm close to something big, but I can't quite make sense of it. "Do you know how much longer my mother will be in surgery?"

The nurse gives me a kind smile. "Probably hours more. The surgery itself will take time, then recovery, and the surgeon's ordered some tests to be done. I promise to come get you when he's available to update you."

"Do you have any information about her condition at all?"

"I don't, but Dr. Salahi is the best orthopedic surgeon we have. She's in excellent hands."

It's ironic that it took a horrific assault for my mom to finally see the specialist she's needed for years.

"Can I give you my cell number? I'd like to take a walk."

"Of course." She writes down the number I give her. Then she peers at me. "You should probably go home and get some rest rather than sitting here alone in that room."

"Thank you," I say hoarsely and take the stairs from the unit, not bothering to wait for the elevator.

The moment I'm outside, I gulp in the brisk, cool air. Tying my unruly hair in a topknot, I see the valet and a few people stopping in the driveway do a double take at me, but I don't care. No matter what I do, they'll believe what they want. That I'm poison. The only opinion that matters is my mother's.

I keep my phone gripped in my hand, volume turned as high as possible so I don't miss a call or text. I start to walk, no destination in mind, my only goal to clear my head. I marvel at the clean streets and palm trees languishing under a blue sky. How can this beauty coexist with so much ugliness?

Taking someone's life is a desperate act. To commit that heinous a crime, with no regard for human suffering, there has to be a very strong motive.

Lauren knew a dark secret. She texted Jesse to tell him that she wanted me to know it. He must be involved.

That secret might explain why Mack or Rachel stalked me. Mack would have done it to protect his investment in a rising star. I don't believe for a second that he had any romantic interest in me. But Rachel might have suspected we were sleeping together and followed me to catch us in the act or find some way to hurt me as revenge.

What if Mack's warning to me about being careful wasn't a threat at all? What if it was to protect me?

There are only three people left alive: me, Jesse, and Rachel.

I stop in the middle of the sidewalk.

Jesse and Rachel. The amount of time that Jesse spent at her house with Lucy and Liam, Rachel's comment to him about our chemistry, knowing how steep the road is to Jesse's cabin. Their guitar lessons.

As the pieces come together in a twisted puzzle, I feel ill. Did they use me, Mack, and Lauren as a cover for their clandestine relationship all these years? Is that what secret Lauren threatened to reveal to me, and Jesse refused to let his and Rachel's reputations suffer? Or maybe they thought that the only way they could be together was to get rid of their spouses. How could I be so oblivious? Maybe, just like my haters, I believed the story that was spun for me.

Quickly, I book an Uber. The driver is here in two minutes. I slide into the back, and he takes off. I watch the time of arrival on the phone mounted on his dash. Six minutes. Five. Four. Three. Finally, he pulls up to the motel, and I hop out and race to my car. I start it up and place a call to Tanaka.

With no preamble, I say, "I think Jesse and Rachel might be together at the cabin. There are a lot of places to hide out in that area." I tell her my theories.

"I know where it is. I'm already in the car, so I'll head straight there and keep you posted," Tanaka says. I hear her turn signal, then she hangs up.

Tanaka didn't tell me not to head there, too, though I doubt she'll be happy about it. I'll let the detective hunt them down. Hopefully, she'll get there before me. I won't risk my life. But I will confront the two people who've tried to steal everything from me.

DOWN AND OUT

Breaking News

Westcott Gives a Walloping

September 30, 2014

We have the never-before-seen, appalling video footage of Ivy Westcott assaulting her supposed best friend, Lauren Malloy, at Caleb Hill's memorial. As Hill was laid to rest in the Pacific Ocean, Westcott laid into Jesse Rafferty's ex-girlfriend for reasons unknown. Shrieking at Malloy, Westcott shows more emotion than we've seen from her as Juliet Jones as she then smacks the grieving actress with a heavy Tiffany necklace. That girl is poison.

CHAPTER
TWENTY-SIX

Then
September 30, 2014

With her head down, Ivy walked silently with her mother to the end of the pier, replaying her entire argument with Lauren. Was she wrong to have screamed at her? Ivy definitely shouldn't have shoved her. She'd snapped. Now she regretted it.

Ivy had never lost someone close to her before. Not someone she'd known and loved. Surely Lauren would forgive her. Ivy would call her tonight, after they'd both had some time to process the emotional upheaval of the day, the agony of Caleb's death, and the devastating, unfinished end of *Hello, Juliet*. Wherever they went from here, Ivy and Lauren would stick together. All they had left was each other.

"Ives, honey, what can I do?" Elizabeth asked when they reached the sidewalk.

Ivy looked up and down Ocean Avenue, unsure where she was supposed to go. The limo was parked a few blocks away, but she'd let Lauren take it. Would Lauren go home, or straight to Jesse's place, which Ivy had never seen? She was supposed to go with him after the Snake Pit. That night was supposed to be the best night of their lives.

"Mom, you know Jesse. Is he really the kind of person who'd leave his best friend to die?"

Looking pensive, her mother tucked Ivy's hair behind her ears. "Maybe he was scared and panicked. Jesse was there when his father died. That leaves a scar that doesn't heal. I wasn't there when your dad died, but I ran too."

"You had no choice. You were pregnant with me." Ivy pulled her hair forward and twirled a curl for comfort. "But what Jesse did to Caleb, and to me and Lauren, was selfish and heartless. He's a coward."

"Perhaps." Her mom tapped her chin. "It is odd that he didn't show up for Caleb's memorial. I hope he's okay."

Ivy was sure that Jesse wasn't okay. But he didn't care enough to check in on her, even though she'd phoned him five times and texted even more than that. Every call and message had gone unanswered. It seemed like he had been talking to Lauren, who was taking Jesse's side, despite the bitter truth that he'd been doing drugs with Caleb, when he'd promised Ivy and Elizabeth that he'd stopped.

And Lauren had all but admitted that Jesse gave Caleb the Molly that killed him. Even if it were Caleb's choice to take the drug and mix it with alcohol, if not for Jesse providing the Molly, Caleb might still be alive.

Caleb's family deserved justice.

"Mom, can you call a car? I'm going to run over to that cart and get a bottle of water."

Elizabeth craned her neck to where Ivy was pointing. "It's not too busy there, but any second, someone's going to spot you. Want me to come with?"

Ivy shook her head. "No. I'll be quick."

She ran toward the cart, turning to make sure her mother was occupied and not watching her. Then she googled the number she needed and raced over to the pay phone to the right of the cart near the sign for the pier.

"Anonymous tip line for the LA Regional Crime Stoppers. Would you like to report a crime or a tip?"

Ivy shut her eyes tightly and spoke. "Jesse Rafferty was in the back room at the Snake Pit the night Caleb Hill overdosed there. He left before the police came. I think he . . ." Ivy hesitated before destroying Jesse's life. Then she whispered, "I think he supplied the Molly that Caleb took."

The second she hung up, her stomach churned. She'd hid the call from her mother. Because even though Jesse should be held accountable, her mom might disagree. She might take Lauren's side, that Caleb, not Jesse, was responsible for his own choices.

Ivy had just ruined Jesse's future. She felt sick. But the damage was done.

She slunk back to her mother right as the limo pulled up to the curb. The driver got out, held open the back door, and Ivy and her mom slid inside. Ivy closed her eyes, like she had on the phone to the police, blocking out both her irreparable action and the entire torment of the day.

"Sweetie, we're home," her mom said a little while later, shaking her gently.

The car had stopped. Ivy put her face in her hands, not wanting to move.

"Come on. Let's go inside. I'll make you some tea and you can nap on the couch." Her mother thanked the driver, then took Ivy's hand to lead her down the narrow stone pathway and up the three steps to the front door.

While her mother checked the mailbox, Ivy unlocked the door. The moment she stepped inside, her despondence was quickly replaced by an icy terror that rushed through her veins. It was as though a tornado had swept through their living room.

The couch was slit open, its stuffing pulled out like someone had gutted it with a knife. Broken glass was strewn all over the floor. Their framed photos lay in pieces next to the tattered pages of Ivy's books, her first friends. Perhaps the most painful violation was the jagged shards of the blown glass vase Caleb had given Ivy for her birthday.

Before she could whip out her phone to call the police, her mother screamed, "Get out!" so loudly that Ivy's ears rang.

She backed herself against the wall near the open front door, and her mom put a finger to her lips. They both listened for footsteps frantically running around the house or the sound of someone fleeing out their back door. There was nothing but their shallow breathing. But that didn't mean someone wasn't hiding.

Ivy gestured for them to go outside. Once they were on the street, where their neighbors were all inside or away from their homes, her mom took out her phone. She gasped, and in a frantic voice, said, "The security cameras aren't connected. The Wi-Fi is off."

Ivy ran to the circuit breaker at the side of the house. Someone had flipped all the switches to cut the electricity. There was no exterior camera in the pathway between the houses to catch whoever had been there.

She trudged back to her mom and told her about the circuit breaker.

Her mom shivered, pulling Ivy close to her.

"They either watched us or they know us well enough to be familiar with the alarm system." Ivy burst into tears. "I can't take this anymore. I don't want to be here."

Her mom stroked her hair. "I know, honey. We'll call the police and stay at a hotel for the night."

"No! I want to leave LA and never come back." Ivy didn't mean for her wish to come out as harshly and childishly as it did, but she meant every word. "Please."

"What about your work?" Her mom released her hold to peer at Ivy. "And Lauren?"

"I have nothing here anymore. I'll call Lauren once we're settled somewhere and make things right. We have enough saved to go away until everything that's happened with the show and Caleb and Jesse is less intense. I don't feel safe, Mom."

That was all her mother needed to hear to take action. "Right. We'll pack up and call the police from the road. We've done this before many times. You know the drill."

"I don't need anything from here. Do you?"

Her mom looked at her and nodded. "All I need is you."

Ivy and her mother had left many homes in a hurry, usually because they couldn't make the rent. Never because Ivy felt like she was in danger. She thought about the call she'd just made to the police. Could Jesse have found out already? She hadn't given him a key to the house, but he could have easily copied her spare without her knowing. She always kept it in her dressing room at the studio, which was unlocked when she was on set. He might have seen the breaker box any of the myriad times he was at the house. Was this revenge for turning him in? Or was he looking for something?

Ivy locked the front door, though she didn't care about any of the possessions inside, while her mother climbed into the driver's side of the baby blue Mini Cooper they shared. Ivy treasured this car because she'd bought it for them with her own money. Now they'd use it, plus their savings—which had been for a down payment on a house—to escape. Wealth didn't matter anymore. It was Ivy and Elizabeth against the world, as always.

When she got in the car, her mother took out her phone from her bag and tapped, then enlarged the image with her fingers.

"We used to do this when you were really young, remember? Before you landed *Little Marvels*. I'd get a map, a paper one"—her mom let out a tinny laugh—"and ask you to point to where you wanted to go in LA on my days off."

Ivy smiled sadly. "I remember."

"Close your eyes. Point to a place in California, and that's where we'll go."

Ivy did.

"Santa Cruz. Perfect. A coastal town, away from the LA grime."

Her mother started the car. Ivy laid her hand on her wrist. "Can I drive? It's almost six hours from here."

"If I need you to drive, I'll tell you, okay? Please let me take care of you. That's what I need."

"Okay." Ivy leaned her head against the window as they left LA, Sunrise Studios, and *Hello, Juliet* in the rearview mirror.

By the time they hit the 1 into Monterey County, the video of Ivy shrieking at and pushing Lauren, slapping her in the face with the Tiffany necklace, had been uploaded, shared, and reshared over a million times.

The footage was taken from far away, the focus completely on Ivy. Even though their words, every accusation Ivy had made about Jesse—leaving Caleb to die on the floor of the Snake Pit back room; giving Caleb the Molly that killed him—were impossible to make out, her clenched fists, her enraged face, and her physical altercation with Lauren were clear enough to make Ivy look totally unhinged.

By 9:00 p.m.—as the moon crested over the Santa Cruz Mountains on Ivy and Elizabeth's way to their new home—all over social media, #PoisonIvy was trending at number one.

CHAPTER
TWENTY-SEVEN

Now

I don't recall the name of the road where Jesse's cabin is located, but I do remember the back route he took. In forty-eight minutes—a good five of which I struggle up the dizzying incline in my already-battered old car—I make it to the driveway of the mahogany A-frame.

Though the structure looks the same, the branches of the pine and cedar trees that framed the cabin now bend dangerously low over the wraparound deck, and the wood on the exterior shows signs of neglect.

Tanaka's black sedan isn't here yet, but there's a squad car parked in the gravel driveway. I hear the whir of helicopters, probably still searching the lake for Mack's body. The sound brings me back to Caleb's memorial, when his ashes were scattered over the Pacific. My heart twists, but I won't cry. I'm not here to mourn but to finally find out the truth about what Jesse has done to me and Lauren.

Relieved that I'm not alone, I park and get out of my car. Craning my neck, I can barely see through the grimy windows at the front of the cabin. Jesse's bedroom appears to be empty, but someone is in the main area, close to the door. I can't make out a uniform from here, but I'm assuming it's a police officer. The person's build is too short and stocky to be Jesse's. I dial Tanaka.

"I'm at the cabin. There's an officer inside, I think."

"You're at the cabin?" Her voice is shrill. "Jesse's truck was located near the lookout. He's—"

I don't hear Tanaka's next words, because a hand slaps over my mouth and an arm snakes around my waist, gripping me as tightly as a boa constrictor.

"Don't scream," a voice whispers into my ear.

I drop my phone in fright. My limbs turn to liquid. I'd know that gruff commanding voice anywhere—and the barrel chest shoved against my back.

"Ivy?" I hear Tanaka call from my phone on the ground.

I watch a black boot smash into my phone, pulverizing it. Tanaka's voice goes silent.

"I don't want to hurt you, Ivy," Mack says from behind me, tightening his arms around me even more so I can barely breathe.

Fighting my shock and terror, I buck against him, but Mack doesn't release his hold. I thrash and reach my foot back to kick as hard as I can but only hit air. He presses his hand harder over my mouth, digging his elbow into my rib cage. Then he drags me backward, my heels scraping the dirt, as he yanks me to the side of the cabin where the overgrowth of trees and shrubs is so thick that no one will spot us.

I should never have come here.

I scramble to push my heels into the ground, but I can't find purchase. I can't stop him. Mack's much stronger than me. My flip-flops fall off. As he pulls me farther into the woods, broken twigs slash at my bare feet. Above me, the sun peeks through the canopy of trees, but inside the forest, haunting shadows close in on me.

There's no doubt in my mind that Mack is going to kill me. I let myself go limp, hoping that this man, back from the dead, will think I'm giving in and loosen his grip so I can escape. But he only holds me tighter, grunting as his sweat drips onto my hair.

Suddenly he stops, but he doesn't let go of me. Wrenching my body like I'm a rag doll, Mack veers to the right, pulling me deeper into the brush, farther from the cabin. It gets colder and darker with his every step.

He controls where and how I move, like he always did. And a rage so powerful gives me the strength I need to stiffen so he has to tug me harder. I hear him pant. The only way out of this might be to exhaust him so he has to release his hold. No matter where he's taking me, what he plans to do with me, I'll fight him with every fiber of my being. There's no way in hell I'll let this man decide how my life ends.

He slows. But he keeps dragging me over the sharp pine needles covering the rocky ground until my lower back slams against the hard edge of something. I yelp, the sound muffled against his palm. Frantically, I move my eyes left and right.

He's pulled me into a decrepit shed. With Mack's hands still keeping me prisoner, he spins me around on the splintered floorboards so I'm facing the back wall, where rusted tools sit on a metal shelving unit. Behind me, I feel his chest jerk and his leg kick back. The door slams shut, shaking the entire structure. We're in total darkness.

"I didn't kill Lauren," he says, his breath hot in my ear, voice scratchy and pleading.

I slam my head back and hear a crunch. He drops his hand from my mouth, a whimper coming from his. There's a click. Then a tinny sound. The room fills with a dull light. Pushing myself from the floor, I stand, breathing hard, fury and fright competing inside me.

Then astonishment takes over, because in front of me is a hunched, withered old man in a black Henley and jeans. Lines crisscross Mack's face, and his steely blue eyes are sunken, ringed with deep-purple circles. His shaved head has a thin cover of gray stubble. Blood pours out of his nose, dripping onto the crumbling floor of the dilapidated shed. He looks nothing like the man who once had so much authority over my life.

I try to maneuver around him to open the door he's locked, but he blocks me, still so much bigger and stronger, despite his deterioration in the many years since I last saw him. Scanning for a weapon, I find logs stacked against the wall opposite a window so filthy with gray dust that I can't see a sliver of the outside.

The metal tools are a few feet behind me, but I'd have to turn away from Mack to reach for one. Even if I manage to get a pair of gardening shears, Mack could grab them and attack me. He looks that desperate.

I open my mouth and scream, "Help!"

Mack shakes his head. "No one will hear you in here. It's too far from the cabin, and the walls are too thick. It's an old shed." Tears leak from his eyes. "I just want to escape and start over, okay?"

His tears do nothing but increase my wrath. But I can't give in to it right now. I have to be careful what I say so I can figure a way out of this shed alive. "Why do you need to escape? You said that you didn't kill Lauren."

He wipes his cheeks, smearing the blood. "I would never have hurt Lauren. I didn't want to hurt anyone, you included."

His meaningless, self-pitying admission makes it impossible to control the fire I shoot at him. "You hurt me every damn day on that show! Your wife thinks you're obsessed with me."

Mack nods calmly, as though he has nothing left in him. "That's why I need to go. For my family, Ivy. I did everything for my family." Then his eyes spark with comprehension. "You saw Rachel?"

"Yes. She's broken. Your kids are a wreck. They all think you're dead." I grit my teeth. "Rachel showed me a box of photos. Of me. Copies of every tabloid piece, interview, message board about me. She stalked me, Mack. Did you know that? Because she's in love with Jesse."

His eyes widen. He backs himself against the door, giving me no possible way out.

I keep talking because I have nothing to lose except my life, which I know he's going to end somehow. He can't escape while I'm still around. There's nothing in here to tie me up with. And this is my last chance to confront him the way I should have the very first time he belittled me years ago.

"Rachel stabbed my mother. My mom is in surgery. She could die! Wake the fuck up and look at the destruction you caused! Whatever secret you've been hiding with Jesse has ruined so many lives! For what?"

Mack blinks over and over. "You don't understand, Ivy. I'm sorry. So sorry that I wasn't strong enough. I'm a coward."

"Strong enough for what? Just tell me. I'll help you. Please," I plead, with no intention of ever helping this monster of a man.

"I need to protect my family, Ivy." He raises his hand and moves away from the door.

I rear back and cover my face with my hands.

But he doesn't step toward me. Instead, in a fractured voice, he says, "I broke into your house in Culver City after Caleb's memorial. I killed Caleb."

Then he whips open the door. And he runs.

For a second, I freeze at his shocking confession. Then like a shot, I'm out of the shed and chasing after his black shirt, but he's fast. Mack seems to know these woods better than me and zigzags through the massive tree trunks that rise in front of me every which way I turn. Instead, I follow the sound of his gasping breaths and scream, "Help!" over and over, my cries echoing uselessly in the damp, dense forest.

There's a clearing up ahead. I'm not paying attention to my surroundings. Disoriented by the sudden sunshine and change of terrain, I clumsily clamber after Mack down a rocky trail, the jagged stones cutting up the bare soles of my feet, the sharp branches that arch over both sides of the trail ripping apart the skin on my face and arms.

"Stop! It's over, Mack!" I scream.

But he keeps running, and I keep following, down an embankment, where I skid—heart in my throat when my knee slams into the knife-edge of a craggy stone. Mack jumps into the shallow creek. I race after him, but I slip, my hands landing in frigid water.

I won't give up. I won't let him get away. Ignoring the sting in my knee, the bruise on my back, my bleeding feet, and the rising water, I leap up, launch myself onto Mack's back, and bring him down. My chin hits his shoulder hard. I taste blood. Mack stills.

"How did you kill Caleb?" I yell.

I don't get an answer, because there's shouting from behind us. Mack and I both turn our heads. Tanaka and Reyes rush toward us, guns drawn.

"Mack Foster, put your hands behind your head now!" Tanaka bellows.

Mack complies, deep sobs racking his chest. Trembling from shock and exhaustion, I'm limp, and I feel someone gently peel me off Mack's back and help me sit up.

"Ivy, are you hurt?" Jesse asks. His gray eyes, full of fear, lock onto mine, and he holds me so I'm sitting in the glacial water.

"Where did you come from?" is all I can ask.

"Jesse was here the whole time looking for Mack. We found you because of him," Tanaka tells me as she cuffs Mack's hands behind his back.

I pull away from Jesse. "But where's Rachel? My mom. She could get to my mom." I moan.

The detective shakes her head. "Your mom is safe in surgery. Rachel's in custody."

Reyes lifts Mack out of the water and leads him away. I allow Tanaka and Jesse to each place a hand under my arms and carefully hoist me up so I'm standing between them.

Still wary, I look questioningly at Jesse. "How did you know Mack was here?"

"The minute I heard that his car went off the cliff at the lookout, I suspected that he was trying to fake his death and go on the run. He's a born drama writer." He shudders out a long sigh. "I figured out he'd been staying at the cabin since Lauren died. Then when the police came, he bolted for the shed. I didn't think he'd go in at all since it's on the verge of collapse, so I spent all day searching the trails, creeks, and woods. But I think he was hiding in the shed until you drove up."

"He told me he killed Caleb," I tell Tanaka, weak and unsure, both from the sting of my injuries and because I don't know what's true. "But not Lauren. What about Lauren?" The adrenaline is wearing off, and my knees start to give out.

Before the detective can help, Jesse's arm circles my waist, keeping me steady. "I don't know, Ivy, who killed Lauren. I really don't. But there are things that Mack has to tell you himself, no matter how much you'll hate me for it."

"Jesse—" I start.

"Please, Ivy. It's for Lucy and Liam's sake." He doesn't look away from me to hide the agony that twists his face. "But I can tell you that Caleb's contract wasn't renewed. He's the one Mack was killing off the show. Caleb asked me for the Molly, because he wanted to pretend everything was okay. He didn't want to ruin our celebration. So, I did it. I gave him the drugs." He swallows hard, as if to consume his guilt. "I should have said no."

"You've paid enough of a price," I say hoarsely.

I finally believe that. I look at the detective, who nods, and seems to think Jesse's got me because she takes her hand off my arm.

Jesse pulls me closer, his body trembling against mine. "I was never with Rachel."

"I got so much wrong," I whisper.

"Me too," Jesse says, as Tanaka's phone rings from her pocket.

She pulls it out and answers, then looks at me. My stomach goes into free fall.

"Let's get you to the hospital. Your mom is out of surgery."

SCOOPS AND SCANDALS

February 23, 2019

Nina Johnson. I'm Nina Johnson with *Scoops and Scandals*, here on the red carpet for the Independent Spirit Awards, where I'm joined by the gorgeous and talented husband and wife power couple, Jesse Rafferty and Lauren Malloy! Hello, you two! Congratulations on both your nominations tonight for director and best female lead! I absolutely loved *Never Go Home*!

Lauren Malloy. Thank you so much, Nina. It's such an honor to be here.

Nina Johnson. This film is romantic and heartbreaking. What inspired you, Jesse, to write the story of a reclusive painter who creates art that she rolls into bottles, then sets out to sea for her lost love to find?

Jesse Rafferty. I'm always searching for stories that will resonate.

Nina Johnson. Well, you two have had quite the resounding journey from your time on the small screen to critical acclaim in indie films. How have your challenges helped you both?

Lauren Malloy. Jesse and I have been a team for a very long time. We admire and respect each other, and we love working together. We're both committed to forgiveness and healing. Our art is our focus.

Nina Johnson. And your marriage, too, I'm sure? You're such a beautiful couple.

Jesse Rafferty. We love each other very much.

Nina Johnson: You heard it here, folks! Love can make anything possible!

CHAPTER TWENTY-EIGHT

February 24, 2019

Her head pounding, as usual, Ivy burrowed under the pale-pink blanket her mother had knit for her when she was a baby. It was unevenly stitched and lopsided, which made Ivy love it even more. An artist Elizabeth wasn't, but she was an excellent mother and manager. Ivy was sick of disappointing her and tired of feeling sorry for herself. Enough was enough.

For the first few years after they'd moved to Santa Cruz, they'd been able to live on their savings and the residuals from *Hello, Juliet* reruns. Even with just twelve episodes, the show was a cult hit on college campuses.

At home, always on the phone and trawling Actors Access and Backstage, her mom worked so hard to get Ivy auditions. But no one wanted to hire her.

Well, not no one. Deemed unpredictable, unstable, and difficult, Ivy mostly received job offers for spreads, literally, in *Hustler*; soft-core porn films; and celebrity rehab shows. She accepted everything else, including B slasher films in which she was the first to die. Yesterday, she'd wrapped on her latest role as the naked victim whose throat was slit while bathing in a claw-foot tub.

Shoving away the blanket, Ivy snatched up her phone from the small glass coffee table in front of the three-seater sofa she and her mom had found at a secondhand furniture shop. They didn't need a bigger sofa, because Ivy didn't invite anyone over.

Luckily, the eight-hundred-square-foot bungalow they were renting was on a quiet residential street with inobtrusive, well-maintained homes, and neighbors who mostly kept to themselves. It was a twenty-minute walk to the ocean, but at least it got Ivy out of the house.

Her phone screen was open to a photo of Jesse and Lauren, hand in hand at an after-party for the Independent Spirit Awards. Both glowing and successful. Ivy deserved a second act too. But first she needed to put the past to rest.

Inhaling a deep breath and exhaling, she opened her email and hit Compose.

Lauren,

I miss you. Congratulations on your success.

Ivy

She read it over ten times to make sure it struck the right tone—generous but not simpering, respectful but not cold, friendly but not desperate. And after five years of no contact, she pressed Send.

Her mom came into the room with a steaming mug in her hand and put it on the coffee table. "It's hot. Give it a minute before you drink it." She sat beside Ivy, who put her feet in her mother's lap. Her mother began digging into the soles with her strong fingers.

Ivy debated whether to tell her that she'd reached out to Lauren after all this time apart. But she decided to wait until Lauren responded. Her mother was her best friend, but Ivy's friendship with Lauren was between them. Only the two of them could truly understand the experience of working on *Hello, Juliet* and the utter devastation of its tragic ending. As much as Elizabeth had loved Caleb, he had been Ivy and Lauren's best friend.

"What goes down must come up," her mom said, smiling at her.

Despite the anxiety that clung to her like a barnacle, Ivy laughed. "I think it's the opposite."

"Nope. I found us a place to live that overlooks the water."

Ivy sat up, imagining awakening to the waves. It calmed her instantly. "Where?"

Her mom scrolled on her phone and showed Ivy a photo. "There's a four-story Airbnb on La Selva Beach. Greer, the owner, is looking for a cleaner and manager. And we can live in the bottom unit for reduced rent."

Ivy gaped at her. "How did you even find this?"

"I'm resourceful." Her mom grinned. "Anyway, I can clean, and I don't think managing the unit would be too taxing for you. It's mostly running the listing, booking the guests, keeping an eye on the property, and making sure everything's stocked and secure. And you could keep auditioning. Or not. You could do something else altogether." A concerned look swept over her mother's face. "I know how unhappy you are."

And Ivy knew how much pain her mother was in. Elizabeth couldn't hide how slowly she was moving, as though the stiffness in her back could be alleviated by shuffling instead of lifting her feet off the ground.

"I could clean, and you could manage it. You'd be much better at it than me," Ivy suggested.

Her mom faked an expression of horror, slapping a palm to her chest. "Ivy Westcott cleaning? I don't think so. This is a blip, honey. A rough patch."

Ivy snorted. "I don't think a rough patch is supposed to last five years." But her mother was right. Ivy was unhappy, and as always, her mom was offering exactly what she needed: a fresh start at the water's edge. "When can we see it?"

"Greer said to stop by anytime this afternoon. So how about some herbal tea, a hot shower, and we'll leave in an hour?" She lifted Ivy's feet from her lap, got the mug from the table, and handed it to Ivy. "I made it with some extracts that will ease your headache."

Ivy rolled her eyes, but she was smiling. "Bark and berries?"

Her mom shrugged. "Something like that."

Ivy drank the tea, took a shower, and got dressed, insisting that she drive to La Selva Beach. She had to stop letting her mom do everything for her. It was humiliating and not fair to Elizabeth.

By the time they got to the beach complex in the used Toyota they'd traded for their Mini Cooper, Ivy's headache was gone.

"That tea worked. Thank you," Ivy said, suddenly energetic as she got out of the car and looked at the few surfers riding the Pacific waves and a couple of people walking dogs on a secluded stretch of golden sand.

Her mom joined her. "I'll always look out for you, Ives. Ready to make a change?"

Ivy was ready. And as she watched her mom's hair—still sleek but with strands of silver at the temples—flow in the breeze, and she breathed in the crisp ocean air, Ivy felt something she hadn't for years. Hope. Hope that Lauren would respond to her soon and that, though they might never be close again, they could at least forgive each other. Hope that Ivy could let go of Jesse and all his mistakes and lies. And hope she'd find the best path for herself, whether that was acting or not.

Ivy laid her head on her mom's shoulder. "No one will ever love me like you do."

Her mom pulled Ivy close, the wind carrying her words toward the water. "That's the truth."

CHAPTER
TWENTY-NINE

Now

I leave my car at the cabin and ride with Detective Tanaka back toward the hospital to see my mom. She lets me use her phone to speak to the front desk nurse, who only tells me that my mom is awake. I ask her if the surgery was successful, if my mom is okay, but she says that I need to discuss that with the surgeon.

Tanaka lent me a pair of sneakers that are a size too large, but they're soft on my lacerated feet. Small cuts sting the inside of my mouth from when I slammed my chin into Mack's shoulder. My injuries are superficial; my emotional wounds are deep.

I gaze out the detective's window at the arid terrain off the I-405, reeling from what transpired today. Sergeant Reyes has taken Mack into custody, and Jesse has driven away in his truck. I'm not sure where he's going.

Once we're far enough from the cabin that all the adrenaline has worn off and fear for my mom sinks in, I ask, "Did Rachel admit to stabbing my mother?"

The detective flicks her eyes over to me. "She did not. She said that your mother asked her to come to the motel."

I balk. "Why the hell would my mom do that? Unless she was trying to be kind and offer condolences but wasn't feeling well enough to leave the room." I furiously rub my head. "Nothing makes sense."

"I know," is all the detective says.

I can tell from the soft, careful way she's speaking that something is wrong. There's something she's not telling me.

When we pull up to the curb outside the hospital entrance, I unbuckle my seat belt so I can get out while the detective parks. But she turns off the car and gets out too.

"Perks of being with the LAPD. Let's go in together."

We head to the elevators, but there are too many people waiting to go up, so I point to the stairs at the end of the hall. I fling open the door and try to take the steps two at a time, but it hurts too much, so I hold the railing and slowly progress to the fourth floor. Tanaka is sure-footed behind me. I appreciate her presence. It's comforting.

Finally reaching the surgical unit, I collapse against the desk.

The same nurse on duty smiles at me, but then she takes in my face, which I haven't looked at yet. It must be covered in gashes and blood. "Are you all right?"

"Yes," I half lie. I'm far from all right, but all I need to know at the moment is if my mother is okay.

"I'll page Dr. Salahi. Please take a seat." She gestures to a row of blue chairs against the wall opposite the desk. "It won't be too long. Meanwhile, I'll get you cleaned up."

After the nurse applies bandages to my feet and face, I sag in one of the chairs, bouncing my leg up and down. Tanaka sits quietly next to me. Waiting is excruciating. I should be used to it after spending practically my whole life in the entertainment industry, but I'm not.

It feels like hours but has probably been only minutes when the door to the surgical unit opens. Expecting it to be the doctor, I sit up straighter.

It's Jesse. He looks awful, but his face lights up when he sees me.

"I can't talk right now, Jesse," I tell him when he's in front of me.

He nods. "Is it okay if I just sit next to you?"

"Yeah," I answer in a hush, unsure at all how to feel about him, what to say, where—if anywhere—we go from here.

It's so uncomfortable sitting in silence, counting the minutes until I find out how my mom is doing. "Fine. Go ahead."

Jesse shifts so he can face me full on and runs his finger around the skin where his gold wedding band used to be. "Lauren married me because I once saved her."

He has my attention. "Saved her from what?"

"I never wanted to be the one to tell you and shouldn't be. But our secrets tore us apart. It's enough. When we were eighteen, we both had guest roles on the same sitcom. Do you remember *Order Up*, the show about the family-owned burger place?"

I nod. Of course I remember it, because I auditioned three times for a guest spot and never got a callback for any of them.

Jesse rubs his lips and sighs. "The producer, a big force in Hollywood, asked Lauren to come to his office to discuss a larger role. She was so excited, and she deserved her big break."

I already know where this is going; it's the oldest tale in Hollywood. But I'll let Jesse unburden himself. We've carried so much trauma for too long.

"He didn't know I was waiting for her, because everyone else had gone home for the day. I heard her scream from the hall. I kicked his door in and found him on top of her on the floor. I pulled him off, punched him in the face, and got her out of there."

"Did she report it?" I ask, glancing at Tanaka, who has her head bent over her notebook, likely to allow us as much privacy as she can while also getting any information she might need.

"What do you think? This was before Me Too, and Lauren was terrified that her career would be over before it started. I had to stand by whatever decision she felt was right for her. Even if it meant he might do it again." He drops his shoulders heavily. "He did and was finally caught. It was Roger Hawkins."

I inhale raggedly at the name of one of the most notorious sexual predators, who was front-page news a few years ago. I imagine beautiful, young Lauren—who mostly acted because it was what her parents wanted, then stuck with it because, like me, she was lonely and sought friends she could call her family—in the claws of that vile man.

"I kept Lauren's secret, and she kept mine. Right or wrong, I keep my word, Ivy," Jesse says grimly.

"Even when it hurts so many people?"

He closes his eyes for a moment. "I've kept my word for Mack because I didn't want Lucy and Liam to lose their father. I still don't. He has to be the one to admit his part in Caleb's death. And maybe I shouldn't have gotten Lauren involved. But she only cared about protecting the people she loved, so I let her." Standing, his knees pop, and his face is haggard. "I'll leave you alone for now. I really hope Liz will be okay."

And Jesse walks out through the doors, leaving me with more questions than answers yet again.

I'm frustrated and want to call Jesse to come back. But I know that he still cares about Mack and his family, and nothing I do will make him reveal the secret that's clearly destroying him to keep.

My frustration turns into worry when a moment later, a dark-skinned man in blue scrubs, holding a silver chart, walks toward me from the other end of the hall.

He stands in front of me. "I'm Dr. Salahi."

When he flips open the chart, my stomach flips too. I can't take much more today. I don't like how Tanaka has shifted closer to me, like a buffer from whatever news the doctor is about to impart.

"Elizabeth Hardwick was brought in with severe blood loss and a lacerated radial artery from a stab wound. We managed to stem the blood flow quickly, so no transfusion was required, and there's no evidence of acute hand ischemia at the moment." He looks up. "In regular speak, that means her fingers and hand are working correctly without numbness or paralysis. I performed a vascular ligation and sutured the wound closed. Your mother is very lucky and should recover well with time and rest."

"But?" I ask, because I know more is coming.

The doctor clears his throat and glances at the detective, who closes her notebook. "You marked on her forms that your mother might have spinal stenosis and, at the least, osteoarthritis of the spine. Correct?"

"Yes. I don't know for sure, but she's had tingling and numbness in her legs and feet for years and debilitating back pain that gets worse and worse."

"We took x-rays and did an MRI." The doctor's expression turns quizzical. "Was your mother ever formally diagnosed with spinal issues?"

"No. She was afraid of a diagnosis because it might separate her from me. She was scared that something would go wrong during a surgery. And we didn't even have the money for a surgery. It'd break us financially."

Detective Tanaka is watching me. My right leg starts vibrating.

The doctor closes the chart. "According to the radiology reports, there's no evidence of any spinal damage."

I furrow my brow. "What does that mean?"

"Does your mother have any history of self-harm?" the doctor asks me so gingerly that my guard instantly goes up.

"What?" I ask loudly. "No. Never. Please tell me what's going on. I just want to see my mom."

That's when Tanaka gets up and crouches in front of me. Everyone's treating me like some kind of fragile object about to shatter. Maybe I am.

"Ivy, the medical information Dr. Salahi has presented confirms my suspicions. I believe that your mother lied to you about her pain."

Before I can absorb that blow, the doctor tells me, "And I believe that she stabbed herself."

I hit the floor so fast that neither the doctor nor the detective has time to prevent my fall. My knees slam into the tiles, but I don't feel the pain. I can't feel anything other than complete and utter shock.

"But Rachel was at the motel," I finally say to the room. "It was on video."

Tanaka puts a hand on my arm, like my mother usually does. And that's when I get very scared.

"Rachel's fingerprints aren't on the nail file. Yes, she could have worn gloves. But she left the motel at twelve forty p.m. Your mother called you at one oh three, because you called me right after. That's twenty-three minutes."

Dr. Salahi adds, "With an injury that severe to the radial artery, it's highly likely that in twenty-three minutes, your mother would have bled out and died by the time you arrived at the motel." He looks at Tanaka before saying to me, "She has other cuts on her neck. It appears that she tried to cut herself on other parts of her body, finally choosing her inner forearm, an accessible location. She sliced too deep." He glances at the detective again. "She doesn't appear to have any defensive injuries."

"I'm sorry, Ivy," Tanaka says. "What the surgeon is explaining is that her wounds are more consistent with a self-inflicted injury than an assault by another person." She looks regretful. "This confirms my belief that she waited until Rachel was gone to stab herself to make it look like attempted murder."

I refuse to consider any of these wild accusations. "That's not possible. I need to see her." Using the floor for leverage, I rise.

If Tanaka and the surgeon try to dissuade me, I don't hear them. I march down the never-ending hallway, frantic to piece together their evidence into anything that makes sense. My mother faked her pain. She might have stabbed herself with a nail file to implicate Rachel. *No.* My mother loves me. That's the only truth I know right now.

At the end of the hall, we reach a room with the door closed. Dr. Salahi points at the door and slides my mother's chart into the slot. "You can go in. If she appears to be in any medical distress, page me. She's my patient, and I have a duty to ensure her care."

He walks back toward the desk. Tanaka opens my mother's door.

"Can I see her alone, please?" I ask in a shaky voice.

The detective screws up her mouth and says, "I'll wait here. Keep the door open." She puts both hands on my shoulders. "I think your mother's dangerous, Ivy."

"She'd never hurt me." I walk into the room.

My mother lies in a hospital bed, tubes running from her nose, arm, and chest. Her right arm is bandaged around her hand, all the way up to her bicep. A few gray hairs peek through the caramel waves matted around her pale face. Her warm-brown eyes are open but hazy.

I edge toward the bed, and my mother smiles, but it comes out as more of a grimace. "My love, I'm so happy to see you. Come over and sit near me."

I glance over my shoulder. Tanaka's not visible from here. Do I tell my mother about the accusations against her? Or do I simply hold her and tell her that I believe her?

"I'm not going to break, honey. I'm fine. I promise. Come here."

I take the chair against the wall and pull it close to the bed, but I can't sit. I'm too frightened. Not of my mother, but what she could have done. She'd do anything to protect me. "Mom, we need to talk. You can tell me everything, okay?"

She shakes her head, wincing. "Sorry, honey. I'm groggy from the anesthetic and pain medication. You know how much I hate medication. I'm not sure what you need." She squints. "What happened to your face?"

I touch the bandages covering the injuries I forgot were there. They don't hurt as much as my invisible scars. "Did you pretend you were in pain? Did you . . . Did you stab yourself?"

Her eyes, suddenly alert, narrow into cold slits. "Who told you that?"

"I did, Ms. Hardwick."

Tanaka comes into the room. My mother's face hardens. She grabs my hand with her unbandaged fingers. Her skin, abraded from all those years of doing whatever she had to so I could live my dream, scrapes against mine.

261

"Ivy, you know me better than anyone. They're trying to tear us apart because they want to use you against me. Pit us against each other. That's how it always is for women. I've sacrificed everything for you. I love you."

She stares at me with the watchful gaze that's shielded me from harm, as best as she could, every day of my life. She's waiting for me to say I love her more. The words are stuck in my throat.

Before I can say or do anything, Tanaka steps over, pulls out handcuffs, and snaps one over my mother's wrist, securing her to the bed railing.

My mom yanks at the handcuff. "What the fuck do you think you're doing?"

"Elizabeth Hardwick, you're under arrest on suspicion of first-degree murder in the death of Lauren Malloy, extortion of Mack Foster, obstruction of justice, and falsifying a crime. You have the right to remain silent. Anything you say can and will be used against you in a court of law. You have the right to an attorney. If you cannot afford an attorney, one will be appointed for you."

My mom rattles the handcuff on her wrist so it clangs loudly against the railing, matching the slams of my heart against my chest. She's not saying anything.

This is absurd. Tanaka has it all wrong. My mother wouldn't harm anyone. She loved Lauren like a daughter. She wasn't even at the studio until I texted her to come. Then I realize I have the proof to put an end to this lunacy.

I yell at Tanaka, "Stop it! My mother did not murder Lauren! Or extort Mack!" I dig through my bag for my phone. Then I remember it's in pieces on the ground outside Jesse's cabin. Clenching my fists, I cry, "My mother couldn't have killed Lauren! I have a photo she sent me! Look at her phone. She was in a doctor's office. Someone's lying to you. You're making a huge mistake."

Tanaka says sternly, "Ivy, I understand how hard this is to hear, but you need to listen to me. Your mother is lying to you. We spoke to the receptionist and the doctor. Your mother never made an appointment. They have no idea who she is. She was in that waiting room for the photo op and an alibi."

"Your mother only loves and protects herself."

I whip my head toward the voice at the door but not before I see my mother's jaw drop. Mack, handcuffed and held by Sergeant Reyes, shuffles into the room. The blood has dried, caked all around his crooked nose.

"It's been a long time, Elizabeth," he says.

"You don't know what he did," my mom seethes to Detective Tanaka.

"They know everything. I can't hide anymore. And I can't continue to let Jesse pay for a crime he didn't commit." He looks at me, with tears rolling down his face. "Elizabeth found a ledger and bags of Molly in the air vent at my Wilshire office while she was cleaning it, after Clarice sent you the invitation to audition for Skylar."

I can't hold myself upright any longer. My knees give out, and I grab onto the bed railing for support. I want to cover my ears so I don't hear any more. My mother won't even look at me. She shoots venom at Mack through cold, hard eyes.

"She extorted you?" I ask Mack weakly.

Mack nods slowly, then hangs his head. "I sold drugs to my actors. I did it to keep them safe from dealers on the street and so they wouldn't get caught buying it and ruin their lives. I wanted to protect them."

Fury explodes inside me. I catapult toward him, but the detective blocks me. I stand down, but I don't hold back. "*You* gave Caleb the Molly that killed him? And let Jesse take the fall?"

"I sold it to Jesse. He never told the police who gave him the drugs because he didn't want my family to suffer through the media storm. For my kids to look at their father differently. He didn't want my family to fall apart. And he wanted to go to prison because he felt—still feels—responsible for giving Caleb the Molly. But it wasn't Jesse's fault. It was mine."

"Yes, it was your fault!" I scream at him. "Why did you keep supplying drugs after my mother found the ledger? Why didn't you stop? Caleb is dead because of you!"

"I tried to," Mack wheezes out, his voice breaking. "I told Elizabeth that I was done. I wasn't going to sell them to my actors anymore. But she wouldn't let me because she wanted the leverage to make you Juliet." He looks me straight in my eyes, his still leaking. "To make you famous."

I turn to my mother. Her lips are a tight, thin line. She's not defending herself or trying to convince me she's innocent. She's not even looking at Mack anymore, only staring at the ceiling, like she's bored with this conversation.

"Is it true, Mom?" I implore her. "Did you force Mack into giving me the role?"

It's Mack who answers me. He exhales heavily. "I'm so sorry. You weren't ready for that kind of fame and responsibility, and especially the hate. Elizabeth told me to break you to make you. I will repent for that for the rest of my life. I'm so ashamed."

I believe him. And it kills me.

Finally, my mother looks at me, but there's no guilt, only resignation on the face I've loved my whole life. "Ivy, you're not a good actress. But you wanted to be a star. No one ever took care of me the way I looked after you. There's not a single audition or role that you would have gotten without my help. But Mack's the criminal. He broke into our house after Caleb's memorial to find that ledger. Stupid man. Like I'd keep it there. He's a drug dealer. He murdered Caleb." She sets her jaw. "I've done nothing wrong."

I stare numbly at the one person I've ever truly trusted. And I crumble when I say, "But you strangled Lauren."

Looking proud, she says, "I made you extraordinary." Then she averts her eyes from me and focuses on Tanaka. "I want a lawyer. The best. I can pay for it."

It's my mother who's been the vulture all along.

FAME AND FELONY

A Weekly Podcast on Celebrity True Crimes

July 18, 2024

Yvette Martin. This is the *Fame and Felony* podcast. We're not detectives, but we played them on *Homicide in the Hills*. We take notes on the most scandalous celebrity trials so you don't have to. And have we got a juicy show for you today!

Drea Thompson. That we do, Yvette! This is the first time an actress who was once an extra on our show is involved in an actual homicide. With a plot more twisted than any episode of *Hello, Juliet*, the real-life behind-the-scenes drama of the cursed teen show ended today, six months after Elizabeth Hardwick, Ivy Westcott's mother and longtime manager, was implicated in Lauren Malloy's homicide.

Yvette Martin. It's wild. A total *Mommie Dearest* type of relationship. Drea, we were both allowed in court as media. Before we dive into the sentencing, let's unpack the dramatic, emotional trial. I think we should start with the man who created the show that only half the main cast survived. Mack Foster.

Drea Thompson. Mack Foster was a huge force in Hollywood. He was the producer and director everyone wanted to work with. Turns out that might have been because he was their drug dealer. For over a decade! Now he's serving ten for conspiracy to distribute the Molly that caused Caleb Hill's death.

Yvette Martin. And the plot thickens. Foster was also convicted of obstructing justice for faking his own death! No wonder *Hello, Juliet* was such a hit. The man knows how to hook an audience with melodrama.

Drea Thompson. Right? Foster was convinced that Hardwick would kill him and his family to prevent her extortion plot from being exposed. If he were gone, the secret would die with him. So he smashed the windows on his SUV, put his phone in the console, then pushed the car off the cliff at the Castaic Lake lookout!

Yvette Martin. —where Jesse Rafferty owned the cabin and shed that Foster was hiding out in after Malloy was murdered. Westcott found Foster and brought him down. That girl is fierce.

Drea Thompson. Westcott's been through so much. Which brings us to the lead actress in this made-for-TV murder, Elizabeth Hardwick, Westcott's mother and manager. Perhaps the evilest mother since Norma Bates. She's been convicted of first-degree felony murder, because she killed Malloy while also committing extortion against Mack Foster. Hardwick didn't testify in her own defense, so we don't know what happened that led her to strangle Malloy, but she'd been scheming since Westcott was basically born.

Yvette Martin. What do you think Westcott will do now?

Drea Thompson. Hard to tell. Both her and Rafferty's social media accounts have been deleted. Neither of them has representation, and we couldn't track them down to get a comment for the show.

Yvette Martin. Well, whatever they do next, we hope they'll be happy now that the murderous momager is behind bars for the next twenty-five years.

CHAPTER THIRTY

Now
November 25, 2024

It's been four months since the last time I laid eyes on my mother—the day she was sentenced to twenty-five years in prison for murdering Lauren and extorting Mack. I still can't comprehend the extent of her depravity.

My therapist, Fiona, assures me that whatever timeline I need to process that I was raised by an emotionally abusive narcissist is justifiable. From my first commercial at seven years old, my mother had skimmed from every cent I made, building herself a nice little nest egg. For so long, she didn't even need to clean. She only did it to guilt me into working as hard as I could and so she could collect secrets, like Mack's, and Wyatt Gibson's.

Those important papers Wyatt told me that my mother saved from his office trash were actually pulled from the shredder. She pieced them together and discovered that he was embezzling from his firm. In exchange for her silence, Wyatt had to give her free legal help whenever she needed it. But once the news broke that my mother was charged with Lauren's murder, he never responded to her messages threatening to expose him if he ever spoke a word about her. Wyatt decided to own up to his crimes instead of dealing any longer with the likes of Elizabeth Hardwick.

Today I'll deal with her, for my own gain.

A female guard leads me through a corridor to the visiting area, where I can only see my mother through glass, because she's a level-four inmate—in a maximum security prison for some of the most dangerous offenders.

I don't want to miss her, but I do. I don't know where my mother ends and I begin. Untangling myself from her will be long and excruciating, but I'm so much braver than she thinks I am. Confronting her alone is the first step.

"Take a seat here," the guard instructs, pointing to a plastic chair at a little counter with a telephone to my right. "The inmate will be brought in on the other side, shackled but not handcuffed, so she can pick up the phone to speak to you. There will be guards stationed behind and next to her at all times. You'll be safe behind the glass. And I'm right behind you over there." She indicates the whitewashed brick wall.

I'm not nervous to see my mother like I was when I testified at her trial. From the defense table, she trained her eyes solely on me the entire time I was in the witness box. It was devastating to see her coldness, to reconcile the mother I thought was my constant loving support with the cruel, emotionless shell of a woman trying to intimidate me. Yet I spoke clearly, truly on my own for the first time in my life, as I stared right back at her.

Now the doors open, and my mother walks through, without a hint of a limp or pain because she's in excellent physical health and always has been. I feel nothing at first.

I've cycled through the stages of grief so many times that it seems endless. But as she sits down across from me, the deep ache of loss I will forever feel over Lauren, my best friend who was simply expendable to her, presses heavily on my chest.

I'm also startled by how much older she looks. She smooths her short-sleeved orange jumpsuit, two bands on her wrist—purple for murder and red for an inmate who receives a lot of publicity. My mother must be thrilled about that.

I pick up the phone on the wall, and so does she. "Hello, Elizabeth," I say into the receiver.

The smile drops from her face, and she rolls her eyes. "I'm always your mother. And you wouldn't be here without me."

I nod. "You got pregnant on purpose."

"Ah, you talked to Millie and Robert. Taking their side against me." She shrugs pertly. "Of course I got pregnant on purpose. My parents cared about drugs more than me? Fine. Josh's parents didn't want me? Also fine. I made someone who did."

Shifting blame is what my mother does best. Even now, in prison, she doesn't care about the anguish she's caused. She only cares about herself. And I believe that her parents' neglect is the only truth she's told me. I won't tell her that my paternal grandparents and I Zoom chat once a week. They plan to visit LA when things are more settled for me. I need to close this chapter before I start a new one.

I lean forward to show her that I'm not afraid of her; she doesn't have the power to control me anymore. "The more attention I got, no matter what kind, brought you more attention, so everyone who'd ever hurt you would see that Elizabeth Hardwick could do something right."

"That's what children are. An extension of their parents."

I scoff. "No. That's not mothering at all. I wasn't a doll you could dress up and make perform at your will." And perform I did, because she said it made me special. The reality is, she never thought I was special at all.

"You can twist it however you want, but I was a good mother. I loved you."

"Love?" I laugh harshly, then swallow, because this is harder than I thought it would be. "You isolated me from the kids at school, making me believe they didn't want me as their friend. The lonelier I was, the more I needed you. You forced Mack to create a PR relationship between Jesse and Lauren to drive a wedge between us. And you also needed to keep Lauren from talking to me."

Tanaka told me that an email, sent to me a day after I'd emailed Lauren in 2019, was found on Lauren's phone. I never received it. My mother must have been monitoring my messages and deleted it. Lauren had missed me too. She wanted to see me. When I never responded, she didn't reach out again until she posed as Mack's assistant.

"You engineered my whole life so I could—what? Become Juliet? Or so she would become me?"

My mother shakes her head. "You'll never get it." Her face softens. "You know nothing about mothering, Ivy. About sacrifice. Good mothers would kill for their children."

She says it with such conviction that it chills me to the depths of my soul.

"You believe you killed Lauren for me?"

"If Lauren hadn't decided to be selfish and plan a whole fake reunion to inform you about Mack's drug-dealing history, none of this would have happened. I only went early that morning to make sure your rider was complete and the tulips you wanted were fresh."

I laugh darkly. "Bullshit. You went to make sure that Mack kept his mouth shut. But he wasn't there, of course. Did Lauren tell you that Mack sold drugs to Jesse, so you strangled her? Or did she figure out the monster you really are?"

She clucks her tongue. "You should be thanking me for my hard work. I'm the only reason that you're famous."

She'll never take accountability. She actually believes she's accomplished a lofty goal. "But I never wanted to be famous. And Mack knew that I shouldn't be. He tried to protect me from you."

Mack testified that he'd asked Jesse to keep an eye on me because he was afraid of what my mother might do; he tried to push back with every script change and press leak she'd forced him into.

After that court appearance, Rachel divorced him. Lucy and Liam have refused to visit their father in jail. I don't know where they are. It's best for me not to know, because I never need to see Rachel again.

Unlike my mother, who clearly shows no remorse, Rachel did apologize to me. She wrote a letter, sent to my attorney, in which she took full responsibility for stalking me, slipping the threatening note in my bag before the premiere, and ripping the pink rose petals off their stems in my dressing room, because she thought that Mack had given them to me. I appreciate the gesture, and I'm working toward forgiving her. She's yet another victim of my mother's destruction. We all are.

My mother waves her fingers at her own neck, wrinkling her nose. "That necklace was always too heavy for you. You don't have the edge to pull it off."

I touch the silver link chain. Jesse gave it to me after he cleaned out Lauren's house. She had kept it all these years, and now I wear it all the time. I think about her every day.

"All I ever wanted was friends," I tell my mother, not that she'll really listen. But I need to express myself like I never have. "And you destroyed them too. You made them believe you cared about them."

She sighs, like I'm frustrating her. "They weren't good for you, Ivy. Caleb was an alcoholic, Jesse has daddy issues, and don't even get me started on Lauren."

Hearing their names—the people who genuinely loved and cared for me—come out of her mouth enrages me. But I don't yell, because that's what she expects me to do. "They were young. You were the adult they trusted to look out for them," I say calmly but icily. "Caleb only ever wanted to be loved. How could you get him kicked off the show?"

A slow, satisfied smile crosses her lips. "You heard what Mack said in court. I made him see that Caleb was deadweight dragging us down."

I'm not shocked at her appalling disregard for human life. But I am disgusted. "Because of you, Caleb took the MDMA that killed him."

"Caleb was old enough to know not to drink, then snort a bunch of Molly. And Jesse should have known better than to give it to Caleb at all."

I switch tactics, because my mother's only going to talk about what she perceives as her extraordinary efforts on my behalf. "You gave Nina Johnson the information to make that Tattle TV exposé about me."

She smiles proudly. "I helped her out. She's a single mom like me."

She is. I tracked Nina down and, after inviting me over for coffee, she apologized for using me, and every other former television star, to reignite her reporting career. The day she'd turned forty, her studio let her go, and with two young kids to support, she took on contract jobs that barely paid the bills. When my mother anonymously mailed her an envelope full of photos, gossip, and details of my ordinary life out of the spotlight, it was the spark that inspired Nina to create the docuseries.

"You couldn't stand not controlling me anymore. Once I'd finally left acting behind, you had to find a way to get people to talk about me again." I take a deep breath, then say, "I also know you drugged my tea for years. So I'd lose weight faster, which is why I almost passed out at the upfronts after-party when I drank the champagne. A sleep aid the night before the reunion, so you could get to the studio before anyone else to ambush Mack."

"Drugged you?" She snorts. "I did what was best for you. That was all I ever did, Ivy."

"You're unbelievable," I tell her flatly.

"Thank you." My mother smooths her hair. "Now, if we're done here, I actually have another meeting to take. An interview. I'm quite in demand."

"I'll bet you are." I lift the collar of my white blouse. Normally I wouldn't wear something so formal. Fancy isn't my thing. I prefer understated clothes and a more low-key life. But today the blouse is necessary, because that's where my mic is hidden. I bend my head and say, "Cut. That's a wrap."

My mother's features collapse. I take no pleasure in it.

"Are you recording me? You can't do that."

I shrug. "Actually, I can. You signed a consent form."

She laughs gaily, the sound driving a stake into my heart. "You're the documentary filmmaker?"

I don't respond. She deserves no information about me, and I have all I need about her. Every person I've worked with wants to help me with this film. They're all willing to be interviewed, including Vanessa, the AD, who did actually try to help me by talking to Mack, but he shot her down every time. And Stella, my wardrobe stylist—who managed to track down her friend who owns the boutique on Rodeo Drive where we borrowed our HERVÉ LÉGER dresses for that first photo shoot. Her friend remembered the call she got to switch my dress size, because Stella was so upset about the error. A woman had phoned in the change at the last minute. She'd neglected to give her name. Was it my mother? Probably.

I take the phone away from my ear, moving to place it back into the receiver. My mother opens her mouth, because she always has to have the last word.

"I love you more," she says, dipping her chin once.

I simply put the phone down and walk out of the visitor's room and down the hall to the communications office. I knock on the door.

My mother doesn't know what love is. But I do.

"Did you get everything?" I ask when the door opens.

"Everything," Jesse says.

We thank the officer who allowed Jesse to watch the video from his office and helped us set up the camera that was placed behind me on the wall. My mother didn't notice it, of course. She doesn't care about anything unless it directly affects her. Once this film is done, it will.

Jesse and I exit the women's correctional facility into the cool air and bright sunshine. He takes my hand, and I lean into him as we head toward his red pickup in the parking lot. Once he's opened my door and gotten in himself, he turns to me, gray eyes concerned. "You okay?"

"No. But I will be."

After my mother was incarcerated, I phoned Jesse and asked to meet. I'd watched him take the stand, overcome with emotion but refusing any breaks because he didn't want me to endure a longer trial than I had to. I was also overwhelmed and grateful for his courage.

Then Jesse and I joined forces. We transformed Lauren's house, with all the lush plants and her gorgeous backyard garden, into an artists' retreat—a private, secure space to escape the pressures of fame. We don't charge anything for a stay because it's not about making money. It's about helping people like Lauren always did and creating the safe family environment that she always wanted.

Throughout that process, I've forgiven Jesse for any mistakes he's made, and he's forgiven me. We've found our way back to each other.

Jesse and I are quiet on the ride back to the cabin, where we now live. It's away from the glamour and grit of Hollywood, and we both do our best work there. It was Jesse who encouraged me to tell my story, to finally control the narrative of my life. He and I are producing partners; together we direct, write, and edit.

Once we're in the gravel driveway, Jesse opens my door and helps me out. I breathe in the scent of pine and cedar, immediately feeling a sense of calm in the stillness. I love it here. This is my home.

"We really need to get rid of that tree," Jesse says when we get to the front deck, where devil's cherries spread their poison everywhere. He grins, pointing at my stomach. "It's not safe."

The pregnancy wasn't planned, but it's so welcome. My grandparents are ecstatic that they'll finally have the opportunity to love a child who's a part of my father. I send them updates on our little bean, due in seven months, and ask Millie all the questions about motherhood that I can't ask my own mother.

I look down at the dark-purple stains on the deck. Bark and berries, like what my mother always dosed me with.

"My mom could have given me deadly nightshade, for all I know." I shudder. "She's the one who told me the real name of the berries that morning I left you at the cabin, after our fight. My sneakers were covered in purple. She said it's good for colds and stomachaches in small doses."

Jesse winces. "It's also called *belladonna*. Oddly, it's the poison that many people think killed Romeo and Juliet." He entwines his fingers with mine. "She could have dosed all of us, and we'll never know."

"God, I never even thought of that." I glance over at his red pickup, with all the windows wide open, as usual. And a wave of dread washes over me as unresolved questions from our past suddenly come into focus. I turn to Jesse. "Did Caleb drink from your flask the night he died?"

He squints at me. "Yes. Why?"

My pulse quickens. "I'm figuring something out. Did you?"

He shakes his head. "Caleb chugged the whole thing down before I could. He was so upset about his contract not getting renewed."

"Did he drink anything else, as far as you know?"

"No." He tightens his grip on my hand. "Why are you asking?"

I take out my phone. "I need to call Katie."

After our ride together from the cabin to the hospital, where she stayed by my side as my mother's crimes were revealed, the detective and I built a bond that only strengthened during the trial. Talking on the phone often, we've become friends. Katie's told me that she admires my resilience; I admire her choice to protect people despite the physical and emotional risk to herself.

She's appearing in the documentary and has helped me behind the scenes with some of the investigative research. But this is something no one's yet suspected.

She answers on the first ring. I don't give her a chance to talk before I put the call on speaker and blurt, "I think my mother killed Caleb."

Jesse rears back. Squeezing his fingers, I describe to Katie the afternoon before Jesse and I went to the Snake Pit, when we were in my bedroom and my mom came home after grocery shopping. Neither of us heard her come in. Jesse thought the flask was in the pocket of his leather jacket, but we found it in his glove compartment. He assumed that Mack had put it in there.

I pull Jesse toward me. "I remember the ME who performed Caleb's autopsy questioning how the drugs and alcohol that Caleb consumed would kill someone his size. I think my mom could have slipped something, maybe belladonna, into Jesse's flask the night Caleb died at the Snake Pit."

Katie inhales sharply. "Yes, the ME didn't seem convinced, but he determined it was the seizure that killed Caleb. I suspect, with the media storm and Caleb's family pushing to have his body released to them, the file was closed fairly quickly." I hear her tap. "An overdose of belladonna can cause seizures and cardiac arrest."

I rest my head on Jesse's chest and say to Katie, "I think she was trying to kill Jesse because he and I had gotten too close." Looking up at him, I watch his face fall. "She could have taken the flask from his jacket, slipped belladonna or another poison into it, and put it in his glove compartment without us ever knowing. The windows on Jesse's truck are always open."

I never realized until right now how close I came to losing him forever.

"Belladonna can also cause drowsiness, Ivy. Millie told you that your father fell asleep at the wheel, and it wasn't an intoxicated driver who caused his death, like your mother made you believe."

My mother might be a serial killer. And it doesn't shock me. Nothing about her has that effect on me anymore.

Sickened, though, I ask Jesse, "Do you still have that flask?"

"No. I'm sorry." His voice hitches. "I threw it away that night in a dumpster."

"Well, it won't be easy to prove, because both Caleb and your father have been cremated, but I'll do everything in my power to make sure Elizabeth never sees the light of day," Katie says firmly. "You and Jesse take care of each other and your baby. Send me an invite to the premiere of your documentary."

I smile. "I will." And I hang up, leaving my mother's fate in Katie's capable hands.

I lay my hand on my belly, where our child grows. My mother's parents damaged her, and she damaged me. I won't continue the cycle. I'm not my mother. And I'm not Juliet Jones. I have nothing to prove to anyone but myself because I know my worth.

Jesse opens the door to our cabin and leads me inside. I shut the door behind us. There's no need to look back. I can only look forward to the next episode of my story, which has yet to be written.

HOLLYWOOD HEROES

January 2026

Winners at the Golden Globes last night include *Poisoning Ivy* for Best Documentary. Cowritten, codirected, and coproduced by Ivy Westcott and Jesse Rafferty, the critically acclaimed doc is an investigative exposé on Ivy's mother / former manager, Elizabeth Hardwick. Hardwick is currently serving a life sentence for the murders of Joshua Westcott, Caleb Hill, and Lauren Malloy. Hardwick was previously sentenced to twenty-five years, but the film brought to light further crimes.

Ivy Westcott and Jesse Rafferty weren't in attendance to accept their award as they were home caring for their daughter, whose name isn't disclosed to protect her privacy. They dedicated their box office smash to the memory of Caleb Hill and Lauren Malloy.

ACKNOWLEDGMENTS

Since I was a little girl watching soap operas with my mom, I've loved television. Falling into stories on the screen, whether fictional or real, is one of my greatest pleasures and escapes. To write a book about a television series and the cast's lives behind the scenes was a lifelong dream. I couldn't have done it on my own.

My fearless, dedicated, incredibly hardworking agent, Jenny Bent, has believed in, supported, and advocated for me for over a decade. Without Jenny, I wouldn't have the most fulfilling and exciting career that I can imagine. I'm so fortunate to have her firmly in my corner.

Victoria Cappello, vice president of the Bent Agency, takes care of so much for me. Her ability to decipher spreadsheets and statements is incomparable, and I'm so lucky to be able to rely on Victoria, as well as the entire phenomenal TBA team.

Mary Pender-Coplan, my TV/film agent at William Morris Endeavor, is instrumental in bringing the worlds I've created to life on screen. My debut, *Woman on the Edge*, has been optioned for series adaptation, which is a joy like no other, especially for a TV addict like me.

Megha Parekh, my extraordinary editor at Thomas & Mercer, changed my life when she acquired *A Friend in the Dark* and *Hello, Juliet*. She champions, supports, and helps shape my work with her brilliant insights and invaluable expertise.

And Celia Johnson, my spectacularly thorough and genius developmental editor, guided my way with magnificent notes and comments, polishing my sentences so they shone the way I wanted them to.

A huge thank-you to my production manager, Miranda Gardner, who keeps everything so well organized and on track.

My copyeditor, Anna Barnes, has worked with me on both *A Friend in the Dark* and *Hello, Juliet*, and she is exceptional. It takes an immense amount of work and focus to ensure my every word is accurate, and I'm very grateful to her.

Jenna Justice, my proofreader, who also worked with me on both *A Friend in the Dark* and *Hello, Juliet*, has extraordinarily keen eyes, catching errors that I can't see, despite having read my manuscript ten thousand times. Those final polishes are what bring a book home, and I'm so thankful for Jenna's attention to detail.

And to my cold reader, Angela Vimuttinan, the very last person to go through every word of my book, thank you for your sharp observations and careful diligence.

My cover designer Mumtaz Mustafa's stellar talent is on display in *A Friend in the Dark* and *Hello, Juliet*. Capturing the visual essence of a book is no easy feat, and my covers are such beautiful works of art that I treasure.

Darci Swanson, Heather Radoicic, and the entire author relations and marketing teams at Thomas & Mercer, Amazon Publishing, and Brilliance Publishing work so hard to promote my books to as wide an audience as possible. I'm very thankful.

My Canadian distribution team at Firefly Distributed Lines, including Lionel Koffler, David Glover, and Jeyran Aslanova, ensure that physical copies of my books are widely available, and they work very hard to market and promote my books in my home of Canada. It means so much to me.

There are many unsung heroes when it comes to book promotion—the Bookstagrammers, BookTokkers, influencers, booksellers, and librarians who love literature and authors so much that they make an enormous effort to spread the word, most often without any financial compensation. So I don't wake up in a cold sweat in the middle of the night because I've forgotten someone, I thank you all for the extraordinary time and energy you invest in me and my work.

I must, however, specifically thank Tonya Cornish of @thrillerbookloversthepulse, whose stellar organizational skills, kindness, generosity, and outstanding team of Bookstagrammers has gone above and beyond to help me. And to the Bookstagrammers who've supported me from the very beginning, I appreciate you all so much. A special thank-you as well to Shelley Macbeth of Blue Heron Books, who's been a huge supporter of mine and is super fun to hang out with at events.

My author friends are everything to me, and again, I'll feel awful if I forget to name someone. From the bottom of my heart, I thank you all. My warm, welcoming, wild thriller community, all my online and offline author friends, my Beach Babes—Josie Brown, Eileen Goudge, Francine LaSala, Meredith Schorr, Jen Tucker, and Julie Valerie—and to the Canadian writers with whom I have such a close bond, I couldn't do this without you.

I do have to especially thank my author BFF, Meredith Schorr, who's not only my critique partner, confidante, and cheerleader but also the best roommate in the world. For the first time in my career, I was able to travel for research. Meredith and I spent five days in LA, and it was one of the most glorious weeks of my life. Thank you also to Jon Lindstrom, for patiently touring us around Sunset Boulevard and telling us all the tales of Hollywood that helped shape *Hello, Juliet*. Thank you, as well, to the LA residents and tour guides who answered countless questions as Meredith and I rode buses, sauntered down Hollywood Boulevard and Rodeo Drive, and nearly broke our necks to view the Hollywood sign from the tippy top of a winding trail off Mulholland Drive.

I'm so appreciative of Yasmin Angoe, Kimberly Belle, Seraphina Nova Glass, Heather Gudenkauf, Susan Walter, and Stephanie Wrobel, who took the time to read and blurb *Hello, Juliet*. I deeply admire their talent and am so thankful for their support.

My friends outside of the book business have never stopped believing in me, which was how I kept going through years of rejections until *Woman on the Edge* was published when I was forty-five. I dedicated this book to Miko and Nicole, my two very best friends since our studious days and raucous nights at McGill University. I love and appreciate all my friends so much. I'm immeasurably lucky to have each of you in my life.

To my family—the ones stuck living with an author who sees danger everywhere and constantly interrupts conversations to jot down notes and leave voice texts for herself, and the ones near and far—all of you accept me as I am, the Gemini with the sunny personality and dark, twisted mind who sometimes watches you a little too closely for research purposes. I'm truly the most fortunate woman in the world to be loved by you.

And to my readers, you take a chance on me every time you pick up one of my books. You've given me the life I longed for. I hope I give you the entertainment and escape you're looking for. Every message you've sent to tell me you love my books is a surreal ecstasy. I truly could not be an author without all of you.

ABOUT THE AUTHOR

Samantha M. Bailey is the *USA Today*, Amazon Charts, and #1 international bestselling author of *Woman on the Edge*—optioned for series adaptation—as well as *Watch Out for Her*, *A Friend in the Dark*, and *Hello, Juliet*. Her novels have sold in twelve countries. Samantha lives in Toronto, where she can usually be found tapping away at her computer or curled up on her couch with a book. She's currently working on her next domestic suspense. You can connect with her on Instagram at @sbaileybooks and on Facebook at @SamanthaBaileyAuthor.